THE WITCH'S DAUGHTER

WereHuman BOOK 1

GWENDOLYN DRUYOR

A WYRDOS UNIVERSE NOVEL

Chapter 1

Spring 2025 - Foothills, OR

"Mom!"

The young boy's piercing voice woke Laylea from a fitful sleep. She shivered and blinked. No brothers snuggled up next to her. Last night Mama had kissed her goodbye before tucking her makeshift bed into a corner of the wraparound porch.

"She's tinkering, Bailey." A man with blue eyes that matched the little boy's joined him in the doorway. He smelled like a nap.

The boy reeked of soap. Laylea crinkled her nose as he leaned in to get a closer look at her. Peeking out through the folds of a baby blue towel, Laylea could see the gray of early morning sky beyond the two humans. Bells jingled lightly against the doorway and she shivered again at the cold breeze. A yawn stretched through her whole body and she tucked her nose back under the old towel.

"Woodford found it."

Laylea cracked an eye. The skinny boy pointed behind her. She smelled earthy warmth and turned her egg sized head. She and the ratty towel lay tucked in amongst the plastic grass of an Easter basket. Behind her, one enormous brown and black paw rested on the edge of her basket. She followed the leg up to a massive barrel chest and on up to the droopy jowls and tired eyes of a mutt. She reached toward him for a nuzzle.

The hound let out one low bark and she jumped backwards, toppling out of her bed. He was on her in an instant. She yelped. But the warm, soft hands of the man lifted her away and she was curled into the dad's chest in a moment.

"Mom won't let us keep it," the boy fearlessly wrapped himself around the big mutt.

"She will let us bring a scared puppy into the house though, Bailey."

The dad carried Laylea through the doorway as the little boy grabbed her towel. Underneath the towel, tucked into the wicker, he found the note in a small white envelope with their names written on the outside; Clark, Bailey, and Dr. Sher.

"Dad, there's a letter!"

"So, bring it inside. I don't think all the neighbors want to hear our business."

"Old Lady Rucker does."

Bells jangled as the front screen slammed shut between the boy and his dad.

Laylea craned her neck, looking around in the dark house. The front hallway led to carpeted stairs straight ahead. One side opened off to a brown room with softness everywhere. The man turned away through an archway that led to a green room centered on one giant wood table. The house smelled fluffy. Not like the basement at all or the car.

"Clark Hillen, where did you get the puppy?"

The dad stopped at the sound of a voice coming from the dark hallway beside the stairs. Laylea dropped her head back over the man's arm to sniff out the stern voice and he fondled her velvet ears with a hand that smelled of food. Her belly told her to twist around and suck on his finger, hoping for milk even though Mama hadn't given her any in days.

"No, Clark." A tall woman with hair a shade darker than Laylea's pale fur and arms full of lavender scented bedding stopped at the archway to the table room. "You can't keep it." The smile that wrinkled the corners of her brown eyes faded when she looked away. "Bailey, shut the front door."

This woman was clearly the mama and alpha of this little pack. Laylea tucked her tail and lowered her head as the woman came close to lift one of her paws with a finger. She talked tough but her touch was gentle. And she smelled like dogs, lots of dogs. Beyond her control, Laylea's tail popped out and thumped against the dad's chest.

"How old is it, Mom?" Bailey bounced over to the trio with the big dog on his heels. The boy stuck his muzzle up into the puppy's face. She licked his nose, remembering no teeth, like Mama said. He giggled. "There was a letter in the basket."

The mom dumped the laundry into his arms so she could take the envelope. He was barely able to hold it all.

"Take the laundry upstairs and then come join us in the kitchen. She's a few weeks old. Barely old enough to leave her mother, I'd guess."

Bailey charged out of the room yelling back at them. "Wait for me!"

The parents didn't bother to respond. They carried Laylea through flapping wooden doors into the most delicious room she'd ever smelled. This room was filled with silver and stone surrounded by pale green walls. A silver kettle whistled on the stove and the dad jostled Laylea jogging over to pull it off the flames. He poured water into two travel mugs as the mom pulled ceramic bowls out of a cabinet and dished something warm and cinnamony into them. She stopped the dad before he could turn away again.

"Here."

The alpha slipped a cold metal tube into the dad's pocket. Laylea craned her head around to sniff the new tube resting beside a warm one already clipped to the fabric.

The dad shifted Laylea to look at the tubes himself. "Another new pen, Sher?"

"The rifling is quieter." She plucked the warm pen from his pocket and tucked it away, glancing at a flat disk on her wrist as she did. "Less noise to distract anyone from looking at the focal isolator."

The mom scooped crunchy bits from a bin on the floor into a plastic bowl which she set on the counter beside the mugs despite the brown hound's big eyes begging her to give it to him. The dad added a spoonful of powdered creamer to her mug even as the mom lifted it to her lips.

"Do you ever consider, when you're tinkering," he reached one handed into a cabinet and pulled a plastic bowl from the top shelf, "making tech that could take down the Consortium?

"Clark." Laylea cringed at the mom's voice. "I gave that all up six years ago when you asked."

The dad squeezed Laylea closer. He bent and dipped his bowl into the bin of crunchy bits. "I didn't ask you to give it up."

"I can't fight them and keep Bailey safe." Sher took the little dish of kibble from Clark and turned away to the kettle. She dribbled a little water into the bowl.

Laylea looked up at the warm man's chin. His neck had gone tense and she could feel him struggling to calm his breath. His voice rumbled against her tiny body when the mom turned and reached past him to set the bowl on the counter.

"You say you want out of the fight," he said, "but you keep developing tech."

A breath hovered between them. Then her bright eyes turned up to his.

"This is just to protect my family." Sher choked on the last word.

She would have walked away but Clark pulled her to him with his free arm. Laylea had heard tears in her voice but there were none in her eyes. Her head rested on Clark's chest and it and Laylea both rose as the dad took in a deep breath.

"I'm sorry. You are protecting us." He kissed the top of the mom's head and whispered into her hair. "And them."

Sher nodded stiffly. She pulled out of Clark's arms just as Laylea risked reaching out to lick her nose. The puppy missed.

Sher turned away to hold a fist out at the hound. "Sit, Woodford," she said, the stern back in her tone.

The big dog sat.

The dad took a sip from his travel mug and smoothed the fur on Laylea's head just as Bailey bust through the swinging door hollering, "I'm here, I'm here, I'm here!"

The noise scared Laylea so much she piddled on the nice dad.

He yelled. "Whoa!" In a lower, slightly less panicked tone he said, "No. Not in the house, little girl. You need some fresh air." He ran through the house and out the front door with her. When they got to the grass in front of the porch, he set her down.

The grass tickled her belly. Laylea chewed at it. She looked up when he started talking again.

"You go to the bathroom outside. Never in the house. Okay?"

Laylea watched the dad closely. She yipped, waiting to see what happened next in this game.

"Here, Dad." Bailey tore down the steps in a tangle of legs.

Laylea yipped at him but he just tossed his dad a small towel. It was wet and warm and felt like Mama's tongue when Clark rubbed it on her belly. It reminded her of how Mama would encourage her and her brothers to relieve themselves after they ate. Her bladder relaxed.

The commotion Bailey and Dad made scared her again but she was pretty sure they were happy with her so she wagged her tail and danced around. Then she found herself in the dad's arms again, going back into the kitchen.

"Mom, the letter." The boy kissed Laylea's head before he went around to his stool. He picked the letter up from where Sher had dropped it and held it out.

The mom ignored him. She set a bowl in front of each of the boys as they settled at the counter, leaning down to reward Woodford at last with his breakfast. She directed the dad to set Laylea on the counter right in front of a bowl of soft mushy kibble. Laylea tripped forward on the slick plastic placemat beneath her tiny paws and buried her face in the food.

Bailey giggled. When his eyes were firmly on Laylea, his mother took the letter. She settled on her stool, took a bite, and unfolded the single sheet of notebook paper.

She took another bite and washed it down with tea before Bailey complained.

"Mom."

A grin tugged at her lips. She didn't raise her eyes from the letter. "Hm?"

"Mom," he repeated, dragging the word out until she flicked her eyes in his direction. "Out loud."

"Oh," the mom's coldness melted for a moment and she earned another groan from her son by saying, "why didn't you say so?"

Then she read.

Dear Hillens,

I met you several years ago. You won't remember the incident but your kindness saved my life. I hope that your kindness can extend to my little Laylea as well. There is an evil man who would do experiments on Laylea and her brothers. Because of this, they have spent their lives thus far in a basement not seeing anything of the world. Two days ago, this man found our sanctuary. We escaped but I dare not foster any of my pups together or to people that know me. I know Laylea would be safe with you and that you are up to the challenges that raising her will present. She is a very special little girl. Please take care of her. Though I am heartbroken to leave my puppy, I am comforted knowing she will be as happy as Bailey and Woodford were when I knew them. She is eight weeks old and just weaned.

With Great Appreciation for whatever help you can give her,

Mama

The boys scraped their bowls clean while Sher folded the letter and grabbed a few bites of her food. Laylea mashed her muzzle around the mess in her bowl trying to lick up every last crumb. Down on the floor Woodford stared up at the silent family, hoping against experience for more.

"That explains why she wasn't dropped at your clinic." Clark picked up the three clean bowls, leaving Laylea to keep working on hers.

Sher tucked the letter back into its envelope, moved, but always and forever practical. "Your big heart gets us too much attention, Clark. Bailey, get your backpack." The boy started to protest but she cut him off. "Your dad and I will have to discuss this before any decisions are made. I'll take her to work today and check her over, see if she's ready to start her vaccinations."

Clark laid a hand on his wife's shoulder. He spoke in a low, quiet voice. "It really sounds like she's one of us, Sher. No past. No family."

She brushed off the hand. "Don't try to manipulate me." She finished her tea and handed it to him for a refill. "It sounds to me like once we've got her vaccinated she should go to one of your hermits off in the wilderness. Much less likely this scientist will find her there than here in the middle of town."

Clark scoffed at her. "You're adorable. This town has five hundred people in it. And we came here because it is so far from anywhere." He scooped Laylea into his arms and kissed her nose sadly. "But you get her healthy and I'll take her on my next delivery. If she belongs with one of the woodsfolk, at least I'll be able to keep an eye on her."

Bailey clambered up onto a stool to reach his mother. He solemnly laid a hand on her shoulder and intoned, "Mom, Laylea should stay with us."

Sher grabbed her son and dangled him upside down. "No conditioning the family!" she hollered.

Through his giggles, he hollered back, "Except for shoe."

She swung him up and kissed his forehead. "Except for shoe."

When she said the word, deep and quiet, Bailey looked at the floor.

"Your shoe is in the air, son," Clark pointed out.

Sher let the kid's feet drop back to the floor. He found his balance before he said, "Yeah, but looking down is the response you really want." The boy squeezed his mother tight and dashed out of the kitchen, the swinging door flapping in his wake.

The parents stared after their son. Laylea tried to grab another lick of her bowl as Clark cleared it to the sink. "I don't think your conditioning has taken on that kid at all."

"That's okay, as long as he does look down."

"Yeah," he raised his eyebrows at her, "but it's making me question your magical abilities."

Sher grabbed the placemat from the table and tossed it into the sink. "That's not magic. It's science."

"You keep saying that, dear, maybe it'll make it true."

The mom left the kitchen yelling instructions to her son.

Laylea yipped. Clark looked down. "Hello, Laylea. Don't be scared. We'll protect you, one way or another." The dad wiped her face and paws with a wet cloth while she tried to chew on his bright orange bracelet. "Now. How do you feel about bicycles?"

Laylea sang. Her tail thumped wildly in the dad's arms.

Chapter 2

Spring 2025 - Consortium Biotech HQ, CA

Trask stopped at the mirror just inside the door. With a sharp intake of breath, she turned to it. She smoothed her black bangs and straightened the new tortoiseshell glasses that set off her eyes while hiding much of her face. Done, she turned to examine the room designated as her new office. The Biotech team was scheduled to start the move from the temporary lab they'd been working in for eight years to this new state of the art facility on Monday. She clearly planned to get the lay of the land first. First was good. All the projects her division worked on were firsts. They were perfecting the human condition. She laughed quietly and straightened the deep gray suit jacket over her matching pencil skirt.

This office was vastly different from the rest of the sterile building. The walls had been paneled with a dark wood wainscoting. The entire length of the back wall held a window looking out over a large courtyard with paths winding through bright green grass, trees and flowers. The window had a deep, cushioned inner sill and warm gray curtains with a brocade pattern of birds. This was designed to be a room where one could feel comfortable and relax. Trask hated it.

A large partner desk stood in the middle of the room with her monitor, keyboard and file boxes of supplies on one side, ergonomic black and steel rolling chair pushed neatly in. The far side of the desk held a laptop set on a calendar blotter covered in writing. Standard issue office supplies were arranged in a neat, almost OCD semi-circle around the blotter. Scattered haphazardly around the rest of the far side were spiral-bound notebooks covered in doodles, a tipping bird toy, a pencil cup filled with packs of black jack chewing gum, a set of wooden perpetual motion balls, and a plastic buffalo.

Trask set her briefcase on the desk. She pulled her cell phone out of it as she ran her fingers over the scars on her forehead. She was scanning through her contacts list when Walter drummed his fingers on the window finally revealing himself in the corner of the room where he perched on the windowsill behind a set of oak finished file cabinets.

"There doesn't appear to be any mobile reception in the building." He spoke with a clipped British accent.

Trask didn't look up. "That's as I requested. Which is why I'm looking for the number to dial on the office phone."

"What office phone?"

She looked again at the desk and then turned to look beside the door where the phones were hung in the laboratories and exam rooms. No phone. She pulled out a leather-bound notepad and added to a growing to do list.

"Dr. Trask, I presume."

She looked sharply in his direction. "Do not call me doctor."

The man smiled. He wore jeans with a vest but no suit coat. His tie hung loose but his gray hair was more or less neatly pulled back in a queue. "You needn't call me doctor either. Although I am a doctor. PhD. My mother called me Boy and my friends have called me trouble. But you can just call me Walter, Trask. I'm the head of--"

"Our assignment together has nothing to do with your division's," she took a breath and spit out the word, "experiments. We are to establish superior surveillance and tracking systems throughout the Americas. And that is all I am required to do with you."

"And in exchange you get this state of the art facility, your pick of experiment materials, and Consortium support of your search for Gamma Subject." Walter strode over and perched on the edge of her desk. "I hear you haven't had much luck in tracking that lost experiment since he blew up your headquarters along with three other Biotech Research divisions eight years ago immolating your records as well as your genius lead researcher."

Trask set her notebook sharply down on the table. "And the Director, bless his heart, has sent you to me so that I can help you track down your personal research assistant who absconded with all of your experiment subjects, essentially shutting down your entire department."

Walter took the smoked glass desk nameplate from one of her file boxes, a smile playing across his eyes. "Tsk tsk tsk. Control yourself, Trask. Your Georgia upbringing shows when you're being a bitch."

Trask turned to leave. "I'll have my things transferred when I find my office."

"They want us together, Trask," Walter said. "And as I'm sure you've heard, I quite like bitches. I do think that my division can benefit from yours, Ms.," he read off the nameplate, *"Supervisor of Biotech Division, Homo Sapiens Operations.* And I know that I can help you find the fellow who destroyed your face."

Trask stopped with her hand on the doorknob.

Walter continued. "We have different styles, yes. But we each want to catch someone quite badly. The Consortium Director is willing to give us the resources to do so as long as we work together."

She turned. Her eyes briefly met his. Then she walked over to his side of the desk. She picked up his buffalo and raised her eyebrows quizzically.

"There is a Navajo legend of—"

A wave of her hand cut him off. She crossed to the window, taking the curtains in one hand. After several deep breaths, she shook her head at the view and tossed away the grey and white damask material. She stalked back to Walter and set the buffalo exactly where it had been.

"I can see the benefits of having help in my search. And I can even see the benefits of having a team of . . . biologists from a different discipline influence my work. But there must be some decorative changes. And I must insist upon the strictest of privacy in this office. You will take no meetings in here. You will most definitely not allow your research assistants in here. I will allow no recording of any kind in this room. You must disable the camera on your laptop before I will agree to this arrangement."

"Oh, I entirely agree to all of your stipulations. I have already disabled the laptop's eye. I plan to personally install an additional lock on the door with a code known only to you and I. And we should have maintenance install a privacy curtain around the door as we have in some of the exam rooms. But I see nothing amiss with the decorations."

"There are birds on the curtains."

"I rather like birds."

———

WHILE HIS NEW Biotech Research team continued negotiations, the Director smoothed the perfect crease of his slacks and lowered the volume on the audio of Trask and Walter's monitor. He had other more promising projects to look in on. He turned from the display of the many feeds from their office to the single view he had so far been successful at implanting in Chief Morioka's office at the Homicide Unit headquarters in Chicago. Morioka was speaking with a female the facial recognition software identified onscreen as Officer Deirdre Morton, nobody the Consortium was concerned with. He moved on to glance at another of the hundred monitors in his viewing garden.

CHAPTER 3

SPRING 2025 - FOOTHILLS, OR

"How's it going, Michelle?" Sher set her clipboard on the reception counter to fix the collar of her lab coat. "You figuring everything out okay?"

The new receptionist stood, using the low desk and higher reception counter for an assist. Her braids barely cleared the counter. "I was having some trouble with the billing software but Nick here noticed what I was doing wrong and he got me straightened out in a heartbeat."

The man in the corner with a gray muzzled golden retriever at his feet waved the ladies off when they looked at him. He reached down to clean some gunk from the corner of the dog's eye.

"Well, I'm crazy grateful, no matter what he says. He may have designed the system but that doesn't mean he'd be a good teacher. He is though." She raised her voice to Nick who had returned to reading his book. "He should never have left the school system. And not just anyone would adopt an older dog like that. Lucky Rufus. Your mother," she noticed he was trying to pay her no mind, "his mother would be so proud if she'd just lasted another week." Michelle waddled to the swinging door that led into the back rooms. "Can you watch the front for a moment, Dr. Hillen? This little guy has been kicking my bladder for ten minutes."

Sher turned to Nick as the barefoot little woman disappeared. "I didn't know your mother just passed. I'm so sorry."

Nick shook his head. "It was not unexpected."

"I didn't know you were a teacher." Sher crouched down to massage the old dog's hips.

Laylea tripped out of the giant dog bed in the corner. She bounded over to the mom and stood on her knee. The golden poked his wet nose in her belly for a sniff.

"That woman is, well," Nick stumbled over his words, "she just asks questions." He reached down and scooped Laylea into his lap since Sher was ignoring the puppy. "And she's just so tiny and pregnant," he added.

Sher nodded, her focus more on the elder dog. "She's harmless," she said and then corrected herself, "she looks harmless. Interesting."

Sher pulled the stethoscope from around her neck and settled herself on the ground. She stuck the business end in an armpit while attaching the earpieces. "Mind if I examine Rufus right here? He's comfy. I'm not expecting any more clients today." She let Rufus sniff the shiny disc before she pressed it to his side.

Nick nodded though Sher barely noticed. When she reached over to listen to the other side, Rufus bared his teeth at her. Nick saw and quickly reprimanded the dog.

"Rufus."

The golden turned at the sound of his name.

A treat hit Nick in the chest. With his hands busy scratching Laylea, he barely caught it. Sher gestured with her head so he tentatively reached out and offered the treat to his dog.

Sher mouthed *Good boy* at him and Nick repeated, "Good boy."

Rufus took the liver treat and laid his head back down on the floor.

Sher reached over again, this time scratching the nape of his neck with her other hand. "You want to reward him when he looks to you for direction. You want to schedule the positive reinforcement as quickly as possible, whether it's a treat or a pat or a *good boy*, so he knows what he's being rewarded for. Rufus is smart but he didn't get a lot of training from his first family."

Michelle pushed through the swinging door. She stopped at the sight of her new boss sitting on the floor. "Dr. Hillen, do you want me to get Chris to carry Rufus into an exam room?"

Sher looked up and smiled widely at her new receptionist. "Thank you for asking Michelle. That's a great idea. We'll be okay here for now."

Nick chuckled. "Nice scheduling."

"What?" Sher asked. "I didn't reward her."

"You thanked her, told her it was a great idea. And you smiled. You never smile, Dr. Sher."

The doctor looked away from Nick, acutely aware of her natural frown. She watched Michelle lower herself out of sight and then turned her eyes to Laylea when the four-pound puppy yawned.

This was Laylea's third visit to the clinic, her third set of vaccinations. Sher had noticed the abandoned dog responded faster to conditioning techniques than any other animal she'd worked with in the six years since she'd shunned her human research. She'd also noticed how naturally Bailey applied operant conditioning in his interactions with the dog. He used verbal and kinesthetic cues, appropriate scheduling, and randomized reinforcement like he was born to it. Which really, he had been. She'd have to be more careful. Clark was never going to stop letting strangers into their lives so it was up to Sher to do a better job of covering her past. If this software designer could spot her behavioral manipulation, any high-level biologist or psychiatrist would recognize her mastery of a technique which should only be of passing interest to a veterinarian.

Laylea yawned again.

"I'm hearing more occlusion in the lungs. Did you bring Rufus in for breathing issues, Nick?"

"He's tired," Nick said. "And agitated. This is the calmest he's been."

Sher pulled an otoscope from her pocket and looked into the dog's ears. She examined the membrane around his eyes and along his gum line. She pet the dog's fur in the wrong direction to see his reaction. When she smoothed it back down, the dog relaxed.

"You just relax, Rufus. I know you miss your old dad but Nick is gonna take care of you." While she talked to the old golden, she tapped a dot of lavender oil under each of his paws and rubbed the rest of it into his fur. Then she stood and brushed herself off.

Nick stood with her, juggling Laylea and the book in his arms. Laylea started wriggling, her tail thumping between Nick's book and his belly. A second later, the bells on the clinic door jangled.

"Hi Clark."

"Hey Nick. Let me take her for you." Clark ducked around Rufus and Sher to catch Laylea before she wriggled herself right into a fall.

Bailey followed his dad in. He backed up to Rufus to let the old dog smell him. He whispered, "Hi Mom," before turning to scratch behind Rufus's ears. When the dog dropped his jaw, Bailey reached back to push on his hips just as Sher had earlier. The dog looked up at Nick.

Nick said, "good boy," just a second after Bailey did.

"Good job, mister." The kid smiled widely at Nick and handed the man a treat.

Sher covered her face with her hand as Nick laughed out loud. She put a hand on Bailey's head and directed him over to the reception counter.

"Give me a minute, guys."

Clark took Bailey in hand as Sher reached around him to get her clipboard before returning to Nick.

"It sounds like he has a bit of a cold."

Clark chatted with Michelle about how she was liking the new job. Michelle tried to include Bailey in the conversation but even though Laylea was straining to lick his face, Bailey's full attention was focused on his mother's conversation.

"He's six years old?" Michelle asked.

Clark was startled, "Who told you that?

The woman pulled a stack of sheets from the printer. "Oh nobody. I'm guessing." She stapled the papers and struggled out of her seat to swap the bundle with the sign-in sheets on the counter. "I'm going to have one you see. And forewarned is forearmed as they say. Will mine be that," she searched for the right word, "focused?"

Clark looked to see if Bailey was paying them any attention although you really never could tell with Bailey. He seemed to have ears all over. Much like his mother. "He's pretty smart."

Michelle reached up to scratch Laylea's ears. Her dark fingers riffled the puppy's pale fur like a storm racing through a field of wheat. "Were you like that at his age?"

Clark doubted it. "I have no idea. Can't remember."

"Oh of course not. You wouldn't remember being six years old." Michelle laughed. "Although, that's the year I learned to tie my shoe. I remember that. Does your mother ever talk about you being a gifted child, like Bailey?"

"Alas, Michelle," Clark shrugged, "I'm an orphan and an only child, before you ask."

"Oh, how awful. How did your parents pass?"

Before Clark could address the question, Sher interrupted. "Excuse me, Michelle, Nick is ready to check out now. I'll have Chris bring up his meds if you can just take care of the billing."

"Oh certainly, Dr. Sher. And if I have problems with the billing, Nick can help." Michelle laughed a bright little chuckle.

"Mom? Lavender, Mom?"

Nick answered, "We're going to get a plant from the nursery on Canal St."

"Not the oil?" Bailey asked Nick directly.

"Bailiff." Each parent put a hand out to touch the kid.

But Nick wasn't bothered. "We'll try the plant. See how it goes."

Bailey nodded and bent down to answer Rufus' requests for attention.

"Bailiff." Michelle picked up the phone and hit the button for the back room as she laughed. "That's perfect with your name being Sheriff."

"Your name is Sheriff?" Nick asked.

"Michelle," Sher began.

Clark interrupted. "You seem to have this under control, Michelle. We're gonna gather the doctor's things and get out of your hair."

He set a hand firmly on Sher's back and escorted her to the wide-open back room with cages and the more complicated equipment of a veterinarian's office. Bailey stayed in the front. Clark set Laylea on the enormous wheeled treatment table locked down in the middle of the room. He bent over to kiss her on the muzzle and Laylea licked him back. Sher watched for the swinging door to settle into the frame.

She turned on her son's father. "Clark, that is the nosiest woman I have ever met."

Clark spun. "Yes, she's fabulous!" He slapped a hand on the exam table.

It broke.

Laylea yelped as the slick surface tilted beneath her dancing feet. She flew into the air, paws flailing. Miraculously Clark caught the dog before she hit the ground.

"Sorry, Laylea, I forget my strength when I get excited," he said as he peered at the table leg. "Looks like I bent the wheel again." He stood to hand the puppy over to his wife. "The thing with Michelle is you'll know," Clark paused when a Hispanic twenty-something with colorful tattoos covering every inch of exposed flesh exited the storeroom closet. Looking over at the tech, Clark casually reached out to level the tilted table.

"Hi, Clark." The tech detoured to join them, a red pill bottle and bag of hip flex treats in his hands.

"Hey, Chris."

"Is Bailey here?" He didn't even pause for a breath. "You should get him Free Dragon. It's totes creative and you actually gain health when you avoid fights. I can loan you my copy."

"Is that the medicine for Nick?" Sher cut in.

"For Rufus, right?" Chris asked.

"Yes."

Chris nodded, not moving, "Yeah."

"Bailey's in the lobby, Chris," Clark said.

"Cool, I'll grab the game from my locker." Chris turned around and jogged out the door leading to exam room A.

Clark turned back to Sher. "Michelle is going to find out everything there is to know about everyone who comes in this clinic."

"What if she's here to get information on us?"

"No," Clark shook his head. "Her pulse never changed. She's not being deceptive. She's just curious. I love her."

He bent to the foot of the table, giving Sher time to realize the benefits of having such a gatekeeper. With his bare hands, he straightened the steel stem attaching the caster. The lock down mechanism flipped open easily and the wheel spun. But he'd still have to replace that stem. When he stood, the shadow had cleared from Sher's face.

"Yeah," Clark hopped over to the wooden pegs he'd installed by the back door. He lifted her packed messenger bag off with one hand. "And she never has to know who you are. You can train her not to ask us questions. She should be easy for you."

Sher directed the bag onto the repaired table when he approached. The wheel held. "It's not easy to train someone to deny their natural inclinations. Look at you." She pulled her new portable ultrasound from the bag and set it on the surface with a thump. "You loved movies. But they didn't want you to sit still that long or, I'm guessing, to think creatively." Glancing around the room for anything she needed to take home, she spotted her journal lying out on the cluttered desk in the corner. She collected it, snapping each of the three rubber bands in turn to be sure they hadn't been moved from the grooves long worn into the leather binding. "But I couldn't wipe that interest. So, I redirected your need for stories into the way you delivered mission reports." Sher tucked her journal into the front pocket of her messenger bag and tossed the much-lightened bag over her shoulder. "And that memory came back. It was the one thing I was able to retrieve." Clark took the puppy from her arms, kissing it on the head. "I don't know that I *remember* liking movies. I think maybe I learned to like them again because I got to sit in the dark with that beauty." He held the puppy up to look at Sher. Laylea curled her tail into her belly until Sher pushed her back into the safety of Clark's arms. "I guess I really hated writing."

Sher laughed. "Yeah. That was easy to condition out of you. I wish I knew *why* they'd want a soldier who can't write."

Clark stepped over to Sher. He pulled her into his free arm and kissed her. Laylea whimpered, afraid of being crushed in the tight hug. Sher reached a hand up to support Laylea's hindquarters and she let herself be kissed the way a woman ought to be kissed.

"Come on, Doctor, let's go home and watch a movie."

CHAPTER 4

SUMMER 2025 - FOOTHILLS, OR

Three rays of the afternoon sun shot into the couch room despite the heavy curtains Sher had pulled across the two windows. Laylea's leg cut through one of the beams as she pawed at the mom's sleeping face. It startled her and she looked around to see if the boys had come home.

The beam had hit her paw as she tried to wake Sher. Maybe it was saying that was a good idea. Another beam struck the spine of a leather book on the shelves beside the TV. Did that mean Laylea should read the book? Even if she could read, she could never get that book off the shelves. It was too high. The third beam didn't help at all. It just pointed at a little Martian guy on the oriental rug. Could a Martian stop Sher's nightmare? What was a Martian and where could she find one?

Laylea looked back as the mom flailed again. The puppy had grown accustomed to Woodford flinging legs about in the throes of his dreams. He often kicked her in the head. But she had never seen one of the humans do it. Most nights she slept in a piled-up comforter on the floor of Bailey's bedroom but she'd slept a couple of times with Woodford in the parents' room so she had enough experience to know this wasn't normal. Dr. Sher showing any emotion wasn't normal.

Her practical haircut was mussed now. Sweat plastering the short blond strands against her face. They didn't move as she tossed her head from side to side. Laylea surfed precariously on her chest. She pawed at her face again and stood on her chin to lick a drop of salt water rolling down one cheek. Another violent breath sent her tripping backwards. The puppy dropped to her belly to keep from falling. The mom didn't wake.

She whimpered quietly, afraid to disturb the doctor but just as scared to let her sleep. She braved the beam of sun to set her cold nose against Sher's neck. With all her heart, she wished the boys were home.

But it was Saturday and they'd gone on a big hike to celebrate Bailey's seventh birthday. All the boys. After the birthday bread pudding was devoured and the dishes washed up, the boys had hiked off the porch, down the street, and between the stone walls to reach the path leading past the rental cottage in the curve of the cul-de-sac.

Sher had tinkered in the hidden room until the sun came up. Once the dew evaporated, she'd settled Laylea in her bicycle basket and ridden to the clinic for her final vaccination shots.

They'd picked up pastries from the Cuban bakery near Bailey's elementary school and then ridden home using the front streets. Laylea knew they were near their street when she saw the two trees that Clark said looked like a couple of drunks. When they turned into their little cul-de-sac Laylea looked up at the thin green sign on top of a pole that told strangers the street name. A small yelp escaped her even though she tried to be stoic when it was just she and the mom. A bright light flashed at her from the sign. It felt like a spike through her eyes into her brain. It was a bad sign. She wouldn't look at it again.

"My deterrent works on dogs too?" Sher had asked her. "But you can't read."

Laylea had curled up in the basket, tucking her nose under her tail. She'd stayed there when Sher stopped to chat with the Old Lady Rucker who was out working on her roses. The OLR's grandsons, Parker and his younger brother Davis, raced to a spigot to wash their hands when the mom gave the neighbor their pastries, saying they were extras.

The Old Lady Rucker had called the renters from the end house over to share the bounty. Laylea expected Sher would hurry home when they came over. But she stayed and talked with them about shoes. She even pet each of them a little. Laylea had peeked out of her baby blanket, hoping to get some petting herself. Davis spotted her and squealed. He scratched her ears without even offering his hand for a sniff first. It was nice. But it wasn't pets from the mom.

After that, they'd gone home. Laylea got to sleep in Woodford's nighttime bed while the mom showered.

She got to curl up on the couch with Sher downstairs as they watched a girlie flick. Lots of sexy men and sword fights and a little time travel. Then Sher had tucked Laylea into the curve of her belly, pulled the afghan up over her head, and they'd napped. Laylea had never napped with the mom before. She smelled different when she was asleep. She smelled happy. For a few hours. Now she smelled angry and sad and Laylea didn't know what to do.

Laylea looked at each bright beam again. The bookcase. The carpet. Her paw. No answer revealed itself. Holding her breath, she nipped at the mom's nose.

Sher shook her off.

THE DOCTOR SHOOK off her grief, wiped the tears from her cheeks and the vomit from her lips. She set aside the silver emesis basin and escorted the soldier known to her as Gamma Subject out of her exam room, through the halls of the lab, to the front entrance. Gamma Subject's deep black skin and dark green coveralls stood out against the white walls. But he stood quiet, as good as invisible when they encountered other Consortium personnel. Sher greeted every one. She touched them; their arms, hands, chest, shoulder and said "sometimes you need fresh air." Each nodded and let them pass.

To get out the front door of the laboratory building they had to stop for a moment in an airlock. While they waited for the standard security interrogation that was protocol before being buzzed through, the soldier quietly dropped a knife from his sleeve into his hand.

The doctor hid her mouth from the guards on the other side of the window by looking at her feet and rubbing at her eyes. She spoke in an unnaturally low voice. "No."

Gamma Subject bent and let the knife slip into his boot, responding automatically, "I will not kill another soul today."

Static sounded in the small room. "You've forgotten to take off your lab coat, Doctor Coogan."

The doctor leaned in to push the button on her side of the protective glass. She spoke quietly. "Beer o'clock, David. Sometimes you need fresh air."

The desk guard stood and gestured for the door guard to open the airlock. As the doctor stepped through, she put a hand on the second guard's chest and leaned in to catch his eyes. "Sometimes you need fresh air."

"Would you like me to pull the fire alarm, Doc?" David held the door for the other guard to go outside.

Coogan smiled at the man. "Yes, please, David."

David turned back to break the glass on the emergency alert box as the doctor continued out the door propelling the soldier ahead of her. Gamma Subject led the doctor away from the building toward the distant parking lot. He noticed a trickle of people leaving the building from all exits. The doctor took no notice, walking as quickly as she could away from the building. Moments after they heard the alarm, the trickle grew to a swarm.

The soldier wondered at it. He turned to the doctor, amazed. "You conditioned them."

"Yes." She kept walking swiftly away from the lab.

Hundreds of people exited the building in a calm unhurried manner. "All of them?"

"Yes."

As they reached the parking lot, the soldier pulled the doctor behind a large white cargo van. Two rugged mountain bicycles leaned against the vehicle.

Coogan was underwhelmed by her subject's preparations. "You're kidding."

"Trust me, Doc."

They got on the bicycles and had almost reached the back of the parking lot when the muffled first explosion reached their ears. It was far inside the building, hopefully driving any remaining employees outside.

The doctor had timed the explosions for least loss of life. But as she glanced back, a part of her hoped that Trask remained trapped inside.

Hundreds of long white coats continued to stroll away from the explosions. They walked into the trees, folded into the lines of cars in the parking lot, and steadily made their ways across the open field between the research building and the highway. Everyone walking away. So, it was easy to pick out the one figure running. The one figure heading toward the building. The woman's black bouffant hairdo stood out against the white building as Trask ran back to the exit nearest her offices. Coogan watched that hair catch fire as the bomb disguised as a fire extinguisher just outside Trask's office went off and sent the bitch flying violently through the air. The doctor's smile didn't have time to hit her lips before she had to help Gamma Subject who knelt, vomiting into the grass at the edge of the woods.

"I will not kill another soul today."

"Not today," she agreed and got him back on his bike and into the woods before they were seen.

A few miles away the soldier stopped by a rushing creek. He rifled through his backpack and pockets, taking out cell phone, GPS, Smart-Pad, camera. He took off his watch and his heart monitor. "Dump all your tech. They can track everything."

The doctor dumped her phone and her watch. But she held on to a small scanner and pulled an alcohol swab from her lab coat pocket. "I need to borrow your knife."

She had the tall soldier turn around and kneel as she wiped the knife with alcohol. Then she pulled up his shirt and scanned between his shoulder blades. When the device whined, she swabbed the area and dug the knife's tip into his flesh, extracting an electrical device smaller than a thumbnail. She dropped it in the water and almost dropped the scanner as well until a thought stopped her. She handed the scanner to the soldier and turned her back on him. Taking off her lab coat she unbuttoned her shirt. When the scanner whined, she pulled more swabs from her pocket and sterilized the knife.

"Where are we going?" she asked, handing the soldier his weapon.

His voice went distant as he focused on his task. He wasn't as familiar with delicate knife work as the doctor. "We're going to the

Consortium's testing grounds. For our final exam, they drop us in a mountain range. If we get back to the lab, we pass. Perhaps I can catch you some more Conditioned Force soldiers to fix."

"You can help me," she replied. "I'll teach you how to recondition."

"Can you get my memories back? My name?"

The doctor winced as he pulled the transmitter from her skin and wiped more alcohol into the cut. "I don't know. I'll—" Coogan fell to her knees. "No." She shook her head violently. "No, I'm lying again. I'm sorry. I don't think I . . . we used drugs. We changed you. I don't think I can do this."

The soldier tried to lift her up. "You have to."

"They killed my brother." She caught his eyes and she knew that they'd made him kill people's brothers. She looked away, fell to the grass before she could wonder if he had been the one to kill her brother. She lay there, frozen, her life blown up.

Gamma Subject knelt beside her. Then he lay down in the wet grass and reached one dark arm up to weave his fingers into her pale ones. They clutched at the grass together.

He whispered into her long black ponytail, "I don't need a name, Doc. I've seen lots of toe tags labeled J. Doe and I've wondered who he was."

She snorted. He laughed.

Another moment passed with the wet seeping into their clothes and the distant fire smoking the air over their heads. The doctor sat up. She could hear voices starting to question each other. The fire and strangeness of the day was breaking down her conditioning. They had to run.

J. Doe took her hand and brushed himself off. He looked back at the flames licking the air on the high horizon. Together they listened to the crackling flames and the intermittent explosions as the fire reached new labs in the building.

"Doc, they've changed you too."

Coogan inhaled sharply in an almost laugh. "I blew up the lab."

"Yes, you did." He smiled encouragingly. "They'll know better than to mess with your family again."

She looked in his eyes. A smile came to her lips now. "I blew up their building."

J. Doe nodded. "Look out, Consortium. There's a new sheriff in town."

It was the push she needed. They climbed back on their bikes and rode away.

"MOM!"

Laylea tumbled from the couch as Sher sat up. The doctor's hand shot out and grabbed the puppy just before she hit the carpet. Laylea stared into her eyes, wanting to see that she was okay. That the dream was over. But the mom just set Laylea on the floor.

"Our wandering champions are home," she called. "The girls are in here."

Woodford continued through the swinging door into the kitchen. But Bailey flipped around, bounced off the dining room wall, and barreled into the family room. Laylea found herself scooped off the floor as Bailey told them both all about the birds and the bugs they'd seen and how you could answer a question any old way you wanted to even if your answer didn't answer the person's question.

Sher folded the blanket in her lap, inviting the bouncing kid to sit with her. "You learned how to keep a secret?"

"Secrets aren't always a bad thing. Like if you don't want to hurt a friend's feelings, you can tell them you like their new haircut even if it looks like they fell into a box fan."

"Really?" Sher glanced up at Clark leaning in the archway. She asked again, "Did you learn how to keep a secret?"

Bailey stayed on the couch. He pet Laylea and bounced. But he also looked his mother directly in the eyes. "I learned that there are so many different species of bugs that we don't have names for them all and that's okay because not everything needs a label."

Sher took a breath to ask again. Bailey cut her off. He lifted a small bag from his hip, making her look away from his eyes. "We collected lots of sage. Sage belongs in the kitchen, doesn't it?"

Sher let a smile grow on her lips. When she looked up, Laylea could still see a little fear deep in her eyes, but the smile was starting to replace it. "Pharmacologically, sage can be used to enhance your short-term memory recall."

Bailey doubled up in giggles. "Which is why Dad puts it in everything!"

"Hey Bailiff," Sher let him catch his breath, but only just. "Did you learn how to keep a secret?"

His giggles renewed. "I'll never tell."

Laylea licked at his face, missing as he kept bouncing.

"Did you learn—" the mom didn't even get to finish her question.

The boy popped up and headed out the door. "I'll go lay the sage out to dry."

Woodford came trotting out of the kitchen, water dripping from his muzzle. Bailey stopped in the dining room to scratch the dog and Laylea nearly tumbled out of his arms onto the big hound.

She heard Sher sigh, "Oh, Clark, what have you done? We aren't gonna get a straight answer from that kid for weeks."

The dad called out, "Hey Bailey."

He rescued Laylea from the kid's arms as Bailey flipped around and stumbled back into the family room. Woodford followed at a leisurely pace.

"Mom! You can pick any word out of the question and free associalize on that word, like you did with *sage*. Or you can change the subject. Or you can make a joke. Or you can just walk away like you didn't even hear the question. But within the family we don't keep secrets. Like I should be honest about how much I miss you when we hike without you. Even though I know it makes you sad because it reminds you that you can't ever see *your* mom again or your dad or your sister or your aunts and uncle or your cousins."

Laylea felt the temperature dip. She tucked her tail tight in her belly, remembering the smell of her mother and her brothers wiggling all around her.

The mom stiffened.

Bailey stiffened too. "Are you sad, Mom?" He added, in a tiny voice, "no secrets."

"You're sad when I'm not around?" Sher asked.

Clark mumbled into Laylea's fur, "Deflection."

Sher's eyes darted up to his. Then she looked at her kid and joined him in nodding.

"Can I hug you, Mom?"

Laylea flipped over to see Sher. The cold fled from her eyes.

"You can always hug me. My mom said I didn't know when I needed a good hugging."

"Your mom hugged you?" Bailey asked, his eyes glued to hers.

A smile tugged at Sher's lips and then disappeared again. "My mom hugged us every single day. Said hugs renewed her magic."

"I like that," Bailey declared. "I'm gonna hug you for your mom every day."

He bounded over. After an instant, he backed away and kissed her on the cheek. Then he climbed into her lap and wrapped himself around her neck, holding tight.

Laylea wiggled when he hopped off. Sher's eyes glowed bright and warm.

"Two hugs, Kiddo?" Clark asked.

"Have to keep her magic strong so she can keep us safe!" Bailey hollered back as he ran off to the kitchen.

"A hug every single day," Clark said. "Are you gonna be able to handle it?"

Sher dragged herself off the couch. She set the folded afghan on the arm and then knelt on the poofy bolster of Woodford's bed. The mom gave Woodford a full massage, working from his ears all the way down to his tail. When she was done, Woodford rolled on his side and let her examine his belly. She finished by picking gunk out of the corners of his eyes.

She stood. She wiped at the corners of her own eyes.

"You didn't have to use your rope bracelet."

Clark threw his head back and laughed so hard he frightened Laylea. "Deflection!"

"No, sir," Sher corrected with a laugh. "That was free assocializing."

Even though he laughed with her, Clark didn't let her off the hook. "*That* was deflection."

"Yes," she agreed. "And I've gotten you to change the subject for me."

"Hugs." Clark changed the subject back.

Sher picked a little green book up off the TV table. She sighed again. "I'm not gonna be able to handle a hug every single day." She crossed over and wiped Laylea's eyes. "I'd rather go back to fighting the Consortium."

Clark scoffed, "You never fought them. You just blew up their building and stole their experiments."

"I didn't steal you," she argued. "I like to think I rescued you."

"And I like to think I'm rescuing you," Clark approached his wife with deliberate steps.

"No," Sher backed away.

Clark nodded sadly. "I'm willing to do whatever it takes to keep you strong."

Sher was stopped by Woodford's bed. She caught herself before she fell on him. Woodford raised his head.

Clark wrapped one arm around his trapped wife. "A hug every day from all of us! You'll be the most powerful witch in Foothills!"

"Damn Gamma Subject."

"I'm Theta," Clark corrected, squeezing tightly and holding Laylea up to lick the mom's face.

"Yeah. But it was Gamma who suggested I remind you about movies."

"Oh yeah." Laylea licked at the smile that filled the dad's face. "That bastard."

CHAPTER 5

SUMMER 2025 - FOOTHILLS, OR

Laylea's vaccinations took ten weeks. She made the most of every minute she got to spend with the Hillens.

She raced around the main floor of the house with Woodford and Bailey. If the boys took their games upstairs she needed help. The first time they'd abandoned her, she dropped her butt to the ground and bayed in her little singing voice, trying to howl like Woodford. Sher had burst out of the kitchen. As soon as she picked Laylea up, the puppy clamped down on her crying. After establishing there was no physical injury to the dog, Sher returned her to the floor. Laylea tripped over to the step and pawed at it, looking up at the mom with little hope.

"If you address the problem you won't have time to stress over it. Have you even tried to get up the stairs on your own?"

Laylea stretched up, her belly against the step, and pulled with all the strength in her little front paws while her back legs scrabbled at the wood. She got one rear paw up before tumbling back to the floor.

"Good job." Sher bent and gave her a rare belly scratch. "Bailiff!"

Bailey dashed back down the stairs and grabbed Laylea up. They went off and played and had fun. But a small part of Laylea wished she'd gotten just a few more seconds of love from the mom.

Laylea discovered the best place to nap was right beside Woodford.

Though he didn't sleep as much, he would find himself a nice sunny spot with a view of the drunken trees or the other neighbors in their cul-de-sac. Sometimes the Rucker boys would come over to play with them and sometimes they'd invite the dogs and Bailey over to run around in their grandmother's yard if they were very careful to avoid the roses. Laylea didn't want to avoid the roses. Their scent intoxicated her. It changed constantly and they smelled differently from the front porch than when she snuck over and buried her head in the bushes. She just sniffed the flowers. Woodford dug in the dirt beneath them.

Laylea learned quickly. Some rules seemed to come naturally to her and some she picked up with only one or two reinforcements. She tumbled down the stairs several times before they were declared off limits. But she only peed inside the house once more after the first day and that was on the carpet remnant inside the front door. Bailey showed her the bells on the door. He showed her the bells on all the doors. If she rang a bell, one of the humans would open the door. It seemed everyone in the house was conditioned to respond to the bells. Every window had bells too. Whenever the security of the house was breached, Woodford, Laylea, and any humans in the house who weren't in a shower would report to the jingling.

Five days a week Sher left the house to work at her clinic. Woodford got to go with her when she rode the tricycle with the rear basket. Bailey went to school five days a week. But Clark never went away. Laylea followed him everywhere. Most times he took her with him in his bicycle basket as he rode around town and beyond. They'd visit other people's houses and fix things. She got to wear a collar like Woodford whenever they left the neighborhood.

She wasn't allowed to help fix things at the Rick's house across the street just because she chased their cat up the porch, over the roof, and into a tree three times. She did get to go with him to help a nice old lady in a mansion right on the edge of town. Her house was filled with blankets and books and clocks and the lady fed Laylea sausages while Clark rebuilt her bathrooms to be wheelchair accessible. That was a wondrous week.

Many of their jaunts involved shopping. One trip took so long Laylea curled up in her blue baby towel and fell asleep to the bounce of the tricycle and the low hum of Clark's singing. They made four stops and by the time they were pedaling home the dad struggled against the weight of an overstuffed backpack, filled trike trunk, plus Bailey's old trailer topped up with odds and ends. Laylea even had to share her handlebar basket with a shopping bag of feminine supplies.

After each shopping trip, Clark would park the bike or trike on the right side of the garage and unload most of his supplies into the small Chevy pickup that rusted against the far wall. The day of the long excursion, Clark scooped sleeping Laylea from her basket and set her atop a quartet of giant flour sacks in the truck bed. He'd closed the motor operated barn doors leading to the driveway and turned on the ancient yellow lamp overhead.

Laylea yawned and pawed at her eyes. She looked around at the crates and stacks of supplies around her. A misshapen burlap sack leaned against the flour sacks at the tail of the truck nearly hiding the two bags of apples beneath it. Behind the flour, a bag filled with various sized jeans sat on a box filled with small camping gear like a water filter and all-weather matches. Most of the bed was taken up by a grid of crates which rose nearly high enough to block the back window of the cab. Each of these was wrapped in plastic and labeled with a number. Most of the crates held one or two books and a baggie of soaps and toiletries. The feminine products were distributed among some of these. One dusty blue crate contained rolls of thread and a giant cloth bag of mismatched buttons donated by the sausage lady. Two bolts of fabric stuck out of the top of this crate. Clark covered them with a potato sack and bungeed it tightly around the material.

He talked to Laylea as he worked.

"We're going to the mountains, Lee." He hauled a bag of seed corn off the shelves. "I don't really have a lot of marketable skills beyond my freakish perfect recall. And since we can only retrieve the details under hypnosis, and that's not really something we want to advertise, I can't get a regular job." He tucked the bag down into the space between the crates and wheel well. "I help people out around town when I can. But my most important jobs are for my clients up in the mountains. I take them supplies they can't produce themselves. I deliver mail. And I provide an opportunity for socializing." He stopped to run a hand over her fur. "You know how we make sure you get to sniff other dogs when we see them? That's socializing. It's healthy. These folk don't get much of it. That's kind of why Sher calls them hermits."

He worked quietly for a while, rearranging the items in the truck bed to fit snugly. Laylea turned around a couple of times, lost her footing, and slipped off the flour sacks. She clambered up the camping gear box and pushed off the sack of jeans to scramble back up. Keeping an eye on the edges, she turned three times and dropped into a curl.

A shadow cut off the light from the old bulbs. She looked up to see Clark standing over her, shaking his head. She lifted her front leg, hopeful of a chest rub, but the dad slipped his whole hand under her belly and flew her over to a stack of tarps by the kitchen steps. He pulled one of the sheets of blue plastic off the top and set her down on the remaining pile. She gave him the puppy eyes and rolled on her side, opening her whole belly to him. Laughing, he knelt to scritch her.

"I guess we're hermits too. But these people are even more wary of civilization than us. Some of them are still healing from being rescued." Clark kissed her head and turned away. He shook the tarp open over the truck bed. "I suppose I'm still healing from—"

Sher stuck her head out the kitchen door. "Dinner's ready."

"I'll just be another minute." Clark bent his head down as he tied a corner of the tarp to the truck.

Sher leaned on the door. "Are you okay?"

The dad looked up, a bright smile on his face. "I'm always okay."

Laylea tilted her head. She could smell his fear. She thought Sher could smell it too because the mom came down the steps and peered in the cab of the truck.

"Bailey's still pouting," she said. "But he's on the stairs now."

"Why don't you just give him the book you got for him?"

Laylea shrunk into her stack of tarps at Sher's tone when she replied, "Because I don't reward that kind of behavior. We cannot keep the dog. He has to understand that. This family is big enough already. What would we do with two dogs if we have to run?"

Clark moved down to the next set of ropes on the tarp. "We're not taking commercial transportation anywhere. My false ID wouldn't pass that kind of inspection. So why can't we just take them with us?"

"You know it'll be too dangerous."

"So, we leave them both at the clinic." He cinched the knot tight. "They'll find homes."

"And break his heart even more?"

Clark took a breath. He pulled a bungee cord out of the bed. "A broken heart just proves you have one."

"You're saying I'm heartless?"

"I'm saying you could be less logical. You could think with your heart now and then."

Laylea looked from one to the other as the air in the garage thickened. She wanted one of them to say something before they all suffocated. Clark stretched the elastic cord in his hands. In a rush he blurted, "Come with me."

Sher took a step back as if she'd been pushed and had to catch herself from falling. She inhaled a breath filled with thoughts but all that came out was, "No."

There was no arguing with that declaration. There was no arguing with Sher. The mom turned and before the echo of the word had died in the stale air the kitchen door fell shut behind her.

Laylea watched Clark. He closed the tailgate and secured the second side of the tarp. He worked with his back to the kitchen door but Laylea could see he was more than aware of the emptiness that stood there now. She slid and tumbled off of the cold stack of blue plastic to totter over to his feet. She shadowed him as he moved along the side of the truck, chanting as he worked. He laced the ropes and tied them off in a rhythm that matched his words. "I will not kill another soul today. I will not kill another soul today."

He repeated this phrase until the last knot was pulled taut. As he smoothed the tarp around the upright bolts of fabric, his words changed. "Her life is in my hands and I will not throw it away."

Laylea felt a calm descend over him.

"I guess that's it." He spoke to himself and then raised his voice for her. "I tried, little girl." He woke from his trance and adjusted the bolts of fabric so the tarp lay more evenly. "If some evil guy is really after you then you'll be safer in the mountains with one of the other CF soldiers. I suppose you might be a match with a regular old hermit but I hope you'll be a salve for one of us. You've been a salve for me. Whoa!" He hopped to avoid stepping on the puppy. Laylea yelped softly.

"I'm sorry." He knelt and scooped her into his lap. "You came over to comfort me, didn't you?" He held her up and tapped her forehead to his. " I'm gonna miss you."

She swatted his mouth with her paws and licked every part of him she could reach.

"You are sweet and silly and cuddly in ways Woodford will never be." Clark held her in front of him, suddenly serious. "Don't get me wrong. I adore Woodford. Have ever since Sher brought him home. *She* rescued him from a ditch on the side of a busy road. He was filthy and underfed and scared of humans and dogs alike. Do not repeat this, Laylea, but Woodford was even scared of cats." Clark bent his knees to support her little legs. He sighed. She looked up, not licking now, trying to listen closely. "She rescued me because she was the one who turned me into a Conditioned Force soldier. She rescued Woodford because knowing there are other horrible people in the world made her feel a little less awful. Now he's our reliable, even-tempered guard hound and I'm her reliable, even-tempered baby daddy."

He looked down and saw her watching him. He kissed her nose. She kissed his back.

"You and Bailey though. You are love. You're filled with affection and cuddles. Wherever you end up, don't you let that go, Laylea. These CF have all been broken, just like me. Just like Sher. We're all trying the best we can to be happy again. To be like you and Bailey."

The kitchen door opened. Clark's warm smell iced over with fear and he stood brushing specks of debris from his khakis.

"Dad?"

Laylea had been watching Clark. Clark had been examining the tie-downs. When Bailey spoke, he swiveled and smiled. Laylea's tail flicked of its own volition in the joy of seeing the kid. She heard Woodford's tail thump against a kitchen counter in counterpoint to the rain of kibble into plastic bowls. Her own tail sped up under the dad's arm.

"Dinner?" Clark asked.

Laylea chirped a happy bark, thinking he was asking if she wanted some.

She pasted her ears back when Bailey answered, "Yeah."

But Clark flew her into Bailey's arms, unaware of her embarrassment. "Dinner for everyone, then."

Sher stayed distant through dinner. She joined them for night walk but didn't chatter with the boys. Before the sun rose in the morning, she rousted Bailey and Laylea from bed and took the puppy outside for an abbreviated morning walk. Nobody said much or sat much during the quick breakfast of kibble and oatmeal. Bailey carried Laylea with him as he helped his dad pack a few last items into the truck.

Sher emerged from her tinker room with a small round pillow half again as big as Laylea. She attached several straps to loops on the pillow and set the whole contraption on the passenger seat of the truck.

Bailey kissed Laylea a billion times before he handed her to his mother who held the puppy up and kissed her forehead. Laylea was so surprised she barely had time to dart her head out and lick Sher's nose before she was set in the middle of the little pillow. She stood as the pillow settled around her, revealing it was actually a bed of cushiony fabric surrounded by a firm bolster. The blue was the same shade her baby towel might once have been and complimented it nicely when Sher tucked the old thing in beside her.

Clark and Bailey pushed open the single right-hand panel of the carriage doors. Then Clark slid into the driver's seat and Bailey reached in the passenger side window to pet the puppy one last time.

Sher came running from the kitchen when Clark started the engine. "Hold on. Two more things."

She reached through the window with a green book about the size of a package of hot dogs. "This is for the new guy. He needs it."

Clark reached to take the book but Sher didn't let it go.

She repeated, "He needs it."

"Got it." Clark set the book on the dashboard.

"And here." The mom tucked a patchwork stuffed lizard no bigger than her hand into the crook of Laylea's belly. "Something for her to cuddle while you're flying."

Her husband laughed. "A lizard?"

"She doesn't seem like a teddy bear kind of dog, right?" She looked to Bailey who nodded enthusiastically. "So why not a teddy lizard?"

Laylea smelled warm joy wash over the tension that had ruled Clark's morning. "I love it when you surprise me, Sheriff."

Sher smelled to Laylea like a mix of burnt popcorn washed with rain. She stood up on the armrest, but Sher turned away. And Clark's joy faded. He put the truck in gear and they rolled away from the mom and the kid. Laylea pawed at the door. She couldn't keep a small cry from escaping.

And when Bailey broke from his mother and ran to the window for one more kiss, Sher caught Clark's eyes.

He stopped the truck.

Laylea lapped at the tears pouring down Bailey's face. She wanted him to pick her up out of her new bed. She wanted Clark to leap from the truck and spin Sher in his arms. She wanted to stay.

But the mom wrapped her arms around Bailey and pulled him one step back from the truck. She waited until Clark had pulled Laylea from the door and settled her again in the new blue bed. Then she bent awkwardly to catch his eyes.

"Fair winds."

Clark breathed. "I love you."

The truck rolled out of the garage and Laylea stared out of the window at the mom and the boy until she couldn't see them anymore. She shut her eyes before they reached the entrance to the cul-de-sac with its drunken trees and painful sign. But in her mind, she could still see her second family waving goodbye.

CHAPTER 6

SUMMER 2025 - FOOTHILLS, OR AND DEEP IN THE MOUNTAINS

C lark let Laylea sit in the pilot's seat of his single engine Cessna Cardinal while he loaded the cargo. She watched as he unloaded the truck and packed everything into the plane. Once the supplies were stowed, the dad backed the Cessna out of the dusty shed and hopped out to park the empty truck where the plane had been. Laylea raced back and forth in the cockpit, hopping from one blue seat to the other and back to find some view out the windows where she could see him. When he returned to the plane, she calmed. He set her in the new blue bed and attached the straps Sher had rigged up to allow the bed to be buckled in. He buckled himself in the left seat, finished his checklist, and keyed the radio.

"I'm about to take the runway."

Laylea watched him work the controls, confident and trusting. Until they started rushing down the runway.

Squeezed against the back of the bed she dropped her lower jaw to bark but found she couldn't. For terrifying minutes the world rushed by and then everything slowed down. All she could see was sky in every direction. She stood on the side door, trying to find the earth she knew but it wasn't there. The whole world was blue. Her tummy gurgled. She twisted around to snap at it. Something inside wanted out. Terrified of making a mess on her brand-new lizard, she half-leapt half-tumbled out of the bed. A bag of clothes on the floor of the cockpit cushioned her fall. And after she threw up, her tummy felt much better. She couldn't figure out how to get back up to her bed without stepping in the sick so she wandered over to Clark's feet to curl up. He scooped her into his lap.

"Try to go to sleep, little girl. We're just gonna have to suffer with that smell for a few more hours."

Laylea turned around three times, navigating his bony knees and the seat belt and the yoke over her head. She climbed over into her passenger side bed and dragged her stuffed lizard back to his lap. Holding the lizard by the tail, she tried to circle three times again, kneaded his left thigh a bit, and finally collapsed, unconscious before she hit his legs. She slept like a baby for the next few hours.

Silence woke her when Clark landed in a clearing. She cleaned her lizard sleepily as the plane slowed until she noticed the view held more than just sky.

She stood on the yoke and saw trees in every direction. Greens of every shade punctuated with browns and the piercing blue of the sky over it all. Not knowing how a plane worked she couldn't be amazed at Clark's ability to land in such a small clearing but she licked his nose anyway.

Clark set a rock in the leather sling hanging from his belt and scooped Laylea into his chest as he got out.

"Ah, fresh air." He inhaled deeply. "Don't worry. We'll clean out your accident after we meet these guys."

This world smelled even better than roses. She craned her head around looking at the enormous trees and got stuck in a backbend watching two men approach. One walked far in front of the other, moving swiftly towards them. She tried to bark, choked, and twisted around so she could look at the hermits upright. Clark seemed to expect their appearance so she tried to take it in stride as well, barking through her teeth just to let them know she was taking their measure.

"Hey Captain, nice pup. Keep her close or the coyotes around here will grab her for lunch." The taller man stopped about four feet away from Laylea and the dad. He stood alert, feet set in a way that could take him quickly in any direction. His empty hands hung at his sides but Laylea saw the thick muscles of his biceps flexing beneath his waffle-cut shirt. A slight wiggle in the fingers of his right hand drew her eyes to the knife sheathed on his hip. The closure was unsnapped.

Her hackles stood of their own accord. Clark smoothed them down. "Thanks for the advice, Stretch. You and Mike have any need for a hunting dog?"

"Yeah." Stretch responded tersely as his quiet, loping friend caught up and passed him. "You got one hidden in the plane?"

Mike held a hand out for Laylea to sniff. Her nose stung at the smell of burning wood and rotten eggs. But then she caught a soothing undertone of frothy dirt which curled into her belly like broth moistened kibble. Underneath that she smelled loss and sorrow and kindness. She approved his smell by tucking her nose under the hand and when he scratched her ears, she peered up into his face, wondering if this was one of the CF Clark wanted her to help.

A smile softened Mike's face when he let Laylea look into his eyes. But then he glanced at his tall friend and shook an apologetic no at Clark.

Clark nodded. He clipped the end of a rope onto Laylea's collar and set her on the ground. He attached the other end of the rope to the plane.

"You stay close," he said. "Holler if you need me."

Laylea sniffed Stretch's legs. Her eyes watered at the sharp scent and she sneezed. But Clark put an arm around the guy and led him away so Laylea tottered off to chase bugs and leap on flowers until she passed out under the plane. When she woke, the world was all blue again and she lay on Clark's lap with her lizard under her head. The stench of sick had been replaced with the scent of oranges. She craned her neck to watch Clark sing softly.

I will
not kill
Another soul today.
Their life is in my hands and I will not throw it away.

She yawned. Her front paws pushed against an object in the zippered pocket on his thigh.

"Hello there. Stretch and Mike didn't think you were their kind of dog. Are you disappointed?" He waited for her response but she just tilted her head. "I didn't think you would be staying with them. But at our last stop, you're gonna meet a few families and we'll be spending the night. I can think of one little girl that's gonna love you. You let me know if you don't like her. Okay?"

Laylea uncurled and stretched. Then she stood up on his chest and tried to lick his face. She couldn't reach.

"I need you to stay in the plane at our next stop. Jay just rescued Red a few weeks ago. She's still learning to control her impulses. Chances are she left her payment at the tree and I'll just trade it for her clothes and medicine and we'll be on our way. But if she is there, I'd feel safer with you here in the cockpit. She got some memories back that . . . well, she makes me glad I can't remember a thing."

He talked to her throughout their descent, yawning a few times right in her face. She yawned back and felt her ears pop open. Clark's voice mixed with the suddenly loud droning of the engine distracted and entranced her so that she didn't realize they were on the ground until Clark cursed as he battled the plane to a stop on the rocky outcropping. Laylea rolled into his body as he flexed every muscle in his legs. She bounced against his flexed abs, claws fully extended with nothing to grip.

She relaxed when the bouncing stopped but Clark tensed more. He lowered an elbow to keep her from sliding off his lap when the plane banked left. They kept turning until they were headed back onto the bumpy ground they had just escaped. Laylea trembled and the dad talked to her.

"This plane" he told her, "is a solid piece of equipment. Made a few modifications, of course. I may make a few more. But you don't need to worry. Gonna park way back here. You keep your head down and stay quiet. Looks like Red isn't about, but you never do know."

His monologue slowly ran out of steam until, by the time he shifted Laylea to her little blue bed he was just chanting, "I will not kill. I will not kill."

Laylea tucked herself down into her poofy bed. She glued her eyes on Clark but he didn't say anything else to her or even look her way. She ducked low when he tilted the seat back over her to pull a black garbage bag wrapped with duct tape from the cargo space behind them. He hefted the bag under one arm and slipped out of the cockpit. He set a rock in his sling and just before he clicked the door shut, he held up his palm and pushed it firmly into the air.

The Hand of Stay.

Laylea wanted to watch. She wanted to jump over to his seat and stand on the door to watch him through the window. But she was a good girl. She stayed. She snuggled down in her bed with her lizard listening to Clark chant.

"I will not kill another soul today."

"That's mine."

Every hair on Laylea's tiny body stood up when a strident female voice cut through the comforting rhythm. She sat up and then dropped to a crouch when she remembered her orders.

"It is." Clark's voice held steady, even friendly. "And this is mine. Right, Red?"

The pause was too long. Laylea's muscles vibrated though she kept silent. Feet scuffled among leaves. A rock pinged off the plane. Laylea held her position even when she heard Clark grunt. A sharp sound of flesh on flesh echoed in the mountains followed by a series of flat thuds. Clark never grunted again but she heard Red cry out. The puppy perked both ears and rotated them toward the sounds. She didn't hear anything except heavy breathing for several moments. Fear overwhelmed the minty brightness of pine and water that had blanketed their runway. Laylea ducked her nose, wiped at it with a paw. She was about to disobey the Hand of Stay and leap to the window when Clark inhaled deeply.

He sang.

I will

Not kill

Another soul today.

Red's breathing calmed to near sleeping levels as Clark softly sang in her ear. When he got to the last line, her crisp soprano tones joined him.

His life is in my hands and I will not throw it away.

The silence returned after the final extended note of the verse drifted into the wind. Laylea kept her head down because Clark had told her to. And because the smell of fear had drifted away with the final note.

"I'll see you in the fall." Laylea's tail bust out as she heard his steps returning to her.

He'd gone seven paces when Red called out, "Can you use some jerky?"

Clark hesitated. "Yes. But I don't have anything else to give you right now."

"No. Later. When you come back in the fall. I know how to make jerky."

"Sure." A genuine smile warmed Clark's voice. "I'll trade for jerky. Good idea."

Red hummed the tune of the chant. Clark opened the plane door just enough to get in. He ignored Laylea as he stowed several large bundles of plants in the cargo area. His face smelled funny. A distant sweet smell like Sher's hands after she escaped from her tinkering room. That smell was overwhelmed by the sharp odor that hit her from the plants. She blinked the sting from her eyes as she leaned in close to examine the dad's face. His cheek glowed red with bright blue and purple lines outlining the shape of a hand. As she watched, a streak of blood absorbed into his skin.

Fighting a whimper, she crawled forward to reach him. But Clark, without glancing in her direction gave her the Hand of Stay again. She backed up to her crouch in Sher's bed. The fabric poofed up around her as she forced herself to settle in. Her eyes watered from the fresh plants so she shut them as they bounced along the ground, picking up speed. Laylea imagined she was running through the grassy field of their last stop. Bailey rode his bike beside her but he still couldn't keep up.

In no time, they were in the air, soaring through the blue again. Laylea rolled on her back and shut her eyes when Clark reached over. He hummed as he rubbed her chest. She tried to harmonize but her long thin tongue, so good for picking prickles out of her paws was no good for singing. Her ear brushed his wrist and she turned to lay her muzzle on his hairy arm. A perfect pillow.

CHAPTER 7

SUMMER 2025 - DEEP IN THE MOUNTAINS

Clark recovered his arm while Laylea slept. She woke to find the teddy lizard under her head. A huge *pff* turned into a yawn. She stretched out her back and legs with a long downward dog and a quick up dog, after which Laylea hopped over onto the dad's lap.

"Welcome back, sleepy." Clark rubbed her belly.

His freezing hand startled her. Laylea rolled to look up at him. One entire side of the dad's face glowed red. Even from his lap she could see the fingerprints swelling. He gave her ears a cold scritch and then took a white bag from the dash and held it to the bruise with the back of his hand.

"That stop went well. I'm very proud of you. Next stop is our last for the night, so one more easy landing like that and you're clear until tomorrow."

They flew on in silence for a while. Laylea rolled again. Cold air issued from a vent below the yoke. She reached her head toward it, breathing deeply but her stomach still churned. She sat up and raised her muzzle to the sunlight streaming into the cockpit. Closing her eyes, she leaned back against the dad's abs and focused on the flickering patterns the clouds made on the inside of her eyelids.

"We'll be with these folks for a night so there are some things you should know. The people I help out here don't in general like anybody nosing about their business."

He worked his jaw from side to side for a moment. The bruise had shrunk in toward his eye. Red still glowed from the swelling but it didn't smell so bad. Clark flexed his hand and rotated the wrist. Laylea watched, mesmerized as the green bruising around his knuckles danced and faded through yellow to the natural color of his skin.

"Some of them are like me and don't have any memories. Some don't even know Sher's helping them. So, don't you go asking personal questions." Laylea perked her ears up at the funny accent he affected. "We all get to be whoever we want to be at the powwow. They call me Captain and I call them whatever they ask me to. I think we'll just call you LG while we're up here. What do you think, little girl?"

He fell into his thoughts again and Laylea turned to look at the dark clouds gathering out the side window.

When Clark moved his arms, the plane tilted to go higher into the sky. Laylea watched what he was doing. She sat up and licked at the recently bruised hand. Then she reached up and stood her front paws on the thing he was holding.

"That's the yoke. Tells our plane where to go. I push it away from me and we go down." Clark demonstrated as he spoke. "I pull it toward me and we go up."

The plane moved up but Laylea's stomach dropped. Nothing to do. She clambered off Clark's lap and leaped to the passenger seat where she threw up on the clean smelling spot on the clothing bags. Her stomach lurched again but nothing came up. Still she lay on the cold blue vinyl with her head draped off the seat, her legs tucked under Sher's bed. She breathed.

"Sorry kid. Maybe you won't ever have to fly again after today."

Laylea dragged her muzzle along the seat to look at the dad. His eyes flitted from the horizon to the instrument readings to his map to the radio doohickey. He didn't look over at her.

She pulled herself to her paws and dragged herself to the edge of the seat. She did not have the energy to leap across the void. One paw didn't get his attention. She sat back and tried to wave at the dad with both paws. And lost her balance.

She fell forward. He caught her.

"Silly girl."

He swooped her over to his lap. Laylea turned a couple of times to find her balance and she stood up, front paws on the yoke. She leaned forward with all her weight until the yoke moved away and the plane tilted down.

Clark lifted her off. "Not quite yet, sweetheart. We have a little farther to go. Try to go to sleep."

Laylea gave up. She curled up in the dad's lap with a paw on her lizard. Soon the drone of the engine and Clarks quiet singing lulled her into the world where memories are as real as life.

ONE OF LAYLEA'S first memories was of trying to sleep while her four brothers crawled over and around her and the rag blankets in their cardboard box. They tossed each other about just as the plane did.

Laylea's little mind flew back through the weeks of her life to that box in the basement of the bicycle shop. The sharp gasoline and the dad's musk in her nose was replaced with the rubber, grease, and sleepy smell of her brothers in the shop. Her brothers who stepped on her face. When they did, she chewed sleepily on their legs wishing Mama would come back because the boys behaved better when she was there. The shop door opened upstairs. The boys stopped fighting. Footsteps that weren't Mama's. They huddled close together and tried to be invisible in their cardboard bed because Mama had made it clear to them that they were not welcome in this basement and they must be very quiet if anyone but her ever came in. So, they were quiet.

Boots clomped down the stairs. A light turned on that hurt Bayard's eyes. He whimpered, just a little. Rhemy bit his nose. But they all knew it was too late because the footsteps turned toward them. Their box was jostled in its hiding spot under a workbench. Laylea saw the hand coming down to take Rhemy, her largest brother and the only one who could get out of the box without Mama's help. She jumped on his back and got herself snatched instead. The hand grasped the fur and loose skin on the back of her neck like when Mama carried her around but this hand was not gentle. There was no warm soothing breath on her neck either. Just cold as he pulled her from her brothers and set her on the filthy workbench. She curled her tail protectively into her belly and huddled, peering up at the man who smelled sickly sweet and mean.

"Not so well hidden after all, are you?" His voice sounded very different from the owner of the basement who sometimes came downstairs to gather tools or work on bicycles. When Mama was around the owner pretended he didn't know they were there. But when she was out hunting, he would talk to the puppies and leave water and treats for them. They could all smell the treats. But Rhemy was the only one who could get them and he wouldn't share. This sweet man's voice was smoother, deeper. His words clipped and unsmiling.

"Not so well hidden at all. Only six weeks it took me. Perfect timing in fact since I don't need to let your bitch live anymore." As he said this, not really talking to Laylea at all, he ran his hands along her ribs, felt her paws which tickled even as she hated it, and looked into her ears and eyes. "Do you know? Or are you still just a stupid puppy?" She resisted as he tried to roll her onto her back. "Like mother, like daughter, eh? Curse all blondes. Well, you'll learn to mind me soon enough, girl." He grabbed her nape harshly and dangled her in mid-air before him. She tried to curl around her belly until he got her so close to his face that the stink of his sour breath overwhelmed the sweet mean smell of his body. The man was so intently examining her that he didn't hear the second footsteps or smell the Milkbones. The bike man's footsteps. The guy who owned the basement crept down the stairs like he was hunting. But he yelled when he saw the dangling puppy.

"You let my dog go!"

"Your dog?" The sweet man laughed at him. "These are not your dogs."

"Put her down." The owner stepped forward.

The man holding Laylea sneered and turned back to bend in to inspect Laylea's fuzzy belly.

Laylea's fear got the better of her self-control. She peed right into the man's face. At the same moment, the Milkbone man lifted the fork of a bicycle over his head and smashed it into the side of sweet man's head. Laylea fell, landing on the edge of the workbench on her left haunch. She yelped and caught her breath as the bike man scooped her up. The sweet stranger lay still on the floor, a little red leaking from his skull. Milkbone man bent with her to snake the bed out from under the workbench. It was empty.

"Come on, big boy. Bring them out here. We'll go find your mother." He leaned over and peered farther back under the table. "It's okay. It's gonna be okay," he crooned.

There was some growling and then her littlest brother Josh ventured into the light followed by Bayard and Rhemy. The owner tilted the box toward them. "Can you get in? Easier to carry the bed than all five of you."

Josh barked, high-pitched and desperate. He was the first to hear the third footsteps. Their Mama's steps.

"Rick! Rick, the door's unlocked. Where are you?" The false concern in her voice changed to real panic when she reached the bottom of the steps and saw him holding Laylea and the boys out of the bed. "Rick, I'm sorry. I had nowhere else to keep them. Please. Please, don't turn them in."

Mama sounded scared of the Milkbone man. To reassure her Mama that the owner was good, Laylea turned and bit his muzzle.

He giggled as he chastened her, "No teeth, baby girl."

Laylea licked the man's muzzle.

"It's okay, Rhea." The man started to explain but Bayard had tottered away from his brothers and the bed and he half-barked at the still body of the sweet man.

Their mama saw and screamed. But just a little.

"He was hurting her. So, I kinda hit him."

Mama took Laylea from his arms and nuzzled her.

Rick assured her, "They're welcome to stay here. It's okay."

Mama sighed. "It's not safe anymore if he's found us." She put Laylea in the bed and started gathering up her brothers. "Thank you. But we have to go."

"Here's some money. Take it. I'm betting you can't access your bank accounts without being traced. Consider it a loan if you like." He bent and scooped up Bayard, pulling him away from the unconscious sweet man's pant leg. While he was bent he slipped something from the man's pocket. "And here, take his money. Seems he owes the baby girl something for scaring the piss out of her."

Mama took the wallet and Bayard from Rick and added both to the box. "Police processing will take longer if he has no ID. Thank you, Rick. You've been a better friend than I knew."

"I'll be here if you need anything, Rhea." He gave her the turn away but Laylea knew that with humans it didn't mean he was mad at her.

The Milkbone man bound the monster's arms together with zip ties. Mama stopped at the foot of the stairs.

"You'd better call the police," she said. "They'll wonder why you waited so long."

He turned with a gentle smile that looked just like he smelled. "I'll give you a few minutes to get out of the neighborhood. We'll be fine here."

Laylea would never forget the warmth in her Mama's voice and the rich, busy scent of gratitude on her breath. "Thank you."

Mama carried them up the stairs and out of the shop that had been their home since she'd stolen them out of the laboratory. A crash of lightning split the sky and Mama tripped on the threshold sending Laylea flying through a beam of sunlight. She landed with a thump in the dad's lap.

He scooped her up with one hand between her legs and under her belly. She woke up a little more as he swung her over to her plush blue bed.

"We are experiencing some light turbulence. Please remain in your seat with your seatbelt fastened until the captain has turned off the seatbelt sign."

Laylea stood. She took a step forward to jump back to his lap when the plane lurched again. The puppy dropped to her belly. She watched as teddy lizard flew through the shaft of sunlight breaking through the rain into the cockpit. Both of Clark's white knuckled hands gripped the yoke. He didn't notice the little stuffed animal bounce off the console and tumble into the puddle of sick on the floor of the plane.

Laylea swallowed back the fresh sick in her throat as she was tossed against the thick bolsters of her bed. The thick pillow kept her cushioned and safe from tumbling out like Lizard. Laylea's only concern was that she not get sick on both of Sher's gifts until the rank wave of fear rolled off of Clark and filled the cabin. Then she closed her eyes and imagined with all her heart she was being tossed about in Bailey's sticky arms.

Chapter 8

Summer 2025 - Consortium Biotech HQ, CA

Rain pattered nearly soundlessly against the double panes of faux leaded security glass in the office. The glass had been replaced when one poorly conditioned Force soldier had found his mind and tried to bring down his creator, or rather shoot her down. Now the branches of the protected species of sycamore around which this wing of the Biotech Research building had been built scraped against the classiest bulletproof glass money could buy.

Walter traced a dry erase line from leaf to leaf, hopping over the leading. He had discovered by error the marker only washed off of the glass. Seven leaves touched the windows. As the storm moved the leaves, Walter erased his diagram with his tie and began over. Occasionally he glanced down at the park below.

Seven figures in the slate gray pants and deep green snap-shut shirts of the CF uniform performed their individual assignments unconcerned with the weather or each other for the most part. Walter's newest pet had been assigned to stalk the Conditioned Force soldiers and to take down the weakest without being caught. Walter had assigned the komodo-altered subject no time limit but they were nearing the final minutes of the exercise period. He clearly expected some action soon as his eyes flicked more often away from the sycamore leaves.

The glow of Trask's computer screen filled the storm darkened room. For hours, the only sounds in the office had been the tap of Trask's French manicured nails on the keyboard, the scrape of the sycamore branch against the window, and the very occasional squeak of Walter's tie wiping the window. Neither had spoken since their new combined budget arrived with an Edible Arrangements basket at eleven that morning.

Walter had rifled through his copy and tossed it onto his doodle-covered blotter. Trask pored over the document line by line and immediately began working up rebuttal arguments for the cuts and the combining of resources. She was, of course, as aware as Walter that the Director would not change a penny of the allocation but her sense of outrage would only be assuaged with a formal recording of her arguments.

Had she hackles, they would be up.

The wind picked up, spattering rain against the glass like knuckles. The seven-fingered branch of the sycamore demanded attention in a crash of scraping fingers.

"Why don't they cut that down?"

Walter answered without turning from his seat on the cushioned window bench. "The Western Sycamore is an indigenous protected tree in this state."

"Yes. Yes. I mean the branch," she drawled. "We can cut the branch off, can't we?"

"Cut off one branch, two will grow back."

"That's the hydra."

Walter looked away from his hunter. "I am so very proud of you right now."

Trask refrained from responding.

The Brit smirked. He wiped his latest doodles from the window and strode over to pop a fresh stick of black jack between his teeth. "The branch reaches our window in order to encourage the violent subjects to climb the tree instead of shooting out the window again."

"Your experiments may prefer the tree. Mine will go for a gun every time."

The screen reflection in Trask's glasses flared as Walter switched on his reticulated desk lamp. He swept the budget report to one side. Several pages of the stapled report dangled off the desk.

He folded his hands on the cleared blotter in front of him and tapped his thumbs together before addressing his office mate, "Do you really believe that a gun is always the most efficient choice of weapon?"

Trask kept her eyes glued on her detailed listing of Walter's failures to follow protocol. "It's the most expedient and gets the quickest response."

"But didn't your genius doctor imbue her subjects with more interesting abilities than exceptional point and shoot skills?" Clearly aware the reminder would irk Trask, Walter averted his eyes after asking the question.

He pulled a green suede folder from his side drawer and laid it on the desk. The concentric circles of the desk lamp caught the pixie face of a laughing blond woman in its bull's-eye as Walter violently flipped the trifold portfolio open. Rhea. He shunted the failed attempt at a security badge photo to one side, instead flipping rapidly through a series of black and white stills printed from the security cameras in his old office. The small woman wore a hoodie pulled up over her blond hair. She carried a duffle bag casually over one shoulder. Walter flipped the photos along the desk with his middle finger with much the same care as a teenager would flip through smart phone snaps. His fingers betrayed his thoughts when he slowed his shuffling at three pictures with a technician in frame. The first revealed the duffle on the ground. A small fawn dog with blotchy black patches on her haunches and over one eye lay curled up beside it. The technician bent in the second photo to scritch the tiny black ears on a puppy climbing out of the duffle. The third photo from that camera showed no dogs, no duffle, and an unconscious tech. Walter punished himself for the failure of his hunting komodo with a review of his own failure. Rhea and the subjects still eluded him.

"My genius doctor imbued our subjects with abilities the rest of my scientists can't even explain." Trask caressed the one worn file folder that never left her desktop. "Dr. Katherine Coogan worked alone. Even when she permitted observation, others were unable to follow her techniques. They accused her, to her face, of being descended from the witches of her hometown."

"She was from Massachusetts? Rhea was recently spotted outside of Boston." Walter continued shuffling the pictures as he half-listened. "How sad for her parents that Katherine died in the fire so soon after her brother's suicide."

Trask removed her glasses to rub at her eyes. One lens of the spectacles reflected the dark raindrops outside and one the bright charts on her computer screen. "I wish we hadn't killed him. He understood her private journals."

Silence returned to the office. Distant thunder and the muted rain kept the buzz of white noise from overwhelming the sensitive microphones. Photos danced across Walter's desk in an entrancing rhythm.

He spun the still with the unconscious technician for several seconds before he commented, "Your witch kept private journals?"

"Dr. Coogan lived for her research. I never needed to give her any reason for my requests. She didn't care about the why. She was a woman focused on her world, her brain, and what she could do with her brain. She never cared much who she did it to. The success she had with every task given her was only surpassed by the experiments she herself initiated." Trask set a fist on the file where another, less controlled individual might have punched it. "And we can't recreate any of her work."

"But haven't her journals helped you? Rhea's diary exponentially increased my understanding of therianthropes."

"The doctor's surviving notes leave much to be desired." In a rare admission of weakness, Trask pulled a file folder from her drawers and tossed it to Walter's side of the desk. It scattered his security photos. "We knew about the journals because we saw her brother take them out of a safe our cameras had never seen before in Coogan's apartment. It took weeks to find a safecracker who could open it and the journals turned out to be written in code. We've managed to translate most of it into English but the results are hardly more useful than the original. Mistress Coogan of Salem stumps us again."

Walter opened the dun colored file to find photocopies of barely legible scribblings stapled to one side and a print out of the translation on the other.

While the ten percent myth is a laughable fallacy, it is true that most humans do not make full use of brain capacity. Most current research is attempting to increase intelligence. But the brain is much more useful. If we can more directly connect a subject's impulses to the appropriate unconscious centers of the brain we can create the superman. Human weaknesses and emotions limit our capacity to believe we are capable of great power. Belief and faith have been supplanted by the religious communities which has caused scientists to shun the reality of such esoteric constructs. But observation shows faith can change the outcome of something so simple as a game of checkers. Task A) increase subject's self-faith/ faith in physics—requires a subject highly educated in physics or natural law / faith in odds—requires wide knowledge of odds, perhaps a high-level poker player can be acquired for study. Task B) a more likely scenario, disconnect subject's actions from awareness - possible? Explore throat monks. Reality vs. Perceived Reality likely to cause apparent cognitive disassociation. Have faith, Katherine.

Walter lifted the bottom of the translated stack up and allowed the pages to descend in a waterfall of words and phrases. He asked, "Did she map the action areas of the brain versus the intuitive areas?"

Trask watched as he rifled the stack of photocopies. "We can identify areas related to creativity and deep thinking. We know that unconsciousness is related to a lack of communication between the thalamus and any other part of the brain. We believe that Delta and Theta level brainwaves emitted in the unconscious mind regulate instinct and emotion and that will occurs at the Gamma level. But we don't exhibit multiple wavelengths at any one moment. There is no way to match Gamma levels to Delta levels. That's a difference of forty hertz."

"I understand you less than I understand Katherine's notes here."

A piercing whistle droned through the thick glass. Exercise time was over. Trask glanced at the storm but Walter didn't even consider looking out the window for his hunter.

He popped a green pen from the hand-thrown clay mug beside his blotter and tapped it on the translation. "Let me ask you, Trask, have you ever studied music?"

The tippity tapping of the keyboard fell silent. Walter grinned as he peered up at Trask, her burn scars standing out white in her cold expression.

"The physics of sound tell us that we can identify a tone resonating at 440 hertz simply by recognizing it as an A." He sat up straight, sucked a breath deep into his gut, and sang. One clear high note rang in the sterile air of the office. "That's very nearly the top of my range. You hear one note but the vibrations within the cavities of my head create a standing wave pattern of multiple frequencies of A. Certain Tibetan monks can sing overtones, two notes at once. AKA multiple wavelengths. It's called throat singing." He circled the words *throat monk*. Closing the folder, he tossed it back to Trask and got up to crack his neck.

Outside the leaves of the holy sycamore brushed wetly against the glass. Flashes of light glinted off the droplets. They caught Trask's eye. As Walter bent forward into a downward dog stretch, a disco party flashed on the ceiling of the office. Trask strode to the window. Technicians and security had gathered flashlights to help them clean the storm darkened courtyard.

An impulse crossed her face in the light of the wild torches and she returned to the desk in two strides. She selected a security still at random from the collage on Walter's side and sat, contemplating the image.

"My division utilizes your old office building as an observation zone now."

"That makes sense," Walter said, walking out his hips in the stretch. "Some of my employees hiked in those mountains you use as your testing grounds."

"How far away was the bike shop where you were beaten up?"

Walter walked his feet to his hands. "The shop to which I tracked my assistant was fifteen miles from the office."

"And how old were Rhea's puppies?"

"When I found them, they were six weeks old."

"How far can puppies that age really travel?"

Walter had no reply. He stopped stretching and let his eyes fall on the photos.

"You've gotten several facial recognition hits on Rhea. Los Angeles, Tucson, Chicago, Philadelphia."

"Boston," he added.

"Boston," Trask repeated. "And that's where you've been searching."

"Yes."

Trask handed him the picture. "Did she have five scruffy mutts following her?"

Walter took the still but his mind wandered far away. "She ditched them." He crossed to the cabinet behind her desk and unfolded the wide panels that hid the display board holding Trask's training ground map. One hundred miles square with a row of barely civilized towns along the eastern border. One finger tapped a particularly isolated spot tucked away between cliff faces and a manmade lake while his eyes roamed to the nearby towns. "She hid them in plain sight."

"You can task my drop and recovery teams to check in on local veterinarian clinics if you'd like."

"Thank you, Trask. I should have spotted that."

Trask reached out and rubbed a hand on the taller man's shoulder. She waited until she had his attention. "You were silent for an hour, Walter." Her voice dropped to about a hundred eighty hertz with harmonics fluctuating around G-flat. "You will always be rewarded for silence."

Walter nodded and patted the hand on his shoulder without saying a word. He closed the cabinet and traced his fingers along the window before he settled into his seat. He bundled the photos together and quietly tapped them on his lap to align their bottom edges. The photos went back into the green suede file. He pulled a spiral notebook from another pocket in the folder and a pen from his clay cup. He tapped the end of the pen on the felt head of his drinking bird, setting the bird into silent motion. He then flipped the pen around and used the business end to flip to a blank page. The pen hovered over the ruled paper.

Trask smiled. She affixed the cabinet latch, glancing out at the angry clouds. The lights that danced around the window earlier had gone. She settled into her ergonomic chair and returned to her complaints about the totally inadequate budget versus the enormous cost of designer security windows.

"The missing CF who burned your," Walter changed his word at the last moment, "lab. What was his designation?"

Trask sighed. She looked across the desk to see Walter playing with the bullet embedded in his buffalo's hide. "Gamma Subject."

Walter tucked the buffalo in against his chest and stared out the window. Trask watched him for a moment then flicked her eyes to her screen. As soon as she was focused on the budget report, he spoke again.

"Was he one of Mistress Katherine's?"

She kept her eyes on her work this time. "Yes."

Walter watched her work. One thumb pet his buffalo's authentic fur.

Rain fell and leaves tapped on the window.

Walter peeked up at Trask. "So, she named him."

"Yes." Trask exploded in her gentle Southern way. She set both hands on her desk, piercing Walter with her full attention.

He pet the toy. "And human will occurs when the electrical signals in our brains experience Gamma wave frequencies?"

Her body didn't move. But her eyes flashed to the empty space over his right shoulder. Gamma waves seemed little involved in her response. "Yes."

Walter sat up and placed his buffalo between the coffee cup filled with sticks of black jack gum and his hand carved Newton's Cradle. He lifted two spheres. "It occurs to me that might have something to do with why she named him Gamma Subject."

Trask's eyes darted to Walter's and then to the hand holding the balls of the perpetual noise toy. "Thank you, Walter."

He set the balls gently back into place and picked up his pen. "Not at all."

Trask closed the window displaying her report. "I think this arrangement is going to be more useful than I originally thought."

A knock at the door interrupted the bonding moment.

Trask stood and swept through the privacy screen. Walter began scrawling notes in his physician quality scribble.

"Yes?"

Trask opened the door to an older man with a neatly trimmed if overly fashionable gunslinger mustache and no hair. She found him straightening his impeccably starched uniform. A pallor of embarrassment and fear paled his skin but he reported in a clear, confident voice.

"Subject One Four Two appears to have terminated his training prematurely. Ma'am."

On the far side of the curtain, Walter sat up straighter in his chair. A smile wrinkled one cheek.

"Did I hear you right?"

"In the courtyard just now, Ma'am, during Exercise. They're waiting on your attendance at the autopsy in D wing."

Trask said nothing else. She left the security agent in the hall to retrieve her briefcase and a Dictaphone from the desk.

Walter stood as she returned. He flung his backpack over one shoulder and trotted out through the privacy curtains with her. "I'll just go see how my folks are doing after Exercise."

Trask let him pass, her lips tight and her scars glowing white again. Walter stopped. He twitched her bangs into place and held the door.

Trask's heels echoed sharply in the corridor, followed by the security agent's hesitant steps. Walter's face broke into a full and joyful smile watching them hurry away. He headed for an elevator in the other direction.

THE DIRECTOR BRUSHED a stray crumb from his chin. He buzzed for his secretary to retrieve the lunch plates. Combining the Consortium's Biotech Research divisions was proving to have been an excellent idea. He felt certain the animosity would provide results in time as well as his ongoing lunchtime entertainment. With an unexpected sense of disappointment, he switched to the array of feeds from a certain highly-decorated five-star general's not-so-secret love pad where five high placed military leaders stood around a three-dimensional live feed of Colorado's El Paso County.

CHAPTER 9

SUMMER 2025 - DEEP IN THE MOUNTAINS

Golden sunlight bathed Laylea's belly. The fur of her chest waved as a blessed breath of wind blew through the cockpit. The puppy dropped her jaw and licked at the air, four paws thrown out to the sides, tail buried in the folds of blue fabric beneath her.

"It wasn't *that* bad, was it?" The dad laughed. Droplets of cold water soaked into her fur where he tucked teddy lizard in beside her.

She shot a breath through her lips and teeth, all the response she could muster.

Clark had popped the doors the instant the plane rolled to a safe stop in the clearing. He unknotted the paisley bandanna around his neck and wrapped his hand up in it before reaching over to shove the plastic bag of clothes out through the right-side door. Dribbles of half-digested kibble fell to the floor in the process. Clark scooped it all up in the handkerchief and tossed that out his own door.

"Thank goodness your belly is so teensy, little girl." He hovered over Laylea and laid a warm palm on the abused muscles of her stomach.

She lifted her head to lick at the hand and her tail popped out, slapping the bolster that had kept her from tumbling around the tossing cockpit. The little rat tail curled right up into her belly at the memory.

"Come on. We'll get you some fresh air and grass. You'll feel better."

Laylea dropped her head back. She pffed at him doubtfully but he gently rolled her over and lifted her to his chest.

Laylea's protest turned into a bark of alarm. An old man stood at the door. He rested a weathered brown hand in the window, holding the door open. The puppy inhaled short, sharp sniffs to get his scent. Under the cloying scent of lavender soap, she smelled sharper chemicals. When he opened his mouth, she jerked her head back and growled deep in her throat. His breath smelled like the plastic bin in the kitchen.

"Hello, Captain. Looks like you flew right through the heart of that little squall." As bad as his oral hygiene seemed to be, the man's voice was so musical Laylea's growl stuttered. "We're lucky the rain never reached us. We'll have a dry powwow."

White hair curled out of the man's ears. Laylea followed his gaze and saw that the plane rested in a large field. Low brush and tall grass littered the ground for a hundred yards beyond the nose of the plane to a forest that climbed away to the clouds. Six spots of color broke the vista of mossy trees, a village of tents with more hermits watching them. Smoke rose from the fire crackling near the last tent. It obscured a figure bent low over a large stewpot. Laylea could see a difference in the air over the pot where smoke gave way to steam.

A heady scent thick with browning meats and burning wood wafted into the cockpit. Laylea twisted in Clark's arms. She continued to growl at the stranger, warning him that she would defend her pack. But her fierceness was mitigated by her searching nose. It was hard to keep up a growl and investigative sniffing at the same time. If this stranger had brought them food, he might be safe.

Clark clipped the long lead onto her collar and climbed out of the plane, unfazed by the stranger or the amazing smells. "I'm glad we made it to the powwow, Ahab." He held a hand out to the old man. "See, he's okay, LG. Everyone here," he glanced over at the new people arriving at the plane, "is okay. I trust them."

Ahab shook Clark's hand, showing it was empty of weapons. Or food.

"Hey Maggie." Clark nodded at a woman with fiery curls bursting from her head in a cloud.

Ahab reached out and scratched Laylea's ears without asking permission. He had rough fingers that felt good on her fur though, so she didn't object.

"You've acquired a co-pilot." A scar on Ahab's hand caught at Laylea's ears.

Clark laughed, "A temporary one, alas. Think the Disneys' girl could keep LG here occupied while we unload the plane and divvy up your goods?"

The old man sent a stone-faced teenage boy back to the encampment. "She'll be here in a moment."

The redhead paused with her hand out when she saw how small Laylea was. "This one looks hardly old enough to be away from her mother. But she's flying with you?"

Laylea shoved her nose into the scent of lavender and pine. She leaned in as Maggie set to massaging her velvet ears.

Clark grinned. "I wouldn't share her story any more than I would share yours, Maggie."

"A mystery woman, eh? Maybe she should stay up here with us."

"That might be something I was thinking." Clark handed the puppy to Maggie and turned to unload the plane. "But right now, let's get the work done. I want a taste of whatever it is Abuela is cooking."

Laylea sniffed the freckled woman's face and snagged a lock of curls to chew on.

The teenager returned accompanied by a younger boy with less serious looks but matching brown eyes. They trotted over in as close to a run as they could manage through the calf-high grass. Following at a more chaotic pace, three lighter brown kids joined them from the tents. The matching set of boys, just a few years older than Bailey, fought with each other as their older sister hurried them along. This girl had long black hair tamed into two fuzzy braids hanging down her shoulders. She'd woven silver ribbons into the plaits, and the fabric caught the bright sunlight each time she turned to yell at her little brothers.

Ahab directed the boys to take things from Clark as he emptied the plane while the big sister hustled over to Maggie and Laylea to meet the puppy.

Maggie introduced them. "Flo, LG. LG, Flo."

Laylea's twitchy nose pulled her nearly out of the woman's arms.

The girl smelled like heaven. Laylea sniffed onions, carrots, potatoes, and cheese. She willingly let Flo run her fingers through her fur. Laylea twisted her head around when the braids bounced off her back. The girl had tucked her nose into Laylea's neck.

"Mmm, you smell like heaven." She kissed the puppy's head. "You can call me Flower if you want to."

"You're not a Dithney!" A bouncing little blond girl ran up and stood on tiptoe to see Laylea. "I'm a Dithney. You can call me Mickey!"

Maggie set her on the ground to meet Mickey. Laylea looked to the back of the plane where Flower relieved one of the boys of his overly ambitious armload. She saw Clark watching her. He nodded encouragement so she led Mickey around the vomit filled handkerchief to underneath the nose of the plane where they played while the others worked.

The plane quickly emptied. A few secret compartments revealed their treasures. And then Clark locked up the doors and took Laylea's leash from Mickey who had it tangled around her.

Laylea focused when her new friend led them over to the temporary village. Mickey took them directly to the source of the smells. Led by her nose, Laylea pulled toward the food, tumbling ahead of Clark and Mickey and straining at the very end of her long leash.

Waves of eye stinging air washed over her, hotter than Woodford's belly after a sunlit nap. A tongue of fire tried to draw her in. She yelped and tumbled rump over reason before gaining her feet to race back to the dad.

"Como está?" Laylea's head whipped back around at the rich craggy voice that croaked out of the old woman commanding the fire. She pronounced her words very differently from the family.

"How's tricks, Bela?" Clark smoothed Laylea's hackles but he didn't scoop her into his chest.

Mickey ran right up beside the fire with no fear. She tugged on the cook's jacket.

"That'th Elgy." Mickey pronounced her words differently too, but it was more like she was trying to sound like Clark but couldn't work it out. Laylea barked. She couldn't talk like Clark either.

"LG is looking for a home, Bela." Flower joined them, handing her grandmother a brown paper bag. "Don't worry. Feranda already said no. Captain, they're starting. You might want to go head off some fist fights."

Clark chanted, "I will, not," but then his eyes cleared and he handed Laylea's leash to the teenager. "LG needs some dinner. She left her breakfast on the cockpit floor. No human food." He pulled a small baggie of kibble from one of his many pockets. Laylea sang. "This is hers. But her stomach is a little off. Mickey," he crouched down to hand the baggie to the little girl, "can you find a bowl and ask Bela for a dribble of broth?"

Mickey held the baggie carefully with both hands, her eyes wide. She bobbed her head slowly up and down and walked with exaggerated care over to the old woman.

"I'll keep an eye on them, Captain." Flower dropped to the ground beside Laylea and set the puppy on her chest.

"Thanks." Clark took a deep breath. He ran his knuckles over the rapidly healing bruise on his cheek. The swelling was gone and Laylea could barely see the one finger of green dulled with dark yellow. She turned her attention to the girl blowing in her face as the dad walked away to the small crowd of loud voices gathered around the supplies.

WHEN THE DISPUTES were settled and nearly everyone had paid Clark, six small piles of things stood in the clearing between the plane and the tents. One for each of the families plus two for the men who most fit Sher's designation of hermit. Flower and Mickey were called away to help their families move the goods to their tents.

Bela wouldn't give Laylea anything from the stewpot so she tottered over to find Mickey in her tent, playing with the small green bound book Sher had given Clark at the last minute. She pounced on her playmate's foot and the two tumbled all over the tent. Mickey grabbed for her ears. Laylea dodged away. She tripped over the book and rolled into a set of ankles.

"Careful there, LG." Mickey's mom crouched to set the puppy on her feet again. "You are a tiny little thing, aren't you? Think you could make it out here in the wild?"

The woman's voice trailed off. Her hand left Laylea's ears to flip over the green book still lying on the floor of the tent.

"David." She turned to Mickey's dad.

"Call me Donald, babe." The man continued reorganizing their packs.

"Donald." She growled between her teeth. "Mickey took Hardknock's book."

"Minnie." The man bit off his words. Laylea cringed at his sudden sour smell. "How do you know it's Hardknock's?"

She pointed at the three men still standing where the piles had been lain out. "He's yelling at the Captain for forgetting it. Won't pay him for anything else."

Donald stopped his work. Fear poured off of him. "We can't return it."

"We can't return it," Minnie agreed. "He'll kill us for taking it."

"We have to return it." The dad spit a harsh word. He muttered it three more times. "We have to return it."

"Yeah." Minnie looked over her shoulder at her daughter. "But how?"

Minnie and Donald argued, trying to come up with ways to return the book. The tent grew cold. Laylea tripped away from Mickey, who had frozen in the face of her parents' anger. She tilted her head at the book. She shoved it with her nose. It wasn't very heavy or very thick. But it took her a few tries to get her teeth around one corner.

None of the family noticed her leave the tent. She ran down to the far side of the encampment and batted the book around in the field until she was playing just a stone's throw from the argument between Clark, a craggy wild-haired man, and a bald hermit who smelled like soap.

"You can't expect me to pay when you don't even do your job." The wild man's voice cracked.

"I'm sorry, Hardknock." Clark held his tone even, controlled. "I can check the plane again."

"No." The pock-faced man ran a hand down his beard. He slunk towards a rucksack sitting alone in the middle of the trio. "I'm taking my stuff and leaving."

"You can't leave until you've paid the Captain, Hardknock." The bald guy stood tall with his feet spread.

Laylea stood up to see this man better. His skin was dark, deeper in a way than Michelle's at the mom's clinic. He wore pants like Clark's, covered in pockets but his single pocket black t-shirt didn't hide his muscles the way Clark's button-downs did. He also had a silver pen stuck in his breast pocket.

Laylea took a step forward to smell the man and tripped over the book.

Hardknock noticed. The hermit dove at the ground and yanked a fist-sized hunk of obsidian from the grass at Clark's feet. Clark stepped back but Laylea saw his hands come up, stiff as blades. He relaxed when Hardknock threw the rock away. But his muscles tensed again at Laylea's fearful yip.

She'd run away when he released the rock so Hardknock missed her. But he hit the book. An edge scraped along the cover. The sound of the rip sliced through the thick air.

Laylea tripped and rolled to a stop in the grass. She looked to Clark for directions but Clark was conferring with the bald hermit. Nobody breathed except Donald and Ahab, hurrying toward them from the tents.

Laylea's ears twitched when the wild hermit inhaled. He breathed out, "I'm gonna kill that dog."

She was still looking to Clark when the steel toe of Hardknock's boot crunched into her side.

Laylea yelped over and over as she rolled, some from the pain, some from the memory of the sickly-sweet man dropping her on that same hip. She curled up, protecting her now twice injured haunch. Her foot had gone numb and she licked at it while her eyes darted from side to side, trying to keep up with the fight high above her.

The dad and the dark hermit grabbed Hardknock. They struggled. Hardknock screamed curses.

Clark caught another blow to his bruised cheek but he grabbed the hermit's wrist on the follow-through and twisted it, stretching the arm out and folding his hand back. Hardknock tried to turn into the stressed shoulder but the bald one had wrapped an arm around his other shoulder and braced a hand on the back of Hardknock's neck.

He whispered into the man's ear, "I don't want to say it."

"I'm sorry. I'm sorry." Hardknock relaxed. He stopped fighting. "I lost my mind."

"You're okay?"

He repeated, "I lost my mind."

"Okay." Clark let up the pressure on his arm. He untwisted the hand, the elbow and lowered the arm before he released it. "Try to remember, *I will not—*"

Hardknock looked into Clark's eyes. "I lost my mind and *I will not* ever find it again."

He pulled a gun, flipped off the safety, and aimed at Laylea.

A thunderous boom cracked the air.

Chapter 10

Summer 2025 - deep in the mountains

Laylea's cries filled the world. Her hip burned. Her nose stung. And she couldn't hear her own voice over the ringing in her ears. Her heart felt like it would burst out of her chest. She leaped up to run away. But fell as her left leg failed to take her weight. Crying louder, she dug her tiny claws into the dirt and tried to drag herself away.

Then Clark was there. He lifted her, shifting his hold when she shuddered. He cradled her against his chest examining the rest of her as her left leg lay limply over his wrist. Laylea buried her nose in his armpit, ashamed of her cries. Her lungs pulsed with her slowing heartbeat but she couldn't draw in a full breath.

Clark paced as he palpated every inch of her body.

Hardknock lay on the ground with the bald man holding one arm doubled up behind his back. A trickle of blood shone on the craggy hermit's face. He'd fallen on the very rock he'd thrown at Laylea. The bald man yanked the body backwards to pull Hardknock's hand from his gun. As soon as the fingers uncurled in the dirt, the old man Ahab dashed in. He flipped the safety and stowed the gun in his own waistband.

"Captain. How's the dog, Captain?" Donald approached Clark.

Minnie holding a bawling Mickey, hung back. Most of Minnie's face was buried in her daughter's blond hair but Laylea heard her humming the same tune Clark had sung with Red in the rocky clearing. She focused on that sound while Clark ran his fingers lightly along her throbbing hip.

Clark finished examining the puppy before he answered. "He missed. But he hurt her with the kick."

Donald leaned in to Clark's ear, "Captain, LG didn't take—"

Clark cut him off. "You all go back to your tent. Mickey, LG is fine. We'll come see you in a bit." He turned away from them, still cradling Laylea. "Jay. The man has been subdued and disarmed."

"You're bleeding." Donald didn't leave. "Captain, your leg is bleeding."

"Yeah, the ricochet. It's not bad. Don't worry about it."

Minnie walked past the men in a daze, approaching the two hermits on the ground.

Clark kept both hands on Laylea. His voice was enough to stop the woman. "You've got Mickey there."

The woman turned. She caught Clark's eyes as she passed, before she buried her face again in her daughter's hair. Donald followed his wife away from the conflict.

Clark faced Hardknock. "Let the man up, Jay."

The bald man pushed Hardknock's arm further up his back, "Do you promise to control yourself?"

"I don't promise nothing, Jarhead."

"There's gonna come a time you need me again, Tracy Hardwick. You remember this." Jay loosened his grip and backed up so he was out of reach when enough feeling came back that Hardknock was able to move his arm.

Ahab reached out a hand to help Hardknock up. The hermit knocked it away. He pushed himself up to his knees and awkwardly to his feet, brushing grass from his filthy jeans.

Still picking twigs from his flannel shirt, he said, "Give me the dog."

Clark picked up the book. "The dog is my cargo, same as your book. I have promised to deliver it safe."

"You didn't deliver my book safe."

"If you'll take it, I think you'll see it's come to no harm." Clark held it out to the man.

Ahab and Jay stayed close on the hermit's heels as Hardknock stalked to Clark. He knocked the book away. "Give me the dog and we'll call it even."

Jay chuckled. "Hardnose—"

"Hardknock."

"You haven't paid him yet. You're nowhere close to even." The bald man picked up the book and flipped through the pages. "Book is fine. Unless you're afraid of a little dog slobber. Afraid of a little dog slobber, Hardnose?"

"Pay the Captain. Take your book. And let's go eat. No harm, no foul, eh, Mr. Hardknock?" Ahab put his hand on the man's shoulder and Jay had to put Hardknock on the ground again to keep him from breaking it.

Clark knelt. "There are words Jay could use." He murmured so quietly that only Hardknock, Jay, and Laylea could hear but the hermit's head snapped up like he'd been slapped. "But I'd rather we behave like free men."

"You're one too." It was an accusation, not a question.

Clark barely nodded.

"He had no right to wake us up."

Clark glanced at Jay who gazed off at the mountain peaks. They both knew they'd felt the same way at times.

"Let the man up, Jay." Clark recovered the book and slid it in his back pocket. "We've got to end this, gentlemen."

Jay helped Hardknock stand this time, keeping a hold on his arm.

"Let him go, Jay."

"Don't feel comfortable with that, Captain. And no offense, but these are my woods."

"Okay, Jay. I can see your point. Hardknock, I have delivered the goods you requested, including the book. Are you going to pay me?"

Hardknock stopped struggling. "We were all chosen because of who we are. And they didn't pick any tree hugging dog lovers." His eyes glowed. "I'll pay you if you kill it."

Clark sighed. He looked down at little Laylea trying her best not to whimper. She could feel her leg now and her hip screamed. The dad kissed her forehead. "That's your choice, Hardknock." He turned to Ahab who had been joined by Flower's mother, Feranda. "Could one of you hold LG here while I put Hardknock's supplies back into my plane?"

"You can't take them back!" Hardknock sprang at Clark but Jay was still holding his arm.

Clark didn't respond. He handed Laylea to Ahab and gathered up a few of the disputed items. He took them over to the plane as Hardknock struggled.

"He can't do that!"

Jay held tight. "Yes, he can."

"Mr. Hardknock," said Ahab, "The captain paid for all of this. He paid for the plane and the gas to transport it here. You have not paid him. So, the items still belong to him."

"Except the chili," Jay put in. "The chili is a gift."

"I have medicine in the bundle."

"No Mr. Hardknock," corrected Ahab, "the captain has medicine in that bundle. You have what you've paid for."

"Jay." Redheaded Maggie sidled into the conversation. Her voice shook. "Jay, would you mind escorting Mr. Hardknock away from camp? He's not welcome."

"It's not for you to say." Hardknock was momentarily distracted from watching Clark unlock the plane.

"You're not welcome." Ahab backed her up. "My vote is he goes."

Flower's mother held a shotgun at her side. "I don't want you here."

"I don't mind if you come back when you've calmed down but you're awfully worked up right now and maybe that's why you choose to live alone but you really shouldn't be around people right now and I don't feel safe with you here." Maggie added. "Minnie and Donald clearly don't want you here."

"It's unanimous then." Jay pushed Hardknock away.

Clark came back over the group. He stepped in front of Hardknock and put a bottle in the man's coat pocket. "You have to learn control. And that means you can't kill a puppy because it ran off with your book."

Hardknock didn't look in Clark's eyes. He avoided every face around him. His gaze settled on Laylea trembling in Ahab's arms. "Give me the book. I'll pay you."

Clark took the book out of his pocket. "If you pay me, I'll give you everything."

"Can't afford everything."

There was silence as everyone assessed the fact that Hardknock had tried to kill the puppy to distract them from the fact that he couldn't pay. Maggie spoke up first.

"I can buy some of his things if you'll take more herbs or another blanket. He can buy them from us with some meat later in the season."

"We can do the same if you've got need of more molasses," Feranda added.

Mickey pulled on Clark's pant leg, "I make bird feederth out of pine coneth."

Donald ran in. He scooped the girl up and backed away. "We'll help in any way we can."

So Hardknock's supplies were brought out of the plane again and divvied among the families who offered to pay for them. Hardknock paid for the book, his medicine, and despite objections, a fifth of whiskey. He was escorted far into the forest by Jay, Feranda, and Ahab. They had a conversation with him before sending him on his way.

Clark, Laylea securely back in his own arms, helped Mickey drag Minnie out of their tent to join the others around Bela's campfire.

Bela had the most healing skill of any at the powwow. He convinced her to step away from her precious stew by promising to bring paprika on his next run free of charge. Flower was given the chef's spoon and strict instructions. Bela, her back not allowing may other positions, examined the pup while Clark held her right there in the middle of the gathering.

"What I can't understand," Maggie was saying to Minnie, "is why the dog ran off with it. What does a dog want with a book?"

"Isn't it usually Mickey who steals everyone's books?" Flower asked.

"Stir," Bela instructed, not taking her eyes off of the dog in question.

Flower pulled a face but kept her mouth shut.

Donald spoke quietly, "Mickey did take it from Hardknock's pile. LG took it from Mickey. I'm sorry, Captain. We were going to return it but we turned around and she'd taken it. I don't know why a dog would play with a book like that."

"You thed the book belonged to Mithter Angry," Mickey reasoned, also not taking her eyes off of Laylea. "He boilth kidth for breakfatht. But Elgy ithn't a kid. Can you make her better, Bela?"

Bela took Laylea from Clark. She resettled her with one of the matching grandsons, Cockroach. He sat in a low chair and Bela showed him how to hold the dog with her left side out, supporting her paws. "Ven aqui, Mickey." She took the icepack Feranda fetched from their tents and squeezed it cold. "Fold your blankie in half and lay it over her hip there."

"Gently, Kayl... Mickey."

"I know, Mommy. Eathy."

Bela laid the icepack on Laylea's hip and taught Mickey how to hold it so the puppy's tiny body didn't have to take all the weight. Mickey was told to keep an eye on Laylea and if it looked like the pain was getting worse, she should tell Cockroach who couldn't see the dog's face.

"Serve up the stew. The warriors have returned victorious!" Jay pounded a wooden bowl on his chest.

"Is it ready, Bela?" Flower lifted the ladle to her grandmother.

Everybody watched as Bela took a sip. "Perfecto. But only give the warrior a small bowl." She patted Jay's rock-solid abs. "He wants to keep his girlish figure."

Jay danced with Bela as Flower filled bowls. Maggie sliced a loaf of fresh bread and served it from a low table near the fire. When Bela shoved him away to get his food, Jay settled beside Clark. Slowly conversations started up around the fire; some that had been interrupted by Clark and Laylea's arrival, some age-old arguments that were renewed each of the rare times the families met.

Jay spoke quietly with Clark. "He knows you now."

"That was my choice. Yours was to let him live."

"I will not kill another soul today."

"You give us all a sleep word, don't you?"

"Well, Sher gave you yours as she gave me mine. But when you take away free will, you take a man's life. I'll never use the words." Jay whispered the oath and then spoke up as Ahab joined them. "You're a peacemaker, Captain. You didn't need to give him his order."

Clark smiled gently. "Peace is found, not made. And some of Hardknock's peace is found in his medicine."

"The whiskey?" Ahab asked.

"No," Bela responded from her special chair. "The pills. The Captain may have saved our lives with his peacemaking. Men can go loco in the woods. Do crazy things."

"Especially if he started out crazy before he got to the woods." Donald turned to Clark, "Bipolar? Is that what the drugs are for?"

"I won't share his story any more than I would share yours, Donald."

"You don't know my story, Captain."

"I know you have three nephews," Clark shot back, "and a rich, stingy Scottish uncle."

The crowd around the fire laughed.

"And he's married to a mouse!" Ahab roared.

Minnie tossed a slice of bread to the old man, "What makes you think we're married?"

"Ohhhh!" General pandemonium broke out.

Clark gazed past the fire to where Flower had joined the kids around Laylea. No patient had ever been better attended. But the flames reflected in the puppy's glazed eyes showed her pain. She lay more still then he'd ever seen her awake.

Jay saw. "You really love your dog, don't you, Captain?"

"To be honest with you, Jay, I didn't know she was my dog until he tried to take her away from me." He looked off into the trees. "He needed a night of socializing."

Jay laughed. "He wasn't gonna stay, Captain. You didn't see us break down a tent for him, did you? Don't worry, he's got spring cleaning chili for dinner." Jay elbowed Clark, laughing at his hangdog expression. He too gazed off in the direction Hardknock had been escorted. "Whatever Sheriff expects that book to do for him, I hope it works quick magic." He pulled a flask from his thigh pocket and sipped.

Clark turned it down when he offered it to his oldest remembered friend. "What book was it anyway?"

Clark laughed. "James Thurber. The Secret Life of Walter Mitty."

Jay sipped again and tucked the flask away. "Why?"

"You're asking me? You've known her longer."

Jay laughed long and hard at that. Then he called over, "Maggie. Do you have your guitar?"

She flipped around to show them the backpacking guitar strung on her back. "Right here. With new strings thanks to the captain."

Jay stood. He stomped on the ground in a rhythm that woke Laylea from her doze. Minnie joined in, clapping an opposing rhythm. Maggie added block chords and after a moment Feranda sang out the tune Laylea had been hearing over and over.

I will

not kill

Another soul today.

Their life is in my hands and I will not throw it away.

The twin boys, mindful of Laylea, sang out a breakdown of the first four notes. They wove in and out of each other until they settled into a pair of rhythms that set a bass line for Donald to join Feranda, harmonizing on a repeat of the verse. Ahab, his boys, and Flower all joined in on the melody, singing quietly beneath Feranda's rich alto.

Clark stood, singing along. He murmured to Jay, "Feranda is the only Conditioned Force soldier singing."

"I'm singing," he replied. "You're singing."

"I never stop singing it," Clark said.

"Don't worry. Minnie likes the second verse."

Clark looked at him. "Second verse?"

Jay laughed. "Feranda wrote a second verse."

Right then, as everyone drifted off on the last note of *away*, Minnie, her blond hair hanging loose in her face, opened her mouth and wailed. She hollered a wordless descant over the rhythm and bass laid down around her. Bela joined in the clapping. Ahab called out a joyful ululation and Minnie surfed off of that into the second verse.

I find

my mind

By listening to my heart
Together they will keep my soul from fracturing apart

Everyone joined in as they repeated the second verse adding variations until Ahab ended the song with a final cry.

The hermits called out songs they wanted. Maggie played. When it got late, the kids were sent to bed and Maggie set down her guitar to take over icing Laylea's hip while Jay helped Clark set up his one-man tent.

When Bela got tired, she mixed some of the turmeric Clark had just delivered into Laylea's kibble and softened it with broth she saved from her stew. The turmeric, she said, was anti-inflammatory and should help if the puppy could keep it down. She wished him luck and shuffled off into her tent. Feranda quietly said her good nights and followed the old woman who had taken her in and treated her like a daughter.

Laylea didn't want to eat. Clark dipped two fingers into the mush and encouraged her to lick it from his hand. She lapped up two bowlfuls of water while Clark tried to scrub the yellow from his fingernails.

The powwow broke up a short while later when Ahab fell asleep in his chair. Clark took Laylea from Maggie's lap and as soon as she was cuddled against his chest, the little dog finally shut her eyes. She didn't wake as he said good night to everyone. Jay escorted them to the tent, carrying a supply of gel packs donated by Bela and himself for icing Laylea's hip in the night. He had to insist Clark take them.

Clark slept uneasily. He tried to lay Laylea in her blue bed, but the puppy woke. She stared at him with her big, glassy eyes until he lifted her into the sleeping bag with him. He slept fearful of crushing her. Several times throughout the night, he woke to Laylea staring at him. When his eyes opened, she'd paw at him and whimper quietly. He'd break an ice pack and hold it on her hip, feeling guilty that he'd allowed her to get hurt, feeling guilty that he was depleting the hermits' first aid supplies.

Feranda had assured him that Bela had an ice-pit at their compound that did a much better job of keeping perishables and providing ice for the kids' many injuries. Jay told him he knew where the compound was so he could deliver more any time Clark could fly out for a quick drop.

But still, Clark wrestled with the reversal of roles. He was supposed to take care of the hermits.

Going to bed he'd been hopeful that Laylea would feel better after a good night's sleep. It became clear to him, long before dawn that she needed more than rest. It took until after dawn, until after breakfast and goodbyes, until he was in the air with Laylea beside him in her bed before it became clear to him that if he took Laylea home, he would never try to give her away again.

CHAPTER 11

SUMMER 2025 - DEEP IN THE MOUNTAINS AND FOOTHILLS, OR

L aylea threw up once on the flight back. She didn't even crawl out of Sher's bed. Clark talked to her at first. Telling her what a brave girl she was. He explained how the plane worked, trying to talk in a soothing voice that would keep her calm. But he soon noticed that she was twitching, running in a dream. So, he stopped talking to her and sang to himself. Dire Straits, jazz standards, show tunes with his own lyrics, and for about an hour he sang the new verse of Sher's song. The song that kept him from giving up, which is what he'd wanted to do nearly every moment since Sher had woken him from the conditioned trance she herself had placed him in. He felt worthy and purposeful when he was with Sher and when he was with Bailey. And for this entire trip, with Laylea.

When they landed he taxied directly to his hangar. He hopped out, telling Laylea to stay where she was with hand gestures and stern verbal commands. Laylea didn't even lift her head. Clark looked around. He saw no one else at the small airstrip and considering his enhanced senses he felt confident the place was deserted. He'd regularly scanned the place for cameras and unless someone had bugged the loose collection of hangars in the last twenty-four hours, he was safe.

The mountain folk had paid him with handwoven fur blankets,

molasses, wooden carvings, canvas bags of fresh herbs, mesh bags of wild carrots, jars of Bela's berry spread, Red's garlic, Hardknock's pair of cured otter skins, and a brace of geese. Clark arranged it all on the protective pallet that lived on the floor of the plane. Setting Laylea and her soiled bed on the floor, he folded down both cockpit seats. He held his palm out at Laylea again, reminding her to stay.

Maneuvering the stack through the door was tough but he only lost the carrots. Everything else he successfully transferred from plane to truck bed in one trip. He swapped the plane for the truck in the hangar and got it battened down, only hastily wiping up the sick that fell out of the bed.

He lifted Laylea as carefully as he could, holding her against his chest as he untangled the mess that he'd made of the bed and its tie-down straps. He transferred the contraption to the truck and belted Laylea in, then took an icepack from the glove compartment and set it, wrapped in his river-rinsed handkerchief, on her hip with the seat belt to hold it in place. Her eyes followed him as he shut up the hangar and climbed into the driver's seat. While the engine warmed up, he smoothed the fur on her wrinkled forehead, petting around to scritch her chin with his fingers. She laid her muzzle down in his palm.

The route home took twenty minutes. Clark drove the whole way with one hand and his knees so Laylea could keep her hand pillow.

At home, he parked in the garage and rushed around to gather Laylea and the icepack into his arms. The door opened before he could get his keys in the lock. Bailey yelped with joy at the sight of the puppy. They heard Sher sigh in the kitchen.

"Sher, I need your help." Clark warned Bailey off with a hand but the boy had already noted Laylea's tucked tail and glazed eyes. He held the door as Clark rushed in to find fruity oaty cakes sizzling on the griddle. Sher leaned against the counter facing the stove. She held a book in one hand and her to-go mug in the other.

"Laylea was wounded."

As soon as she saw them, Sher flipped the gas off and tossed Bailey a hot mitt. "What happened?"

Clark started to set Laylea on the island counter but though she took the ice from him, Sher had him continue holding Laylea as he described the pertinent details of the hermit's attack. Sher palpated the leg and hip and when she touched a spot that hurt worse than the puppy could handle, Laylea whimpered and showed her teeth. She licked Sher's hand.

"That's no good, huh?" Sher asked. "Okay, Laylea, I'm gonna give you something to make you feel better and reduce the swelling. Are you hungry?"

Clark answered, "She had mushy kibble with turmeric for breakfast about four hours ago."

"Hopefully she'll eat again. We'll try to make it appealing. Bailey." Sher rolled her eyes. "You're gonna love this. Grab me a can of tuna and scoop a little kibble into your old Muppets bowl."

The mom fetched a medicine bottle from Woodford's cupboard along with a mortar and pestle. She took the tuna from Bailey and set it on the counter in front of Clark while the kid dipped the plastic bowl into Woodford's food. Clark pushed a thumb into the metal top of the tuna. He opened just a small hole and poured the juice over the kibble in Bailey's bowl. Sher mixed some of the powder from a ground pill into the mush.

Then Laylea cuddled in the dad's arms while Bailey fed her out of his hand. Woodford howled at being left out. So, Clark and Bailey sat on the ground and fed him tuna. Sher sat on the stool above them, scratching Woodford's belly with her foot.

"Did he want the book?" Sher asked her husband.

Clark looked up. Bailey was well occupied. "Hmm?"

"The newest rescue. Did he want the book I gave you?"

Laylea rubbed her face against her dad's pale green button-down. She left a streak of mush on his chest. Clark kissed her forehead.

"He remembered his name."

Sher choked on her coffee.

"Yeah," Clark agreed. "But he's going by Hardknock instead."

Sher reached down and pulled off one sneaker so she could wiggle her toes into the muscles of Woodford's thigh. "He must be one of Trask's newer CFs."

Clark hummed a few notes of the song into Laylea's head. "Well, the conditioning may not be up to your quality but your recovery tricks don't seem to be working as well either."

"He remembered his name." Sher crowed a little.

"It's not doing good things for his sanity."

"Hardknock should have needed the book. Was it important to him?"

Clark nodded for a while. Laylea leaned into him, one step from sleep. Bailey offered her bowl to Woodford to clean.

"I didn't get much breakfast. Think you could finish those pancakes for me?"

"Sure." Sher slipped her shoe back on. "Was the book important to Hardknock?"

Bailey stood with the clean bowl. "Can Laylea have some more?"

"As much as she would like." Sher sent her son off to the food bucket. "Did he want the book?"

Clark finally relented. "The book," he said, "is what set Hardknock off."

Sher stood. She took two strides towards the swinging doors and froze. Realizing her coffee mug was still in her hand, she walked over to the French press and poured out the last drops. She drank it. Grounds from the French press went into the compost bin. She washed the press and her mug in the sink, dried them, and put them away into the cupboards.

"How much medicine, mom?" Bailey asked. "Same as before?"

Sher reached over and tapped more of the powder into the mush. She flashed a smile at her son but he darted back to the dogs and her eyes darted among the different recipes taped to the backsplash over the stove. Split pea and barley soup. Peanut butter oatmeal muffins. Fruity Oaty cakes. Banana bread. Chick Pea Chili. Fingerprint Cookies written out in Baileys block letters.

Her voice was subdued when she spoke. "Tell Jay to check in on him and make sure he's reading." She looked over at the counter. Clark's elbow stuck out but the rest of him was hidden. "He'll feel better. He'll be better."

Sher snapped the plastic lid onto the bowl of pancake batter. She considered putting it away in the fridge but left it beside the half-browned circles on the griddle. Bailey laughed and then apologized when the puppy yelped. Sher selected a towel from the five hanging on the oven handle and crossed to pull a reusable gel pack from the freezer door. Laylea's cry made the hair stand up on her arms. The wail quickly subsided to a barely audible whimper. Sher imagined the puppy was trying not to cry. Flexible cold compress acquired, Sher wrapped it in the yellow flowered towel. She found herself working as quickly as if Bailey were the one crying.

Clark's voice, husky and raw, froze her.

He sang.

I find
my mind
By listening to my heart
Together they will keep my soul from fracturing apart

The tune was hers. The words were new. Laylea stopped crying at the first note.

The emergency ice pack from the truck caught Sher's attention as she listened. It sat on the counter over the boys' heads where she'd tossed it. Clark had insulated the cold with his paisley handkerchief. Worn from seven years around his neck and being shoved in his back pocket, the oversized square of cotton frayed at the edges. Listening to Bailey join in, humming her song, Sher swapped the crisp new kitchen towel for the ratty, wrinkled bandanna.

As the song ended, she lowered herself to sit on the floor with everyone else. Bailey knelt beside Woodford. He held two fingers up for the injured puppy to lick clean. But Laylea's eyes were fixed on Clark. Sher watched her son try to get the little dog's attention. She risked a glance at her husband.

Clark's face was one that would draw anyone in. It took effort for him to turn his thin lips down into a frown where Sher had to concentrate just to not look angry. His eyes might hold a wealth of secrets but he couldn't remember them, thanks to her.

"You woogied the book, didn't you?" Clark kept his eyes on the wounded puppy.

"I didn't—" She started to correct his invented verb then just nodded. "It was supposed to help him. It will help him."

Clark hummed.

"I'm sorry." She reached out to the little dog. Laylea looked away from Clark. The puppy tapped her palm with its little nose and a smile brightened Sher's face. She scooted closer to her husband and wrapped a hand around the dog's muzzle as a bitch would do with her mouth. Then she slid her palm up the warm face and massaged the loose fur at the nape of Laylea's neck. "I didn't mean for you to get hurt. I'm going to do everything I can to help you get better."

The little dog turned her sleepy head and licked Sher's finger, leaving a mess of mush. Her glazed gaze searched Sher's face. If Sher had believed it could, her heart would have melted.

Clark offered her a white monogrammed old-man handkerchief from his back pocket and Sher considered it. But at the last moment, she reached over and wiped her hand clean in Bailey's hair. The boy giggled. Sher scooted closer, snuggling her hips in next to Clark and shoving him over so she could lean on the kitchen island as well. She slipped a hand between the dog's paws to feel her heartbeat. It pumped strong and her breathing was regular. Laylea licked her again.

"Laylea?" Sher asked.

The puppy dropped her head back to look up at the mom.

"Would you like to stay here?"

Laylea tried to sing. Her joy came out in a rolling howl and they all laughed at her except Woodford who never took his eyes off Bailey. Clark shifted Laylea to free his right arm which wrapped around Sher. The mom brushed her fingertips against the tiny yellow bruise on Clark's cheek, healing it. Bailey lay on the ground to let Woodford lick the mush out of his hair.

Laylea thought about her brothers and their basket in the bike shop. She remembered her mother's bouncy curls and the warm thick milk from her belly. She remembered playing the game of hide in the bag when her mama was so scared. She didn't remember why Mama had left her but knew it had something to do with the sweet-smelling man who had found them. She trembled, remembering how he dropped her on the hard table, on the leg that still hurt now.

Three hands reached out to comfort her. Laylea blinked her eyes, trying to look at them all at once. The sweet man couldn't hurt her here. And that's what her mama wanted.

Laylea tried to sing again but it came out as a sad little *wff*. The family laughed at her again. She sighed and fell asleep, safe in the arms of her family.

CHAPTER 12

SUMMER 2025 - FOOTHILLS, OR

"Dad, is it time yet?" Bailey stuck his head in the kitchen to ask yet again.

Woodford waited for the door to stop swinging before he pushed in after the boy. He padded between Clark's feet and the blanket he held to get to the water bowl beside the back door.

Clark replied, yet again, "It is not time yet."

He folded Maggie's rabbit wool blanket and tied it with a silver ribbon, attaching a card he'd printed with an invented story of its origin. He set the bundle on the counter beside the bunches of labeled herbs. He'd strung the sturdy plants together by their stems while the crumbly fronds lay in individual sized mesh bags. The air was filled with the sweet scent of boiled blackberries. His tools lay clean and drying in the dish rack, the preserved jam jars packed with newspaper beside Bela's berry spread in two cardboard boxes on the stove.

Bailey climbed up onto a kitchen stool. He fingered the rolled-up otter skins. "What are you doing?"

"I am packaging the payments I got in the mountains. You and I are going to hit the farmer's market regulars before we go to pick up Laylea and your mother."

"Yay!" Bailey fell off the stool and rolled over to Woodford's bed beside his food bucket. A quick belly rub and the boy was off, the kitchen door flapping behind him, the hound on his heels.

Clark shook the water from the cleaned greens of Ahab's wild carrots. He laid them on a pair of kitchen towels as he braided the stems together and tied them with a thick twine to which he attached a crafty label with another clever lie of the vegetable's provenance.

Normally he tried to offload the hermit's goods as soon as he got them home. But Laylea seemed most comfortable in his arms so Clark had delayed. Sher ordered forty-eight hours of observation. But when Laylea hadn't improved by dinner the next day, Clark reiterated that Hardknock had been wearing steel-toed boots.

A short argument ensued over whether he was reiterating or stating the fact for the very first time. In the end, Sher had decided to spay Laylea a little earlier than she would prefer in order to take advantage of her unconsciousness to get a closer and more clinical look at the hip.

Bailey backed into the kitchen. He held the door to let Woodford skitter in before he set a shoebox up on the counter.

"Can we sell these? The bald lady sells slabs of bark with google eyes."

"That's a man," Clark corrected.

He set the carrots on top of the jams and peered at Bailey's offering. Polished rocks sat in an even layer on the bottom of the box. He had two stunning pieces of agate surrounded by a mix of small brownish red carnelians and clear blue opalite. It was all bordered by a dozen of the most colorfully patterned jaspers Clark had ever seen assembled.

"These are beautiful. Are you sure you want to give them away?"

"I don't want to give them away." Bailey looked at his dad as if the old man had lost his mind. "I want to sell them. Laylea is another mouth to feed. I have to pitch in."

"Oh kid." Clark lifted Bailey onto a stool. "You don't have to pitch in. She doesn't eat that much and I've got a way with the vet. I'm sure we can negotiate her bills. Don't worry." He picked up a blue and purple jasper. "How did you find all these?"

"I don't know." Bailey pulled out one of the agates to show him the reverse side. "I just see them. You know, like when you make me shut my eyes and tell you all the different kinds of trees around us. I remember the rocks too."

"That's really cool, kid. You got any you want to keep? Cuz I'm pretty sure we could sell all of these to Ms. Audrey."

Bailey shrugged, flipping the stones in the box. "I'll find more." Then his face lit up. "She's the lady who makes jewelry."

"Yeah. And not the ugly stuff. We'll stop by her shop while we're out. Don't take less than fifty cents a stone. And make sure you say there's more where that came from."

"Yeah, there's lots more. All over the ground. I found this one on the playground at school." He held up a large opalite. "Why would she pay me fifty cents for a rock?"

"You just look around at the jewelry in her shop while I make small talk." He set a carnelian back into the box. "Hey, what do you say we have her set one of these in a necklace for your mom?"

"No." Bailey pulled the box away. "I'm looking for a labradorite for mom." He stood and took the box with him as he bent to nuzzle Woodford. "Can we get Laylea now?"

Clark made a mental note to look up labradorite the next time he stopped by a library. "Go get your shoes."

After successfully unloading all of the hermits' stuff, Bailey negotiated a dollar per rock for the agate and jaspers with the rest thrown in as "a gift to a new customer." He raised the price by pointing out she could advertise all of her stones as local and ethically mined. Clark enjoyed the looks Audrey shot him assuming he had put the words in Bailey's mouth. Bailey sealed the deal by asking if there were any colors she'd like him to keep an eye out for in particular. Audrey, playing along, showed him a necklace a customer wanted some matching earring for. Bailey had stared at the pendant until Clark ushered him out of the store.

Once at the clinic Bailey gave his fifteen dollars to Michelle and asked her to apply it to Laylea's bill.

"Now where did you get fifteen dollars?" Michelle took the fives and faced them before she tucked them away in the locked top drawer.

Bailey watched her drop the key into a side drawer after she secured the cash. "Don't you have a register?"

"No need. Most people pay with credit cards. Your mom just had an envelope tucked into the filing cabinet under C until I suggested we make this pencil drawer our kitty." She snorted. "Get it? Our kitty? Oh dear, I peed a little. Do you ever have accidents?"

Bailey shook his head. Heat rose to his ears. "Do you need to go to the back? I can watch the desk."

"Oh no." Michelle leaned in and whispered, "I wear diapers. Kenneth just loves kicking my bladder. Were you a runner in your mommy's belly or did you sleep?"

Bailey's eyebrows knit together as the heat raced past his ears to fill his head. He leaned in and whispered his confession, "I can't remember."

Michelle laughed at him again. Bailey worried that she would have another accident. Before she could ask him any more questions, he dropped below the counter and crawled over to curl up with Woodford in the dog's bed.

Clark came out of the back room, followed by Sher sans white coat. She stopped and held the door open for a six-foot man wearing tailored purple scrubs with black piping.

Bailey jumped up at the sight of Laylea tucked into the tech's arms. "Can I take her, Armando?"

His forehead rose in amused wrinkles, but the man crouched so Bailey could see the woozy pup. Laylea looked even tinier tucked into her ratty blue baby blanket with a white clinic sheet wrapped around it. Her lips hung open with the tip of her tongue sticking out between her teeth and her eyes didn't move when he tilted his head down to catch her gaze.

Bailey's face scrunched up with the effort to keep tears from escaping his eyes. He clasped his hands behind his back, knowing he couldn't hold her. Not safely. He only remembered to breathe when Armando stretched out his chin and tickled Bailey with his thick beard.

"It's okay. She looks funny cuz we gave her drugs. You're gonna hold her in the truck, Baileo. But it's like hospitals and wheelchairs. I have to carry her out there. Cool?"

Unable to speak, Bailey dove back onto Woodford's bed.

"She looks so much better." Michelle rolled her chair over to have a look since Laylea was at her level too. "You had Dr. Sher worried there for a moment, Laylea."

Armando tickled Michelle's cheek with his beard. "All thanks to your positive thoughts, Misha." He grunted a little as he stood up to his full height. "And Dr. Sher's magic touch."

"Bailey, can you get Woodford in the truck?" Clark put a hand on Armando's back, encouraging him toward the front door.

Bailey grabbed Woodford's leash from the hook above his bed, but he didn't clip it on. Woodford led the way out to the curb where the truck was parked. He didn't really need Bailey's help beyond opening the door, which took some effort for the kid.

The rusty door successfully wrenched open, Woodford hopped up and settled on the carpeted floor mat. He rested his head on the hump, looking over at the pedals. This was his customary spot in the family vehicle. Sher helped Bailey hop up and scoot over to his customary spot in the center of the bench seat. She buckled him in and backed out of the door.

Armando leaned in and set Laylea on his lap. He told Bailey to hold her carefully and showed him how to keep her secure without hurting her. Bailey asked questions. Bailey asked more questions. Sher abandoned Armando to help Clark put the trike in the truck bed and tie it down. Armando uncurled the puppy a little to show Bailey the stitches on her belly which would keep her from becoming a mom and doing other icky girl stuff. He then showed him the stitches on her hip, where Sher had repaired some of the damage done by dad's client.

Clark buckled himself in the driver's seat and got some basic instructions from Armando on where he should not hold Laylea if they had to stop short. He shook hands with the tech and started the engine. Armando backed up to give Sher her seat.

"Wait." Bailey stopped him. "How long before she can resume her normal activities?"

Armando stopped. He shot seven-year-old Bailey a funny look and appealed to Clark. "It's a kid, right? Not a cleverly disguised midget?"

"Little person, Armando. You should know better, working with Michelle."

"Michelle is a good 5 feet tall. I believe the cut off for LP is like 4'10" or something."

Bailey spoke up. "I'm not a Little Person. I want to know how long before she can play with me."

"I'm sorry." Armando folded the towel up over Laylea. "Your Mom will let you know when you can run around with her. But it should be about a week of rest. She's got painkillers, mostly for the hip, but they'll help with the belly too. She'll want to move around more than she should. So, you need to find quiet ways to entertain her. If you have any more questions, you can call Chris."

Clark sighed. "Really, Armando?"

"He already has his number, Clark." Armando tickled Bailey one last time and hopped out of the truck.

"Thanks for your help, Armando." Sher suffered the tech's hug. "You'll check in on Dash every hour?"

The tall man grinned guiltily. "I'm in the middle of Dean Koontz' latest. I was just gonna pull a stool up to Dash's cage and hang out with him all night."

"That," Sher shoved him out of her way, "works too."

"Doctor," Armando held onto her arm. "I mean yeah, she's just a dog." He scuffled his feet in the grass. "But she'll be able to walk and that's no little thing." He frowned at a grass stain on his pristine white Chucks, then caught Clark's amused grin when he looked up again. He shrugged his lanky shoulders and let his gaze rest on Laylea's drug goofy face. "I just . . . good job."

He flashed a smile and ran across the sidewalk and into the clinic. Sher slid into the truck and shut the door. Laylea looked up at the sound. Sher yawned at her, a canine calm down signal, and the puppy dropped her jaw in a return yawn. Her pink tongue curled at the end and retreated fully into her mouth as she laid her head on Bailey's arm.

Clark put the truck in gear. "Ready to go?"

"Ready."

"Ready to go, Dad."

"Bailey," Clark asked, "why do you have a vet tech's number?"

Bailey looked away from Laylea just long enough to give his dad a scathing look. "Cuz you don't know how to play video games."

Clark looked over him. "Sher?"

"You vetted him, Clark." She pointed out. "Don't you like Chris?"

"He's twenty-four years old." Clark tried to catch Sher's eyes but she wouldn't look away from Laylea.

"Yeah," she agreed. "But he's a boy. You guys are all the same age." She ignored their protests. Instead she tucked Laylea's tail into a fold of the baby blanket. "Maybe it'll be good to have another girl around the house."

She looked up when she noticed the truck wasn't moving to find both her boys staring at her. She straightened up and turned her gaze to the street. "It's been a long day, Hillens. Let's go home and play card games."

"Yes!" Clark put the truck in gear. "I'm good at those."

Bailey and Sher both laughed. "No, you're not."

CHAPTER 13

SUMMER/FALL 2025 - FOOTHILLS, OR

Laylea ruled Bailey's life not only for the next week but for that entire summer. Bailey took the bedrest instructions literally. Other than for bathroom breaks, he and Laylea hadn't left his room. Three days after the surgery, Sher officially announced that Laylea could go outside. She carried the puppy downstairs where she got her medicine-laced breakfast on the floor beside Woodford.

After breakfast, Sher went to work and Bailey asked his dad to hold Laylea while he brought her bed out to the porch. He brought his sleeping bag out too and his stuffed bear, Casey along with her teddy lizard. Another trip up and down the stairs and he brought out a pile of books. Then some pillows. The chess board. Finally, he gathered snacks in the kitchen and took out a tray which included a bowl of water for Laylea. Then he came and got her from his dad.

When Clark looked out later Woodford was snoring on Bailey's legs and Bailey napped with one arm encircling the bed. Laylea had laid her head on the bolster so she could clean Bailey's ear. Clark saw her take a deep breath and sigh into sleep, staring at her boy.

Clark checked on the trio again at lunchtime. Bailey sat up with Laylea on a pillow beside him. He had one of his old picture books laid out in front of them. His finger pointed at a word as he explained to

Laylea. "This says *puppy*. You are a puppy. This says *boy*. I'm a boy. This says *dog*. Woodford is a dog. When you grow up, you'll be a dog. When I grow up, I'll be a man. If I were a girl, I'd be a woman. But you'll still be a dog. This is *mother*. Sher is our mother. She's a woman. But this is the puppy's mother so she's a dog. Your mom is a woman cuz you live with us."

Bailey sounded like he had confused himself. He paused to sort it out. Then let it go.

"You and I are siblings now. And we take care of each other. Woodford is your big brother and you can chew on him. But if he says stop it, you stop. That's the deal. He's older and wiser and knows a lot more about life and Mom and Dad's secrets than either you or I. They both talk to him a lot. He's a really good listener." Clark's breath caught in his throat wondering how much Bailey overheard.

He went on. "I'm your big brother too and I'm working on being a good listener. If you ever need help you have to ask me. That's what families are for."

Clark smiled. He stepped out onto the porch. "How are you guys doing? Are you ready for lunch?"

Laylea's tail wagged wildly and she tried to stand. Bailey picked her up to keep her from hurting her leg. "Dad?"

"Yes."

Bailey had always been allowed time to think. Sometimes conversations with him went quite slowly.

"Dad."

"Yes, Bailey."

"Where is Laylea's first mom?"

"We don't know, Bails. She had to give Laylea to us because she couldn't keep her."

Bailey took a moment, kissed the top of Laylea's head. She looked up from chewing on his fingers and licked his chin. "Do you remember your mom?"

Clark leaned back against the doorjamb, trying to act like the question didn't hurt. "Nope. I can't remember her or if I had a big brother to listen to me or a little sister to take care of."

"That's why we're so important to you." Bailey nodded sagely.

Clark grimaced at his kid, "Your mom remembers her family and you're just as important to her."

Laylea growled. The Rick's cat sat beside the Old Lady Rucker's rose bushes.

"Laylea," Clark chuckled. "What are you going to do with that cat if you catch her?"

"Hey dad," Bailey closed the book, "what *is* for lunch?"

"Cheese and tomato?"

"Awesomesauce."

Woodford hopped up the stairs as Bailey led the way inside.

"Hey kiddo, do you remember what a secret is?"

"Pff, yeah Dad, practically everything."

The screen door slammed shut behind them, jangling its bells.

BY THE TIME SCHOOL STARTED, Laylea could walk normally. She could tumble down the porch stairs all by herself. Bailey set up a box, a stool, and a chair next to his bed and taught her how to use them to climb up and down. She'd doubled her size and still weighed in at only seven pounds according to the scale at Sher's clinic. She no longer whimpered in her sleep and no longer dreamed of four brothers crawling on her. When Bailey came home from school with work to do for the next day, Laylea sat at the foot of his desk, listening when he talked through the math. Any reading homework was done on the bed so that she could follow along and look at the pictures and words.

During the days when Bailey was at school, Sher at the clinic, and Clark doing errands he couldn't take her on, Laylea sought out Woodford to curl up next to him. But at night, Laylea climbed her personal staircase and slept in the crook of Bailey's belly.

CHAPTER 14

SPRING 2026 - CONSORTIUM BIOTECH HQ, CA

S unlight wormed its way through every gap in the drapes. Walter hopped up from the desk with his puppy tongue tape dispenser and sheaf of papers he'd just shaded black. The man whistled as he worked.

"Correct me if I've misunderstood but you did not find the silkies you were looking for in Scotland?" Trask set her sweet tea on its coaster and wiped her cool hand along her neck and chest.

"I did not see the *selkies*." Walter smirked at Trask. "I did not catch a selkie. But I know where they hunt." He did a jig on the window seat.

He taped a paper to the ceiling and tucked it behind the curtain rod. This blocked the one ray that actually had been bothering Trask. She turned back to her request for increased volunteer applications. Her researchers were continuing to fail. The brain wave adjustment procedure was creating massively unstable CFs with most of the volunteers terminating training before their first off-campus excursion. She had been most hopeful about a candidate volunteered by one of the rare returns. Instead of killing the survivalist who witnessed him leaping from tree to tree, the CF had tied the man up and brought him back. They'd had to sedate the CF when he'd strenuously objected to the intake coordinators taking his pet away. After a successful return, Trask hadn't wanted to rewipe the man but he wouldn't stop crying for his prize. The subsequent conditioning failed to take so Trask had rid herself of the volunteer by quietly funneling him through Walter's intake department.

His prize however had been their first success with the gamma wave surgery. Until last week when the seizures had begun. The doctors said there was no way to wipe him clean and start fresh. The seizures would continue no matter what they tried.

The office shook. Walter had jumped off the window seat. He flipped the fan around and put his face right up to the blades. "I should have had them start building the pool before I went hunting."

Trask flipped on their intranet to send yet another memo to building maintenance.

"They've moved the subjects outside to the courtyard. The guards and scientists are sharing ice lollies. No one's dropped by to offer us an ice lolly." He popped over to his computer as the intranet link downloaded fifteen messages from the server. "We've got a perpetually distressed volunteer my team think might be a good candidate for your theta wave experiments. Can't stop wailing about a lost prize." Walter peeked up to see Trask wiping sweat from her glasses. "Would you like him?"

"Thank you, no." She avoided his eyes.

"Aren't you losing most of your volunteers right now?" he asked.

"I believe I maintain the same retention rate as you."

"Hm." Walter typed a response to his intake team. "He seems to like heights. We'll try a basic primate integration and send him out to your mountains."

"You've advanced to off-campus testing?" Trask couldn't hide the shock in her voice. "I hope Gamma has met some of yours."

"This would be our first foray, not counting the carnivore blends who killed each other in the first six hours out." Walter climbed back up to the window. "Do you ever send your warriors out in pairs?"

"They're soldiers." Trask shut down the intranet and opened a downloaded tracking report on the prize. They'd released the man back into his environment with a short supply of antiepileptics and no return order. The man had learned enough from their training to find his way back to his compound. He had a wife and son her intake team had failed to discover in their interviews.

"What's the difference?"

"Hm?" Trask skimmed the report to find sections relevant to the son. They'd successfully captured the boy and executed a 300-series wipe.

"What's the difference between a soldier and a warrior?" Walter grabbed her stapler and did a quick basting job where the two curtains met. Trask didn't object. She hated the bird curtains anyway.

"A warrior fights for himself. A soldier obeys orders."

"So, Gamma is turning your soldiers into warriors."

"Until we get successful surveillance on Gamma, we won't know what he's doing with my CF. For all we know, he's killing them."

"But you don't think so."

"No." She pulled a hand fan from her top drawer and leaned back to finish her tea. "How goes the search for your dogs?"

"It turns out the dog pounds around the mountains don't keep good records." Walter stapled the last piece of paper to the ceiling. "But my techs are developing some interesting new data mining worms." He hopped off and wiped the cushions with his hand. He set the stapler on Trask's ever-present Gamma folder. "Why don't you try conditioning a CF team? Humans are pack animals after all. A team might have better luck avoiding Gamma or even teaming up on him." He grinned. "Get it?"

"Yes, Walter. I got it." Trask turned back to the report on her new 300. The kid did have a mother. Keep her maternal instincts intact and she might make the perfect guardian. She wiped the sweat from her face and put her glasses back on.

"Yes." Walter pulled five more sheets from his notebook. "I think we'll definitely send the new man out into your training grounds." Starting from the top left corner, he painted a paper with black marker. "Maybe he'll find his prize."

Walter focused on his scribbles. Trask glued her eyes to her computer.

THE DIRECTOR TYPED a quick sequence into the tablet attached to his thigh. His screens filled with acquisition photos and stats on Trask and Walter's volunteers. He tapped another command and this array whittled down to those who had *terminated training*. Another command eliminated those CF known to have been retrieved by Gamma Subject. Quick math by the system informed him Trask's failure rate was 97.394%. A little smile brightened his stout features. The director transferred the details to Records with a memo for them to organize it into a report cc:d to the Biotech Research supervisors. A little inter-division competition should set a fire under the team. That would guarantee him entertainment for years.

He pulled up the prison feeds and set the audio to scan for the keywords physics, survival, and soldier. The feed on a tenth of one screen blanked out as he watched. The Director diverted his attention to have his voxbox call in an anonymous tip to the Superintendent of Angola that Camp D might be about to experience an escape attempt. As an afterthought, he sent code to the Biotech Research building to release the air conditioning shut down.

CHAPTER 15

SPRING 2026 - FOOTHILLS, OR

A week after Laylea's first adoptionversary as Bailey declared it, they shoved the chairs and couches aside so Clark could lay his tent and tarp out in the family room for repairs. Bailey slumped on the couch in a pout. Until Sher stopped by.

"Do you have a problem, Bailey?" she asked. Grease smudged her forehead and she held a plastic toy in her hands that she seemed to be trying to break.

"I want to go."

"And you can't go." Clark summed up, "So that's a problem."

Sher peered down at a patch on the tent. "It's better to address a problem than stress over it."

Bailey stood up and addressed his father, "Please can I go flying with you?"

Clark set down the patch kit and looked at his son. "No."

"Laylea is going."

The puppy in question perked up from Woodford's bed.

"You'll be at school and your mom at work. Lee is too young to be left alone all day."

Bailey almost stomped his foot which would have gotten him into real trouble with his mother. He took a breath and tried to put his distress into words. "She got hurt last time," he said. "She's going to be sick."

"Now that seems like a problem you can address." Sher smiled at Bailey. She patted his head with a greasy hand and went back to her tinkering room.

"I can't promise she won't get hurt," Clark said. "And yeah, the airsickness was pretty unpleasant but she was little. It probably won't be as bad this time."

Bailey turned to look at Laylea. She flicked her ears at him. He gave her the Hand of Stay and stomped out of the room. Laylea tilted her head at Clark.

"Don't know, little girl. But whatever happens, it'll be interesting."

She barked and laid her head down on Woodford's butt.

Clark packed up the repaired tent, the tarp, and his lights and toiletries in the hotel bag. Sher came out of the tinkering room to cook dinner so Clark could spread his maps out on the dining room table and work the math aloud. Laylea stood up on his leg. Clark picked her up and showed her how he was making a flight plan and recording his plans into a code that only Sher could understand so she could find him if he didn't come back. Bailey wandered in. He set a canvas bag on a chair and climbed up after it.

"Hey kiddo, what's that?" Clark set aside his dictaphone.

"It's a better first aid kit. In case you guys get hurt with mom all the way down here." Bailey leaned over and traced the line of the mountains with a finger. "I'm still working on Laylea's kit. What are you doing?"

"Plotting a flight plan. We're looking at the weather reports—"

Bailey tickled Laylea's belly. "Can you fly anything, Dad?"

He thought about it. "Fixed wing, yeah, probably. I'd need to glance at the instruction manual."

"But you can't fly helicopters?"

"Well, I haven't been in one since your . . . since I can remember."

"What are these circles?" Bailey tapped a finger on the possible landmarks.

"We need to pick some ground checkpoints and it's a little more complicated because I'm deliberately not flying the optimum route."

Bailey's head fell forward onto the charts. He snored.

"Is that your mother calling you?"

Bailey popped up. "Yes! I hear her too." He raced out through the kitchen door.

"Am I boring *you*?" Clark asked the little girl lying belly up, chewing on his pencil.

He took it from her and looked over his charts again. He leaned on his forearms and marked a few more options, lakes he knew of from previous flights, a bare ledge too rocky to land on but easy to spot from his maximum altitude. He was caught up in his thoughts, trying to keep the numbers straight in his head so he was startled when Laylea stood up to lean on his face. She licked his forehead and his eyelids.

He gave her a little love and lifted her to the far side of the map. "I'm working here."

Laylea blew air through her teeth. She stood and padded over the map to sit against Clark's chest. He smiled and continued quietly searching for the most convoluted route his gas tank could afford.

She barked and stood.

"What?"

At the sound of his voice, she sat again, eyes on his pencil.

"You like my voice?"

Laylea barked and looked up at him.

Clark kissed the tip of her nose and started talking through his thoughts as he figured the distance, time, gas, and coffee needed for their trip. Laylea didn't interrupt him again.

After dinner, Clark carried Laylea with him into the small closet he'd turned into an office and radio room. He set her on the table as he fired up his old HAM radio. While it was warming up, he stepped out to snag Laylea's baby towel off the couch. He came back to find her tilting her head at the headphones hanging off the reticulated lamp arm. Clark dumped the towel on the table and slipped the cans over his ears. He chatted with some strangers for a bit while he watched Laylea rearrange her towel using her teeth and occasionally a paw to drag it into a comfortable bed. She turned around seven or eight times and dropped onto the towel, curled into a tight ball over her tucked under tail. With one last look at Clark, she shut her eyes.

Clark fiddled the dials with his left hand and gave a shout out to Jay

Doe. He settled in to wait, repeating his call periodically. He watched his baby girl, wondering at how quickly she could fall asleep. Laylea startled herself, waking at a little snore, then settled again. Shortly her eyelids began twitching. One paw flapped from the wrist, maybe as she tried to trap the Rick's cat in her dream.

The radio crackled.

"Jay Doe to Captain Crunch."

"Crunch here. Getting soggy. Where you been, Jay?"

They verified the powwow landing coordinates. Jay passed along last minute special orders. Clark approached the subject of Hardknock carefully.

Jay showed no such reserve. "He won't be attending, Captain. I've a gorgeous black bear skin to trade for his order."

"I haven't got anything near worth that. Just his scrip, his beverage of choice, and a few small toiletries."

"Not bringing him any books this time, are you?"

"That's a negatory, Jay. No reading materials."

"Good. He's like a teenage girl and a telephone with that thing."

"Come back?"

"He doesn't ever put it down."

"Hey Jay, think maybe you had a sister?"

"Open channel, Captain."

"Affirmative. Sorry. You have anything else on your list?"

"Will you be bringing your copilot again, Captain? The families all asked after her when I went around for their orders. I think the Disneys are interested in taking her off your hands."

Clark looked over at the puppy. Laylea yawned, her long pink tongue curling up at the tip. He smiled. "Yeah, she's coming with me. But she's my co-pilot. Can't fly without her."

"Maybe you can find a more useful type for them."

"I'll keep an ear to the ground."

"For me too, as long as you're looking. Bigger, stronger, but just as sweet as LG if you can manage it."

Clark chuckled. "She's yours if I find her." He picked his pencil up and scratched behind Laylea's ear with it. "Need any other sweets from the pantry?" he asked, offering to get Sher on the line to answer any clinical questions.

Jay paused for a moment and then replied, "One kid in the cottage, Captain. Breadcrumbs are sparse. He's an Obi one."

Clark repeated this into his dictaphone. "Over and out, Jay. We'll see you in the place at the time with the things."

Two days later after Clark had gathered the additional supplies, Bailey helped him buckle Laylea's bed into the truck. The kid cracked the lid of a shoebox. Inside he'd stacked a sour cream container inside an empty butter tub. A bottle of water sat beside them. He pulled out a medicine bottle with nail holes poked in the cap.

"Ginger. I ground it and some is liquefied."

Clark examined the bottle. "How do I get her to eat it?"

"You don't." Bailey took it back. "She smells it. You can see if she's looking green and hold it up to her nose. It'll calm her stomach. If it loses its odor by the time you're coming back, you can open the lid and smoosh the shavings a little and that should refresh it. You want me to show you how to open the lid?"

"Let's just see if she likes it, wise guy."

Bailey giggled and reached through the window to hold his home-made diffuser under Laylea's nose. The puppy jerked back at first but then she darted her head forward a few times to check it out. She seemed to be okay with the ginger so Bailey put it back into the box on the seat beside her bed.

Clark swung Bailey into a bear hug. He swept Sher into it when she came out to the garage with a new and improved set of flashwipes for the plane.

"I understand how the flashwipe on our street sign deters people from looking at it again or really reading it at all, but how does this help me fly under the radar?"

"The sequence works on technology as well as human brains. Your plane won't show up clearly on radar or pictures and I improved the three-sixty for direct visual contact deterrence."

"And you're pretty." Clark kissed his wife.

She waited with Bailey by the bicycles while he got in the driver's seat and buckled in, setting the flashwipes beside him with exaggerated care.

Sher leaned in the passenger side window. She set her handwritten instructions on the dashboard and tucked teddy lizard in the bed with Laylea. "You'll be careful with the new guy?"

"I promise." Clark crossed his heart.

"Fair winds."

"I love you."

LAYLEA COULDN'T SETTLE in the cockpit as Clark loaded the plane and performed his checklist. She paced around her bed once he had it buckled into the seat. She tried to fluff the stuffing. She jumped down and paced on the floor until he needed the space. She climbed over to his seat and then up onto the instrument panel. From there she could see out the window and calmed a bit. But Clark lifted her from the perch and set her back into her bed when he started up the plane.

He took Bailey's bottle from the shoebox and offered her a sniff. Laylea took it from him and buried it under a bolster. Laughing, he showed her the instructions written on the lid of the box. She tasted it. He cracked the water bottle and poured a little into the sour cream container. Bailey had magic markered "Water" on the side.

"Go easy on this." He set it on the tarp-covered boxes lining the passenger side floor.

He showed her the butter tub. Bailey had written "Barf" on the outside of this one. And inside on the bottom.

"Try to aim for this. Okay?" This one he left on the seat next to her bed. He keyed the radio, "I'm about to take the runway."

Laylea barked at him. Then curled up into a tight ball of dog and covered her eyes. When they started rolling, she wiggled around until her nose disappeared under the bolster, near the ginger bottle. Clark got them in the air as smoothly as he could.

Fifteen minutes into the flight Laylea let out a growling sigh and rolled onto her back. Clark reached over to rub her belly but she swatted at his hand, threatening to chew it off. She climbed off the seat and lapped briefly at the water. Then she hopped back up and stood up on the door. She could just barely see out the window.

When she tried to climb up the side of the door for a better view, Clark reached over. He took Laylea in his right hand using what he thought of as the crane grip. Her belly rested on his arm, a leg on either side. His palm and fingers supported her chest. When he felt her relax, he swung his arm across his chest so that Laylea could see out of his window. With a sigh, she leaned forward and pressed her nose against the Plexiglas.

Clark's bicep was just starting to seize up a few hours later when he noticed Laylea had leaned her whole face on the window. Steam blocked his view out that side. He lowered his hand and slid her onto his lap without waking her. She stretched and dreamed but didn't wake again until they were safely on the ground.

"An entire leg with no barfing." He woke her with a hand cupped around her muzzle. "I'm very hopeful. Now, this is a quick stop. Find yourself a bathroom and don't eat anything Sher would disapprove of." Clark lifted her down into the grass and let her run free while he found a rock to prep in his sling. She immediately leaped after a possible grasshopper and tripped, rolling under the plane. She danced over to the far side of the wheels to relieve herself. Then she ran around the plane a few times just to stretch her legs. On her third lap, she broke off to growl at a pale boy approaching from the nearby woods. She tried to jump sideways to get between Clark and the stranger but tripped and went rolling again.

Despite the bag on his back and his stick thin legs, the kid dropped to a crouch to see her better. He reached out and Laylea jumped back when she saw his hand. The pinkie finger ended in a rough scar before the second knuckle. He didn't notice her reaction. His ice-blue eyes couldn't have gotten a very good look at her before he bounced back up. A shaggy translucent ponytail hanging down his back kept bouncing as he jogged in closer. "We didn't order one of those, did we?"

"Nope. That's my in-flight entertainment." Clark shook the boy's offered hand. "Here, let's empty your bag."

Clark and the boy quickly transferred sixty pounds of smoked salmon from the large bag balanced over the kid's shoulders to the cooler of dry ice Clark had ready on the plane. He dragged the appropriate crate out of the back and set it on the ground with a bag of corn meal.

"I've got your scrip here in the cockpit." Clark reached into the bag he kept beside the pilot's chair.

He stopped at the sound of a choked sob. When he turned, the perpetual motion boy had frozen in place. His head started shaking and he found his voice.

"Don't need the Lacosamide anymore." Another strangled whimper brought Laylea to Clark's feet. The kid spun away and began stuffing supplies into his empty bag.

Clark rolled the vial up in its paper sack and tucked it into a side pocket of his flight bag. When he turned around, the crate was empty. He glanced down at Laylea. Her eyes were glued to the boy.

"I'm sorry."

The kid didn't look back. He was still tying up his pack as he thanked Clark and jogged back toward the woods. He was in such a rush that he didn't notice when something fell out of the bag. Laylea saw. She barked and ran toward the parcel. The boy turned and shouted in alarm as Laylea picked up the giant Snickers bar with her teeth and ran it to him. She stood up on his leg so he wouldn't have to bend as far and upend the bag on his shoulders. He took it from her gingerly. She didn't recoil at the short finger this time.

"Thank you."

Laylea barked and ran back to attack a grasshopper near Clark's feet.

"That was food, you doofus. You're a dog."

He looked up to see the boy standing still with the candy bar in his hand, watching them. He waved and the kid ran off. "A normal dog would have eaten it."

Laylea looked up at Clark and listened for a clue to what he wanted. She sat. She lifted a paw. Clark bent down to shake the proffered paw and she got her a cookie from his righthand pocket. His glorious righthand pocket. When she was done with the cookie, she noticed Clark swinging teddy lizard in her face. She lunged for it and they had a good game of keep away there in the field around the plane.

Chapter 16

Typically, Clark spent a flight singing or mentally listing all of the things he knew about himself. He could fly any plane he'd seen. He loved movies and the smell of popcorn made him smile while the taste didn't thrill him all that much. Plants of all sorts thrived under his care but each time he dug in the dirt was like his first time. He loved Sher with all of his heart. He would give everything in his power to give Bailey a normal life. And he could eat Caprese salad for every single meal and die a happy man.

It was a short list. So, he would add the more mundane. He preferred paste to gel when it came to dental care. He believed anyone who didn't agree that Harry Connick Jr's rendition of anything was far superior to Old Blue Eyes' was off his head. He didn't care for chocolate. Han shot first.

And then he would sing Sher's song to make himself feel better.

But with Laylea in the cockpit, Clark found his typical buoyant spirit maintaining the fore. He didn't sink into dark thoughts. During the next leg of the short journey to the powwow, Clark explained to her what each of the instruments told him. He explained to her how they differed in other planes he'd flown since Sher had reactivated his long-term memory storage. He explained to her about the magic Bernoulli fairies who ran on the clouds with their steel-toed combat boots for kicking birds out of the way. They wore tutus and plaid shirts and all of them, the girls and the boys, had thick beards. He explained how the Bernoullis held the plane up. And then he explained the math of Daniel Bernoulli's Law of Differential Pressure.

Laylea watched everything he did. She loved his chatter and Clark took cues from the tilt of her head and turn of her ears on whether to expand on a subject or move on. She seemed most interested in things he could point at.

He stopped talking when he needed to focus on their second approach. The selected rendezvous provided only a tight landing field. Not for the first time, Clark dreamed of somehow adding hovering capability to his little Cessna. Laylea lay down when he stopped speaking. In his focus, Clark didn't really notice her kneading his thighs. And when they hit the ground, he didn't dare look down to see where she went as she crawled off his lap. The sound alerted him. She made it to the appropriate tub to throw up the cookie.

"Maybe I shouldn't take you flying." Clark sighed as he shut the plane down and unbuckled. "This could be animal cruelty." He climbed out of the plane and reached for her.

Laylea backed away.

"What's wrong, little girl? Don't you want to get out and stretch your paws?"

She whimpered a little and curled up on the far side of her bed. She stared at Clark until he got the message.

"You're not getting out. Okay. I'll leave the door ajar if you change your mind."

Laylea tilted her head.

"Ajar means open."

He washed out the butter tub, replaced it, and went on about the business of trading items with a young couple. All these two had to give Clark were envelopes. Clark opened the passenger side door to put them in a locked box in the floor of the plane and Laylea tumbled over to the floor on the pilot's side so he couldn't reach her. She relaxed when he was back in his harness with the doors shut. Once they were in the air she climbed over to his lap and tried to get on his right hand so he could crane her up to the window. This was a longer leg. She divided her time between staring out the window and at the instrument panel. For a little while she even lay on her back in Clark's lap and stared up at his face as he chattered at her.

The third time they landed she was awake and did not throw up. But she curled up in her bed with her nose tucked by the ginger bottle when Clark told her they were descending. Clark held the water tub up for her after he shut the plane down and before he unstrapped.

"This is the powwow, little girl," Clark said. "I hope you don't remember what happened last time. But Hardknock won't be here." He unbuckled his harness and added, "And I don't care how much anybody likes you, you're coming home with me." He leaned over and nuzzled his face into her fur, growling, and mushing an ear between his lips.

Laylea twisted her head up to lick his face off. She whined back at him and wiggled into his touch.

A knock on her door startled them both. Still kissing the top of Laylea's head, Clark reached over to push the door open.

"Hi Mithter Capitan. You brought Elgy!" Mickey offered her hand to the puppy. Laylea flipped around, smacking Clark in the face with her butt. She crawled out of her bed and tried to climb down out of the cockpit onto Mickey's head.

"Hang on there, beaver." Minnie jogged up to assist Laylea to the ground where she wrestled with Mickey under the plane. "Hi Captain. I take it LG is doing well. Oof." Minnie grunted as Laylea bounced off her legs.

"She's feeling much better. Thank you for thinking of her." Clark unbuckled and got out to organize the deliveries.

Maggie and her partner, Trey, piled a hundred pounds of flour onto a travois and dragged it over to the campfire where the kids were put to work dividing it into seven bundles. When the flour was repackaged Flower and Judah, Ahab's eldest, hauled the bags over to the clearing where Clark had laid out each family's goodies. Mickey tried to explore the piles, but before any adult even noticed, Laylea herded her away.

When he'd been paid and the return goods locked away in the plane, Clark carried the last three items over to where Laylea was being buried in flowers.

"Hey Mickey." Clark crouched. "Do you still make pine cone bird feeders?"

The tow-headed little trouble maker looked up at him with enormous eyes and nodded.

"Great." He showed her the books in his hands. "I would like to offer you a trade."

Mickey squealed and reached for the books but Clark stood.

"This is a proper trade. I've got to see your product first." He gestured for the girl to lead the way and when she figured that out, she grabbed his hand and pulled him toward her family's tent, weaving through the woodsfolk transferring all of their newly acquired goods.

An unfamiliar hermit approached the center of the clearing once everyone else had gathered their belongings. He sported a neatly trimmed beard and had dyed his Consortium issue pants with red leaf buds. With the nearly white beard and green snap front shirt, the kids had dubbed him St. Nicholas. But the short hermit himself had so far refused to choose a name. Hardknock remained the only rescued CF to remember his real name.

St. Nick paid for his camping backpack with camelback insert and basic survival kit in medicinal herbs. Before he would let Clark pack them away he'd used Clark's gifted pen and paper to label each bundle, stressing in his note that he didn't know what they were for, just what they were called. He also wrote a promissory note for the extra goods he felt he owed for the unexpected tent. Clark tried to explain that the tent was a gift but the old man wouldn't discuss it. He walked away.

While everyone else organized their deliveries or did Bela's bidding at the campfire, this man crouched in the clearing redistributing his worldly goods into his new pack.

Laylea shook the weeds out of her fur. She trotted over to the plane and retrieved her toy from behind one wheel. Stalking up on the silent hermit, she dropped the lizard on his sack of flour. She bounded backwards and stuck her butt in the air, growling. The hermit brushed the toy off and fit the flour in his backpack. Laylea leaped forward and grabbed the lizard, shaking it madly. She lost hold of it and the stuffed animal flew over to land on the hermit's tent roll. She bounded after it, startled when the roll rolled and teddy lizard fell off the far side. She dropped low and growled at the tent. She stalked it from side to side, dashing in to nip at the green fabric.

St. Nick saw a patch job in his future. He left his packing and fetched the lizard from behind the tent roll. The colorful lizard soared through the air. Laylea barked and bounded off to catch it. She was too slow. Scooping the patchwork lizard up, she ran it right back to the hermit. Dropped it at his feet. He ignored it. She growled. She bowed. She darted in, leaping away before she could grab it. He ignored her. She leaped around his legs, nipping at her lizard. He found it hard to avoid stepping on her. So, he picked up the lizard and sent it flying farther.

It took her five returns before the hermit gave up his packing. Laylea sang when he sat on his tent roll. She dropped to her back and showed him her belly for an instant before leaping to her feet again.

They played tug-of-war. One of them was a bit rough with her teeth and the lizard's side seam ripped open. St. Nick confiscated the toy. Laylea tried to get it from him but he put his hand up flat in the stay gesture. She dropped her butt. He pulled a matchbook sized container from a side pouch on the backpack. Laylea watched as closely as she could from her seat. She tilted her head and craned her neck forward. The hermit threaded a needle and did a delicate patch job on the lizard. He was just tying off the knot when Clark set a campstool down on the other side of the backpack and offered the hermit a beer. The older man looked at it suspiciously for a moment. Laylea twisted the top half of her body to look back at Clark without lifting her butt from her seat. She sang out with a musical growl.

Clark laughed and released her. "Okay."

She ran over and licked at his nose then returned to her spot to watch the hermit. He'd watched her with an admiring smile on his lips. He tossed the patched lizard at Laylea's feet and took the beer. She cleaned every inch of her toy and then trotted over to drop it at the man's feet.

The hermit picked up the lizard and stood. He tilted his head at Clark much as the puppy would have and raised an eyebrow.

"I'd love to." Clark stood and the two of them walked over to the campfire.

The hermit dangled teddy lizard just out of Laylea's reach. She could have stolen it from him when he sat on a log beside Jay Doe, but she was distracted by the smells of all the incredible food she couldn't share. To keep from begging, she hunkered down against Clark's feet until Flower and Mickey lured her away.

They soaked her kibble in a lake of broth and with the captain's permission, even added a few chunks of rabbit meat.

Dinner was cheerful, filling, and lasted long past Laylea's bedtime. She played with every person in the encampment except Feranda. When the little kids grew too tired to play, she napped with them by the fire until they were sent to their tents. Ahab carried Laylea to his wife's lap. When she had to go settle a fight between her boys, Laylea was traded to Maggie's care. Bela even took her for a bit when the stewpot was cleaned. But at the end of the night, she lay cuddled in the dad's belly soothed by the whistling noise of his deviated septum.

She leapt out of their tent in the morning. While Clark took care of his boring human morning things, she bounded around the field searching for the nameless hermit. She tumbled with Mickey for a bit. She let Maggie carry her over to the campfire for breakfast and chewed on the woman's irresistible curls. She ate the kibble Flower mixed with a spoonful of oatmeal. But her head stayed on a swivel the whole time, searching for her friend.

"Morning, LG." Jay Doe snuck up behind her. "The new guy said you left this with him last night. Didn't want you to forget it."

He sat on the ground and set teddy lizard by her bowl. She glanced at it while she snatched up the last bits of food.

"He's a different kind of guy. So afraid of what might come out of his mouth that he won't talk at all." He played with a leather knife sheath as he chatted with her. He tightened the decorative braiding on the closure and drew the knife to trim the extra. "He freaked when I gave him his knife." Jay flicked his thumb on the blade. He poured river water from his own canteen into Laylea's bowl. "Didn't want to take it at first. And he asked me to hold it for him during the powwow."

Laylea finished the water.

"I made this. Panned for the metal. Built a little forge. Pounded it into shape. I've caught Elk before but this antler came from a buck who lost it in a mating fight. He won the fight so I guess that's good luck for the knife. Right? I've been working on this weapon for seven years. Can't wait to see what the Captain gets for it."

"I'm not selling that knife, you idiot." Clark approached the pair.

"You have to. It's my payment."

Clark bit into a crisp red apple. He picked up Laylea's bowl and popped it flat before he hooked it to a belt loop. "Oh, I'm taking the knife. But there is no way I'm letting that go to a stranger."

"What do you need with another knife?"

"What do I need with another dog? But she's mine and I'm hers and we're gonna take your knife and go home now. Want to come?"

While Jay considered the offer, Laylea took Lizard's tail in her mouth and dragged it over to the log St. Nick had stayed on throughout the evening, throughout the singing and stories and camaraderie. She cleaned the new stitches.

"Sounds good." Jay sheathed his knife and handed it off to Clark. "But the new guy needs looking after. Hardknock randomly comes to me for rebooting. And with what Maggie and Feranda did to each other last week, thanks, maybe another time."

"Any time you like. Let's talk tomorrow."

"I won't get to my equipment by tomorrow. Dusk after?"

"You got it."

"Tell the Sh . . . folks at home I'd love to see them." Jay pushed to his feet. Laylea turned her big sad eyes up as he moved but kept her head down on the lizard. "Look at that. Think she remembers the hermit sat there?"

"Definitely," Clark tucked the exquisite knife into his belt. "That is one smart little dog."

CHAPTER 17

SPRING 2028 - FOOTHILLS, OR

Laylea's ears grew up and flopped over. The light blond of her coat darkened into a light fawn, setting off her one dark brown paw and the white triangle over her eyes. Her tail looked like she could be part Fox Hound. Her thin body and face called Chihuahuas to mind, while her stout, muscled legs let her leap like a Jack Russell. Clearly though, she was bred from the smartest dogs of whichever breeds made up her genetics.

She topped out at twelve pounds, small enough that she continued climbing under the covers to curl up in Bailey's armpit throughout the winter and well into the chilly spring to keep from shivering.

"Hi Lee." Bailey flung the blankets over his head and snuggled down to kiss Laylea on the nose.

She licked him back. He kissed her. She licked him. It was a good game and they kept it up until Bailey yawned and Laylea got a swipe at the inside of his mouth.

"Ewwwww!"

Laylea yawned. She stretched her paws out and then tucked her nose back under Bailey's arm.

"No!" He sat up, letting cold air in. "Don't you know what day it is?"

Laylea rolled over and laid her muzzle on his neck. She blinked sleepily at him and let her eyes drift shut.

"Wake up, Laylea! It's your adoptionversary. You joined the family three years ago today."

Laylea sat up. She watched Bailey dart about the room. He yanked his hiking pants from the chest of drawers and grabbed a stinky t-shirt from the floor. His excitement was infectious. The dog dropped her jaw, her tail shaking her entire body.

A knock at the door set her tail spinning.

"Morning kiddo. You ready?"

"In a minute, Dad. Laylea tried to sleep-witch me."

"Sleep-witch?"

"Yeah." Bailey dropped to the floor to pull on a pair of socks he found under the bed. They didn't match. "She gets all cute and yawny and lays her head on my shoulder so I can't get up without disturbing her. It's like she wants to woogie me back to sleep."

"Ah, and that's why you're late for breakfast every day?" Sher leaned in the doorway. "Get fresh socks. Your green wool ones are clean. Then get downstairs. I'm mixing up shmancakes and you're manning the grill." She turned away, calling over her shoulder, "And you're magical, not her. So, who's been sleep-witching who?"

Bailey dropped his socks. "I don't use magic on Laylea, Dad."

Clark tossed him the green ones. "I know you don't. She knows you don't." He turned to Laylea." Good morning, adopt—" Clark looked to his son.

"Adoptionversary, Dad."

"Good morning, adoptionversary girl. You want a crane all the way downstairs?"

Laylea picked her way over the piled-up blankets to the edge of the bed. She had to be careful because her wagging tail threw off her balance. Woodford never seemed to have a problem with his tail. He was a good dog.

The dad slipped his hand between her front legs and lifted her off the bed. "Stop helping, little girl."

He said that every time. Laylea couldn't help it. She loved his one-handed carries and like her tail spinning, she couldn't help but hop up and down when she saw the crane coming. She flew with Clark on all his trips and though she had bad days where she had to spend the entire flight with her nose tucked into Bailey's ginger bottle, most of the trips were hours long cranes, looking at the instruments and staring at the clouds in the dad's firm grip.

"If you don't hurry, Bails, I'm gonna get the spatula."

"I'm coming. I'm coming." Bailey lay on the floor by his dresser, pulling on the fresh socks.

"Dad!" Bailey cut the whine off in mid D. He repeated the word in a tone that Laylea knew meant he was about to apply logic. "Dad."

Clark recognized the tone as well. He backed out of the room and dashed down the stairs like a kid. The bells jangled on the front door as he grabbed a jacket and Laylea's leash from the coat tree in the front hall. He stepped back to let Sher in. She handed him a basket of sweet cherries to hold while she shed her poncho and hung it on the tree.

"The Rucker boys are here."

"Here?" Clark asked, "on our front porch?"

"Here," Sher took the basket, "visiting their grandmother."

"Good. It's spring. She probably has a long list of chores she won't let me help her with."

Clark slipped out the door and shut it without jangling the bells. It was a trick Bailey was trying to master. Laylea had seen Sher changing the bells just so Bailey couldn't leave silently. But Clark never had any trouble.

He set Laylea in the grass. She expected him to slip her collar over her head while she did her business. He didn't. She looked up at him in confusion when she was done dancing at the pee. He glanced over at the Old Lady Rucker's yard.

Her grandsons waved. They were throwing around a football. Clark glanced down at Laylea and swung the leash and collar in his hand as he walked away towards the brothers.

"Hey boys. Parker, you have doubled in size since I last saw you. How old are you?"

"I'm seventeen, sir. Davis turned fourteen last week."

Parker had grown his hair out. It stood like a halo of tight curls two inches from his head. His little brother was trying to imitate the afro but only had a fringe of hair. Davis wore the same green and yellow shorts as his brother and though his shirt was different, it advertised the same band. Laylea wished she could dress like her big brother to show him how much she loved him. Her collar wasn't even the same color. Her collar was light blue. Her collar was swinging from the dad's hand.

Laylea perked up. Then she pinned back her ears and ran for the rose bushes. Scents of lilac and clove dripped on her head with the dew. Moss rose in the scent floor and she thought she detected an undertone matching the mom's rare glass of red wine.

"Mr. Hillen?" Davis' shy tone wasn't enough to get Clark's attention.

"And has Davis joined you on the football team, Parker?"

"Excuse me. Mr. Hillen?" Davis tried again.

"Davis, I told you to call me Clark."

"Oh shit!" Parker corrected himself instantly. "Shoot. Oh shoot, Laylea's in the roses, Mr. Hillen."

"Clark," Clark insisted.

Laylea took advantage of every second he stalled. She sniffed the petals and the leaves and the dirt and covered her nose in yellow pollen buried deep into the center of an open bud.

"Oh no. I am so sorry." Clark put a hand on Laylea's scruff. She backed out. "You didn't do any damage to Mrs. Rucker's prize roses, did you, little girl?"

"She never does no damage to my roses." The boys stood up straighter as their grandmother, just an inch taller than Davis, let the screen door slam behind her. "She never digs like your other dog."

"I'm sorry, Letitia. Has Woodford gotten into your roses recently?"

"Not for about a year now, I don't think," Mrs. Rucker drawled. "He's learning." She brushed dirt out of Davis' hair and straightened Parker's shirt as she passed her grandsons. "And this little terror hasn't watered my roses once since we had our little conversation. She knows where she's to do her business."

Laylea shook the dew from her fur. She trotted three feet over to squat by the Rick's deep pink azalea bushes.

"Oh my." Mrs. Rucker pushed past Clark to stand at the property line. "What a bad little doggie you are."

Laylea sat at her feet on the Rick's side of the line. The old lady bent and waggled a finger in her face. Her other hand dropped a piece of cheese in the grass.

"Oh dear. Oops. Just can't get these old hands to grip no more." She turned and hung on to Clark's arm. "Help me back up to my door, Clark. Spring is supposed to be warmer than this. It certainly was down home."

Clark escorted the OLR up her three steps to the front door. "Letitia, I hate to deprive you, but I'm going on a hike today. Would it be okay if I invited Davis and Parker along?"

"Take em." She waved a hand over her shoulder. "Get em out of my hair."

"Can we go, Mr. Clark?" Davis scooped Laylea up into his arms without asking permission. "Can we go with you?"

"Of course. You have good walking shoes?"

Both boys automatically looked at the ground.

Davis smelled concerned. "These are the only ones I brought besides my church shoes."

"Then those'll do fine." Clark slid the collar over Laylea's head. "We're gonna finish our walk and get breakfast. Can you be ready to go in a half an hour?"

"Sure, sir. But we have to be back in time to clean out the shed before dark." Davis gestured with the football in one hand. He dropped it.

"We'll get you back. Bring water, okay?" Clark took Laylea from Davis and set her on the ground. "And hats."

He led her past the Rick's house to do a circle of their street. The new renters at the end of the cul-de-sac were on their enclosed porch, drinking coffee and ignoring each other through newspapers. The wife waved at Clark. The husband ruffled his paper and muttered something unintelligible.

Clark waved and then bent to pick up what Laylea laid down.

"Just dump it right there in our trash," the woman called out. "It's no problem."

"Marjory." The man scolded her from behind his paper.

She didn't even glance his way. "Really. No problem at all."

Clark and Laylea moved along after he secured the lid of their bin. People could be very sensitive about poop. Bailey had a book all about how everybody poops. But he still made faces sometimes when he picked up after the dogs.

Laylea veered over to walk on the curb by the ghost house. An unhappy German Shepard lived behind the fence and Laylea wanted to be far away when the wood splintered against his weight. She wasn't allowed to walk in the street so the curb was as far away as she could get without breaking any rules. Her trick left hip gave way though and she fell into the gutter.

Quick as she was, jumping back onto the curb, Clark noticed. "Hey, are you up for a hike? Is your hip giving you trouble?"

Her hip had troubles on cold mornings and if she were tired. But most of the time it didn't bother her. Whenever it did, Bailey would notice. He'd haul out his old children's books and read to her. He lay beside her and put the book down on the bed so she could see the pictures like when they did homework together. Sometimes she pretended her hip hurt just so that Bailey would stop running around and read with her.

But there was no way she was going to let that stupid old injury slow her down. She bounded away into their own yard and rolled over in the grass before pulling Clark up the porch stairs.

"Okay. Okay. I get it. You're fine." He hopped up the stairs after her, sitting on the top step to let her climb into his lap. "Come here. I'm so glad you stayed with us, Laylea." He kissed her head and unclipped the leash. "There, if I leave your collar on, will you believe you're coming with? Because this hike is for you, Adoptionversary girl."

Laylea barked. The bells jangled.

"Dad!" Bailey banged out onto the porch.

Clark herded him back in the house. "Inside with your big news, Bails. Old Lady Rucker doesn't want to hear it."

"Dad, she always wants to hear."

Sher rushed over and kissed Clark on the cheek as she grabbed her riding jacket. "So sorry about this. We'll think of something special for dinner." She tossed Bailey his riding jacket and scooted up the stairs. "Meet you in the garage."

Clark and Laylea watched her.

"Bailey?"

Bailey zipped his jacket and pulled gloves, a bandanna, sunglasses, and ear warmers from the pockets. He explained as he wrapped himself up against the cold, "Thomas Bevery from school rescued a great dane named Mitzi. She was malnourished and pregnant and she just went into labor and his mom is really worried and so she called Chris from the clinic cuz he's a friend of theirs and Chris called mom and she invited me to go help."

Sher hustled back down the stairs, the medical pouch from her go bag in hand. Clark took it from her so she could pull gloves and all from her pockets and dress against the weather. They went through the kitchen to the garage.

"The batter's all made if you still want to have shmancakes." Sher grabbed her messenger bag from its hook as Bailey dragged open the door.

"No." Clark helped her fit the medical kit in the bag. "We'll have them for dinner. The celebration wouldn't be the same without all of us. You go help Mitzi."

"Mitzi?" Sher stopped.

"Dad, they renamed her."

"Okay, well then you guys go help?"

"Chewbacca."

"Right." Clark kissed both of them. Bailey kissed Laylea. "You're friends with Thomas?"

Bailey threw a leg over his bike. "Not yet."

The pair took off and Clark shut the garage door.

"How do you feel about a scrambled egg, jerky, and kibble casserole for breakfast?"

Laylea sang.

CHAPTER 18

SPRING 2028 - FOOTHILLS, OR

Clark and Bailey often went on long hikes into the mountains. If they were jogging, they left the dogs behind on Sher's orders. She worried that the walking hikes were even too strenuous for Laylea and Woodford's short legs. Laylea tried not to let it show when her paws got sore.

Davis noticed. Although Laylea wondered if maybe Davis called her out because he wanted to turn back, she couldn't be sure. In any case, they did turn back after only a few hours. And Clark was carrying her when he tripped over a protruding root and nearly face-planted on top of her in the dirt.

Clark worried over Laylea while the grandsons and Woodford worried over Clark.

"Mr. Clark, your shinbone is sticking out of your leg." Davis smelled like Laylea felt on bumpy flights.

Parker hit him. "Shut up. You can't tell a guy that."

"It's bleeding really bad, Parker." Davis managed to keep his breakfast down but it was a near thing.

Woodford howled.

Laylea contorted herself in Clark's arms to lick the dad's nose. She was shaken up but that was all. He needed to take care of himself.

"You're sure?" he asked her.

She barked as fiercely as she ever had and wriggled out of his grasp. The leg was bleeding all over the pretty rocks that had spilled from Davis' bag. They'd all had their eyes peeled to collect for Bailey since he couldn't come. Laylea ran around the boys and sat her butt beside Woodford. Finally, Clark focused on himself.

"Whoa." Clark reached out and held onto Parker's shoulder when he got a look at the broken shin. "That's not good." He breathed deeply and Laylea could just hear the rhythm of the song in his exhale.

Parker laughed and stopped himself, blushing. "Sorry."

"No. Laughter is good. Could you boys look around and see if you can find a solid stick or something we could use as a splint?"

"Sure thing, Mr. Clark." Davis turned away from the leg with super-human speed.

"Shouldn't we tie off the artery first, sir?"

"Yes. Thank you." Clark held himself up with one hand while the other untied the paisley bandanna from around his neck. "Aren't you a teenager, Parker? Why are you so polite?"

The lanky kid took the ratty old bandanna when Clark started trying to tie it one-handed around his own thigh. "Down here, Mr. Clark, just above the knee is better."

He pulled the tourniquet tight but didn't complete the knot. "If Grandma asks, I'm polite because she taught me so, sir." He placed a stick against the kerchief and completed the knot around it. "But really, I'm polite because," he turned the stick, pulling the bandanna tighter until the blood flow slowed. "I'm polite because my moms wasn't." Parker tucked the stick under the edge of the bandanna and stood. "Sir."

As soon as Parker turned his back, Clark lifted the leg. His gasp of pain was covered by Woodford's impressive howl. He grasped his knee in one hand and the ankle in the other. Laylea could barely hear him chanting.

"I will not kill another soul today. I will not kill another soul today."

He pulled. Laylea smelled pain rolling off him in the sweat pouring down his face and staining his armpits and groin. The hand on his knee slid down and pushed the protruding bone back into place. When he released the ankle, several wrinkles smoothed from his face. Clark lay back into the dirt and rocks and leaves and breathed. Woodford stopped howling. He stepped forward into the puddle of blood and sniffed up and down the gash. When he found what he was looking for, he pointed his nose at the break and planted himself in place.

Laylea whimpered. She stood on Clark's shoulder to lick his salty face.

Clark didn't open his eyes. "Yeah. It's better."

Laylea cleaned his entire face. She turned her back on the scary, coppery leg and licked every inch of skin she could reach. By the time the boys returned with the perfect splints and a thin log to use as a crutch, Laylea had climbed to Clark's chest and was watching his twitching eyes.

At Clark's direction, the boys cut up the dogs' leashes to tie the splints against his leg. They had to physically shove Woodford out of the way to do it with Clark crooning to him the whole time just to keep him from snapping at the well-meaning boys. Laylea chewed on Clark's orange rope bracelet while the boys destroyed her leash.

The walk home was easy compared to getting Clark on his feet. Once they let Clark use the makeshift crutch on the side of the bad leg and supported him under his opposite arm, they were able to ignore Woodford keeping pace more with the wound than with the group. Laylea trotted in front of the parade while Parker and Davis explained football to Clark.

Davis thought he was putting them on, that he was pretending not to understand to keep them from worrying about him. But Parker told him that Mr. Clark wasn't that kind of an adult.

"It's you teach me football or I teach you the math that makes me so good with my slingshot."

As they struggled over the uneven forest floor, Davis eventually got into the subject. They had begun explaining how specific football games had changed the rules over the years by the time they reached the rental's back yard.

It was hard to tell where the forest ended and the yard began. A chair missing much of its caning sat in the middle of the weeds. The heavyset woman named Marjory rocked in another chair. Wavy brown hair hung loose to her waist, held away from her face by a hot pink headband. She had her head down, focused on the bar of soap she was carving with a dull pocket knife. Both fell to the ground when she spotted the trio hobbling out of the trees.

When her screams had finished echoing through the forest, the woman scrambled to her feet. "Oh, dear god. Come here and sit. Have you called an ambulance?"

"Thank you, Ma'am." Clark grinned at Parker on the *ma'am*. "I'm fine. I'm just gonna get home." Clark felt the boys' reactions to this and added, "and drive to the hospital."

The renter trotted alongside them as they made their way step by step across her yard. Laylea had to dance lively to stay out from under her feet. Woodford ignored her as he did everyone else. "Did a bear get you? Or a lion?"

"We don't have lions in these mountains. Ma'am," Davis pointed out.

"Mountain lions." Parker corrected his brother. He took Clark's weight as they turned to go single file through the short stone walls that led out to the street.

Davis rolled his eyes at his brother. "Those are cougars."

"No, my sister-in-law is a cougar." Marjory snorted.

Clark smiled, "I just fell. I've done worse to myself."

"Oh, I used to see all kinds of strange injuries at my job. Strange animals too." Marjory finally noticed Laylea running alongside them all. "Well, you look just like a dog we used to see running around the grounds." She bent to look more closely. "Smaller, but Rhea had that same color fur and those floppy ears. Why your leg doesn't have any blood on it at all. Your pants are a mess but your leg is—"

Clark swung the ripped ends of the pant leg aside to show her the gash. She stopped talking for a good minute.

"We washed the wound."

Parker glanced at Clark's water bottle. The boys hadn't brought enough and he'd given them the last of his shortly before his fall. Laylea jumped out onto the curb when they reached the ghost house. The fence shuddered from the shepherd's paws before the dog even started barking. Marjory the renter didn't even flinch.

"Yes, yes. I would offer you a ride to the hospital but my husband has the car. He's fishing. I can't bear it. I will never hurt another animal as long as I live."

"Thank you so much for offering, Marjory."

Her head jerked so hard Laylea thought she could hear the vertebrae crack. "How do you know my name?"

Davis tripped on the curb. Clark reached a hand out and caught him by his shirtfront before he fell. He never took his eyes from Marjory's suddenly cold face. Before he could judge the reason for her fear, Parker spoke up.

"Your husband yells your name, Ma'am. Everyone in the neighborhood knows you're Marjory. But we can keep it our secret, if you want."

The chubby cheeks reddened and puffed up as the smile popped back onto her face. "Oh, my goodness. You mean you can hear it when we're—"

"When we walk by, Marjory," Clark interrupted. "He gets your attention by yelling your name when you're talking to us."

"Oh, of course he does. I never listen. I just haven't been the same since they closed the office and I lost my job." Marjory seemed to forget they were there. She stopped walking after a few words but kept talking, heedless of the vicious barking on the far side of the fence. "I was a supervisor too, in the Therian Division. Making very good money. But the things I heard and worse, the sounds I saw, I am glad they shut the whole project down. Paid me enough to send the kids off to school and we go to a different little town every summer."

Clark and the kids kept moving towards the house. Laylea watched Marjory, more concerned about the woman than about her arch enemy the shepherd. Eventually Marjory turned and, still talking, returned to her own back yard. "All this moving about though. I just don't. . ."

When Marjory was out of sight, Laylea caught up to the boys.

Parker had an arm around the dad but he wasn't really helping him very much. "Mr. Clark, sir, you're walking pretty good for a guy with a broken leg."

Clark leaned on him a little more. "I can take a lot of pain."

"Sure." Parker helped him limp along a few more steps. "But won't it heal better if you give the leg a rest? I mean, sure we're just kids, but we can help you."

Davis threw a rock into the street. "We can't help Marjory."

"Yeah, she's scary," Parker agreed.

Clark stopped. "Guys, I was just trying to give you a rest for a little while."

"Sure you weren't trying to get away from Marjory?" Davis asked.

Clark pursed his lips and raised an eyebrow at the kid. Davis giggled.

"What do we need a rest for?" Parker asked. "We're here."

Laylea hopped up the six steps to the porch.

"Now we need to get me up those steps and onto a couch."

"Oh."

"No problem, Mr. C," Davis squeaked. "Grandma's coming over to help."

With Old Lady Rucker's invaluable supervising, the boys got Clark into the house. While the OLR settled him on the couch with pillows and the phone nearby, Laylea and Woodford led the boys to the kitchen. They rinsed the blood off the dogs' feet and their butts where they'd sat in the puddle. Woodford emptied the water bowl as they cleaned him. They refilled it and Clark's canteen and fetched several ice packs from the freezer.

"You call me if you need anything at all and I'll send the boys back over. Should we lock the door or leave it open?"

"Lock it. Thank you, Letitia. Thank you, Parker and Davis." Now that he was safe at home, Clark let a little pain show on his face. "Sher will take care of everything when she gets home."

Laylea walked the family to the front door. Woodford stayed glued to Clark's side.

Parker was uncertain about leaving. "Grandma, his bone was sticking out."

"Now it's . . ." Davis stopped at a look from his grandmother. "Shouldn't we make sure he gets to the hospital?"

"You are very thoughtful. But in this neighborhood, we mind our business. If the man wants our help, he knows perfectly well how to ask. Now git. I've a big pot of soup needs eating."

Old Lady Rucker shooed the boys out of the house. She made Parker check the lock and the bells rang as they jiggled the handle again from the outside. When Laylea got back to the family room, Clark had passed out cold.

CHAPTER 19

SPRING 2028 - FOOTHILLS, OR

Clark slept for the rest of the afternoon. Sher and Bailey came home from a successful day birthing eight Great Dane and possibly Irish Setter mixes. Bailey cuddled Laylea and Woodford and reviewed absolutely everything he had learned. He described for his dad, in excruciating detail how they had to gain Chewbacca's confidence and help her get the pups out.

When he started explaining a board game Thomas taught him, Sher hustled him into the kitchen to help her finally make their special pancakes for Laylea's adoptionversary. Laylea and Woodford stayed in the family room with Clark. The dad dropped back into a doze the instant the kitchen doors swung shut behind his son. In all the excitement, nobody ever moved the afghan off of Clark's legs. Nobody noticed he was still wearing his hiking clothes. Nobody told his doctor wife that his shin bone had been sticking out of his body earlier that day.

The family ate dinner in the family room. Both Woodford and Laylea got shmancakes with their kibble. To celebrate her adoptionversary, Laylea got a giant peanut butter flavored rawhide from Bailey and a new harness with her very own flashwipe like the ones on Clark's plane from Sher. Especially for trips outside of the neighborhood, she explained. But the best gift came from Clark.

He sent Bailey off to his radio room to get the small package, wrapped in Sunday comics. Laylea ripped into the paper, trying to tuck her nose under a flap for leverage. She ended up with tape on her muzzle and a paw wrapped in Calvin and Hobbes. In front of her lay two braided leather collars dyed deep blue.

"She's outgrown baby blue and Woodford's collar is tatters," Clark explained to Sher. "So, I had Maggie make these."

Sher slid off her end of the couch to the floor. While she picked up the collars, Woodford crawled out of his bed and wandered over to nuzzle her for some attention. "They found Maggie? You didn't tell me."

"Well, Maggie found Jay. She's still hiding from Trey."

"I wish we knew which one of them needs help."

"Sheriff, they both need help. We all need help. Everyone needs help."

"I need some help." Bailey said.

"We're here to help you." Clark replied.

"How does this clasp work?"

Clark helped Bailey work the clasp as Sher unbuckled Woodford's old collar while acceding to his demands for ear scratches.

Laylea watched them. Her body shook. Every muscle in her vibrated with joy while her tail drummed a paradiddle between the coffee table and couch leg. She whimpered just a little when Bailey replaced her store-bought nylon necklace with Maggie's handmade one. Woodford's new collar laid smoothly in his thick neck fur. And like Davis Rucker, Laylea was now dressed just like her big brother. She couldn't contain the thrill in her heart any longer. It burst from her in her pitiful singing howl. She danced around the room, bouncing off the couches and comfy chair.

Sher laughed. Bailey rolled around with Laylea jumping his limbs. She tagged Woodford over and over with her nose and finally grabbed a mouthful of neck and worried it until her brother swatted at her with a paw. He chased her around the couch until she got a little scared and leaped into the mom's lap.

"I think she likes it." Sher adjusted the collar so it laid smoothly on Laylea's short fur. "I wonder if she could make a collar for our human son."

"I'll ask," Clark offered. "Come here, Bails, let me measure your neck."

Bailey screamed and ran to wrestle with Woodford and Laylea in Sher's lap.

Sher sent Bailey for a blanket from the second couch and the four of them cuddled on the floor, leaning on Clark's couch. Woodford snored while the rest of the family watched an episode of *Firefly*. Laylea could have stayed like that forever.

But the next day was a Monday and after the girls on the TV rescued the boys from Siska, Sher hustled Bailey upstairs to get ready for bed.

Clark stayed on the couch to read for a little while. According to his self-imposed rules, Woodford was required to stay up with Clark. Laylea stayed because she'd just made herself comfortable with Sher's pre-warmed blanket. They both fell into a doze.

When he finally closed the book and got up, Clark winced a little. Laylea woke at the intake of breath. Woodford got up from his bed and followed Clark into the kitchen. Woodford sniffed up and down the leg, turning his head from side to side.

"Whoa, sorry boy." Clark almost stepped on Woodford as he took off the tattered remains of his pants and leaned into the garage to toss the bloody things in the trash bin.

All the hair stood up on his legs as he completed the nighttime routine in nothing but a smelly, sweat-crusted high-performance shirt and his boxers.

Woodford followed at the dad's heels as he checked all the doors and windows, ringing each bell in its turn. Laylea stayed with the pair as they went through the house. Ignoring the great gash in his leg, Woodford found a spot on Clark's right foot, just below the ankle and tried to tag it with his nose. Whenever Clark stood still, Woodford put his nose on the spot.

Clark dug a pair of pajama pants out of the laundry basket in the hall and put them on before checking the windows in Bailey's room.

Normally Laylea would have left the parade here and hopped up into bed, but Woodford smelled upset and she stayed with him.

The older dog howled once when Clark got into bed. He patrolled back and forth brushing the dust ruffle on Clark's side. Laylea tried to play with him, to distract him. But Woodford pushed her away with his haunches.

So Laylea went into the hall bathroom where Bailey was getting ready for bed. She tagged his leg with her cold nose. He bent over to pick her up while he brushed his teeth. After he rinsed, he carried her into his room and set her on the bed. But she hopped down the chair, the stool, and the box to the floor. She stood at the door, looking back at him. When Bailey noticed, she took a step out into the hall. She led him to Sher and Clark's room and put her nose against the closed door. She had to tag it a few times before he knocked.

Clark called out. "Come on in."

The door opened and Laylea bounded in. She pranced to the far side of the bed where Woodford still paced. Laylea stretched up as far as she could reach on the mattress. Clark reached a hand down and she climbed on it to be craned up onto the bed.

"Hello, little girl. You and Bailiff come to say goodnight?"

Laylea got out of his hand and walked down to sit on his foot.

"Ow."

She looked pointedly at Bailey.

"What's up?" Sher came out of their bathroom. She had toothpaste on the corner of her mouth.

"Mom, Laylea wants you to look at Dad's foot."

"Clark?" Sher turned immediately to her big baby.

"It's fine," he protested. "I was a little stiff after sitting on the couch so long. But I'm fine."

Sher walked to the far side of the bed. She picked Woodford up and set him on the bed. Then she untucked the top sheet and lifted it off of Clark's legs. Woodford tagged the spot on Clark's foot. Clark winced at the touch.

"Bailey, would you get me a bag of corn from the freezer?" She set Woodford down so that he could follow the boy. "You think I didn't notice all of our ice packs hidden under the couch? You owe it to us to take care of yourself. I shouldn't have to hear from a dog that you're not healing." She was silent for a moment as she examined the foot. She was not gentle. "It's not just a bruise. You have a broken foot. You have broken your foot. How have you been walking around on this?"

Before Clark could prevaricate, Laylea tagged his shin and looked to Sher. She repeated the motion until the dad pulled up the leg of his PJs.

"I didn't notice the foot because I was distracted by this."

"Clark Hillen!"

Laylea curled up on Clark's chest while Sher went on. She talked a lot when she was angry. Clark knew better than to interrupt or argue with her. Sher put pillows under the leg and pressed in places that caused Clark to sharply draw in his breath. It made funny noises. Laylea licked at his muzzle when he made the sound again and he giggled. She licked his nose and looked contritely at him, lowering her head.

"It's okay, Laylea," he whispered to her. "You did the right thing. But I hope you're up for a Python marathon because I think I'm being put on bed rest."

"Clark." Sher stopped working and sat beside him. "What happens if they find us and you can't walk?"

"It's been over ten years since you left. Nearly that long since you rescued me." He put a hand on her face. "Jay saw the obituary. You're as dead to them as to—" He broke off.

"As to my family." Her face drained of feeling. Her standard way of dealing. She avoided sad and instead went cold.

Laylea sat up on Clark's chest. She tried to lick the mom's muzzle. Sher turned her face away. Laylea shrank back to sitting and then slunk off Clark's chest, her tail tucked, ears flattened to her head.

"No, Doc." Clark took Sher's chin in his hand. He didn't turn her head though. "You promised me you'd never go away."

"I'm right here."

"No, you're not. That's a turn away you're giving us. Look at Laylea." He let Sher take her time to look at the little dog curled into a tight shivering ball. "That's how I feel too."

Woodford tore into the room ahead of Bailey who slowed enough to be careful of his dad's foot. "The ice packs are all gone. I got—" He saw his mother's posture and pulled up short. "Uh oh."

Clark took Sher's hand and kissed it, then put it on Laylea's back. He turned to Bailey. "It's an emergency, kid. Forget about the peas. Mom needs hugs. STAT."

Being careful not to crush Laylea, the boys tackled their woman and hugged the coldness out of her.

Distracted by the healing and the hugging, Clark's spotty long-term memory forgot about the strange renter who noticed his bloody pants and clean leg. He forgot she knew a dog that looked like Laylea. Had he remembered, he probably wouldn't have reported to Sher that the woman had worked at the Therian Division because he had no idea it was an arm of the Consortium. And with limited access to his mental dictionary, he couldn't know the Therian Division worked with shapeshifters.

Chapter 20

Fall 2028 - Consortium Biotech HQ, CA

"Subject 397a just checked in at the perimeter gate. He's on his way to containment now." Walter stood from the desk as Trask came into the office. He jogged over to catch her before she turned around again and left for the containment outbuilding. "Wait."

"Why?"

"You don't want to let him know how important he is."

"He's not that important."

"First to return in two years. First with my teams' enhancements."

Trask let the door shut and pulled the privacy curtain as she brushed past Walter into the room. She crossed to a new teak cabinet set in the middle of the wall of file drawers. The carpenter who designed the expanded cabinet would have been impressed with how thoroughly the two had utilized his designs if he hadn't been recruited before being paid.

Trask unfolded the doors hiding the display board. More than just a training ground map now, the panels held a white board to the right covered in subject numbers and statistics and to the left, corkboards covered with yellow legal pad pages, pictures, printouts, maps, and a physical schematic of the final testing field for Trask's Conditioned

Forces. The map had been expanded from its original size to include printed out maps of the surrounding villages and towns.

Walter and Trask believed that by keeping these details in physical form, they were subverting the expected Consortium surveillance of their computers.

Trask glanced at the map then moved to the waterfall of printouts and notes on subject 397a. She tapped her pen against the board as she flipped through the papers. "He should have returned months ago. Where has the child been?"

"What does his tracking implant tell you?" Walter stood right behind Trask, reading over her shoulder. She was used to this.

"We didn't implant a tracking device. We conditioned a strong desire for Snickers candy bars," she paused while he snorted, "thinking we could follow a purchasing pattern since you've started the surveillance system on the surrounding towns. But we haven't picked up any unusual patterns."

"It's a good idea but perhaps you want to implant a fetish for something less popular, like those chalky wafers you Americans give kids at Halloween. Looks like he's the youngest subject you've ever conditioned." Walter reached over her shoulder and lifted a medical workup to see the notes underneath. "Trained him for longer too."

"Which is why we let you experiment on him. Perhaps his heightened animal instincts interfered with his basal ganglia on a scent level and negated his Snickers desires."

"I don't think there is any feralization that would interfere with food hoarding. Maybe you try a type of jerky next time." He left her to make a note on his blotter. "All those little towns in and around your mountains are going to be stocked on jerky but I'll search for a less popular variety you can try."

The wall phone buzzed.

Walter continued, thinking out loud as Trask stepped over to answer it. "I'll have Sarah design a program for tracking all movement of that particular brand throughout the states. Even if you don't use it, it would still be a practical application for creation of a micro-trace system. Yes, specific is better."

Trask had stopped listening. She twitched aside the privacy curtain and punched the button to put the call on speaker. "Start over, 397. Tell Walter why you're three months late."

The sound from the speaker rang with echoes. The containment outbuilding was large, designed to hold all evacuees from the three laboratory buildings in an emergency. Now it likely held only CF subject 397a and a couple of extremely low-ranking doctors. The subject's already thin voice was swallowed up by the empty space around him. "Good morning, Walter sir. Trask ma'am, I made it out of the mountains with such little trouble I was concerned that I was being tracked. I wasn't sure though. I didn't see anyone following me. I know how to lose a tail if I know I have one."

Walter stood suddenly from where he'd been sitting on the corner of the desk. "What's that?"

"I said I know how to lose a tail, sir."

"But not how to grow one back," Walter muttered.

"Excuse me, sir?"

"Autogenetic regeneration." Walter was not listening to the speakerphone anymore. He appeared to be looking over the desk but his eyes were focused much further away.

Trask rubbed her itching scars. "Go on, soldier."

"Yes ma'am." The CF sounded thrown. Trask, it seemed, had finally become accustomed to Walter's moments of abrupt introversion.

"I wasn't sure I was being followed but I didn't wish to risk returning home until I knew I was clean. I initiated a standard randomization of my travel, but it occurred to me that I could appear random while still pursuing information for one of Walter's goals. So, I travelled to each of the veterinarians in the foothills of the training field, both those with offices and private practices. There are three who remember patients matching the descriptions of Walter's missing subjects around the time that they were lost."

Walter came back to the present. He was on his feet and crossing to the map as he asked for details. Trask took a seat. She wouldn't get her answers until after the post hypnotic debrief. The CF wasn't aware of the information he had been gathering for her search. In the meantime, she typed up a record of her thoughts on the retrieval.

Subject 397a return ETA+99

It is a concern that this kid is showing initiative in pursuing Walter's goals. He was extensively trained to follow orders and not think for himself beyond immediate goal achievement. This is a serious breach of the conditioning. This sort of failure never happened when Dr. Coogan was in charge. Why did she never experience such reversals? How can we achieve her level of success when we are still chasing her shadow? Her work in this field was exemplary and ground breaking and we must seek to improve upon it rather than simply trying to imitate.

A separate team must be created to focus purely on interpreting her diary and those few personal notes we were able to recover after the fire. We need to recruit new researchers from the top schools. Note: Perhaps we haven't combed the depths of disenfranchised researchers. Coogan's notes remain so far above the abilities of myself and my current team as to be useless. We must continue improving our other methods even as we devote resources to finding a scientist who can understand Coogan's methodology.

Consider scrapping the three hundred series

The 300 line represents a radical shift from my original goals. I have conceded that it is not an ideal method of erasure. Yet another setback caused by Gamma Subject's bombs. But 397a has returned. He is the first subject with no tracking device and one of the few successful live retrievals. The only conclusion is that Gamma Subject is in possession of the ability to track our implants.

"Trask, ma'am."

The researcher saved her notes and closed the screen. "Yes?"

"The doctors want me to sleep for a while. Is there anything else you need from me first?"

Trask crossed to the wall phone. She straightened her bangs in the mirror and wiped at the lines of stress around her eyes. Once the doctors recommended it, sleep should have been his only desire. This independent thinking was a problem.

"No. Do as you are ordered, 397." She disconnected the line. She would be contacted when debriefing was complete.

Trask closed the privacy curtain and returned to her desk chair. She fingered the scars on her neck as she thought. Her history made clear how vehemently she despised micromanagement. But still she stood and gathered some items into her briefcase.

"I'll be in containment. I need to oversee 397a's debrief myself."

"Why don't you give them names?"

"Excuse me?"

Walter had left the map. He crouched at his side of the desk gathering items into his own knapsack. "Why call them by numbers? Names would be ever so much easier."

"Names would make it easier for them to start thinking they're individuals."

Walter turned to the coat tree in the corner, hiding the journal they used to write notes to each other following the required monthly bug sweep by the Consortium. Until they completed their own private sweep, they would only allow small talk in the office which, with these two, meant no talk. The head of the Therian Division swung his coat off the tree and onto his arms in a dramatic swoop.

"Makes sense. But I think you're going to need two-way communication with your CF if you want to be a queen bee. Redesign the implant with that in mind." She watched him pull his dopp kit from the bottom drawer of a file cabinet. "Can I borrow a conditioner?"

For a moment, she thought he meant for his hair.

"Someone low level should be fine. Someone you can spare for a few weeks or so."

Trask leaned forward and typed a message to her head of personnel. Human Resources had a different meaning in her and Walter's divisions. "Go speak with Perino. I'm sure he can find someone qualified who doesn't disdain your operational objectives."

"Thanks." Walter flipped through some papers on the corkboard.

"Any other ideas you recommend I pursue in your absence?"

"Compensatory epigenesis as a tracking program methodology." He took down three pages of dog sketches. He slid them into a hard cover folder and then into his backpack. "We should have software that could switch from monitoring say the sale of Snickers to trail mix at its own discretion without alteration of the primary program design."

"You want to encourage independent thinking in our computers."

"In a way." He stopped at the door. "Honestly you're reprogramming humans to be more like computers. Why not try the reverse?"

Trask swept her briefcase off the desk and joined him at the door.

"Please keep an eye out for Gamma Subject in your travels. And if you find a doctor who happens to be a genius in conditioning, send him my way."

"I'm going to be visiting veterinarians."

Trask raised her eyebrows in a rare expression of feeling. "How do you think we train animals except through conditioning? You have heard of Pavlov, right?"

"Look at you thinking outside the box. I'm so proud. If I find any genius Russian vets, they're yours."

Walter slipped a piece of black jack in his mouth. Trask straightened her skirt. And the two left the room.

THE DIRECTOR HIT pause on the playback. He picked up his stylus and requested his assistant find a biologist who could explain the last three minutes of the conversation to reassure himself that the two hadn't developed some secret code. He reached under his glasses to rub his dry eyes. The doctor had ordered him to get out in the field more. Instead he washed down a couple of vitamin D capsules and stretched his neck. He swiped to a video marked as priority level four that had been cut together from several Washington offices. Not desperately important, but Washington was always good for a smile.

CHAPTER 21

WINTER 2029 - FOOTHILLS, OR

Laylea was almost four before she got to spend a day at the clinic with Sher again. Clark picked up extra work flying to small airports and airstrips judging their safety for a private firm. He was going to be gone long hours, sometimes not coming home every night and with Bailey at school, Sher didn't feel comfortable torturing Woodford with the younger pup all day every day. So, the mom planned to alternate taking Laylea and Woodford to work with her.

On the morning of her first day at work, Laylea woke up before Bailey's alarm. She stuck her nose in Bailey's ear and snored a few times before she did up dog with her paws on his chest. She hopped on him and did down dog with her back paws on his hip. Once certain he was awake, she barreled down her steps and out the door.

Spring thaw had come early and the parents had been sleeping with their door cracked to get a cross breeze so Laylea was able to get in and stretch on Clark's side of the bed. She stood there staring at the dad until he reached down and craned her up. She clambered between them and licked Clark's face until his eyes opened. Then she leaped off the bed by way of his bladder. When he got out of the bathroom, she herded him, Bailey, and Woodford outside for a good long walk in an early spring drizzle.

Back home, Sher had oatmeal and kibble ready for everyone. After breakfast, Bailey gathered his schoolbooks and homework, Clark tucked his lunch into his hiking backpack and Sher slipped teddy lizard into the back pocket of her cycling jacket. But then they all three stood around the garage door talking about where each of them was going to get dinner and who was going to get home first to feed Woodford or some such inanities until Laylea sang a growl at them and grabbed her leash from its hook.

"Oh," Clark teased, "are you ready to go?"

The little girl barked and spun around. She leaped onto the dog food container, from there to one of the stools and then up onto the counter where she grabbed the rubber Kong toy stuffed with tasty treats. Before any of the humans could grab her, she bounded down to the floor in the same way and ran to Woodford's bed in the family room. She dropped the Kong and covered it with a blanket. Then she ran back to the garage door, picked up the hook end of her leash, and firmly put her butt on the ground staring at the knob.

Clark swung his pack onto his back. "I'd feel a little insulted if I were you, Woodford."

Bailey tried to give Woodford some love. But the hound was already hunting down his Kong. Sher finally scooped Laylea up and they all went out to the garage. Laylea settled in her basket on the front of Sher's bicycle. Woodford barked when the garage door opened and all the humans yelled goodbye to him in their own ways.

Laylea tried to be a good girl and sit crouched low in the basket. But the speed was too enticing. She rested her chin on the edge of the basket and licked at the wind, reveling in racing through the countryside with her pack. The overnight rain had soaked into the earth and released a treasure of rich odors. Scents melted together as they sped away from the OLR's roses, through the old neighborhoods, and down the hill to Bailey's school.

Laylea dreamed of going to school with Bailey. Woodford had gone to Show and Tell but he only got to stay for an hour. Laylea wanted to go and sniff every book in the library. She would sit quietly at Bailey's feet and not help on tests.

She stood when Sher rolled to a stop by the paved playground.

Bailey rode on through a thin patch of wet grass and hopped the curb. He tucked his front wheel against the side of a rack filled with kid's bikes. Most were half-heartedly connected to the rack with U-locks Bailey could open with a pen. He wrapped his back wheel, frame, and front wheel with his Abus cable before securing the end around the thickest pipe of the rack. He used to slip the cable through his helmet straps and leave that outside. But someone had sliced the strap once just to be mean.

"Look, it's the genius." A much bigger kid wearing a camouflage rain poncho stuck his muzzle right in Bailey's face. His friends surrounded Bailey from behind.

Laylea barked.

"Michael Asher," Bailey stepped around his bicycle and put a shaking hand on the bigger kid's arm. His childish tenor didn't drop as deep as Laylea knew he'd like it to, but he soldiered on. "Inside. I'll talk to you inside."

"Inside." Michael scoffed. He splashed through a puddle on his way toward the school building. He muttered over his shoulder at his crew when they didn't keep up. "I'll see him inside alright."

Bailey ignored the chatter. He jogged over to Sher's bike and gave Laylea a kiss on the head. Laylea wiggled.

"Bailey."

He didn't look up. "Yeah, Mom?"

"Did you condition your friends?"

Clark laughed quietly but he didn't interrupt.

"I conditioned Michael and *his* friends." The kid stuck his chin out and looked his mother straight in the eyes. But Laylea felt his hand still shaking as he pet her.

"You can't do that."

"Yeah, I can."

"Bailiff Hillen." Clark dropped his voice to a ridiculously low and quiet tone. "No. No training your friends." In a normal voice, he added, "Or your enemies."

"He's not my enemy. He's a thirteen-year-old in sixth grade with absentee parents and a bleep bleep uncle."

"Don't you—"

"I *didn't* swear, Mom. Gotta go." He kissed Laylea again and ran across the emptying playground to catch up with a heavyset kid dressed in black from head to toe. Thomas had entered his goth phase early.

Sher sighed.

Clark whispered, "I love you, kid." He rolled up next to his partner and kissed her. "We made him."

"That doesn't scare you?"

"It's a rough world and I think he's gonna be prepared for it."

Most parents dropped their kids off at the turnaround in front of the school so the two were the only adults in sight. The kids who rode their bikes to school were used to seeing Bailey's folks. Some of them even waved hi.

Still, Sher lowered her voice. "He's got your skills. And mine."

"Skills." Clark chuckled at her choice of words.

"What happens to him if the Consortium finds out we had a child?"

"The Consortium thinks you're dead. And how could I pass along my skills?" He watched a girl struggle with her too-large cruiser. She took off her equally large backpack to better fit between the crowded bikes. "Unless you altered my genetics?"

"Of course I did." Sher didn't notice Clark grip his handlebar a little more tightly. "You haven't noticed he heals as quickly as you? He can remember everything in a room at a glance."

The school bell rang as the girl squeezed her cruiser into the rack between two dirt bikes. Without locking it up, she ran for the school. Halfway to the doors, she remembered the backpack she'd left on the ground.

"Bailey can remember everything in a forest at a glance," Clark said. "That's more than I can do."

"Biology is designed to improve us with each generation."

"Subtly, I thought."

The good science teacher leaned out the back doors, encouraging the little girl. She raced for the doors, her pigtails flying as she clutched the dripping backpack to her chest.

"How strong is he going to be?"

"How can we know? He's still growing." Clark waited until the door fell shut. "How strong is his magic compared to yours?"

Sher hissed, whipping her head around.

Clark took her hand. "There's no one in earshot, my sweet witch. How strong is he?"

Sher whispered, "Not as strong as me. Not as strong as my father. But puberty will change everything. He could lose it all or grow more powerful than Great Gram Coogan."

"I imagine we'll start getting a measure of his physical strength then as well."

The final bell rang and a dozen students in matching sweatpants and jackets blasted through the gym doors onto the soccer field.

"Sit." Laylea did as Sher ordered and they rolled away from the school. "I worry because he's so different from these other kids."

"They're all different, Sher," Clark laughed, pedaling beside her. "Everybody is weird. Michael Asher there deals with it by bullying anyone he's afraid won't like him. Bailey deals with it by befriending the absolute weirdest kids in class."

"I could make it easier."

"You are. We are. We're keeping him safe. Don't worry. He'll find his way, just like you did."

"I found my way into a lab where I messed with your genetics and your mind. And Jay's. And Trey and Maggie, and—"

Clark had to stand to chase her down. "Sher. Stop. If you want to go after the Consortium, I am ready. Just say the word."

"No. We can't risk Bailey." She turned onto the main boulevard into town.

"Then you need a little of my disease. You need to forget."

Sher looked askance at her husband. "I can't forget."

"Can you give yourself a break? Let down your guard and enjoy life for a day?"

Sher pulled over at the stop sign at the east end of town. "For a day?"

"Bailey has band practice after school so you don't have to worry about him. Just forget about your past for a day."

A couple cars passed them, rushing to get to work before the rain began in earnest. Clouds passed in front of the early morning sun. Clark shivered. Laylea stood up on the edge of her basket, every sense glued to the mom. Sher laid a hand on Clark's face. The hazel ring around her brown irises widened, gold sparking as she captured his eyes.

"Until I see you again, I will forget about the Consortium. I will forget about Trask."

"You will enjoy your life."

"I will enjoy my life."

Clark jumped as sparks ran from her fingers through his hair. The gold sank into the brown. Sher blinked and her plain face again looked at Clark from under the blue visor of her helmet.

He leaned in and kissed her. "It's gonna be a good day."

"Every day is good that I get to spend with you."

Laylea sang her agreement and ducked back down into her basket as Sher rolled back into the trickle of cars that constituted rush hour in Foothills. Clark followed when he'd caught his breath.

Five blocks later Sher rolled to a stop at the four-way stoplight. Clark was going right, out to the airfield. Sher and Laylea were headed straight. When Clark stopped beside her, Sher kissed him.

"Fair winds."

"I love you."

Clark kissed Laylea goodbye too, took his right on red and rolled away.

Laylea leaned out of the basket and watched him until he was out of sight.

"He'll be back, Lee. Don't you worry."

CHAPTER 22

WINTER 2029 - FOOTHILLS, OR

Sher rolled her bike right into the clinic. She plucked Laylea from the basket and handed her off to a tiny woman with her hair in dozens of twisty braids. Laylea tasted them.

The receptionist remembered Laylea from her visits to the clinic as a baby and she squealed with delight at seeing her even though Laylea didn't remember the cute little woman.

"You obey Michelle as you would me." Sher turned back halfway through the door to the back room. "As you would Clark. You got me?"

Michelle laughed when Laylea barked as if she understood.

Laylea's day at the clinic went by in a flash. She greeted all of the dogs that came in. Some were friendly and energetic. Most of them were nervous and skittish and just wanted to leave. Some were in pain. Laylea yawned at a lot of dogs to calm them. She jumped up and took a short nap in the lap of a very nervous mom waiting for her old dog who'd had surgery the day before. She bowed and invited a puppy to play to get him in the door. She growled at a frightened terrier who snapped at Chris.

The cats all came in portable cages. She kept her distance from most of them. But one sick kitten smelled worse than the rest. Laylea caught a whiff the instant she was carried in the door and crept to the edge of the counter to sneak a look. The three-pound calico lay listless in her plastic crate. While her exhausted dad talked with Michelle, Laylea examined her from around the corner of the counter.

Even though the sun had finally come out from behind the clouds, no light glinted off this kitten's fur. It lay matted against her thin body as if she'd been rolled in the wet grass. Her dull eyes stared at the bars of her crate.

Laylea sat up and took a couple steps forward. The kitten looked over at her but then ignored her. Didn't hiss or spit or even turn away like most of the other felines. Laylea dropped to a lie down. She set her chin between her paws, mirroring the kitten. Nothing. She army crawled right behind the dad's feet to the door of the crate. Her nose twitched at the sour smell, but Laylea stayed there. Finally, she reached out and rested a paw on the metal bars. The kitten just had time to swat at the paw before her dad carried her away to an exam room.

At the end of the day, last day patient sent home, the doors locked and Armando and Chris swapped out for night techs, Sher came into the lobby to find Laylea sound asleep in Woodford's bed, half a giant Milkbone sticking out of her mouth.

"Well, Michelle, was she any trouble?"

Michelle switched off the computer. "I think this is the first nap she's gotten. Your Laylea has been a very busy girl."

The bells on the front door jangled as a young woman came in. She wore a silk tweed pantsuit with perfectly coiffed hair and one inch heels. She guarded the leather purse strung over her shoulder as if she were entering a tattoo parlor in Detroit. Sher noticed that she looked back for approval from a man waiting outside. Sporting jeans and unkempt hair, he kept his back to the clinic, looking around at the other folks closing up their shops. He pulled a copy of the local paper from the vending box and leaned on a telephone pole as the suit greeted Sher's receptionist.

"Good evening." She held her hand out to Michelle who took it and as they shook, the suit put her left hand on Michelle's arm. She held on to her a bit too long. "You are a lovely woman...?"

Michelle filled in the blank as she was expected to. "Michelle. Welcome to Foothills' finest veterinarian clinic."

Sher added, "Foothills' only veterinarian clinic." She picked up a stack of magazines from one of the benches and smiled benignly as the suit held her hand out.

Thrown by Sher's failure to notice her outstretched hand, the suit tried to step closer and touch Sher's shoulder as she asked her name. "And you are?"

Sher smoothly dodged the touch by taking the magazines to the reception counter. "Done working for the day," she replied with an easy smile.

Michelle flipped the sign on the front door. "The office is closed now. But we open again at 8 in the A.M. You can bring your pet by then. Where is your pet?"

Sher laughed silently as she maintained her turn away, fanning the magazines on the counter. The suit was consciously trying to manipulate their behavior but she was falling victim to Michelle's natural curiosity.

"We are new to town." Too slow. The response was a lie. "Thinking of getting a dog." The woman gave up trying to catch Sher's eye. She took both of Michelle's hands in her own. "You'll keep an eye out for any pretty little fawn colored dogs for us?" The statement was barely a question and Sher had a sudden impulse to forestall Michelle's response.

Too quickly, Michelle asked, "You're looking for a dog like Laylea here?"

As the suit, whose name they still didn't know, followed Michelle around the reception counter to see Laylea, Sher went on the offensive. She stepped in front of the dog to finally offer her hand. The suit automatically took Sher's proffered palm even as she stared at Laylea. Sher encased the suit's hand with hers, waiting for eye contact.

Not until the suit looked in her eyes did she speak. "Laylea can be very temperamental, Ms... Mrs... Miss? I'm sorry, what shall I call you?"

The suit was caught off guard, paying more attention to Laylea's sudden growling than to her answer. "It's Dr . . . Jones."

Michelle trilled. "Like Indiana. I just love Harrison Ford."

Sher didn't stop shaking Dr. Jones' hand. First names worked better but you used whatever self-identifier the subject gave. "Dr. Jones." She waited again until Jones looked away from Laylea's low insistent growling, which Sher considered an acceptable replacement for the deep white noise she would use in a formal conditioning. She lowered her own tone to match. "Dr. Jones. Laylea is not the dog you want. You want to go outside now." She let go of the woman and changed her tone just slightly, turning her head away to look at the front door. She also put a hand down to silence Laylea. "It is such a beautiful day. We'll see you when you've adopted a pet."

The doctor looked a bit dazed. But she didn't look at Laylea again. After a moment, she followed Sher's gaze and looked out the door.

Sher prompted. "Thank you."

"Thank you both so much." Dr. Jones' fake smile snapped back into place. She started to reach out to Sher. Sher didn't move. Dr. Jones seemed to think the better of it and she turned to rub Michelle's shoulder instead. "Dr. Indiana Jones. Ha ha. I want to go outside..." she hesitated, uncertain, "and enjoy this beautiful day. It's been very nice meeting you, Michelle." This she said as her feet took her to the door. With one last smile that ignored Sher and Laylea, she left.

"Bye bye." Michelle waved a bit as the bells jangled. When the door closed, she lowered the blinds. "I don't think she's going to fit in here at all."

"Nah," Sher took the magazines back to the bench where they belonged. "She's just Big City. Foothills will do wonders for her." And remembering that Foothills was a nice place, not at all like the other worlds she'd lived in, she decided to take a risk. "Michelle, Clark is away tonight and Bailey has band." She faltered, for some reason uncomfortable at having given out that much personal information. "Shall we go out on the town?"

Michelle goggled. "I'm shocked. Woodford won't mind?"

"He'll deal. Would Jim mind?"

"Not at all. I'll call and tell him he and Kenny can have breakfast for dinner cuz Mama's got a girls' night." She sambaed over to the phone at reception.

Sher pulled Laylea's leash off the hook on the wall. The sleepy girl stumbled over to her and Sher bent down. "Good instincts, Lee. Something about her irked me too."

Laylea growled at her, showing her teeth. Then she jumped back and bowed, wagging her butt in air.

The ladies locked up the clinic and walked over to The Witch's Tit for fine pub fare in the open air, never noticing the scruffy guy in jeans still watching them from behind a local paper.

Chapter 23

Spring 2029 - Consortium Biotech HQ, CA

"Um, you only owe four eighty-seven, ma'am." The pimply faced community college grad tried to hand Trask's dime and pennies back.

"Yes. I'm giving you a five and twelve cents so that you can return to me a quarter." Trask kept her hands firmly on the steering wheel. "I'm actually making your life easier."

"Hold on." The barista failed to attract someone's attention inside the coffee shop. "I don't know if I can take more than you owe."

"The five-dollar bill is more than I owe," Trask pointed out.

"Uh."

She shifted to park and folded her hands in her lap. "I'm happy to pay less than I owe."

"I'm gonna have to get my manager."

Trask glanced in her rear-view mirror at the long line of cars behind her late model Prius. "Sure. You do that."

The kid blinked. He took off his headset and walked away into the store.

"Trask, just take the pennies." Walter's voice issued from the after-market blue tooth speaker on her visor. "I will buy them from you with good paper money when I return."

"No." She ignored the honking SUV three cars back. "What's going on? I was expecting you back last week. Have you moved back into your old offices?"

"No. It's been a very interesting trip. Much more interesting than any other so far."

Trask smiled at the conversation between the manager and drive-thru cashier. Another car joined the SUV in honking.

"Development of the four hundred series is behind schedule." She flipped through a file open on the passenger seat beside her. "Your team is not being cooperative."

"Use Steffan to spread a rumor about raises being dependent on interdepartmental review. She's the fastest gossip you'll find in your department. Extremely efficient. We might even see an increase in productivity across all divisions." Walter's voice got quiet as he turned to speak with someone on his end of the line. "Thank you, love. Keep the change. Did you hear that, Trask? I told her to *keep the change*. No math for her. No pennies for me."

Trask sighed. "Yes, Walter."

"Is three nine seven still in the field? I think I spotted him yesterday."

"Three nine seven is dead." Trask reached out the window to take her soy latte macchiato and a quarter from the barista. She sniffed the drink before securing it in the cup holder and shifting into drive. "Three nine seven A should be in the mountains."

"Well, it could have been someone else. I'm not terribly adept with faces. I had planned to come home today but I may need to look more deeply into something strange."

"Is it something I need to be concerned with?" Trask pulled out into the southbound lane despite the clearly posted no left sign.

"I don't know, Trask, there's something about Nicole . . . Dr. Jones. She started behaving oddly after the Foothills Vet visit. Thank you." The call dropped quality as Walter left the hotel restaurant. A brisk wind buffeted his voice and filled the speaker with white noise. "I'm going to go back and check it out myself."

"Was Jones wired?"

"No. Just one cup of coffee in the morning."

"Walter." Trask hit her steering wheel a few times. "Walter, was she wearing a camera or recording device of any kind?"

Walter chuckled quietly at his own oversight. "No."

"Do you have any network equipment with you?"

"Yes. I can set a sync camera to monitor the front door. And I'll wire myself up for the revisit."

"Not too much coffee though."

"You are amusing but I am a tea drinker, Trask."

"I'll keep that in mind come Boxing Day. Do try to remember you're in the surveillance business now."

"I am, as always, gratefully surprised by your brilliance, Trask." A door clicked shut and the audio cleared. "After Steffan has started the rumor, take the red binder from my credenza and walk through the Therian labs. No need to make an excuse or talk to anyone. In fact, it would be better if you didn't talk to anyone. Just walk through."

A rare smile crossed Trask's lips. "My team is afraid of the blue clipboard."

"Lovely. Are you on your way to meet with your friend now?"

"I am. I will pass along your suggestions. Please try to fix Dr. Jones before you return her, will you?"

"I'll see what I can do. Ta."

Trask let Walter cut the connection. She pulled a U-turn with no signal and cruised in the northbound lane, away from division head-quarters.

———

THE DIRECTOR MUTED the sound but let the live feed run. Trask didn't drink coffee. So, what had that whole charade been about? Who was this friend she was visiting? He flipped his pen and used the stylus end to shoot Records a note to go through all of Trask's car footage for the last month. The files in her portable file box didn't appear to ever leave the car. He might need to suggest she have all current CF soldiers check in at base so that he could have his man do a physical check of the files. He made a note to find some excuse for a force-wide recon. The Board wouldn't like it if they found out his researchers had secrets.

A swipe of his hand sent the Bio Research monitoring deck back into rotation and randomly arrayed the Southwest Wasteland Project feeds on his screens. The Director leaned back in his ridiculously comfortable chair and prepared to be bored.

CHAPTER 24

SPRING 2029 - FOOTHILLS, OR

The Hillen household toed the line at spring cleaning time. Sher woke Clark at the crack of dawn to make banana oatmeal energy bars and start his would-be world-famous chili. As in it would be famous if they weren't hiding from the world. Breakfast and lunch would consist of bars eaten on the run. But if they accomplished everything on Sher's list, they would feast in the evening on fresh made cornbread and WBWF chili.

If they didn't finish all their chores, they'd pack chili up for Clark's spring trip to the hermits. Twice the hermits had gotten WBWF chili. Twice the Hillens had gone to bed hungry. It wasn't likely to happen again.

Most of the heavy lifting, painting, and repairs were done by lunch. Sher scheduled light chores around lunchtime that allowed for munching as you worked. Clark gathered and located appropriate homes for magazines, books, and papers while scanning the house for tech. Bailey followed behind. He dusted and scrubbed all the newly visible surfaces and everywhere else. Woodford defended them all from squirrels in the backyard, occasionally cleaning the sliding glass door with his nose. Laylea helped by licking the surfaces Bailey dusted. He said it was gross but he laughed every time so she kept helping.

Sher herself had a bucket filled with soapy water out on the front porch. She set it to the side and started by throwing all dog and boy toys into a box. She called the boys to clear the furniture onto the lawn while she swept the big dirt from the porch rug and hauled it over the railing. Done with the furniture, Bailey took the rug from his mother and shook it out onto the driveway while Clark tickled the breath out of Sher. Woodford and Laylea barked and tangled around their legs.

"Stop it! Everyone get back to work."

"Nope. Son mandated moment of rest."

Sher sighed. "If you insist."

She dropped to the porch floor. One hand smacked the porch railing on her way down. Laylea leaped on top of the mom while Woodford tagged her hand. Clark dropped to join them followed by Bailey after he tossed the rug over the railing. Laylea bounded from one to the other, licking the giggles from their faces. Sher hugged Bailey and pulled him over to throw him onto Clark. As they wrestled, she sat up and rescued her hand from Woodford.

"Ow."

Clark trapped Bailey beneath his legs and sat up. He took the hand and kissed the bruise raising on her pinkie and ring finger knuckles. Sher leaned against him.

"Ooh, sorry baby."

Bailey blew a raspberry. "Walk it off."

"I keep telling you not to listen to Thomas' dad."

"Oh yeah. Sorry mom. Here." Bailey knelt up and took Sher's hand from Clark. He looked at the bruise and then rubbed it lightly like he was brushing away dirt. When he was done, he gave it back to his dad. "There you go."

Clark rubbed a thumb over the smooth skin where the bruise had been. He locked eyes with Sher.

"Parker. Davis." Bailey scrambled to his feet. "When did you guys get here?"

"Hey Bailey." Parker Rucker crossed the lawn to the foot of the stairs. "We just got in this morning. Wondering if you want to come throw a football around with us."

Davis hopped up the stairs past his big brother.

"I would love to," Bailey said evenly.

"But," Sher prompted.

"My mom would kill me."

Clark pulled himself to his feet using the railing. "Spring cleaning."

"See ya!" Davis leapt from the third step and ran back to the OLR's house.

Parker followed, laughing. "Yeah, bye Hillens!"

"Alright, you misfits, back to work." Sher hustled the boys and Laylea into the house. Woodford trotted down the steps and chased a squirrel to the backyard.

Clark let Bailey go ahead. He took Sher's hand. "He woogied—"

"We'll talk later. He doesn't know what he did."

Clark nodded and headed inside. Sher stopped him. "But maybe you tell him to clean up the wine stain under the orange couch."

"Ha! Can't you do it?"

"I'm not good at *things*. I'm more of a *people* person."

Clark leaned in. "A *people* witch."

She kissed him, hard. "Shut up and get back to work."

Clark went inside and upstairs. Sher shut the door firmly behind him to keep the dirt outside. She picked up a tennis racket from her stack of cleaning supplies and attacked the rug.

She worked up a good rhythm and a good sweat beating the rug. The work was like meditation and she was so focused she didn't hear the man approach.

"Good Afternoon, Doctor."

She jumped when she turned to find him standing at the top of the porch steps. "What?"

Clark, clearing old magazines from their bathroom, heard the ice in his wife's voice. He stepped over to the open window and looked down to see a middle-aged man, dressed in dark designer jeans, a button-down shirt, grey suit vest, and wide rimmed black hat. He could not see the man's face.

"I've heard that you rescued a puppy just a few years back."

"I'm a vet. I rescue a lot of animals. What's your name?"

"The dog I mean—"

Sher interrupted him, walking deliberately closer holding the tennis racket ready at her side. "It's well known in this town that I don't talk with strangers. You couldn't have known. But now you do, get off my porch."

"My apologies, Dr. Hillen. I did hear that you are a deliberate woman with little time for pleasantries. I thought I would come directly to the point."

"I haven't heard your name."

Clark dropped the pile of soaps in his hands. He dashed out of the bathroom and nearly collided with Laylea on his way down the stairs. He looked around the front rooms and saw the vacuum cleaner by the empty coat tree. One of his chores was to wrap electrical tape around the cord where Laylea had chewed through the wires. Clark plugged the vacuum into the entryway outlet and folded the cord, holding it so the wires of the chewed section were exposed about three feet from his hand. He stood by the front door and listened to his more-than-competent wife handle the stranger.

The man was saying, "So you see, I have many names. If you like, you can call me Walter. And may I call you—"

"What's your business in the neighborhood, Walter?"

"My wife left me a few years ago. She took our dog and her puppies. That was my dog too and I didn't think she had a right to take all of the 'children' if you will of our union. My lawyers discovered that she had dumped the puppies in various neighborhoods before settling in Boston with the dog who sadly did not survive the trip. You have one of the puppies."

Clark thought, *too many details*.

Sher operating on instinct did something she rarely did. She prevaricated quite often. Avoided almost on a daily basis. She would misdirect occasionally. And now and then evade. But she almost never out and out lied. "Our dog is nine years old. I wouldn't risk his health by bringing a stray into the house."

Walter slipped past Sher and was opening the front door before she could stop him. He moved so swiftly she wondered if he had a military background.

"Stop!"

"Hi there. Have you come by to help with spring cleaning? I'm

Clark," chirped Clark. "Is this a patient of yours from the clinic, dear? Well, not a patient, but a client. You know." He laughed. "I was just gonna vacuum but I heard you outside. Woodford! Leave the squirrels. They're only trying to drive you mad. Get in here. Come on."

The stranger covered his nose. "What is that awful smell?"

Clark turned, looking toward the kitchen doorway as if he had not noticed it before. "Accident in the kitchen. We have a son. And a dog. Life is messy. Do you have children?"

The man looked around the few rooms he could see from the entry-way. There were some old, battered dog toys lying around and an enor-mous green bed with one arm chewed up and sewn. But he could only smell some kind of hound dog under the garbage odor. He saw nothing, smelled nothing that might be one of his missing pups. "Could I have something to drink? I'm parched."

"No, Walter." Sher stepped in front of the man and put a hand on his chest. "You were not invited in."

"Are you sure you don't know a dog named Laylea?"

Sher dropped her tone. "You know nothing." She began again when she captured his eyes, "you know nothing about us. It's time for you to go."

She was about to reinforce the suggestion when two athletic young men stepped in the doorway with a pie. "Hey Hillens."

Sher took her hand from the stranger's chest.

"Hi, Dr. Hillen, Mr. Hillen. Hey there, Woodford. Who's a good boy with a smart nose?" Davis crouched down and gave Woodford's ears some good scratching as the old dog slipped through the door following them.

Parker proffered the pie to Sher. "Grandma sent us over with this. Didn't know you had company." He took another step into the house, putting himself awkwardly between Walter and Sher. "We can come back later."

Walter backed away a step. "It's time for me to go." He said it hesi-tantly though. "Sorry to bother you. I must have bad information."

Davis stood and stepped out of the way. "Goodbye." He reached around Walter to shut the door on the man's back.

Sher and Clark tried to communicate psychically. Woodford ran to the feast of smells in the kitchen. Davis watched his brother keep watch out the little windows at the top of the front door.

Bailey peeked around the wall from the family room. "Mom?"

"Just a minute. Just give us one more minute." Sher took a deep breath and released it, counting to ten under her breath, getting only to six. "What is that smell?"

"I have no idea." Clark grinned at the younger Rucker.

Davis grinned back. "Mr. Hillen, you know that cord could be dangerous if you turned on the vacuum."

"This?" Clark looked down at the vacuum. "I'm just working on the spring cleaning. Since you're here you could help."

Parker turned from the door. "Thanks, but we're supposed to deliver the pie, make sure the guy leaves, and go right back home."

Clark took the pie from Parker. "I'm just thinking of you. You, two football stars, were asking Bailey to throw a ball around earlier. Wouldn't want you to be bored while you're home."

"I appreciate that, sir. Grandma makes sure we're never bored."

Davis punched Bailey in the arm. "You keep an eye on things, right? We'll be working in the yard if that pie is too much for you to handle on your own. Just holler... or whisper. Grandma will hear."

Sher tried to catch the license plate on the deep blue sedan just pulling past the drunken trees as the Rucker boys left. "Clark, did you go outside? Did you see the car?" She dashed into the family room to shut the front windows.

Bailey followed her. "Mom."

Clark unplugged the vacuum and stepped into the dining room to shut the windows there. "I didn't see the car, Sher. He was inside before I realized you needed help. I didn't see outside at all. Come on, Bails." He took Bailey and the pie to the kitchen.

Following them, Sher asked, "Where are all the toys, Bailey? And Laylea's bed?"

"That's what I wanted to tell you, Mom." Bailey turned defensively as Clark stepped into the kitchen. "I didn't do it."

Woodford ruled the room. He waded through garbage beside the overturned trashcan. Bailey's soccer shoes lay nearby.

Sher sighed and ran a hand through her hair. "Bailey. We're trying to make the house cleaner. You can't just throw things out of your way."

"I told you. I didn't."

Clark scooped the nearby garbage inside and righted the can, leaving Woodford to the cheese packaging he looked willing to fight for.

"Bailey, all the evidence points to you." Sher pulled a stack of towels from the drawer. She set most on the counter and began scooping onion peels and butter wrappers into the pail. "Woodford has never gotten into the garbage. Laylea isn't nearly big enough to knock it over."

Clark tossed Bailey a towel. "Accidents happen, Bails. It's no big thing. Mom's just upset you're lying about it."

"I'm not. Dad, believe me. When Mom was talking to that guy, Lee went crazy. You saw her. Something's wrong." Bailey wailed with frustration. He turned to his mother. "My shoes were upstairs. Remember? We just put in new laces."

Sher looked around. She saw Woodford happily chewing on a red cheese rind. Clark scrubbing the floor. Bailey dumping papers in the trash. But no Laylea. "Where is she?"

She didn't come when they called. Clark searched upstairs where he'd last seen Laylea. Bailey searched under the couches in the family room and called into his mom's tinkering room and his dad's radio closet though those doors were always shut. Sher searched the garage and around the house, checking the bells on all the doors and windows as she went.

There was no sign of Laylea. No sign that she had ever existed except for the chewed vacuum cord. All the toys she'd claimed as hers were missing. Her bed was gone from Bailey's room. Her baby towel wasn't bunched up under Bailey's bed. His pajama top which she cuddled against every night in the curve of her brother's stomach had been pulled from under the pillow. Even her precious teddy lizard was missing from its home on the headboard.

When they reconvened in the kitchen, the family barely held panic at bay. Sher stood at the sink going over the last hour in her mind. Bailey wiped tears from his cheeks. Clark held his breath to keep from chanting in front of his son.

"Every door, every window in this house has bells. She didn't leave."

Clark reasoned. "No one came in except through the front door. Right? You would have heard the bells."

"The windows were all open," Bailey swept the towels off the counter.

"The windows all have screens and none of them were disturbed. She's here," Clark insisted. "She's in the house and she is just waiting for us to find her. Okay, buddy? Use your head. Where can she hide?"

"Why was the garbage turned over?" Sher asked from the sink. "The first thing he noticed when he came in the house was the smell."

Bailey turned, dropped, and yanked open the cabinet under the sink. Only cleaning supplies and the compost bin. Sher opened the pots and pans cabinet beside the stove. No dog but she added an item to next year's spring cleaning list. Bailey crawled around the counter, past the trash can as Clark reached for the knob on the pantry but Woodford had settled with his cheese rind leaning against the door. Bailey shoved the big dog along the linoleum and scrabbled at the side of the pantry door to help open it from where he knelt.

Inside they found all of Laylea's toys, her bed, blankets she slept on around the house, her favorite pillow from the couch, her blue baby towel, and Bailey's pajama top.

"Laylea?" Bailey's voice cracked.

Clark pulled items out of the pantry and tossed them aside. "It's okay, little girl."

Sher joined them. She took Laylea's towel from Clark. "That man is gone."

Bailey and Clark both looked at Sher in confusion.

She told them, "He was looking for her. And she hid," she looked to her son, "right, Bailey? She hid when he showed up?"

Bailey nodded, a boneless golden lion in his hand. "She went crazy right before Dad ran down and turned the vacuum into a weapon."

A small whimper sounded from behind the potato sack.

"Laylea!" Bailey dragged the vegetables out of the way.

A muffled cry escaped her and she cringed away from the light, curling tighter into the dark corner. Clenched in her teeth, teddy lizard vibrated with Laylea's uncontrollable shivering. A second cry caught in her throat when she saw Sher.

Sher felt tears well in her own eyes at seeing their little rescue huddled in the very back of the pantry. "You go ahead and cry if it makes you feel better, Lee. Bailey is." Neither boy noticed but Laylea saw a tear spill down the mom's cheek.

"It's okay, little girl. Wanna come out?" Clark took it as assent when Laylea lifted one paw and let whimpers ring deep in her throat.

Bailey stepped aside so the dad could reach in and lift his fearless flying buddy out of her hiding place. Clark folded her into his chest, kissing her head and rubbing her belly. He sat on the floor rocking and murmuring to the tiny dog. Woodford left his cheese remnants to poke her with his nose. Bailey snuggled in close to his dad. He reached into the cave of Clark's arms and caressed her wounded hip as he did when they read together. He added his reassurances to Clark's murmurs.

Laylea stared up at Sher. The mom used Laylea's baby towel to wipe the tears from her face and Laylea gazed in awe at the sight. She forgot to cry herself. When her shivering had subsided in the warmth of her father and brothers' love, she lifted the lizard in her teeth, asking Sher to join them.

The mom knelt down and put her hand on the side of the puppy's face. Laylea dropped teddy lizard to lick her. "I didn't like him either, Lee."

The family sat cuddling on the floor as they had after Laylea's first trip with Clark. She licked each of their hands and Woodford's nose. Gradually the happy scent of out of season pie overwhelmed the rotting reek of garbage. Laylea took a breath deep into her lungs and relaxed in her dad's arms.

He freed one hand to touch his wife. "Who was that guy?"

Sher rubbed the light triangle above Laylea's eyes. "I don't know. There was something familiar about him."

"Why does he want Laylea?" Bailey asked, looking between his parents.

"I don't know." Sher said. "But he's not gonna get her."

Laylea barked at the sharp words. She stretched and climbed from Clark's lap into Sher's. Sher held her hands out of the way until Laylea settled with her head on the mom's knee, nose to nose with Woodford's muzzle on the dad's knee. Another sigh and Laylea relaxed, safe. Sher ran a hand from her ears down to her tail.

Clark took that hand, his voice barely audible as he asked, "Do we run?"

"No!" Bailey buried both hands in Woodford's fur, gripping a little harder than the dog liked. "I heard you, Mom. You told the guy he knows nothing about us. We don't have to run."

Clark rested a hand on Bailey's. "You're right. I heard it too."

Sher looked around at the fresh paint and hand-crafted stools of her kitchen. She shook her head. "I didn't reinforce it."

"Would you trust yourself, woman?"

Her head snapped around to meet Clark's eyes. "If only you'd seen the car."

"I didn't. So, we have to trust you."

"No." She scoffed. "We don't have to trust me."

Clark twisted one of Laylea's ears around his fingers. He smiled. "And yet I do."

Sher stood. She lifted Laylea to the crook of one arm and strode to the knife block. She selected an eight-inch serrated knife. She set the OLR's pie on the counter's rubber trivet and sliced it into six equal portions. She rubbed a cheek against Laylea's head when her back was turned from the boys. Laylea licked her cheek and the mom rubbed her chest as she stared at the recipes pinned to the wall over the stove.

Clark walked over to her.

"So?" He put a hand on the small of her back. "Do we go?"

Sher turned. "No. But spring cleaning is scrapped. We're using the rest of the day to create an early warning system around the house, around the neighborhood, and update our run plan."

"Yes!" Bailey grabbed a handful of kibble from the bucket and scattered it on the floor for Woodford. "I stocked my go bag this morning."

"Good, Bails." Sher bent for a small handful of kibble herself. "Now check it again keeping in mind that I'll change my mind if Walter comes back." She held the food up for Laylea to eat right from her hand. "Nobody threatens my family."

CHAPTER 25

SUMMER 2031 - FOOTHILLS, OR

"Shhh, Lee. I'm sleeping." Bailey dragged a hand up and draped it over Laylea's muzzle, stopping her kisses in his ear.

But it was Bailey's birthday and Laylea was not easily put off. She wriggled under his palm. To reach his chest, she used his face as a ladder. A paw in the ear was a tried and true method of waking her brother up. Once she pushed off his Adam's apple she sat crushing his lungs and focusing her thousand-yard stare on his face until he gave in.

Bailey peeked at her with one eye. When he shut it again, she growled. Bailey exploded in giggles. He grabbed her close as he sat up but she wriggled out of his arms, leaped to the bed, and bounced down to the floor. Her paws pounded across the books strewn over his carpet as she ran out the door. Bailey lay down again. Laylea raced back into his room and up onto the bed. She licked his nose. Gave him a second to decide to give in. And then jumped on his bladder.

He got up.

Laylea waited for him outside the bathroom door with his Bugs Bunny slippers. She ran up and down the stairs until he put the slippers on and followed her. Downstairs the family room was decorated with streamers and balloons. Two backpacks leaned against the coffee table.

One was his Dad's familiar red pack. The other was a horribly clashing neon orange backpack with a bow on it. And it was stuffed full.

Clark and Sher yelled from the kitchen doorway, "Surprise."

Bailey danced around the kitchen as they sang happy birthday with Woodford and Laylea barking in counterpoint. Sher held out a spoon and a pan of bread pudding with thirteen candles in it. Bailey blew out the flames and grabbed the spoon from Sher.

"Hold on, beast." Clark shooed his son away long enough to remove the candles. "As you were."

Bailey buried his spoon in the steaming dish and promptly burned his tongue.

"Better go change," Sher suggested. "You can't wear bunny slippers in the woods."

Bailey whooped and blasted off, leaving the door flapping behind him.

Clark pulled a spoon from his pocket. "Get some bread pudding while you can. When the walking stomach gets back, it's gonna be gone."

"I'll get some after you leave. You eat." She kissed him and handed him the pan. "You're gonna need your strength."

Sher laughed at her husband as she poured herself a cup of coffee. Clark ate a few spoonfuls as he scooped kibble for the fur babies. They sat at the counter while the dogs ate listening to the whirlwind named Bailey upstairs. When he came down, he grabbed the bread pudding pan out of his father's hands and flapped back through the door to kneel with it at the family room coffee table. He unzipped the front of his new pack and started rifling through.

"Nope!" Clark launched into the room. He grabbed the bag and zipped it up. "The deal is, you have to have the Talk with me first. Then you get the rest of your presents."

"Whose deal is that!?" Bailey demanded.

"Mine." Sher sat on the arm of the brown couch with her coffee. "You and your dad can have the Talk in the air and when you land you pretend nothing ever happened. I have acceded to your wishes to have the Talk with the non-medical professional. But there are a few items that I've made your father swear to cover and I promise you," she smiled sweetly, "I will know if he hasn't."

"Mom!" Bailey turned to Laylea to keep from saying anything that might get the whole trip canceled. He scratched her ears and rubbed her down and up again. She stood up on his knees to lick his nose. He reached over and massaged Woodford's old hips. Then he grabbed the backpacks and took them out to the truck.

Clark sidled over to his wife. "What are these items I'm supposed to cover?"

"You know what I want him to know. The really gross stuff about how to be honest with a woman and ask questions. He got the physical how-to from school three years ago." She pulled him in with her legs. "You know what to say." She pulled his head down to hers and kissed him deeply. "Fair winds."

Clark caught his breath, "I love you."

"Oh gross!" Laylea barked at Bailey's quiet entrance. "You don't have to demonstrate!"

"Get out!" Sher imperiously gestured them on their way. "This house is a testosterone-free zone for the next five days. No boys welcome."

Clark pet Woodford as he grabbed his flight bag from the coffee table. "Sorry, buddy. She doesn't mean it."

Laylea stood up on Clark's leg and he almost lost the bag bending over to say goodbye. Then the boys were gone. And it was just Laylea, Woodford, and Sher for the rest of the week.

At ten that night Sher took Laylea and Woodford out for last walk. They didn't see any neighbors and within half an hour they were back home.

Laylea went to the bowl and lapped up enough water to get her through the night. She started up the stairs on Woodford's heels. The sound of the TV turning on stopped them. Sher crossed from the family room into the kitchen. Laylea sat on the stairs. A few minutes later Sher crossed from the kitchen to the family room with a glass of wine. Laylea and Woodford heard the microwave and both got up and trotted into the kitchen when they smelled popcorn. Sher came into the kitchen and poured the popcorn into a large bowl. Several pieces fell to the floor. Neither of them foodies, Woodford and Laylea were content to divvy the popcorn equally. A bratwurst on the floor might have been a different story.

They followed Sher out of the kitchen and she held the swinging door for them. Instead of turning out the lights and climbing the stairs, the mom turned out the lights and settled on the couch. Wine glass in front of her. Popcorn on her lap.

Woodford scampered straight to his bed which often garnered a treat. Laylea wanted to jump on the couch but she wasn't sure of the rules governing a popcorn/couch/Mom scenario. She was not allowed on the couch if the family was eating there. But the rule was not enforced by either Bailey or Clark when they were eating popcorn.

To be safe, Laylea went to her blanket. But she didn't get a treat for it so she detoured to her third favorite spot in the family room and curled up in Woodford's bed with him. They both stared at Sher for a while but no popcorn was forthcoming. Woodford kicked Laylea a couple times, shut his eyes, and went to sleep.

Laylea circled seven times to get comfortable. She perked up when she saw James Garner on the TV screen. Her head tilted as it did when she was thinking hard and after a moment she recognized *The Great Escape*. She circled four or five more times and settled in to watch the movie.

It was already past Bailey's bedtime and she soon fell asleep dreaming of tunneling out with Hilts and Ives. In her dream, the sickly-sweet man was behind them in the tunnel and gaining on them. She twitched and dug and ran and bit Bayard on the nose because he whimpered. Her hip hurt and it was getting cold and loud in the tunnel. Sirens everywhere pierced her ears.

Then the mom was there, picking her up, careful as always of her left side. "It's okay, Lee. When the boys aren't here, we don't watch the end. They all got out. They all escaped Germany and are happy and safe with their families and procedural crime drama gigs."

Sher nudged old Woodford with her stocking foot. She carried Laylea as she put the wine glass and popcorn bowl in the sink. She checked the windows and doors and then she snuggled Laylea down onto Bailey's bed, wrapping the comforter around her and tucking his bear, Casey in beside her.

"Good night, sweet girl." Sher bent her head down as she rarely did so that Laylea could lick her nose.

Laylea watched mournfully as the mom left the room. She shut each door behind her but didn't latch them.

In the morning, Sher nearly stepped on Laylea when she got up to trudge into the bathroom. The dog had dragged Bailey's comforter into the room and fallen asleep right in the doorway.

That night, bedtime happened on time. After last walk, the dogs followed Sher around as she checked the bells. She held open Bailey's door and looked significantly at Laylea who moped in and climbed up onto the remade bed. She lay down and tried to give Sher her best and biggest puppy dog eyes. But Sher had already left.

She really tried not to but a small whimper escaped her. Water rushed through the pipes as Sher brushed her teeth and washed her face. The mom talked to Woodford as she settled into bed. Laylea listened to it all and cried a little more. Could she hear pages turning?

Laylea army crawled to the edge of the bed. She cried in short, hard to ignore spurts.

"Oh, come on." Sher sighed and then raised her voice, "Lee, would you like to join us?"

Laylea leaped off the bed and dashed into Clark and Sher's bedroom. She pounced on Woodford and chewed his ear. Then she ran out again. She went to Bailey's bookshelves and pulled her favorite off the bottom. The book was almost as long as she was and it took some effort to get it down to the other bedroom. She tried to throw it up on the bed but was wildly unsuccessful.

Sher sat up against the headboard with the light on. She held a paperback with no cover. Laylea woofed once, quietly at her.

Sher looked down. "I don't know how the crane works. And once you are on this bed, you had better stay because I am only picking you up once."

She got out of bed and used both hands to lift Laylea up. When she stepped on the corner of the picture book she picked that up too.

"*The Little Crow.*"

Laylea looked at Sher hopefully.

"You want me to read you a bedtime story. Absolutely the weirdest dog. You. With those black alien eyes and your cold tagging nose."

Laylea hopped aside to give Sher room as she climbed back under the covers. The mom held the book up on her lap.

"*The Little Crow, by KJ Knight.*" She looked down at Laylea. "Seriously?"

Laylea climbed up into Sher's lap. She sat between her legs and leaned against her belly so she could see the pictures.

Sher turned the page. "*A mother crow sat on her nest. An egg hopped. 'Oh Oh!' said the crow.* Gotta go get some worms."

Sher did not do the mama bird voice like Bailey did. And she didn't jump along with the book. But Laylea did.

"*The egg hopped. It hopped, and hopped, and hopped! Crack! Out came the little crow! 'Where is my mother?' she said.*"

Laylea tilted her head and looked up at Sher. Sher did not look down at her.

"I don't do voices. *The little crow looked for her mother. Down, she went, out of the tree. Down, down, down! It was a long way down.* So far down that the little crow broke all her pneumatized bones and lay there until a good Samaritan took her to a vet to save her life.

Laylea barked. Sher returned to the book. "*The little crow couldn't fly.* Because she doesn't have any feathers yet. *But she could walk.* But not as far as she's going. '*Now I will go and find my mother.*'"

Sher read it in squeaky voice. Laylea leaped up and woofed. Her tail caught in Sher's pajama top and wagged the shirt.

"*She did not know. . .* stop that." She brushed the tail out of her shirt. "*She came to a cat. 'Are you my mother?'* The cat pounced on the baby crow and bat her around with his paw until he got bored and wandered off. *The cat wasn't her mother. 'Where could she beeeee?'*"

Sher wailed the crow's words in the silly squeaky voice. Laylea's tail slapped back and forth against Sher's chest.

"*Then she came to a dog. 'Are you my mother?' 'I am not your mother, I am a dog,' said the dog.*" Sher went to turn the page. Laylea put her paw up on the book. She leaned forward and tagged the picture of the dog with her nose. She tilted her head at it. Then she leaned back and cuddled into Sher's lap. Sher read on as the little crow ran and tried to bond with the bicycle, the boat, the building, and the excavator. She did more melodramatic wailing for the excavator ride. Even though Sher didn't do the motions, Laylea looked down at the bicycle, up at the building, and she wagged her head back and forth in despair at the construction equipment until it dropped the bird back in its nest.

"The little crow was home. Just then the mother crow came back to the tree. 'Do you know who I am?'"

Laylea wiggled with joy.

"'Yes,' said the little crow. 'You are my mother.'"

Laylea knocked the book onto Sher's legs. She tagged the mother bird with her nose several times. Then she turned and leaped to tag Sher's cheek. Laylea danced out of Sher's lap and tripped over the book. She rolled to her feet and spun in circles of joy on the bed. She barked. She leapt off the bed and startled Woodford with lapping at his muzzle. He growled. She bounded joyously over to a chair and used that to leap back onto the bed, throwing herself at Sher to kiss her nose. She tagged Sher over and over. Then she clambered over to the left side of the open book and nosed the cover. She flipped it shut and climbed back into Sher's lap.

"What was that?"

Laylea tilted her head back and woofed at Sher. Then she tagged the book with her nose and stared at it.

"What?

Laylea tagged the book again.

"I'm supposed to read the book again?" Sher picked up the well-worn, slightly chewed book.

Laylea barked. Sher read the book again, with less edits and more commentary, giving Laylea a lesson on kitten, chicken, and bird biology. And again, Laylea moped for a moment at the dog page and danced and tagged Sher at the end. When Laylea stood on her chest to kiss Sher's nose, Sher picked her up. She held her up with her rear paws dangling and looked into the dog's eyes.

"Am I your mother?"

Laylea sang out and wriggled happily in Sher's hands. Sher set her down again.

"Woodford, am I your mother?"

Woodford lifted his head and looked up at his name. His tail thumped once.

"Lee."

Laylea sat up and turned all her attention to Sher.

"Sweet dreams. And fair winds." Sher turned out the light and scootched down under the blankets. Laylea circled on Clark's pillow. When she lay down she faced Sher. She reached out and licked Sher's ear then settled her head and fell asleep in seconds.

CHAPTER 26

SUMMER 2031 - FOOTHILLS, OR

Every night of the week that Clark and Bailey were off in the wilds having the Talk and other talks as well, Sher read a bedtime story to Laylea. The mom refused to read *The Little Crow* every night. But she did read it one more time and Laylea reacted to the dog and the mother crow exactly the same as she did on the first read.

Clark and Bailey were expected to arrive home Sunday morning so Sher was concerned when Woodford started barking his head off late Saturday night. She had her go bag on her back when she got down the stairs to find the dogs climbing all over Clark and Bailey. The boys reeked.

"Mom!"

"Sheriff!"

"We have returned to you!"

The boys tried to extricate themselves from the dogs to hug Sher. She warded them off with her bag.

"Out. Those backpacks are not coming into my house."

While the conquering heroes backed out of the house, she fetched towels from the backyard clothesline. Sher returned to find them already stripping down, putting the filthy clothes directly into the washing machine.

"Good boys."

She sent Clark up to shower first and fixed Bailey a snack while he told her everything he could about their trip. He was over the moon and talking a mile a minute despite his full mouth. He held Laylea in his arms, telling the stories to her as much as to his mother. The dog licked at his face and hands, even cleaning the peanut butter Bailey dripped on his bare chest.

"Stop it. That tickles. Here, you eat it off my finger, weirdo."

Sher used a napkin to wipe the remnants of peanut butter and dog saliva from her son's chest. He babbled on about rocks and animals and survival skills and Jay Jay Jay.

Clark came down wearing his tuxedo pajamas and smelling like something Sher could allow in her bed. He took Laylea from Bailey and the kid pecked his mom's cheek before racing away. When Bailey and Woodford had turned the corner upstairs, Clark took his wife in his free arm and kissed her hard. Laylea gave them a moment before she kissed Sher too.

"A raging success. Your son is going to be a ladykiller. He's smart, respectful, and not afraid to ask questions."

Sher pushed Laylea's muzzle away with one hand and covered Clark's face with the other. "You didn't brush your teeth."

He laughed and kissed at Laylea's face instead. Sher went to the fridge and Clark settled on a stool. She set a bowl of berries in front of him and grabbed a knife to slice some apple.

Clark waved imperiously at the crockware. "Take away this forest food. The hungry traveler wants cheese and wife."

"You can have cheese and olives." Sher returned the apple to the crisper and pulled out a triangle of smoked Gouda.

"Did you know that Thomas is gay?" Clark whispered to Laylea who did know.

Sher handed a knife to her love, "And how does Bailey feel about that?"

"He asked me if we could introduce Thomas to Armando. So, he would have someone to have the birds and bees talk with."

Sher tilted her head. Clark laughed through a mouthful of half chewed Gouda when Laylea did the same.

She asked, "You did get to the pregnancy part of that talk, didn't you?"

"I knew I forgot something."

Sher gathered the remainder of the kid's apple and a piece of bread onto a plate. Clark added two fingers of peanut butter and another chunk of cheese before Sher took both from him.

"How did the other talks go?" She spun the cap on the peanut butter and stuck it back in the cabinet over the bread garage.

"Ha." Clark attached the occlupanid on the bread bag and tossed it to her. "As you suspected, he knew a lot already."

She kept her back to him. "Is he mad at me?"

Clark leaped over the center island and spun Sher into a one-armed hug. "Does he seem mad at you?"

Sher leaned back to hold the cheese away from Laylea's sniffing. "But all the things I did."

"He gets it." Clark released her to grab his knife from the counter. "As we've always said, he's a strange kid. He's a smart kid and he knows you'd want to scientifically understand how you affect people."

Sher stood from the cheese bin, the fridge door between them. "But that's not why I did it."

"Sher," Clark asked, "did you know why you were doing it?"

Sher blanched. She whispered, "Because I can."

Clark nodded silently. When she started to close the fridge, he bent under her arm and stole a beer from the bottom shelf without slowing her.

"He didn't know how fast I am. He was kind of relieved to talk about it. Said he feels like Superman at track meets."

"Why doesn't he ever win?" The mom stopped with her hands on the plate. "He could win occasionally. That wouldn't give us away."

Clark flipped the cap of his home brew into the trash and grasped the neck in the same hand that held Laylea. He hit the light switch by the garage door and slipped his free arm around his wife's waist, escorting her to the swinging door. "He never comes in first because if he's in front he can't gauge how slowly he should be running."

Sher stared at her husband. "We got so lucky with this kid."

Clark let her take the lead as they headed up the stairs. "Oh, he tells me we effectively educated him on the benefits of secrets."

"We hammered it into him." She looked back at the first landing.

Clark half shrugged. "We needed to. And now we need to train him."

They passed through the steam billowing out of the hallway bathroom. The water turned off as Sher led the way into their bedroom. She'd left her light on but now she flipped on the overhead light as well. "It's time to turn the focus from secrecy to control."

Clark left the door cracked. He tossed Laylea onto the bed. "He'll go on trips with Laylea and I and we'll work in the mountains. You can train him here and maybe at the cabin sometimes."

"You showed him how to find the cabin?"

"Oh yeah." Clark leaned out of the bathroom, toothbrush halfway to his mouth. "He's really curious about how you hid it. I told him it was like a more extensive version of the flash wipes you put on my plane and the neighborhood street sign."

"Well, not that simple. And I think I've improved the tech. We could all go there together soon and he can help me redo it." She slipped back under the no longer warm covers. She picked up her book from Clark's pillow where she'd sacrificed the spine to save her place. "That's not a bad way to figure out how strong he is."

"Oh, he's strong." Clark spit in the sink and repeated, "He is strong, my love."

Sher lowered her voice. "Magically."

Clark nodded with a mouthful of water.

"I wish Grams were here." Sher set her bookmark in the pages and put the book aside. "I wish anyone were here to help."

"We can do it, Sheriff." Clark brushed her knee on his way to the dresser. "We're an amazing team."

A quick paradiddle on the door and their son rolled on in. "Team Hillen to the rescue!" He scooped Woodford from the floor and found him a comfortable bulge of blankets on the bed. Laylea scrambled over her fur brother to cuddle in Bailey's lap when he perched cross-legged beside the big dog.

"I missed you guys." He made monster face and chewed on Laylea's ear. She bared her teeth before diving down to chew on his fingers. "Did you girls have any fun while we were gone?"

"Poor Woodford." Clark sat on the bed and scratched the big boy. "No one gives you any respect."

Laylea fell backwards onto the hound and rolled over to leap at Clark. He caught her and submitted to a bite on his nose.

"Yeah, Dad. Woodford's almost asleep." Bailey yawned his next words. "He's not in the mood to talk."

"Actually, human boys, there is something I want you to see." Sher leaned over to her bedside table and picked up the picture book.

She opened the book on her lap and waited while Laylea tumbled out of Clark's arms to take up her usual position. Sher read *The Little Crow* with assistance from Bailey who hopped with the egg and fell with the little crow. He meowed and clucked and barked in the appropriate spots. When Laylea tagged the dog with her nose and laid her muzzle on the page, Bailey reached over and pet her gently. He looked down and up at the boat and building and shook his head at the excavator. And when the mother crow returned, he crawled forward and kissed his mother's cheek as Laylea tagged her.

"Oh!" Sher remembered all the times that Bailey had come running to find her, kiss her, and run away. Laylea had run with him. This is explained it all. "I don't know what I was thinking. She's imitating your behavior, Bailey."

"It's just how we read the book. Check this out." He reached over and craned Laylea to the ground. "Go get Dad's book."

Laylea ran out of the room. She came back carrying a lighter book. Clark took it from her and craned her back up. He read the title and handed it to Sher.

"*Hop on Pop*. Of course."

Laylea walked over to the book and tagged the pop on the cover. Then she tagged Clark.

Clark kissed Laylea's muzzle and tucked her into his chest. "Bailey. Can you show your mom and I what you were telling me about this morning?"

Bailey hopped up. "You believe me? Yeah. I'll show you." He looked around the room. He reached over to grab the paperback from his mother's bedside table. "We'll use Mom's book."

Laylea leaped from Clark's arms, bounced over Bailey, and landed on the bedside table, knocking everything except the lamp off of it. She kept skating along until she hit the wall. The coverless book ended up behind the table.

"Whoa! What's up with you?" Bailey caught Laylea before she could slide off the marble top.

Clark grabbed a book off his dresser. "Here you go, kiddo. Try this one." He looked at Sher over Bailey's head, raising his eyebrows at her. Sher blushed.

Bailey flipped through the book. "You ready, Laylee? Let's play fetch." He started reading out loud. "*And then his daddy,*" Laylea was up. She tagged Clark with her nose. "*. . . was on the bed,*" She tagged the blankets at her feet. "*Daddy's arm around his back,*" She ran over and tagged Woodford's back. "*. . . asking him what was wrong. Tad dared to look into the mouth*" She yawned. . . . *of his closet*" Jumped off the bed and over to the blue doors of their closet. "*. . . again. The monster*" She ran over to the stationary bicycle. Clark guffawed. "*. . . was gone. Instead of whatever hungry beast*" On the bed, she tagged Bailey "*he had seen, there were two uneven piles of blankets,*" She picked at the wool blanket with her teeth. "*. . . winter bedclothes which Donna had not yet gotten around to taking up to the cut-off third floor. Instead of the shaggy, triangular head, cocked sideways in a kind of predatory questioning gesture,*" Laylea tilted her head at the book. "*. . . he saw his teddy bear*" Laylea ran out of the room and returned with Bailey's stuffed bear. She ran out again and returned with her own lizard. She set the lizard beside the bear.

Sher cocked her head at the toys. "She's brought a teddy bear AND a lizard. I don't get it."

"Sher!" Clark was appalled that this is what she had focused on.

"It's okay, Dad. Sometimes you have to interpret." Bailey picked up Laylea and rewarded her with love as he spoke. "Mom, the bear's name is Casey. And you named the lizard, Teddy. So," he pointed at each in turn, "Teddy. Bear."

"How long have you been working on this? This is amazing." Sher reached over to hug Bailey but he slipped off the bed with Laylea.

"Mom, it's not a trick."

"Of course it isn't. It takes a lot of work to teach a dog how to do that."

"Sher, is it really possible to teach a dog to do that?"

Sher smiled. "Of course. It's basic conditioning. You say *mother* when she gets near me and give her treats and praise and eventually you can condition her to run to me whenever you say *mother*."

Laylea's tail drooped. She leaned her head against Bailey's shoulder.

Clark looked over at Bailey and Laylea. "It seems so amazing."

Sher agreed. "Oh, it is. She is a very smart dog and your son is the most patient kid in the world. But it's still just a dog."

Laylea's jaw dropped at the pronoun. She sang her frustration just as Bailey screamed.

The lamp on Sher's side table exploded.

CHAPTER 27

SUMMER 2031 - FOOTHILLS, OR

Bailey stared in shock at the lamp. Laylea stared at Bailey. Clark watched his wife reach up and pull a shard of pottery from her forehead. Blood poured down her face.

Bailey ran from the room.

Clark chased him. "It's okay. It's okay, Bailey. Please come back. Come here." He wrapped his arms around boy and dog, squeezing them until Laylea squeaked. "Sorry."

"I'm not that patient, Dad. And *she's* not just a dog."

"Okay. Come on back and show us."

"The lamp."

"Don't worry about the lamp. Your mom once accidentally made her brother jump into the Atlantic Ocean. In February. And she liked her brother."

Bailey sniffed. "I liked the lamp."

"No, you didn't." Clark shook his head. "You have better taste than that."

"I can hear you!" Sher hollered from the bedroom.

Clark saw a smile crack on Bailey's face. He led him back to the bedroom. Sher was scooping the last shards of lamp and bulb into the bathroom trash. Her face showed no signs of injury except a trace of blood in her hair. Clark put the can away as Sher grabbed the bathmat and covered the fragments too small to pick up by hand.

"Sit, Bailey." She followed her own orders. "Talk to us."

Bailey took a deep breath. He looked at the mat and at the empty space on his mother's table, now holding only her bookmark. He let the breath out and tried again. "But wait. There's more."

He set Laylea down on the bed and crouched beside her. He picked up his dad's book and flipped through the pages.

"Ready, Lady Laylee?"

Laylea barked, intent on the book.

Bailey ran his finger along the words but he didn't read them out loud. After a couple of lines, Laylea barked. She ran down the chair and out to Bailey's room. Bailey sat back down on the bed with the book in front of him. Woodford grunted in complaint so Bailey ran a hand through his fur. Clark looked over Bailey's shoulder.

"*Baseball.*"

As he read it Laylea ran back in with a blue racquet ball in her mouth. She climbed chair to bed and dropped the ball by Sher. Then she returned to Bailey's side, leaning on his thigh with one paw like she was bellied up to the bar. He ran his finger along the words. She barked.

Laylea clambered up onto Sher and leaned over to the bedside table.

Bailey deflated. "I don't know what she's doing."

Sher picked up the illicit bookmark, a memorial card from her grandmother's funeral twenty years ago. She handed it to Clark. Her Grams had been an animal lover and the prayer card's image was of St. Francis of Assisi.

Clark read over Bailey's shoulder, "The word is *saint.*"

Laylea returned to the book. Bailey laughed at the next word she picked. Laylea ran over to the mirror in the corner while Clark read aloud, "*Dog.*"

He scanned the page as Laylea climbed back up to the bed. When she got to Bailey, Clark pointed at a word. She looked up at him and then went over and sat in Sher's lap.

"*Doctor.*"

Bailey handed the book to his mother. "Here Mom, you do it."

Sher turned a page and ran her finger along the words. *Cujo knew he was too old to chase rabbits.* Laylea barked. She climbed out of Sher's lap and got Clark to crane her down. She left the room a little slowly. Bailey watched her sadly. He adored his mother but he wished she had more imagination.

Clark perched on the bed beside Sher. "What's the word?"

"*Rabbits.*" Sher shook her head. "I don't think she can do this one."

Bailey whispered. "Mom, she is more than just a very smart dog."

"I know you want to think so, Bailey. But when you were three you thought your clown doll was talking to you at night."

"Mom! I'm thirteen."

"Bailey. I'm on your side." Clark got up and rubbed his son's shoulder as he went to his dresser. "Sher, I think you're gonna have to shut off the scientist who knows the facts of life. Our dog is reading these words off the page. The facts of life may have changed."

Laylea stood in the doorway. She would normally have felt the tension in the room and run in doing something silly to break it up. But she knew this time she was the cause.

"Come on in, Lee." At Sher's urging, Laylea padded over to her side of the bed, dragging the slipper. Sher picked it up.

"Bugs Bunny."

Clark exhaled a stuttering laugh. He came back from his dresser with a pencil and a couple slips of paper in his hands. Scooping Laylea up he cuddled her for a moment. "Good girl. You are so smart." He set her in the middle of the bed with the slips of paper on either side. "We're gonna ask you some questions, okay? And you'll..." Before he could finish, Laylea touched her paw to the slip on her right. The slip read *Yes.*

Clark caught his breath.

Bailey laughed at him. "What were you gonna say, Dad? One bark for yes, two for no?"

Laylea put her paw on the *Yes* slip and barked. She put her paw on the *No* slip and barked twice.

She sat waiting for the questions but there were none for a while. The room fell silent but for Woodford's snoring. Sher hid her face in her hands.

"Are all dogs like you?" Clark blurted out the question.

Laylea quickly tapped the left slip and barked twice.

"Do you know what you are?" he asked.

Laylea tilted her head at the question.

Clark yelled out, "Is the sky blue?"

One bark, right slip.

"Is grass green? Excepting Kentucky."

One bark, right slip.

"Is Bailey a girl?"

Left slip, two barks.

Clark clasped his hands. He broke the pencil. "Are you happy?"

Right slip, one bark, singing.

"Am I the best dad?"

Singing, right slip, dancing.

Sher found her voice. "Am I a good doctor?"

Laylea stopped dancing. She stood looking at Sher. Then she picked up the *Yes* slip and carried it over to the mom's lap. One bark. She dragged out the picture book from under Clark's pillow. Laylea flipped it open with her nose. She turned the pages with her nose and then tapped her paw on a particular line. *Are you my mother?*

Sher gathered Laylea up in her arms and barked. Once. When Sher could breathe again, she looked up at her husband. "I think we're gonna want to reread that letter she came with."

Clark nodded his head. "Yeah."

Clark pulled the letter out of his go bag. He invited Laylea to sit in his lap and followed along with his finger as he read.

"*Dear Hillens,*

I met you several years ago. You won't remember the incident but your kindness saved my life. I hope that your kindness can extend to my little Laylea as well. There is an evil man who would do experiments on Laylea and her brothers."

Laylea barked several times. She ran over to Bailey and looked off at Woodford. She tilted her head at Clark.

Sher reached over to her and scratched her ears. "Not Bailey and Woodford, Laylea. I think she means your littermates. You had biological brothers who must be like you."

Bailey blurted out, "She means the creepy guy who came looking for Laylea that spring, when she hid."

Sher's face went hard. "You might be right, Bailey. Walter. He definitely wasn't a good guy."

"How did Laylea recognize him?" Bailey squeezed his sister when she shivered. "You knew to hide from him."

Sher hushed him. "Clark, read on."

"Because of this, they have spent their lives thus far in a basement not seeing anything of the world. Two days ago, this man found our sanctuary."

Bailey nodded his head. "She saw him."

"It's more likely she smelled him."

Laylea barked. She waved at Clark with her right paw.

"We escaped but I dare not foster any of my pups together or to people that know me. I know Laylea would be safe with you and that you are up to the challenges that raising her will present. She is a very special little girl."

"Yes, she is." Sher wiped gunk from the corner of Laylea's eye.

"Duh."

"No shit, Sherlock"

"Clark!"

Clark smirked sideways at Bailey who hid his face.

"Please take care of her. Though I am heartbroken to leave my puppy, I am comforted knowing she will be as happy as Bailey and Woodford were when I knew them. She is eight weeks old and just weaned. With Great Appreciation for whatever help you can give her, Mama"

Sher raised her hand. "So, question number one; Mama? Like I'm her mother or like," she flipped through the picture book's pages to the dog, "her Mother. And if it's her mother, who did she get to write the letter?"

"Or maybe she's a scientist who bred them for Walter to do experiments on," Bailey chimed in.

"Or maybe she helped genetically engineer them," Sher shot back.

Clark put his hands up. "Regardless of how much information we drag out of this note, I think the important thing is not where she came from but how we go from treating her like an adored pet to treating her like a sapient being."

Laylea tilted her head at the exact moment Bailey raised his hand.

"It means, how do we go from *who's a good widdle puppy dog. Do you want a treat? Do you want a treat?* to *I'm proud of you, pup. Would you prefer a Milkbone or Pupparoni?*"

Laylea barked the cadence of Milkbone as Bailey said it.

Clark waved them away. "Yes, I know she would prefer a Milkbone. It was just an example."

"Oh gods," Sher sat up. "She can spell T R E A T."

Laylea barked once for yes.

Bailey added, "And W A L K and D I N N E R and P L A N E R I D E."

"Okay, but hold on." Clark stopped them. "My real point was that I have not slept very well camping without my apparently genius watchdog. I'm tired and we're not gonna be able to figure everything out tonight."

"Or ever," Sher put in.

"Yes," Clark continued. "But we'll think better after some sleep. We're all home tomorrow, right?"

They each confirmed. Laylea with one bark.

"Then let's go to bed. How much more can the world change in eight hours?"

Bailey and Laylea kissed their parents. Bailey grabbed his Bugs Bunny slipper and the books. Laylea climbed all over Woodford in her usual goodnight ritual while Bailey scratched the old dog. And they went to crash in their room, Laylea listening avidly while Bailey told her all about the camping trip until they both fell asleep.

Clark and Sher didn't fall asleep for hours.

When Sunday morning rolled around, Clark and Sher were still talking. When later Sunday morning rolled around they were jolted from bed by Bailey's screams.

CHAPTER 28

SUMMER 2031 - CONSORTIUM BIOTECH HQ, CA

A rainbow of file folders flew to the floor in a crash with the stash of chewing gum. Dozens of photos of black, brown, and fawn colored canines made a taunting river of failure for Walter to wade through. He ignored the pictures. He scooped the remains of the shattered Oogies coffee mug into Trask's wastepaper basket and fished a stick of black jack out of the mess.

"Not what you expected?" Trask asked standing unmoved at the window as she watched the fiasco unfold far below.

Guards flanked the yard though none moved. She had not given word for them to interrupt and so they wouldn't. Her four CF, three new and one check-in remained in the yard as well. Two of the new soldiers continued their training assignments. 343 had scaled the Sycamore and hid in its branches. Trask had a camera feed of those areas of the yard not visible from their leaded window but she didn't bother checking on 343's position. She had diverted funds from her secondary testing team to build an electrified field out three feet from the window. If 343 climbed too close, accidentally or otherwise, he'd soon fall from the tree. If he survived, he'd have to be reconditioned.

Her third newly processed subject watched Walter's maimed volunteer, Sammy, and her attacker. Black eyes sparked out of a dark face painted with even darker tattoos. He was aware and ready to react but otherwise appeared neither repulsed nor enchanted by the human being writhing on the grass at his feet.

Sammy threw herself at the bleeding body. As long teeth descended from her human jaws, she buried her face in the thigh of the man who had cut off her arm. Biting into his neck would have held more of the fantasy element expected from Walter's experiments but the salamander-imbued woman had already chopped the head off of Walter's star subject and thrown it at their beautiful leaded window. A streak of blood and pus to the left mirrored the green and brown patterns of the Sycamore branches pushing against the window to Trask's right.

After a subdued moment dominated by deep sucking noises from Sammy, she tore a chunk of flesh off her attacker's thigh and split the air with a feral scream of power and pain. She leapt thirty feet away from her victim and disappeared into the maze of bushes and trees in the center of the courtyard.

"Why don't they shoot?" Walter begged around three sticks of gum.

"I don't let my forces have guns on property unless they're on the range."

"What about the guards?"

"But would you want them to shoot?" Trask turned away from the entertainment to see her office mate huddled in the corner farthest from the window and video screens. "We're learning so much."

"I know nothing."

"I'm tempted to believe your new mantra. How many different animals did you splice into that woman's DNA?"

Another wet splat against the window dropped Walter to the floor. Trask's heels clicked evenly as she circled the desk to retrieve her sweet tea. She selected a red pen from the top desk drawer with her free hand and opened the display board just long enough to cross off a number.

"You didn't see the head. How do you know which soldier it was?"

"I don't." Trask set the red pen in the center of Walter's blotter. "I'm making a guess. You're the one who told me I need to have more fun with my job."

"Why don't you order the guards to take her down? She's killing your CF."

"If my forces cannot defend themselves, I want my scientists to see what happens when they fail. This will be much more effective than losing a CF in the mountains and simply never seeing them again." Trask strolled back to the entertainment. "Ooh, her face has turned pink. If you want to save your bear cub, you should activate the guard yourself."

"That's right." Walter pulled himself up. "I can activate them."

Trask sat on the window seat. "What is going on with you? I appreciated that nice long trip you took to central Mexico. And Dr. Jones has developed new focus since you stopped taking her on puppy-hunting trips. But you've lost your annoying chipper and I find this helpless you irritates me even more, if that is possible."

Three quick pops followed by a scream stopped Trask's lecture.

"Oh dear. She's going after the guards now."

"What's the body count?"

Trask scanned the courtyard out the window and via the monitors. "I can't see your little bear cub boy but that's the bat girl's leg hanging from the tree there. Can't imagine she survived that excision. Of course, your komodo man got it first. Sammy showed amazing speed there. I would love to learn more about that. I'm extremely disappointed in 433 and 425. The four erasure team have earned the honor of clean-up duty. 343 is safe in our sycamore—or not so safe." Trask took a step away from the sparks flashing off the window. "Plus the two guards. That's a total of four subjects plus one collateral and two employees. So far."

Walter pushed off the wall. He kicked aside the pictures and raced to the alert button.

"She's growing gills, Walter." Trask returned to her chair. "I imagine she'll drown in just a bit."

The female figure had ripped away her standard issue black t-shirt and stolen a bloody green snap-front shirt from one of Trask's CF. Beneath the open folds three slashes on either side of her rib cage grew fuzzy red tendrils while the woman scratched at her throat with one hand and one sucker-toed paw. Her pink face turned a deep shade of red with her mouth twisting open, gasping to pull in oxygen.

The black tattooed CF appeared in front of her. Her gaze drifted from the window to his illustrated face. The two volunteers stood in tableau for two minutes. Walter's hand hovered over the alert button. In a flash too quick to be seen except in digital replay, the CF snapped Sammy's neck.

Walter hit the button. Walter hit the window. Walter raced for the red pen waiting on his side of the desk. He threw it at the cabinet behind Trask's head screaming in eerie imitation of Sammy's earlier cry.

"I know nothing!"

Trask's chair clattered to the ground. She gripped the edge of the desk, nearly shoving it out of her way as she circled to him. He backed away but she grabbed his bare forearms. Her perfectly manicured nails dug into his flesh as she demanded his gaze.

"You will never say that again. Walter, you will never say that again." Her voice dropped even lower as on those mornings when she had worked all night long. "Go find your children."

Walter's breath caught in his throat. Trask flung his arms from her and he stumbled backwards as she walked away muttering, "you sick bastard." She yanked the handset from the wall and hit two buttons. "The cleanup team will stand down. E4 leads report to the courtyard immediately."

Walter straightened his shirt. Without a word, the scientist took his knapsack and jacket from the hook in the corner. He bent to the sea of pictures and selected one composite of five pictures of Rhea and the puppies. He shoved a handful of gum into his bag. Then he pushed past Trask and left the office.

THE DIRECTOR MADE a note to pull his lab plants for loyalty testing. Trask seemed to be improving her conditioning skills. She couldn't be allowed to have too much control over her employees. As much as the Biotech Research divisions amused him, the Director would not permit another disaster like the fire that had taken the genius Kathrine Coogan from them. Their successes were few and far between since Coogan had died and each one was being tested by the secondary team in Rotterdam. The Consortium was taking no chances this time. Coogan should have been more closely monitored.

On a whim, the Director pulled up restored footage from the fire. They had not wired the original division buildings as they had this new facility but there were a few security cameras. The only footage that could be recovered came from the parking lot cameras. Why did nearly everyone leave the building except for Trask, Coogan, and a dozen others? Of the hundreds of people working in that building, only three died that day.

The Director folded his hands and laid his chins on them. He watched the three angles of employees chatting as they exited each of the heavily secured doors of the building in an endless stream. His fourth screen showed only a patch of grass interrupted by a few feet and later flaming debris until the camera was taken out by the last explosion.

His phone sang out a passage from Stravinsky to tell him it was time to check in on L.A. Headquarters. He ignored it. Lights turned on in his little garden and the temperature dropped, both trying to get his attention.

The Director buried his nose in his knuckles and focused on the fourth screen. The camera should have shown the main entrance to the division campus. It showed grass. Someone had moved that camera.

The Director cut the other three playbacks. He pulled the cord of his headphones from the primary jack and plugged it directly into the audio feed of screen four. He turned the volume to ten.

CHAPTER 29

SUMMER 2031 - FOOTHILLS, OR

S her grabbed her go bag from under the bed and followed seconds behind Clark out the door and down the stairs. She was thrown from her feet when they ran into Bailey zipping up the stairs.

"You have to come. You have to come help him!"

Woodford barked furiously.

Clark caught his son when the kid's sudden stop sent him tumbling. Sher pulled her feet in on the landing to stay out of their way.

"We're coming," Clark assured him. "Who's hurt?"

"Mom, bring your bag." Not waiting to catch his balance, Bailey tore back down the stairs.

"I've got it right here. Who's hurt?" Sher scrambled to her feet and followed.

"Davis!" He ripped a blanket from the back of the orange couch. "I saw the tree falling but I couldn't catch it."

"It's okay, kiddo. You aren't infinitely strong."

"No, Dad. I could have caught it. I could have lifted it off him but I didn't because then he'd see."

Sher pulled her son from his dad. "It's okay. We'll go help him. Is he. . . Where is he?"

Bailey led them out the front door. Mr. Rick was crossing the street with his cat in his arms.

He held out his phone. "I've got 911. Can you talk to them?"

"No!" Bailey yelled as he jogged towards the rental cottage at the curve of the cul-de-sac.

Clark slowed. "Tell them to send an ambulance. We'll come back and direct them if we can't get Davis out."

"But how is he hurt?" Mr. Rick whined the question.

Letitia Rucker burst through her front door yelling, "Go get my grandson. Sher, you do whatever you can. Go, Clark. George Rick, you give me that phone."

Clark caught up with Bailey and Sher at the stone passageway. She was already out of breath.

"You boys go. Make a mess and I'll follow your path."

Bailey nodded. "We'll send Laylea back to lead you." He leaned forward to put on speed.

But Clark grabbed his shirt tail. "No. Davis will notice if you get back too soon."

They kept running, but not as fast as the boys could.

"He was half unconscious from blood loss, Dad. If I hadn't cauterized the artery, he'd be dead already."

Sher pushed herself to catch up. She slowed her son even more. "Which artery? Bailey, what happened exactly?"

Bailey stumbled through the trees, trying to slow when his legs wanted to race. "I was jogging with Laylea," he cut off his Dad before he could even ask the question, "Yes, slow enough for her. We heard Parker and Davis saying hi to someone. I ran closer and I couldn't see the guy real well but he looked like a brown Yeti."

"Bigfoot," Clark automatically supplied.

"Yeah. He was chopping down a tree and when the guys stopped to talk to him, he pushed the tree over at them. Parker ran. But Davis got caught in the branches. One broken branch spiked his left leg and the trunk trapped his body. I thought he was crushed. I could have," he stumbled again, pushing off a tree to keep upright, "I could have got there but I kept thinking Davis and Parker and this bigfoot would see and then the Consortium would come for you, Dad." A sob rolled in. "But I did go, following Laylea's pace and when we got to him, there was blood everywhere. Parker was covered in it because it was just spurting from Davis' leg. I know you're not supposed to pull things out but Parker didn't. He saw that, that living stake in his brother and he pulled it out. I swear to god, he didn't see me do it. I made sure my body was between us. And I pulled off my jacket and tied it around the leg after to explain why the blood stopped. Davis was screaming and I wanted to lift the tree off him, but— Dad! Please can we run faster? A . . . A little faster?"

"Bailey," Sher stopped her son. She took him by both arms and held him in place with all of her strength despite her burning lungs. "This is important. You cauterized the femoral artery?"

Bailey nodded. His eyes were too full with tears to see clearly. But Clark saw terror cross his wife's face.

"Go." Her voice was firm but painfully quiet. "Clark," she nodded slightly, giving him permission to run full out, "Go."

Clark took her medical bag and the boys ran. Sher followed as best she could. Five minutes later she could hear distant shouting and she was met by a frantic Laylea, blood dripping from her little body. The dog skittered to a stop. Sher bent over her knees, gasping for breath.

"Do—" She waited another moment, telling her lungs to relax. "Is he alive?"

Laylea barked so hard her head bobbed.

"Go."

Laylea took off, stopping every now and then to be sure Sher was behind her. She detoured a couple of times and after tripping through a rock quarry when she didn't trust the dog, Sher followed her exactly. Clark, Parker, and Bailey waited for her.

"Should we lift?" Clark asked.

At the same time Parker told her, "Clark said to wait for you."

"Give me a second." Sher had to climb through the branches to get to Davis's side. She heard the boy cry out as she moved the tree. She cried back, "Davis, what's your name?"

After a moment, the boy replied, "Davis Fitz Rucker."

His voice was strained but she heard nothing bubbling in the tone. Nothing to indicate his lungs were punctured.

"Boy your mom likes jazz, huh?" She fell out of the branches into wet leaves and barely heard Davis' slow response.

"Dad named us. He plays tenor sax."

"Really?" She liked the strength in his voice. "Bailey plays the tuba. Not much call for jazz tuba these days."

Sher pushed past the three waiting to lift the tree. Parker crouched closest to his brother and Sher laid a hand on him as she looked over Davis. "Breathe, Parker. Let the blood flow."

She didn't wait to see if his body responded to her suggestions. She set a cold hand on either side of Davis' face and crooned, "Sleep. Go ahead and sleep and get warm."

When his eyes floated shut, she hunkered down and reached under his shoulders to grip his armpits. Behind her, Laylea scampered through the leaves, dragging branches aside and nosing at rocks. Pretending to play, she cleared space for Sher to back into.

Sher squeezed Davis' head between her forearms to keep the neck straight. She took a breath, tensed her muscles, and called out, "Lift."

Sher pulled. Davis' body moved a few inches, then stopped when his pant leg caught on a branch. Laylea ducked under the tree and clamped down on the pants. She growled and tugged, throwing her head from side to side as she dug her Jack Russell legs into the dirt. Sher and Laylea both fell over when the pants ripped. Sher scrambled to get her feet under her while Laylea hopped back up and kept watch as the mom pulled Davis all the way out from under the tree.

She laid him down and began a full examination even as she yelled, "Clear."

"No!" Parker yelled as the tree's weight lowered his hands. "The dog."

Laylea barked twice, echoing Parker's *no* as she pulled her rear paws from the pit of mud that may have saved Davis from being crushed. Dragging hard with her front paws, she got herself free, growling fiercely at Sher when the doctor looked like she was going to leave her patient to help. Her legs popped free much as Davis' pants had and she rolled to safety, stopping when she hit the unconscious boy.

"Okay. Clear." Parker fell to his knees when they finally dropped the tree trunk.

Bailey imitated him. Clark rubbed his arms but he moved over, ready to lift Davis on Sher's word.

"Spine seems okay. Some minor cuts. Some worse."

Clark leaned in and murmured, "leg?"

Sher barely shook her head. "Get him to the ambulance."

Clark didn't wait for any further confirmation. He lifted the boy with barely a grunt and sat on the trunk to swing his legs over. He was nearly out of sight before Parker was over and after him. Bailey went to follow but Sher tugged at his sweatpants. "Stay with Parker. Don't help him too much."

Bailey nodded. He cleared the trunk with one hand to assist and jogged after the others.

Sher brushed at the soaking mess of her pajama pants. She hitched her medical kit more securely on her shoulder and looked toward the base of the tree. It looked like several trees had been cleared from an area just beyond. An odd arrangement caught her attention and she picked her way toward it.

One short, high pitched cry drew her eyes down. Laylea looked up at her and quickly looked away. The dog tried to walk along the trunk but the left hip wouldn't take her weight.

"Oh, I hate that man." Sher picked up a rock and threw it into the deep woods.

The rock careened off a tree, crashing to a stop in some leaves. Sher fell silent. She palpated Laylea's hip and massaged it a bit before lifting the dog into her arms. They walked towards the tree stump. When they reached it, Sher glanced off in the direction the boys had run. Then she looked in the opposite direction, toward the remains of a rough lean-to at the edge of the clearing.

"No." Laylea was startled by the mom's rough voice. "Your bum hip is my fault, Laylea." She pushed off the stump and crossed the clearing. "I created this human research program to see what we could turn men into. And I didn't destroy it well enough when I left. Don't hate Hardknock. He's not a bad man. He hurt you because I created the conditioning program that hurt him."

She circled the pile of logs, rolling a few with one foot. She bent to touch a tanned hide that might have acted as a door. Under one corner of the hide she found a scrap of paper torn from a book. She brushed a little dirt from the page and read.

"'*Don't keep telling me what you hope!' Howled the little man. 'Keep listening to what I hope'. He pulled the bell rope savagely.*" She flipped the little scrap of page and read, "*You know where they catch that crook — that guy has a little finger off one hand and wears a glove to cover it up? That's Thurber. Was . . .*"

Sher stood. She looked around the area but saw nothing but trees and leaves and rocks. She couldn't see a forest the way Clark or Bailey could. And suddenly she felt uncomfortable out here by herself.

"Let's go home." She started to say Laylea's name but stopped herself.

She slogged through the wet forest, following the trail of broken branches and crushed leaves left in the boys' wake.

"Davis is lucky to have Parker. He'll take care of him. My big brother watched over me whenever I was hurting. Just like Bailey watches over you."

Laylea barked.

Sher wandered off in her thoughts for a while. When she spoke again it was like she was talking to herself. "He's gonna be okay. We'll train him and he won't make a mistake like this again."

Sher tripped. She caught herself against a trunk with just her shoulders and leaned there for a moment before pushing off to keep trudging forward. They had spotted the sequoia triplets that led to the line of bitter cherry trees that promised the stone walls would soon be in sight when a breeze rustled the treetops. Sher shivered.

"I'm carrying a blood-covered dog through a dew dappled forest in Hello Kitty pajamas and a pair of bright yellow galoshes." She wiped a hand along Laylea's back and down her tail. Her hand came away covered in brown and red. "You are getting a bath when we get home." She lifted Laylea and tilted her head at the dog. "Unless you want a shower?"

Laylea bared her teeth and growled.

"Okay." Sher brushed her wet hackles back. "A nice warm bath it is. For both of us."

Laylea settled into the crook of Sher's arm. She tried to keep her mind off her throbbing hip and Davis' cold dead leg by thinking of the nice warm bath followed by a full body rubbing with a sun-heated towel and a long snuggle with her dad, her brothers, and a book under a thick comforter.

CHAPTER 30

WINTER 2032 - FOOTHILLS, OR

Sher stomped the snow from her boots in the garage. The truck was still gone. She lifted her bike onto its ceiling hook beside Bailey's. A ten-year-old mountain bike leaned against the shelves. Sher hung her headlamp on the bike's handlebars and her heavy coat on the peg by the door. She took advantage of the truck's absence and squirted some oil into the never-used hinges of the rear garage door, mentally adding the escape route to her spring cleaning checklist.

She opened the kitchen door to enter a tropical forest based action film. She hung her bag on the hook by the door and grabbed a handful of nuts from the bowl on the center island. She stopped by the radio closet. The door was open. When she got closer she heard static coming from the set. She shut it down.

Woodford met her in the hallway. His tail circled wildly and when she bent to scritch his head he fell to his side and raised a leg.

"Oh, belly rubs, huh?" Sher complied, scratching up and down the rough fur on his chest and stomach.

Woodford followed her to the family room arch. He trotted under the two boys' legs propped on the coffee table and circled to his bed. Sher watched the boys' avatars swing around in treetops battling a pack of pterodactyls.

"Hey, Thomas."

The boy jumped. His green sweatshirt hood fell back. Nice to see the kid might be moving out of his all black phase.

He turned to smile at her without taking his hands off the controller. "Hi, Dr. Hillen."

Sher let them defeat the horde of colorful dinosaurs. The female avatars high-fived and leaped into their airship.

"Hey, Thomas, do you know what Bailey got on his math test?"

"Yeah, Dr. Hillen. He got a D."

Thomas' red-headed avatar stopped moving. The kid looked at Bailey and then over his shoulder at Sher.

"Gotta go, Bailey." He flipped his hood up and grabbed his book bag from the table. "See ya. Bye, Dr. Hillen."

"Bye, Thomas. Ride safe."

Bailey jumped up from the couch and ran after his friend. He avoided Sher's eyes.

Woodford ran after him. Sher shut down the game system and disconnected it from the TV. She gathered the bowl of popcorn and two empty glasses from the table, wiping away a wet ring with her sleeve. She'd bet Thomas had been the one using a coaster.

Light suddenly flashed overhead, snapping around the mirrors set in the corners of the ceiling. Sher crossed the room to raise the window shades. Her spirits rose as well at the sight of the battered old truck inching into the neighborhood. She felt for him and Laylea and breathed a sigh of relief that both were cold but safe. Lucky Lee lay tucked in Clark's lap under his jacket and seatbelt.

Sher joined Bailey in the garage in time to see Clark stop Thomas. She grabbed her jacket from the hook and went out to take Laylea.

"Welcome home." She kissed him, whispering, "The early warning system worked great."

"Great!" Clark's cheeks shone with the chill. "I'm gonna take Thomas home."

Thomas shook his head. "I'm fine."

"Don't worry. I'll drop you off by the church so you can say you were at the library." He kissed Laylea on the head and then his wife.

"Actually, I need to go to the library. I'm gonna get some textbooks on navigation."

"Drive safe."

"Okay," Thomas swung a leg off his bike. "I can ride home from the library."

"Only if they've plowed Elm. Help me put your bike in back." He kissed Sher again. "What a flight. We're starving."

"I'll have Bailey throw some dinner together."

Clark turned from dropping the gate. "Uh oh."

"We'll talk when you get home. Bye, Thomas." Sher took Laylea into the garage. "Bailey, inside."

Bailey pulled the carriage door closed and followed her. She set Laylea on the center island. They had taped a pad of paper on the counter and collected pencils from the Putt Putt in Hatch. Laylea picked up one of the pencils in her teeth.

She wrote *pairilus flight* and turned her big brown puppy dog eyes up to Sher.

Sher set the kettle on the stove. "Thank you. Two things to talk about."

Bailey shut the door and hustled to the pantry. He took a snake of felt-wrapped rice bags and stuck it in the microwave. Sher planted herself at the end of the island facing Bailey and Laylea.

"First," she began, "how was the powwow?"

Went ice skating! Judah and Flower took me this morning. My fault we're late.

"Not the storm?" Bailey transferred his sandwich fixings to the island.

Sher transferred the fixings back to the fridge. "If you're hungry, start dinner."

Whether wasn't bad in the air. Everyone worked together to dig out a runway.

Sher held Laylea's chin with her hand. "Are you just trying to keep Clark out of trouble?"

No. He was never worried.

Bailey stole a spoonful of peanut butter before his mother got to it. "How many times did you throw up?"

2

"They hit the storm." He snagged the bowl of cherries from the fridge along with an armload of veggies.

Laylea growled at her brother. *Maggie is woried about Jay playing "catch and releese."*

"He's catching CF and not reconditioning them?"

Sending them back.

Sher took the cutting board down. Why would Jay send any of Trask's victims back to her?

Maggie said he dosent know she knows. She gave us the idea to go ice skating. She almost fell on her butt. Laylea barked through the pencil. *Mom! Put a carpet on your scale!*

Sher looked away from dicing garlic when the scratching stopped.

"At the clinic? Why?"

Laylea's writing degraded with speed. *The skale is skary. It's slippery and cold.*

"A carpet would throw off the weight."

Bailey took the garlic. "I can recalibrate it for you."

"Really? Doesn't that take math?" Sher stood. "Laylea, anything else you need to tell us about the trip?

Tons!

"Too bad. Let's talk about you two. Bailey, you've already figured out you're on D I N N E R duty."

Woodford barked. He jumped up from his bed, wagging his tail. Sher dropped her head into a hand.

"When did he learn to spell that?"

Laylea sang. She wrote, *SMRT.*

"And you are not getting any more flying lessons until you can spell every word on this list." Sher pulled out Laylea's red-lined spelling test. She took the pencil and added *perilous, worried, release, scale, scary,* and *smart* at the bottom. "Every single one of these words came from books you've already read."

Laylea ducked her head, her ears pasted to her skull.

"Bailey, you will complete every single one of your math assignments, by yourself, AND pass a retest before Thomas is allowed over again."

"Mom. You're punishing Thomas too."

"Poor Thomas. He's suffering because you let your sister do your homework." Sher hid her pleasure at watching her little cheater pulling food and pans from the cupboards without looking at a recipe. "You will both be doing your schoolwork in the dining room or in here. And your dad and I will be keeping a closer eye on things." She sat at the counter. "Laylea, since you find math so easy, you're going to start studying physics."

Bailey groaned and pretended to barf over the sink. Laylea kept her head down but her tail gave away her excitement.

"While *you*, my son, will be adding canine anatomy to your official biology homework."

The microwave dinged. Laylea and Woodford both automatically looked at it. Bailey detoured to pull the rice snake out and tossed it to his mother. Sher lifted Laylea into her lap. She wrapped the warm cloth around her hips and kissed her head.

"Please stop helping your brother cheat."

Laylea barked once. Curled up with her muzzle on the mom's hand, watching her big brother cook, she wondered if any of her litter brothers had gotten as lucky as she had.

CHAPTER 31

WINTER 2033 - CONSORTIUM BIOTECH HQ, CA

Trask came into the office, turning completely to close the door behind her and take a moment to regain her calm. She ran both hands over her scars, fixed her hair, her skirt, and turned to push brusquely past the privacy curtain, only to stop short. She froze facing the angry muzzle of a ten-pound chocolate colored mutt. It wore a harness connected to a leg of the desk by what appeared to be the chain of a ship's anchor. It stood with front legs spread, back legs crouched as it decided whether or not to pounce from the top of the desk.

Everything that should have been on the desk was now on the floor except for a classified folder with its contents spread across the desk, Walter's blotter, and her gifted legal pad flipped open to a page covered in penciled redactions. Her monitor had hit her chair leaving glass shards on the seat before falling to swing from its cord just over the floor. Trask looked for the hated buffalo and was momentarily cheered to see it had flown all the way to the window and was tangled in the bird curtains' draw chain. Then she looked back at the tiny bared teeth in front of her and the smile faded.

The click of a code being entered on the other side of the door was followed by Walter striding past the curtain with a long pole in his hand.

"You've met Bayard. And how are you getting on?"

The dog finally decided to risk it and pounce. He leaped from the desk at Trask. Even as the chain stopped him short, Walter caught him and slipped the loop of the dogcatcher's pole over his neck. Before Bayard could get his teeth into Walter's hand, the man threw himself backwards and held Bayard at the length of the pole.

"Bayard is one of my missing subjects. The runt, I'm praying."

"Do they get nicer when they're bigger?"

"Smarter, I hope."

Trask smoothed her skirt modestly as best she could on the floor where she'd fallen. "It's trying to kill you at the moment. It can't be that dumb."

The dog stopped snapping at Walter for a moment and turned to glance at Trask at this remark. Walter took the moment to roll onto his knees and Bayard turned his growl back at the Therian researcher.

"I'm trying to give you a better life, Bayard. They were putting you in danger. Just look at you. You're covered in scars." Walter spoke in a sweet voice as he duck-walked over to the foot of the desk.

"Where did you find him?" Trask resigned herself to having a conversation while sitting on the floor.

Walter kept Bayard at a distance, pushing him back with the pole as he moved forward. Trask saw this and scooched back from where she had fallen. She reached the door before she stopped, the privacy curtain bunched on her head. She shoved it aside and halfheartedly tried to fix her destroyed coiffure as Walter unhooked the chain from the desk leg and gently dragged the dog, speaking lovingly to it, over to where he attached the chain to the lowest handle of the farthest file cabinet. Trask smirked. Even the tiny dog could easily rip the handle from the wood of that cabinet.

Walter took a moment to breathe once he had the chain moved. "We found him in a town not far from Hatch."

"Hatch, that's where you found the bicycle shop Rhea was hiding them in before she got the drop on you again."

"Yes." Walter held the little dog still with the pole as he edged along the file cabinets and back toward the door. He handed the long handle of the dog pole to Trask. "Twist it as you hold it to keep the loop closed. But pull him forward a bit like this so that he's at the end of the chain."

Trask slipped off her shoes. She rolled to her knees and took the pole in both hands. Walter kept a hand on it while he used the other to fish in the pocket of his vest. He took out a syringe, uncapping it with his teeth as he left Trask.

"She'd dumped him at the fire station. They have a sign on the front door that says *Don't abandon your baby. Safe Surrender.* That's where Rhea left him." Walter laughed a moment.

The dog lunged at him but Trask pulled on the pole and Walter safely circled around Bayard. The dog could only stare at him from the corner of his eye as Trask held him tightly at the length of the chain. Walter got next to the dog, trusting Trask to keep his head controlled. "The firefighters kept him as their mascot. He didn't even have a home, sleeping at the firehouse and going on calls with them. That's what all the scars are from, aren't they, my precious? Those men did not take good care of my little boy." He stuck the syringe in Bayard's haunches and emptied it. The dog fell into a forced sleep, his lips snarling to the very end.

Trask held the dog pole tight until Walter tugged it from her hands.

"We had a bit of a witness problem when we took Bayard." He pulled the loop over the dog's head, unclipped the chain from the harness and scooped Bayard into his arms to lay him on the desk while he straightened the office up. He flinched when he swept the redacted legal pad off his blotter to make room.

Trask let him clean. "You mean you did some recruiting."

"I've named him Felix."

"I thought its name was Bayard."

"What?" Walter looked up from his examination of the buffalo. "Not the dog. The volunteer. Dr. Jones claimed him."

Trask slowly stood and straightened herself. "Volunteers in my program do not get names. We've discussed this."

She looked at the still form on her desk. The dog was more appealing unconscious. For one, his teeth were hidden. He had shaggy brown fur except for his spotted back left paw and a tuft of white on his right ear. The ears were too long for the face, his body a bit too sturdy for his short legs. He had no extra fat on him though he did have quite a few scars. His tail was cut short but not short enough to be fashionable in the AKC crowd.

"Nicole and I decided to share the volunteer. She thought a two hundred series erasure would be the best base for what we plan." He lifted her monitor back onto the desk and unplugged it. "Division four is closest to my kennels and she says a level four instinctual conditioning would be appropriate to the basic physical reboot my division will oversee."

Once she'd gotten her hair in place, Trask circled the far side of her desk chair and leaned over the monitor to gather the strewn papers on her desk back into the folder labeled Gamma Subject Intake Profile.

"Congratulations on your recovery." She glanced over the still body. "I hope he's everything you've hoped for. I'll go oversee 244's intake."

Walter didn't stop cleaning. "*Felix* 244, please."

Trask tucked the folder under her arm. "Will you be putting Bayard in the kennels before he wakes?"

"For bonding, it's best he stay near me."

Trask crossed to the door. "I'll have a crate delivered. You can keep him in our office only if he's inside the cage when he's conscious. Should he undergo a successful personality transplant we can revisit the arrangement. I will see that Felix 244 is being well cared for and then I'll be debriefing Jones." She pulled the privacy curtain closed behind her.

Trask paused by the mirror to check her hair. A strange expression curled up the corners of her mouth. Trask was happy Walter had returned to his unbearable old self.

THE DIRECTOR FLIPPED to a set of shots showing Walter's yellow college-ruled legal pad. Walter never stayed within the lines. The pages were covered with doodles wherever notes weren't scrawled in his prescription-quality handwriting. The Director focused on three blackened pages. Notes from his previous trip with Dr. Jones into the mountain villages. Notes on directions. An address. The name Laylea, repeated multiple times. Sketches of a woman's face and of a dog. All violently scratched out. When reviewing his notes, Walter had not transcribed these pages. He'd flipped past these three pages as if they didn't exist. The pad sat on his desk blotter, untouched for over a year. Organized clutter continued to rule the blotter side of the partner desk everywhere around the legal pad. Until the chaos of Bayard, the pad itself rested ignored as if covered by a force field.

The Director combined the three cleaned images with the redacted originals onto a screen in his peripheral vision and pinned them there for the next hour to let his unconscious mind consider the conundrum yet again. His conscious mind moved on to the more mundane task of reviewing possible scientific renegades spotted through phone call and text data mined from the University of Chicago's student roster. This job had been made immeasurably tougher by a recent Second City sketch on bioterrorism. A little personal recruiting trip might refresh the Bio Research department's selections, solve the lack of qualified scientists problem, and satisfy his doctor's insistence that he get outside more. He opened a link to his assistant, then remembered how cold it was in Chicago and shut it down again.

CHAPTER 32

WINTER 2033 - FOOTHILLS, OR

"Dinner's ready. Laylea, go get everyone."

Laylea lifted her nose. She peeled an eye open. Bailey stood poised with his wooden spoon over the rice pot. Food was ready. He had a working voice box. She barked twice without opening her mouth and tucked her nose back into her belly.

"Laylea, wake up," Bailey crooned through her dream. She flicked an ear at him.

"Laylea, you caught the rabbit and we made sausage," he tried again. Laylea rubbed at her nose with a paw. She smelled meaty goodness.

Her eyes popped open. Bailey held a hunk of sausage and three triangles of zucchini in front of her. Laylea snatched them. And burnt her mouth. She sat up and let the food dribble out to the red vinyl seat of her kitchen stool.

"Hot?" Bailey grinned.

Laylea barked. She looked around the kitchen. The mom had been cooking when she went to sleep. Her apron was still missing from its hook. Davis' letter was also still sitting on the island, unopened. Laylea stood up and tapped it with a paw.

"He's loving Northwestern. Parker's asked his girlfriend to marry him. She's asked him to quit football. There's nothing in the letter I can't guess."

Laylea barked twice and pushed the letter at him.

Bailey slapped a hand down to keep the white envelope from sliding off the countertop. "The letter ends *thank you for saving my life* and includes a picture of his newest leg." Bailey kept his eyes down, on the return address. "Your sausage is getting cold." He stuck the letter in his apron pocket and turned back to the stove.

Laylea ate the food and licked her stool clean. She hopped down the three steps and ran off to find the parents.

A few minutes later Clark and Woodford dashed into the kitchen. Woodford padded over to Bailey while Clark hid beside the door. He jumped out when Sher came in carrying Laylea and dipped them. Sher and Laylea both protested and kissed him.

"Easy there, Captain. Lee's having a rough day." Sher guarded Laylea's hip with an arm as Clark spun them up out of the kiss.

"The cold weather makes her limp."

"The cold contracts the muscles and that aggravates her damaged nerves." Sher massaged the joint. "If only you were human, Lee. I could make you heal yourself." Sher sunk into her thoughts. She stood by the pantry, massaging Laylea, and looking a million miles away.

"Mom?" Bailey offered her the spoon.

"I got this, kid." Clark kissed Laylea's head and took her from his wife. "Sustenance makes brain work better, woman."

Sher blinked. She didn't laugh but she managed to help Bailey serve up the human's sausage and vegetables over rice while the dad set Laylea on the food mat beside Woodford. He dished up kibble for both of them and took their bowls to the stove. Bailey added a spoonful of juice and a piece of sausage to each.

The humans settled around the island counter. Throughout dinner, Clark accidentally dropped pieces of squash into Laylea's bowl. Woodford considered vegetables on par with poison. Normally Sher would have objected to feeding Laylea from the table, but she didn't say a word. Clark stole a piece of zucchini from her plate to confirm her absence.

"Well, Mom's on a different planet."

Bailey didn't miss a beat. "Mom's from a different planet."

"Be nice now. We're all weirdos sometimes."

Bailey shoveled food into his mouth before returning, "Or all the time."

Clark was finding the teenage years to be just as difficult as advertised. Ever the Pollyanna, he trudged onward.

"We're thinking of going to the cabin for a weekend to do some repairs. What do you say we start training? See what you can do."

"I've got marching band every weekend."

Clark choked back his laugh. "*Every* weekend?"

"Yeah, it's competition season. Not like Foothills High has a backup tuba."

"I get that." He wiped his mouth. "I get that. Not many kids can carry a tuba and march at the same time."

"Yeah, anyone can. Just no one else plays tuba at my school."

The three ate in silence. Bailey took a couple pieces of the squash Clark had pushed to the side of his plate. Sher ate but with her eyes focused on a space deep inside her own mind.

"Okay, kid." Clark tossed the last squash slices into Laylea's bowl and set down his fork. "Do you know what's going on with Mom?"

"No."

Clark looked down at Laylea. She tilted her head at him.

Clark took his glass to the sink for more water. On his way back he bent and poured some into the dogs' bowl. "You don't know what's going on with Mom?"

Laylea licked her muzzle. She trotted over to the Magic Slate they'd taped to the ground. Using a claw, she scratched out *new tek? Early warning lights?*

Clark wrote *tech* and then lifted the top page to clear the writing. "I don't know. This isn't her normal new tech fugue." He rubbed Laylea's ear and returned to the counter. "Hey Sher. What's going on in there? You okay?"

"Give it up, Dad. She's done for."

Laylea and Clark both perked up to hear Bailey start a joke.

Laylea barked twice. Clark turned a stern gaze on his son. "Don't say that."

"No. It's true," Bailey insisted, still eating. "She's done for."

"Bailey, son," Clark gripped the counter, shaking it. "Don't say that."

"Don't waste your time, Dad." Bailey finally giggled. He leaned in on an elbow and whispered to Laylea, "She's totally done for."

"Don't say that." Clark slammed his napkin on the table. "Never end your sentence with a preposition."

The boys laughed. Laylea rolled on her belly and got foot rubs. Sher sat with a spoon halfway to her mouth. When the giggles had faded away, the boys stared at her.

"This is really weird," Bailey admitted. "Can I have her food?"

"No." Clark took the spoon from Sher's hand and she finally looked at him. She raised her eyebrows and gestured at the stolen utensil.

"I said, what's going on in there?" He ate the food and gave the spoon back. "Can we help?"

Sher snatched the spoon from Bailey when he tried to take it. "No. It's a problem with one of my patients."

"What's going on? Maybe talking it out will provide a solution."

"No." She ate a bite. When the boys didn't stop staring at her she added, "Don't stress about it."

Bailey grunted into his next bite, "You're stressed about it."

Laylea barked. She'd scratched *address* on her sketchpad.

Clark laughed. "I believe Laylea is saying if you address the problem you won't have time to stress over it."

Bailey turned to the dog food rug. "Hey, can Laylea help?"

"How could *she* help?" Sher scoffed.

"She's a dog. Your patient is a dog." Bailey kicked his stool back to get more food.

His parents watched him go.

"Sorry." She took a sip of water. "Too many geniuses in one kitchen."

"Tell us the problem and we'll see if there's a way she could help." Bailey picked up his fork. "Or do we keep secrets from each other now too?"

"I have a Schnauzer limping on a paw that has nothing wrong with it. Plus, Herrhund won't let me touch him when the family is present."

Laylea wrote, *I can help.*

"Woodford can pinpoint where the problem is and Laylea can maybe help you understand why he's limping," Clark offered.

"That's a lot of translation," Sher replied. "Pain to dog. Dog to English. English to doctor."

Laylea wrote *Is he in pane?*

Sher took another pencil and wrote PAIN on the sheet as she nodded, "He is."

"Then you should try." Bailey pointed out as Laylea wrote *We make better.*

Sher flashed a glance at Clark, "If I take Laylea to work," she looked back at Bailey, "you have to go to the cabin with us Christmas weekend. You don't have marching band events that weekend." Sher wanted to add a requirement that he submit to their strength testing but Bailey wasn't the easy-going boy he'd been. "And you," before Bailey could reply Sher turned to the dog. "You need to answer one question truthfully."

Laylea nodded, her head low.

"Did you eat all of Clark's squash?"

Laylea pinned her ears back. She wrapped her tail tightly around her feet and lay down. Her big brown eyes ping-ponged between Clark and Sher. When Clark shrugged a shoulder at her, she barked. And then she barked again.

"That's my girl!" Clark scooped Laylea off the counter before Sher could reach her.

The mom calmly picked up her spoon. "Too bad. I'll have to help that sick dog on my own."

"Mom." Bailey sat and picked up his fork. "She's not lying. I stole some of Dad's squash."

CHAPTER 33

WINTER 2033 - FOOTHILLS, OR

The family rose at the crack of dawn. Clark and Bailey followed Sher to work and left her with the two dogs. Even as early as Sher was, Michelle already sat at the reception desk, enjoying a gourmet coffee and the paper.

"Good morning, Dr. Sher." Michelle swung her legs off the desk. "Jim and Kenny are couple of mucus factories. I got em up. Fed em breakfast and drugs. Put them back to bed. It was like a snot symphony serenading me from both bedrooms so I thought I'd come enjoy a quiet morning here."

While Michelle chattered on, Woodford trotted over and curled up in his bed beside the desk.

Sher flipped through the mail. "That can't be from our coffee maker then."

"I used that French press your man brought us. But I stole Jim's birthday coffee. And my mother's French vanilla creamer." She crooned down at Laylea. "Delicious. Oh! Both dogs are here today. First time ever."

Sher searched for an explanation but as Laylea curled up right in her big brother's belly, Michelle provided her own.

"Isn't she the sweetest? She just adores him, doesn't she? Do you think she knows how old he is and that he's not gonna be around for much longer and so she wants to spend as much time with him as she can? I wish that I had had that sense before my father died. I regret now, so much that I didn't take every opportunity I could. Well, you two just enjoy yourselves today. You are a lucky boy, Woodford."

And she gave them each a giant Milkbone. Woodford took his and relocated to the blanket back in the corner of the filing room. Before he could settle though, Sher called him.

"Well you enjoy your morning. Woodford, Lee, come on. Let's remind you where the bathroom is."

She led them to the back. Woodford followed reluctantly but he did as he was told. They followed Sher past the new treatment table to the kennels. Laylea recoiled at the waves of fear. She scooted out of the way as Sher awkwardly carried a fifty-pound schnauzer to the backyard.

After gaining his feet, Herrhund squatted and peed like a girl. When he limped away, Woodford noticed. Sher's big boy sniffed along the taller dog's chest. He completely ignored the limping paw. Woodford scanned the dog until he found a spot on Herrhund's ribcage just behind the leg. Woodford touched his nose to the spot and held there. When Herrhund moved, Woodford moved with him.

Laylea barked once and led Sher toward the door. They left Herrhund to deal with OCD Woodford. Inside, Sher set Laylea and Herrhund's chart on the counter in exam room C.

Laylea stood on Sher's chest. Sher started to pick her up but the little dog grabbed the pen clipped to her coat and used it to point at the chest on the body diagram. Sher took the pen. She flipped off the cap and gave it back. Choking a little, Laylea wrote *breathing hurts.*

Sher stuck the business end of the stethoscope in her armpit while she carried Laylea back out to the yard. Though she'd left the door open, both boys were still standing as they had been. Sher kneeled in front of Herrhund.

"Okay, Mr. Dog, let's take some pictures, what do you say?"

After the x-rays confirmed a broken rib, Sher started Herrhund on a course of steroids and settled the dog in a padded crated where he could rest sitting up which would be easier on his ribs. Laylea curled up in front of the crate.

Laylea stayed with Herrhund for most of the day. Later in the morning, Chris brought the portable ultrasound over to the crate. Despite Laylea's efforts to assure him Chris was a good guy, Herrhund wouldn't let the tech touch him. Sher came back looking for Laylea and got the tests done in a proverbial heartbeat.

"I'm borrowing Laylea for a minute."

"Sure, Doc." As they left the room, they heard him mumbling to the dog. "Something must be really wrong with you, pup. No one likes the doc better than me."

Sher paused in Exam C. "I've got a stoic dog in B. Glover never gives me any clues. Can you tell if she's in pain?"

Laylea barked once and they continued on in to see the patient. The owner sat on the floor with a dappled greyhound leaning on his lap.

"This is Laylea." Sher set her down backwards in front of Glover. "She's one of those dogs that can sniff out a wound. Mind if we give it a shot?"

"Sure. If you think it could help."

Laylea obediently sniffed the greyhound all over. Glover watched the smaller dog with half closed eyes. When Laylea reached her tail, the greyhound grunted. She turned away from Laylea and poked her muzzle under her dad's hand.

Laylea barked twice and then tagged at Glover's tail like Woodford would. Sher carried Laylea to the counter in room C. Laylea grabbed a pen. She waited for Sher to give her something to write on.

Glands. Constipated.

"The one would cause problems with the other." Sher put Laylea on the ground and they returned to Exam B. "Hi, David. You said her bathroom habits haven't changed?"

"No," David said. "She goes out in the yard at six in the morning, when I get home, and ten at night."

Sher waited in case he had more to say. "Yes, but is she actually pooping normally?

"Oh, I don't know that." He looked appalled. "My gardener scoops the poop."

Sher nodded. "Okay. Here's what's going on with her."

Laylea got bored when Sher started her treatment talk. She pushed through the door to reception and curled up with Woodford in his bed.

Woodford slept for most of the day behind Michelle. He'd wake up to get water and stretch. Armando was setting a Bichon mix on the scale while he was getting water once and Woodford turned as the owner stepped up beside him. He sniffed. He left the water, dripping of course on the waiting room floor, and walked closer to the owner. He sniffed his leg. Weigh-in accomplished, the owner followed Armando into Exam B. Woodford went along. Laylea followed them. In Exam B, the owner stopped moving and Woodford sniffed his other leg. He put his nose on the guy's shin and glued it there.

"What's wrong with this dog? Should I be scared?"

Armando shook his head. "Woodford? He's harmless. Did you walk through a flowerbed? I know he likes roses." Armando tried to pull him away but Woodford had a good solid stubborn stance working for him.

Armando stepped over to the swinging door and hollered into the back room. "Hey, Dr. Sher. Can you come look at your crazy dog?"

Sher came with her hands held in front of her, surgeon style. "What is Laylea doing now?"

"Not Laylea. Your big boy."

Sher looked down at Woodford. Then she looked into the owner's face. "Do you have any bruises or cuts on that leg?"

He smiled, flirting. "Just a mosquito bite. Trying to ignore it actually. I know I'm not supposed to scratch, Doctor."

"What's your name again?

"Stephen."

"Do you mind if I take a look, Stephen?"

"Not at all." He lifted the pant leg, keeping a close eye on Woodford as he did.

Sher looked at the spot Woodford had tagged. There was a small bump like a mosquito bite. And surrounding it was a subtler swelling and several rings of angry red. She looked up to see Armando wincing at the wound. He schooled his features when she raised an eyebrow at him.

Stephen," Sher leaned around the owner to make a note on the dog's chart. "You need to stop self-medicating and go to your doctor.

We'll keep Elmo here, free of charge, so you don't have to drop him off at home. But you have to promise me that you won't take any more medications until you are done driving for the day."

"I'm fine," he insisted.

"You're not," she informed him. "You can't help Elmo if you're not thinking straight. You have to put your own mask on first before assisting others. Armando, can you make sure Stephen gets off safely. And get Woodford a cookie. Elmo and I are gonna go get some shots." She picked up Stephen's dog and walked away into the back.

"She... she just took my dog."

"The doctor can be like that." Armando opened the door to reception. "Do you have a local GP you can call? Dr. Pantras is mine and he's a good guy with short notice."

"Yeah, he's my doctor." Stephen followed Armando slowly. He seemed to not fully believe what was going on.

"Fabulous. You can walk. Michelle will call and tell his receptionist you're on your way. Bye." Armando pushed on Stephen's lower back and shut the front door behind him. "Michelle, can you let Dr. Pantras know we're sending Stephen over with a necrotizing spider bite?" Armando took a cookie from the jar for Woodford. "He's got a fever and is probably doing some serious self-medicating."

Michelle picked up the phone. "Elmo?"

"He's staying with us until the doc says otherwise. Thanks, Michelle."

Woodford was asleep before the call connected.

Laylea pushed through to the back room. She found Sher ruffling the Bichon's fur as she set him in a crate. Nobody else was around. Laylea barked. When Sher looked at her, she tilted her head and tagged Sher's ankle.

"I couldn't heal it. He would have noticed." Sher sighed. "We have to stay hidden. For the whole family's safety."

Laylea sighed.

"Come on, Lee. Let's go for a walk." Sher stood.

They left Woodford in the clinic. Sher led Laylea across the town square to the library. Sher carried Laylea to the old people's section. This was the area with shelves that were only filled a few rows above and below eye height. And all the books were printed with enormous lettering.

Sher strolled along each aisle, looking up and down the shelves and crouching down so that Laylea could see all the titles. She barked when she recognized *Cujo*. But Sher shushed her.

"You can't bark in here. Can you tag my arm when you see one you like?"

Laylea tagged Sher's arm with her nose.

"Do you want to read *Cujo*?"

Laylea looked up at Sher and shook her head. Sher laughed.

In the end Laylea picked out five books. Sher's favorite selection was *Mia Dethica's Guide to Patience in Dog Training*. After checking out and being civil to a few patrons who were drawn to Laylea, they strolled back to the clinic.

Sher carried Laylea most of the way so she could speak quietly. "You've been very helpful today. Above and beyond normal family chores. We all work together. You see that. Clark and I do jobs to support the family. You and Bailey are kids so your work right now is school. We push Bailey to learn as much as he can about everything so that when it comes time for him to have an income job, he'll be better equipped to find and land one that will make him happy. He does chores as well, like we all do. And if he does more than his share or something extra like weeding, he gets a reward. For him it's games. Clark gets fancy seeds. I get bourbon. Today you did above and beyond. You should think of something you would like..." Laylea barked several times and struggled to get down.

She ran to a spot of mud. The only person nearby was a blind woman tapping her way along another path. Laylea scratched in the mud. Sher read what the dog had written and wiped it out with her foot. She bent down.

"No. I don't care how above and beyond you go, I am not going to let you eat the Ricks' cat."

Laylea started tracing an *L* in the mud. Sher picked her up.

"No, I'm not going to let you eat it even just a little. I took you to

217

the library as a reward for today." Laylea licked Sher's cheek. "Thanks. You should think of what you might want next time."

Laylea turned her head and bent over to chew gently on Sher's thumb.

"Wish I could help you with that, Lee. I want my family. Clark wants his memories. Bailey," she sighed. "Bailey wants to turn back time. You want thumbs. I don't think there's much hope for any of us."

Sher set Laylea down to walk the rest of the way to the clinic. Laylea stayed right by her side, tagging the mom's leg every few feet.

THE DIRECTOR SWIPED to the camera view showing the front door of the clinic. He set it to auto scan the footage from the moment it had gone operational. It slowed every time a person entered frame. Only two days of footage skimmed by before the good doctor showed up with her little tricycle and the dogs. She rolled the bike inside and waved over her shoulder. The Director skimmed through the listing of angles. He pulled up a wide shot from the nearby telephone pole. They'd been unable to get any cameras working inside the clinic or even attached to the outside of the building. He'd love to know how Coogan had managed that little trick.

He typed in the time code and the wide shot jumped to show two bicycles sticking out beyond an SUV parked at the curb.

"Come on. Come on."

The bikes rolled back. The Director pulled up one of the four traffic cams they'd charged the city to install. Bingo. Two bikes. A man rode one. A boy the other. Jumping from camera to camera, the Director followed the pair to the local school. Two buildings separated by a small courtyard served the entire population of Foothills throughout their education years. The man watched as the boy locked up his bike.

The Director watched as Theta hopped off his bike to hug his son and hand him off to a dour kid in a black trench coat. The kid said something drowned out by the buzz of all the other kids messing around on the playground before first bell. But the son, Bailey, punched him and the two laughed all the way into the school.

He messaged his operative. *Tag the blue and grey hybrid behind the school: audio/video/tracking*

The Director's hand hovered over the archive button as he turned back to the still frame of the little dog nosing Dr. Coogan's leg.

"The witch and the warrior have a son." He chuckled. "Now we have a ballgame."

CHAPTER 34

FALL 2034 - FOOTHILLS, OR

"Mom!" Laylea looked up. Bailey's piercing voice startled her from the book she was reading with Clark on the porch swing. The solar lamps had judged it dark enough to flip on thanks to the dark clouds racing in from the mountains. Woodford, their new teenager, slept on. His muzzle rested on the purple dragon the Ruckers had given him for his birthday. The boys had brought it over along with Parker's toddler and they'd all played on the porch until she'd fallen on Woodford one too many times. Screams rivaling Bailey's pitch still carried from the OLR's yard where the boys rolled around in the grass with Ella.

Bailey sat at the porch table, working on college applications. Laylea had expected him to go inside when the Ruckers came over. She knew how hard it was for him to see Davis showing off his latest prosthetic leg. But Bailey stayed. Laylea wondered if he stayed to punish himself.

"Mom!"

"She's in her tinkering room, kiddo." Clark put a finger on the page to hold his place. "Can I help?"

"Why do I have to go so far away?"

"You don't. You pick the school, kiddo."

Bailey stared across the street. Ella had started crying. Parker held her on one hip as he crouched beside his brother. It took them two tries to get Davis to his feet. Bailey's shoulders rose. He tucked his head. If he had a tail, it would be curled tight against his belly. Great big drops of rain splattered down on the house at the end of the cul-de-sac.

"What's got you scared?"

"We just have so many secrets to keep." He leaned his head on a fist. "Maybe Mom could make me forget everything I'm not supposed to know."

The screen door cracked against the frame. Even the Ruckers looked over before they disappeared into the backyard.

"You would ask me," Sher's voice carried no further than the porch and sent icicles down Laylea's spine, "to maim my own child?"

Dust made her hair the white of a grandmother's. Splotches of grease took the place of blush on her cheeks. She wiped a hand on her white work apron before holding the screen door open.

Bailey tried to explain, "Mom—"

She stopped him. "Inside."

"Mom—"

"Laylea, Clark, take Woodford for a walk before the storm hits. Bailey, inside."

"Mom. It would solve everything."

Sher released the door. She took a step over to put her back to the neighborhood. "I made your father forget. Think he's thanked me? I made Jay forget. Trey, Maggie, Feranda. I made them all forget. And these new victims. I designed the procedures that wiped out all of their memories as well. Do you think, Bailey, that any one of them would thank me for it?"

"You wouldn't do it like that. If you make me forget, it'll keep you and Dad and Laylea safe."

Clark added, "and Woodford?"

"Woodford doesn't have any secrets." Bailey rubbed a foot along the dog's fur.

"That we know of."

"Bailey," Sher put a hand on his papers, "I can't pick individual memories out of your brain."

"Well, how should I know that?" Bailey slammed down his pen.

Sher laughed harshly. She walked away from Bailey and pounded a fist on the porch railing. "You shouldn't. I shouldn't expect you to know anything," she crossed back, "because teaching you how to keep our secrets was more important to me than teaching you about our powers."

Thunder rolled in the distance.

"I don't want to learn about our powers. I won't ever use magic again."

Clark chuckled. Sher threw her head back as silent laughs shook her whole body.

When she could breathe again she told him, "You use it every day."

"I do not. I never use magic." He looked to his father to back him up.

He didn't. "Kiddo, you made that baby girl fall down so that Davis would go away."

Bailey rolled his eyes. "He's my friend. Why would I want him to go away?"

Sher answered. "Because it's your fault he lost his leg."

Lightning lit up the sky.

"Sher." Clark half-stood from the swing.

"Bailey." All laughter had fled Sher's voice. "You listen to me. Or I'll make you listen." She waited until she had his full attention, his eyes. "It's your fault he has *that* leg, the one he designed himself. It's your fault he has a purpose in his life now other than adoring his older brother. It's your fault he's alive." She looked down at the small worktable for a moment and then back into his eyes. "It's my fault he lost the leg."

Bailey stuttered, "You . . . you weren't even there."

"No, I wasn't. I wasn't there when you needed to be taught how to use your powers. I told your father we should let you have a childhood."

"That's bullshit, Mom."

"Bailey," Clark interrupted.

"No, Dad. It's bullshit. I've had these powers all my life. There is nothing you could have taught me that would change anything."

"Really?"

Sher turned and walked into the house. The screen door slammed behind her.

Bailey picked up his pen and engraved some answers into the application.

"Kid." Clark looked at Laylea but his tone made it clear he was giving Bailey an ultimatum.

Rain pounded on the porch ceiling and a gust of wind shuffled Bailey's application papers. He took a breath to argue with his Dad.

"Kid."

The look on Clark's face convinced him to shut up and follow his mother inside.

"We'll be in shortly."

"Okay, Dad."

Bailey stopped in the doorway, listening to his dad mumbling his old song as he encouraged the two dogs down the steps.

"I will not kill another soul today. His life is in my hands and I will not throw it away."

Bailey first looked in Sher's tinkering room but she wasn't there although the place smelled just like the sizzling lightning outside. He started up the stairs but a noise in the kitchen drew him through the swinging door. The garage door stood open. The racket came from out there.

Bailey left his application papers on the kitchen island. He found his mother in the garage working on his bicycle. She had it sitting upside down on the saddle and handlebars. The front wheel spun as she dragged a tire lever along the rim. She snaked the flattened tube out and tossed it to the cement. After working the tire off the rim, she unscrewed the axle and threw that bolt aside. She lifted the wheel out of the dropout, removed the tire, and set the rim, spokes, and hub aside. Bailey didn't know what to say as she repeated the process with the rear wheel.

She dipped the adjusting barrel, removed the chain and grabbed a multitool to split the chain and unscrew the pedals.

"What are you doing?"

She flipped through the wrenches and removed the water bottle cage, brakes, cables, chain rings, seat post, saddle, fork, handlebars, head-lamp, and bell.

"You've had a bike all your life." She handed him the black and yellow multi-tool and plastic lever. "You've got the tools you need."

Bailey stared while Sher wiped her hands on the once-white tinkering apron. She picked her way through the pieces of his former bicycle to open the passenger side door of the truck. She hopped up and sat with her legs dangling out, watching him.

"Put it together."

"Mom, I'm gonna need this to go to school tomorrow."

"So, put it together."

Bailey fumed for exactly five seconds. Then he grabbed the pump from beside the steps and gathered the pieces of his front tire. He reassembled each tire. He reattached the water bottle cage to the frame and the light and bell to his handlebars. He screwed on the right pedal but couldn't get the left one to seat in the threads and when he tried to force it, the wrench slipped out and scraped all the skin off his knuckles. He was working on reattaching the fork to the frame when Laylea limped out. She did downward dog off the bottom step.

Clark laughed in the doorway. "It's raining pretty hard. Can I give Laylea something for her hip?"

"Give her a quarter Tramadol. How's Woodford feeling?"

"He's stiff. But he's doing okay. Already crashed in his bed here."

Clark disappeared into the kitchen. Laylea grabbed a rag from the bucket beside the washing machine and dragged it over by the door to watch Bailey. She dug and pulled at it with her paws and teeth to make the thin fabric more comfortable while her brother worked.

He gave up on the fork and turned to the broken chain. He held the two ends of the chain together but couldn't see how to connect them. Even the tiniest hex on the multitool did him no good.

"Need some help, kiddo?" Clark gave Laylea a piece of cheese with the bitter medicine hidden inside.

"I think that would negate her point."

"No, Bailey." Sher hopped out of the truck. "That *is* my point."

"That I can't do anything right?"

"Yeah, genius. I expect you to be able to put a bicycle together via your psychic connection to the mechanic gods."

Clark, Laylea, and Bailey all gaped at her.

"You are a superhuman. You're unreasonably strong and observant with a possibly eidetic memory from your father. You have an IQ through the roof and magical powers from me." She shut the truck door. "But you still can't fix something if you don't know how it works." She took the multitool from her son and flipped through to the teeny little thumbscrew looking instrument. Showing him how as she did it, she removed another link from the chain and then attached the newly open end to the closed end in his hand.

"Tools are useless if you don't know how to use them. Even dangerous." She rubbed her thumb over the bloody knuckles. "Let's clean that before you heal it with grease inside."

Clark held the door. Laylea followed Sher who pushed Bailey ahead of her to the kitchen sink.

"You need help. You need training." She scrubbed the knuckle with their hippopotamus nailbrush and dish soap. The grease didn't budge.

Clark grabbed an orange from the fruit bowl and ripped off some peel. He bellied up beside the two to rub it on the wound. He flipped on the water and the grease washed away with the orange pulp.

He grinned. "Knowledge is power."

Bailey slapped the faucet handle shut. He dried his hand in his hair and scooped Laylea up from the floor. "I don't want to be a superhuman." He paced the kitchen. "Please, can't you just make me forget those things?"

Sher turned the water back on. She took another peel from Clark and washed her own hands clean. When she wiped her face, her wet hands just streaked the tears.

"My methods have so badly broken the Consortium's volunteers that Jay can't keep them from going back anymore. The best he can do is condition them to resist further conditioning. Those victims, Jay, the hermit who won't pick a name, your father, all the others, they will none of them ever know who they are because I scrambled their brains. The ones we were able to help are still hiding in the mountains up there because they don't know what they've done, who they've hurt down here." She turned, her hands still gripping the sink. "And you're asking me to do that to you because you don't think you're adult enough to keep a secret?"

Bailey stood. "*A* secret?" He faced his mother. "You were an evil scientist experimenting on humans. Dad killed people for your company. Jay still rescues soldiers from that company one by one AFTER they've been broken by your methods. They hide in these mountains right here. Our last name is Hillen because when I was born you went out and found some frozen homeless guy and stole his social security number. Oh, and we're home schooling a dog that was dumped on our porch." He stopped to catch his breath. "Anything I've missed?" He paused and then asked more quietly. "Anything I don't know?"

Clark popped an orange slice in his mouth. "Woodford used to be in the mob. He's in Witness Protection. His name is actually Makers Mark."

"Dad." Bailey didn't smile. "What's your real name, Mom?"

Clark swallowed the last of his orange. He dumped the peel in the sink and went to take Laylea from Bailey. He continued around the island back to the sink where Sher still stood, her fingers gripping the cold metal behind her. Laylea set her head on the mom's shoulder as Clark kissed her cheek.

He whispered, "It's up to you."

Sher took Laylea. She poured herself a glass of wine one-handed and pulled Laylea's baby towel from its hook on the wall beside the fridge. She set the towel and Laylea on the island counter.

"Laylea's secrets belong to her. But since she's a minor and we've agreed to care for her, your father and I have decided to keep her secrets among us."

"I don't think we should be less secretive, Mom. Do you think I'm stupid?"

"Bailey." Clark threw a bulb of garlic at him.

Bailey threw the bulb back. "I'm scared of what happens if I slip up. I'll be all alone. No you. No Mom. No Lee. Do you get that?"

"Bailey, we trust you." Clark smashed the garlic between two bowls.

"I don't have to go to school. I can stay."

Laylea sang out. She pulled a pencil from the cup and wrote on her paper, *Pay up.*

"You took bets on if I'd go away?"

"No, Kiddo," his dad pulled a ball of mozzarella from the fridge. "We bet on when you'd freak out about it."

Sher took the cheese. "My money was on day of."

Laylea barked for their attention again. *You have to go. I want my own room.*

Bailey wrapped her ear around his finger and pet her head. "No, you don't."

Laylea pasted her ears back, tucked her tail, and shook her head.

Sher took a stool. She held the cheese out for Laylea to eat from her hand. "You want to be a doctor, Bailey. You can't do that if you don't go to school. We don't even have internet access."

"To keep the outside world outside. I know."

Clark barked a laugh, tossing the garlic skins in the trash. "Ha!"

"We don't have internet to save money. You can't exactly apply for financial aid."

"We've always known you'd have to go, Kiddo. I think Chicago is a great choice." He slid a cutting board and onion across the island.

"I haven't decided on Chicago."

Clark flipped over the application papers with his knife. "This is the fourth Chicago school you've applied to. Big chunks please." He flipped the knife into the air.

Bailey caught the handle and let the momentum drive the blade through the onion. "My counselor said it was a bad choice. He said a small-town boy would get lost there. Idiot doesn't know that's what I want."

"Respect, Bailey." Clark whisked the onion skins away as Bailey chopped.

"Dad."

Sher took a sip of wine. "I have a friend in Chicago."

"An ex-boyfriend." Clark spun his paring knife around a tomato. The skin landed on the counter in front of Sher as a perfect rose.

Sher picked the rose up and tossed it to Woodford. "He owns a well-established consignment shop. He'll look out for you. If you need help and you can't get hold of us, you go see Orin Morton."

Clark reached over and refilled Sher's empty glass.

She took a deep breath and let it out. "You can trust him. He's the other man I can do this in front of."

Sher shut her eyes and shook her head. The hair Laylea thought matched her fur so well suddenly bounced on the mom's head in black curls. Her deep brown eyes sparkled green out of a pale face covered in freckles.

"Mom."

"He'll help you any way he can. Just tell him that you're Katherine Coogan's son." Sher stared into the wine.

"Mom." Bailey couldn't catch his breath.

Clark sang, "*I will not—*"

"I'm not angry." Bailey shot at his dad. He jerked a hand up to tangle his fingers in his mother's curls. "I have your hair."

"You can have any hair you want."

"How?"

"Change your DNA."

Clark spun away from the stove. "Sher, he'll try it."

"Or just change the melanocytes in your hair. Change the shape of your follicles to change the texture. My sister could just think of blue hair and have it but I need to scientifically understand what I'm doing."

Behind her, Clark rolled his eyes. When Sher caught him, he covered with, "You'll hide your run bag at Orin's place. His co-owners are safe too. Their shop is full of secrets. Yours will be well hidden there."

Laylea barked. *I thought I had Mom's hair.*

Sher shook her head. Her dirty-blond hair came back with deeper brown eyes and a crooked diamond of smooth white skin over her third eye.

Laylea sang and waved her dark paw. Sher toasted the little dog. The skin of that hand had turned dark brown.

"Have you ever made yourself look like Dad?"

"Yes."

"Could you make Dad look like you?"

"Not temporarily."

Clark threw water in his pan to make the vegetable sizzle. "Come over here and stir this, will you?"

Laylea waved at Sher. Sher's hair turned red. Laylea waved again. Mousy brown. She waved. Blue.

Bailey wandered over to take the spoon from his dad. "After I leave, who's in charge of Laylea if you have to run?"

"Your father."

"I am."

His parents answered together. Clark went on, "When you pack, we'll take her things from your go bag and add them to mine. Your mom'll take charge of Woodford."

"You're very smart Bailey." Sher shook her head back to her familiar appearance. She set her wine glass aside and stood to gather plates and flatware. "I'm one of the few people you're gonna find who understands how hard that is. I thought being smart was everything. It's," she watched Clark slice bread, "taking me a while to understand that love is everything. I hurt people because I was having fun being smart. My brother was killed," she set the plates down with a clatter, "lots of people have been killed because I'm smart. It's not easy for me to change. I can make people do what I want. Why should I care who they are?" She circled the island to stand with her husband. "I don't know how your father ended up in my lab. But I will be ever grateful that he did and that he was such a poor soldier we were able to catch him within a year."

"Thanks." Clark kissed her blond hair. "Is that ready, Bails?"

Bailey turned off the burner. He set the sizzling pan on the island trivet. Clark slid the breadboard beside it. He grabbed Sher's wine and handed it to her but she didn't drink. She leaned over the island and lifted Laylea and her towel off.

"Your father has a huge heart. We wouldn't have kept Woodford or Laylea if it were up to me." Sher rubbed her cheek against the dog's head. Clark wrapped his arms around her. "We wouldn't have kept you."

Laylea watched Bailey. She knew her job. She knew Sher would only be holding her if she needed Laylea's comfort. But she wanted to be in her brother's arms. The calm, thoughtful blue eyes welled with tears.

But they dried up as his jaw clenched. He threw the hot mitt onto the counter behind him and turned back around to face his parents.

"So, Hardknock, the nameless guy, all these new victims as you said, their pain is all my fault."

"No." Sher's head popped up. "Why would you ever think that?"

"You quit fighting to keep me safe."

Sher pushed out of Clark's arms. "You didn't tell him that."

"No. I would never."

Laylea barked.

"Yeah. You guys used to talk in front of Laylea." Bailey laughed. "Hardknock would never have hurt her if I hadn't been born."

"And Walter might have captured her if we weren't here to take her in," Clark slammed a hand on the counter.

Sher let Laylea hop to the counter. "And Woodford would have died on the side of the road if I hadn't become a vet instead of a vigilante." She circled the island to Bailey. "I don't regret choosing you."

"How many soldiers has Jay rescued?"

"Conditioned Forces," Sher corrected. "They're not soldiers. They're not responsible for what's been done to them."

"No, Mom. I am." Bailey tore on, refusing to be interrupted. "How many CF has Jay rescued? How many have evaded rescue? How many never even survived the conditioning? *You will not kill another soul today*," he sang the words off key. "How many people have your CF killed since you ran away to keep me safe?"

Laylea trotted around the hot pan and plates. She stood on the edge of the counter, leaning at Bailey. He refused to look at her.

"It upsets you that they're still using your work to hurt people? You could stop them but you don't."

Laylea leaped from the counter. Bailey caught her easily as he pushed past his mother and out through the swinging door.

Sher followed him. "Bailey."

"I'm going for a walk."

Clark held the door. "It's raining."

"I need to go for a walk."

"Sure, but it's raining."

"If I catch a cold Mom'll fix me." Bailey grabbed his slicker from the coat tree.

Sher hushed Clark with a hand. "We don't want you out alone."

"I'm not alone." He turned and gestured with his sister in crane hold. "I have Laylea. She'd never dream of using me as an excuse to do nothing." He wrapped her in the slicker, jangling the bells as he pulled the door open. "It's funny. The only person in the world I trust is a dog."

The bells rang again when the screen door slammed behind him.

Clark let the kitchen door flap shut. "It's raining."

"I think it's worse than that, Theta."

"Lightning?"

"An angry untrained teenage witch with unfathomable strength has just gone for a walk with magic on the mind."

"Yeah. But Laylea's with him."

CHAPTER 35

FALL 2034 - CONSORTIUM BIOTECH HQ, CA

B lue light glowed off Trask's face. The reflection in her glasses effectively hid her eyes but the starkness of her scarring made clear how unhappy she was with the chart on her screen. The drawn curtains bathed the office in a mustard hue. Earbuds lay dangling from the far cabinet where Trask had hurled them after testing a new brainwaves focus training CD produced by her soon-to-be culled Practical Applications division.

Trask punched numbers into a physical calculator and recreated the chart on a legal pad in case her scientists were playing congress with the graphics. But the straight data told the same unlikely story.

She slammed the keyboard tray into position and pounded out a memo to her newest Head of Behavior Reinforcement for an immediate in-person review of all returned CF followed by a memo, less forcefully typed, to the Ops Commander to recall all current CF. Again. The percentage of returns had changed dramatically following the last directorate-ordered recall. Unless Gamma Subject had died, and no CF had reported either killing him or finding the body, she couldn't think of a reasonable explanation. Sure, her teams could have finally improved on Coogan's techniques but Trask had hired each of them and she didn't find that a reasonable explanation at all.

A trumpet sounded from Trask's phone signaling three o'clock. Trask activated the intranet just long enough to send her stack of memos and download the day's reports. She disconnected from the server at two minutes after. Any reports not uploaded to the internal server by three or too large to download in two minutes would be considered late and all employees in the division would have their paychecks docked one percentage point, the rate increasing with each subsequent failure. This negative reinforcement continued despite much positive response because it provided Trask with a salary savings she could apply to security enhancements. No, by far the much more effective reinforcement had been removing all coffee supplies from the break room until the division achieved seven days' compliance.

Fluorescent light flooded the Biotech Research office from the overheads.

"Whoops."

Walter hit the electrical pad again and the fluorescents were substituted with a softer yellow-hued glow from torchiere lamps in the corners of the room.

"He's off." Walter twitched the curtain shut behind himself and Bayard. He danced to the far corner and locked Bayard into his kennel. "That's a good boy." He spun to address his side of the desk and plopped down, feet on the forgotten yellow legal pad. "Does it feel like this every time you send a subject off on his final test? I'm giddy as a schoolgirl. I was homeschooled of course. Had no sisters. Are all schoolgirls giddy? It seems unlikely. But if they are, what is it that they are so giddy about? We discover the answer to that and how to imbue it in your volunteers, and everyone else, no more need for soldiers." He kicked off the edge of the desk and spun around. "My boy is off." He leapt from the seat to hang his knapsack on its hook and grab a bottle of iced tea from the dorm fridge hidden in his paper closet. He filled Trask's delicate Turkish tea glass and tapped it with the neck of the bottle. "To Felix 244."

"Walter. Do you remember we discussed how you are to behave when I am working with the lights off?"

"I know," thinking *nothing* very loudly, Walter scanned the post-it notes delineating the line where Walter's side of the desk was to stop. He put a finger on one and whispered, "that you have a migraine when the lights are off and I should be gentle."

He spun away from the desk and tiptoed back to the doorway. The metal slider of the privacy curtain jangled when he slid it aside.

"Shh." He held a finger to his lips, admonishing the curtain.

The torchiere lights faded.

Walter used extreme care shutting the curtain. He tried to manually muffle the apparatus.

"Thank you."

Walter propped a butt cheek on the side of the desk. "What's got you stressed?"

Trask closed the folder of reports on her screen. She tore the chart she'd hand drawn from the pad and handed it to him. "Do you know what that is?"

"This is a chart."

Trask ripped it out of his hands. She slammed it on the desk. "This is a chart showing our subject rate of return is increasing. Most of the soldiers we send out are actually coming back. 397a has returned seven times."

Walter cocked an eyebrow. "That sounds like progress. Felicitations?"

Her chair rolled to a stop before it hit her cabinets. Trask glared at the hated birds on their curtains. She tried to ignore the earthy scent wafting from the dog crate. "We went from a nearly ten percent rate of return to seventy statistically overnight."

Walter folded his hands. "I reviewed my doctoral thesis and all the related course notes but I didn't find statistics terribly entertaining. Perhaps you can tell me why an increased return is bad?"

Trask clicked her way to the cabinet and unfolded the doors. "You began acting strange after you stopped searching for your dogs. Dr. Jones has refused to report to me on the final visit except to say it was a beautiful day. Was she ever out of your sight on that trip?"

"I'm sure we had separate hotel rooms." Walter waggled his brows.

"You did. Did she do any activities on her own, without you, other than sleeping?"

"I." He faltered. "I'd have to check my notes."

"Please." Trask leaned her back against the map. "Go ahead."

Walter stood. He approached the undisturbed yellow legal pad. He reached for it and noticed a sliver of dirt under his index nail. He cleaned it out with the thumb of the opposite hand and then examined the rest of his nails. "Oh, Bayard, hush. Trask has a headache." His eyes returned to the yellow paper but his legs walked him over to the cage. "You know, I really should take him out. He's been in testing all day. All sorts of bloodwork and CT scans. Must be simply dreadful."

"Walter." Trask didn't move. "Check your notes first. Your plans for that trip were to start in Hatch and end in Foothills. Is that where you went?" She turned and pointed to the area on the map. "Is there any chance you and Jones ventured into the mountains for a day of hiking?"

Walter laughed gaily. "Oh Trask, you dear. I don't hike."

"Jones says you do."

His face dropped.

"I think you went hiking on that trip." Trask examined the map. "I think you went hiking and ran into Gamma Subject. He figured out you were from the Consortium and he conditioned you to forget everything. He didn't do as good a job with Jones so you were probably first. Now he's reconditioning my soldiers and sending them home to spy on us." She spun to see Walter's face drained of color. "Where did you go hiking, Walter?"

Walter dropped to the cage. He squeezed Bayard's prong collar over his head. "Ask the returning soldiers."

"We're going to. But you're here now, Walter. Gamma Subject is somewhere in these mountains and he's getting more dangerous. Walter, where did you meet him?"

"Ask Nicole." Walter stood. He led Bayard around the desk. Trask cut him off at the curtain.

"She's going into interrogation as soon as she returns from vacation." Trask stroked Walter's arm. "Something happened to you, Walter. Gamma messed with your brain. Don't you want to help us catch him? If we don't catch him, he's gonna get Felix 244."

Walter stumbled away from her. He glanced at the yellow legal pad on the desk. In one unbalanced lunge, he grabbed the pad off the desk and shoved past her and out the door. All the way down the hall he could be heard screaming, "I know nothing!"

THE DIRECTOR CHEWED on a slab of Oberto Jalapeño bacon jerky. The reports on Trask's reconditioning of 397a from Snickers to jerky had set an itch in his taste buds. He zoomed in on the map with Trask's notations of the region Walter and Dr. Jones had been visiting. An overlay of plastic covered the map and the good scientist had already begun tracing the routes taken by any CF who ventured into that area. One of the two lines indicated his man had visited the compromised wilderness. She would rightly wish to terminate or re-wipe all CF with indications of tampering. He would have to devise a way to prevent that without a direct order. He must also assure that Gamma Subject survived capture. He might answer the questions Coogan's coded notes did not. If he had figured out how to recondition the CF, couldn't they train a CF specifically to recondition Gamma?

The Director swiped to blank screens. He was getting too involved in the Biotech drama. He should reconsider this vacation home business. He wasn't prepared for field work. He buzzed for his assistant.

"Yes, sir."

"Schedule me a sit down with the Netherlands' Biotech Supervisor."

"Yes, sir."

"Get me a status update on the Foothills remote site."

"Yes, sir."

"And find me a glass of milk."

"Sir?"

"A glass of milk, please. As soon as humanly possible."

The Director cut the connection. He wiped the tears from his eyes as he pulled up Random Selection and let hundreds of feeds paint the room in a cacophony of voices.

CHAPTER 36

SPRING 2036 - FOOTHILLS, OR

"No!"

Bailey flung an arm out. Laylea dodged out of the way when the arm fell to the bunched-up comforter.

"Don't touch him!" The scream rasped out of his throat in a mumbled whisper but Laylea knew what he was saying because he wailed the same thing almost every night. "Don't touch Davis!"

She didn't know if he was telling Parker to not pull out the stick or if he was yelling at himself. He wouldn't talk about the dreams. She'd shown him the book that said it would help but he wouldn't talk to her. He suffered her snuggles. He appreciated when she was able to wake him up. But he wouldn't talk.

Clark and Sher never heard his nightmares. Usually they were sound asleep when the dreams came. But this was a powwow day and they'd gotten up well before the sun. They'd have heard him for sure if they weren't downstairs already. Woodford's hearing was so bad now he probably hadn't heard even though Laylea smelled him lying right outside the bedroom door. If he thought his boy was unhappy he'd have been scratching to get in.

Laylea climbed onto Bailey's chest. She licked the tears from his cheeks and tumbled off to clean the streaks leading to a small pool in his ear. She would have let him sleep but a commotion on the stairs made Woodford bark. Bailey stirred. She kicked him in the throat and dropped into an innocent ball of dog in the curve of his shoulder.

"Happy Adoptionversary, Laylea!" Sher and Clark yelled outside the door.

Bailey wiped at his eyes. "Come on in." He wrapped his hands around Laylea and held her in the air as their parents hopped onto the bed. "Happy Tenth, Laylea."

"Happy Eleventh." Clark leaned in and lay a zerbert on her belly. "Are you still doing Bailey's math homework?"

Laylea barked twice.

"Tenth adoptionversary." Bailey hopped out of bed to lift Woodford up.

"She's been with us for eleven years, kiddo."

"Which makes this the tenth time we've celebrated the anniversary of her adoption."

Sher set the traditional peanut butter, oatmeal, tuna muffin on the bed and handed Bailey a spoon to share the bread pudding his father had already begun devouring. "Save us from Bailey logic."

Laylea struggled out of her brother's arms to get to the giant muffin before Woodford ate it all. She buried her face in the food because she thought it would make Bailey laugh. It did. Especially when Woodford licked muffin from Laylea's head. She spun on her tail and chewed at his neck. Undisturbed, her brother kept picking pieces of tuna from her fur.

"Thanks Woodford, she needs a bath." Clark handed the bread pudding to Bailey. "Here, Bails, you're gonna need your strength to keep up with your mom today."

"We've got four days of fun planned."

"I wish you were going to the cabin." Clark massaged Woodford's old hips.

"We'll keep the magic indoors," Sher reassured him. "I can't leave town with Armando operating on Moe tomorrow. If it were any other dog."

"I know. Nick's a friend."

Bailey licked the bread pudding bowl. "Armando's a qualified vet now."

"He is. But I've got more experience. If something goes wrong I want him to know he can reach me."

"Shouldn't Laylea stay home then too?"

The adoptionversary girl leapt for her paper and pencil on the dresser that acted as Bailey's headboard.

"Lee can't help with an unconscious dog. But she can help keep your father safe."

Laylea woofed through her pencil. She'd written *Copilot*. She kept writing, *magic dangerous.*

Sher frowned, taking the sparkling clean bowls away from Woodford and Bailey. "Magic isn't dangerous."

Laylea scratched out *Bailey's.*

"That's it, you fat little loaf of bread." Bailey grabbed her pencil and raised it like a wand. "I'm turning you into a newt."

Laylea sang out and dove for the comforter. She belly-crawled through the mess of blankets to hide behind Woodford.

"Right." Clark scooped both dogs off the bed. "No newting my copilot. We'll be back late tomorrow. Enjoy your day of hooky."

"It's not really playing hooky if I'm getting homeschooled, Dad."

"Oh, my poor little witch boy." Clark pounced on Bailey. Laylea leaped back up to the bed and bounded over. When Clark had him pinned down, she grabbed his t-shirt with her teeth and dragged it up far enough for the dad to zerbert his belly.

AFTER THE PLANE was unpacked and repacked, the goods delivered and paid for, after she ran around the grassy meadow with Mickey like they were still little girls, Laylea lay in Bela's lap beside the fire. The old woman complained that her arthritis bothered her in the wet weather. But Laylea thought she just liked watching Jay's knife skills. Everyone else got to gather and clean and stir. But she kept Jay chopping everything.

Clark gathered one last surprise from the cockpit safe before he joined the campfire. He called loudly as he crossed the meadow, aiming his cry at Maggie and Trey's tent, the farthest from the campfire. "Mail call. Everyone who wants mail, report to the campfire. Mail for everyone."

Jay dipped a bowl of stew for Bela to test while they waited for the stragglers to arrive. She declared it edible. Donald served everyone and they settled around the fire. Flower served up Laylea's kibble.

"I have here," Clark held up a bulging manila envelope, "letters for everyone from Judah God. He wrote me too and says he's enjoying things in Denver. He aced his GED and is working as a farmhand to earn money for college. I brought paper and pens in case anyone wants to send a response right away. Flower," he handed a folded piece of note-book paper to her, "he asks that I make sure you write him back. Now, Maggie Monster."

Flower's face glowed red. Clark started handing out letters on the far side of the fire from her so she didn't have to suffer too much attention. She bent to give Laylea her food and forgot about her own. Laylea tried to read over her shoulder but Flower sat back against a log. All she saw was a heart on the signature line.

The chilly evening settled into reading hour. Some of the letters were long. Others got only half a page. But since most of these people never got any mail, they devoured the little letters with more relish than Bela's stew. Flower read hers through and left for the tent. Laylea stepped over and cleaned out Flower's bowl while everyone was other-wise occupied. She had just returned to her own small meal when Mickey squealed. The girl ran over to sit on the ground beside her.

She read, "*Tell Clark there is a horse on the farm with a white diamond over one eye just like LG. She is a sweet, smart mare and doesn't mind that I have nicknamed her Little Girl.* Oh my god, I'm talking to a dog." Mickey scratched Laylea's ear and bent to kiss her forehead diamond. She bounded over to Clark's side to read the passage to him.

Laylea saw Judah's dad, Ahab watching Mickey. Her action started everyone talking around the fire. They compared letters and talked about the strangeness of the outside world. Ahab kept quiet. His wife wrapped an arm around their second son, holding him as close as he would let her while she studied her eldest's words.

Laylea lay at Ahab's feet. She put a paw on his booted foot to let him know she was there. Ahab wasn't one of the CF. Laylea didn't know why he and his wife and boys lived out in the mountains but she knew that Judah leaving had terrified him.

Ahab folded the letter and put it inside his jacket. He leaned over to scratch Laylea's neck with one hand while the other retrieved his stew.

Laylea looked away. She heard something. There had been a noise that didn't belong coming from outside of the circle. Not so far outside as Hardknock was. She could smell her old nemesis off in the western forest. Hardknock attended every powwow this way. He'd almost been caught a few times and once Laylea had been the one to distract Feranda before she tripped right over him. Laylea had no hard feelings. Hardknock was the first post-Sher CF. He hadn't lost his mind. It had been taken from him. The same thing might have happened to her if her mama hadn't found the Hillens.

Her ears twitched. A click closer than Hardknock's lean-to and farther south. It sounded like it was out toward Ahab and Caroline's shelter. She ignored the voices growing louder around her. Maggie began strumming her guitar. Laylea angled her ears to focus on the distance. When Ahab offered her a chunk of meat, she turned her head away to keep the smell from distracting her.

Smell. Laylea remembered she was a dog. She paced over to the periphery of the circle, her hackles up though she didn't yet know why. She caught a whiff of unfamiliar sweat. Again, she heard the click. This time she saw the snap of the lens from the flap of Ahab and Caroline's teepee.

She growled. Her instinct was to chase him away and she jumped to do so. But the more-than-dog part of her saw that he was stealing from them as well as taking pictures. So, she barked to Clark for help before she put on the speed.

"Jay!" Clark ran right behind her, calling over his shoulder, "Everybody circle up and stay here!"

She had tiny legs, but she was, as Clark kept reminding her on these visits, a dog. She could run. And she could follow his smell so she didn't need to be able to see the intruder. He was running fast and gaining. She tried to snap branches and brush leaves so Clark could track her but it slowed her down. So, she detoured through a bush with cottony blooms. The flowers dripped off of her as she ran.

When the thief took a hard-to-follow turn, she stopped barking. Maybe the thief would think she'd lost him. He slowed down. She did not. She was just getting her wind. Feet flying, even dashing through bushes to leave a trail, Laylea gained on him. She reviewed in her mind what the mom and dad were always telling Bailey, *We're here to help you.* And what they were always asking her, *What are you going to do with that cat if you catch her?*

She was a very small dog. She couldn't do anything with the thief. Clark and Jay probably could. But they had to catch up to him first. She barked to scare the thief, let him know that she was right behind him. Scared people did stupid things. Clark's horror novels taught her that.

When the trail ended, she ran right past the spot where the thief's scent stopped. She ran on past the clearing and then bayed her disappointment at losing him. She ran back past the tree again to pick up the scent where she'd last had it. She scratched in the dirt. She howled. She ran around the wrong tree and darted off in different directions, nose to the ground.

When Jay and Clark caught up to her she continued baying and sniffing the ground in all directions. It was apparent that she had lost the scent. Jay went to her. Laylea planted her butt. She threw her head back and howled a howl Woodford would approve of. She caught Clark's eye and as soon as Jay stepped away to examine the ground for traces of a trail, Laylea stood. She'd scratched the word *Up* in the dirt. Clark crunched through the leaves, scattering them over the area. He knelt down by her.

"It's okay girl. You tried. Good job. Good girl." He tugged on her collar like he was dragging her away. "Let's go back to camp. Come on."

Clark stood and headed back the way they'd come. Laylea followed. As soon as they were out of sight of the clearing, Clark turned and looked up into the trees. He saw a figure tucked into the bare branches. Dark skin blended into the trunk.

"Huh," He grunted quietly. "That's familiar."

Laylea tilted her head at him. He crouched down beside her. "The way he's up there, that's something the Consortium taught me, I think." He scratched the scruff of her neck as he considered. "Can you draw his attention away?"

Laylea barked belligerently and turned to run off after Jay. Clark looked up. The thief watched Laylea. Clark loaded a slingshot and snapped a rock straight at the guy's stabilizing hand.

"Look up here look up here look up here," he called to Jay.

His second shot hit the perp's forehead just above one eye. His nervous system shut his eyes when the missile approached and that compromised his balance just enough. The thief fell.

"Look out!" Jay screamed from the other side of the clearing.

The world slowed before Clark's eyes. He looked down from the falling body to see Laylea looking back at Jay running towards the tree. Hardknock appeared from nowhere. He dove at Laylea just as the thief broke through the last branch. The crazy hermit swatted Laylea with his green book and she went flying. She hit the trunk with a crunch that went unheard under the sound of the stranger crashing down on Hardknock's back. Jay leaped onto the bodies but Hardknock was already crawling away. Jay got a handful of the hermit's rough spun poncho. The stranger got an elbow up into Jay's nuts and Hardknock slipped away.

Clark had his bracelet half unwoven before he reached the pair on the ground. He looped the orange paracord over the thief's neck and connected it to the elbow trapped between Jay's shaking thighs.

"I've got him," Jay coughed. He grabbed the unraveling bracelet from Clark. "I've got him."

Clark stood to chase after Hardknock.

"LG, Clark." Jay kicked him to get his attention. "Little Girl isn't moving!"

Clark turned. Beyond the two men struggling in the leaf-strewn dirt, Laylea lay sprawled. The tangle of roots at the base of the tree held her head up at an impossible angle. Blood matted the white diamond over her eyes.

Chapter 37

Spring 2036 - deep in the mountains

Clark leapt over the struggle. He fought his sketchy memory to recall every bit of first aid Sher had ever taught him. He felt for blood under her head before he lifted her with an arm splinting either side of her body.

"Come on, wake up." He realized Jay was two feet behind him and added, "Who's my good girl?" without much heart.

He kept her head straight, feeling for any injury to her spine. It was okay. He was relieved for an instant before he realized he didn't feel any movement at all. His little girl wasn't breathing. Her heart had stopped beating.

Clark hummed. He controlled his panic. As gently as he could, he squeezed her rib cage twice with his forearms. He tilted her head back and covered her muzzle with his mouth. He breathed for her. Two compressions and a breath. Two compressions and a breath.

His mind couldn't remember his mother. His mind couldn't remember Bailey's birth. His mind couldn't remember the garage door code. But he remembered that CPR hardly ever worked. The odds flashed through his brain even as he breathed for Laylea. Two compressions and a breath.

"Stop." Jay knelt in front him.

Somehow Clark had fallen to his knees. Two compressions. He leaned over her to breathe.

"Captain, stop." Jay held him upright. "She's breathing."

Clark's entire body shook. He sucked in shuddering breaths through his nose. Their captive couldn't see him, a grown man, crying over a dog. Jay unknotted the paisley bandanna around Clark's neck. He soaked it with water from his canteen and washed away the dirt and blood caked on Laylea's face.

"It's a scrape."

Clark tried to sound strong, "Only a flesh wound."

"Head wounds bleed. She'll be okay. Let's let her rest here while we deal with our photographer friend." Jay shrugged out of the deep green hoodie he wore underneath his coat and laid it on the ground. "Here. Captain? Put her down here."

Clark nodded. He didn't want to let her go. But he folded the warm fabric over Laylea and bunched the hood up to cushion her head.

"Okay?" Jay's eyes were still soft when he made his voice harsh. "Shall we go get some info from this little shit?"

"Absolutely." Clark's voice was stronger on his second try. "I don't like people who mess with my business."

The two men, with no discussion, settled each on one side of the man lying face down in the dirt. His head was held just off the ground by the pull of his neck tied to his arms tied to his legs and covered with Jay's jacket. He unwound his jacket from the man's shaved head and crouched with his shin pressing against the side of the man's face. Clark crouched on the other side, his shin pushing the man's face into Jay's leg.

Jay sliced the thief's camera from his neck and smashed it against a rock.

Who are you and why are you taking pictures of us? was the question Clark wanted to ask but that gave away more information than he gained. So instead he played his part, "What are you doing, jackass? I deliver this shit for money. If you want it, I'll deliver it to you for barter, cash, or information."

As Clark began negotiations, his eyes stealing over to Laylea's gently breathing body, Jay searched the thief's pockets and clothing. Through-out, the two kept up a banter over the guy's back.

Clark pulled a hunting knife from the sheath on the guy's belt and handed it to Jay. "Did you know, the mark of a good martial artist is that they can subdue their enemy without killing them?"

"We are good."

"A great martial artist can subdue their enemy without hurting them."

"We are not so great." Jay pulled the guy's jacket off his shoulders and ripped open the lining. He found a couple more blades which he added to the growing pile at his side. He also found some memory chips and held them up to show Clark. Jay kept talking while they considered. "A master martial artist has no enemies to subdue."

"Because he sent all the novices out to fight them."

Clark pulled down the back collar of the kid's undershirt. His leathery tan stopped just below the collar. They both saw the scar between his pale shoulder blades.

"Think you can question this guy without damaging him?" Jay asked.

"I've got better skills in this area than you." Clark came to a decision. Despite the information it could provide, he did not want to invade the privacy of the CF or any other woodsfolk. He crossed his neck with a finger.

Jay dropped the chips at his side where the thief could see them. "This is information gathering, not martial arts. In my opinion, the more damage the better. And I've got sharper skills than you there." He pulled his own knife from its sheath and held it up for Clark to examine.

Clark made a show of leaning over the body to take the knife. "Yes, that is sharp."

A fierce growl grabbed all three men's attention. Laylea stood, teeth bared, inches from the stranger's face. When he whimpered, she scooped the memory chips up in her mouth and limped back to Jay's hoodie.

Clark found he couldn't breathe. Jay laughed at the relief in his eyes. He said, "There you go girl. Chew them up."

"Don't swallow them." Clark switched to a more appropriate

foolish dog owner tone and added, "You chew em up. That's my girl. Go on, chew em all up."

Laylea spit the chips out uneaten, unchewed. She licked at her sore hip, scratched at the fabric to make it more comfortable, and collapsed facing the interrogation.

Clark handed Jay's knife back, "Tell you what. We don't know who this guy is yet. I'll take the first round. You can have the second."

"Deal."

Jay pulled a couple of ID cards from the guy's back pants pocket and handed them to Clark. Clark glanced at them. Ahab and Caroline's pictures over different names. He pocketed the IDs. As he did, Jay took his very sharp knife and sliced the man's pants from waistband to hip.

Clark protested. "We agreed I get the first go."

"My bad." Jay sliced the man's jacket. Then he flipped the man over and put him in a headlock, propped up on his knees, facing Clark but not allowed to look directly at him.

Laylea saw that he was just a kid. Maybe a little older than Bailey, a boy Mickey might like to meet. He smelled familiar.

Clark smiled. His voice when he spoke was not his voice. It was warm. It was calm. Well-meaning. And terrifying.

"Hi. What's your name?"

The kid didn't respond. He didn't respond to any of their questions. As they continued to undress him and examine his skin, cutting away clothes where the ropes were in the way, the kid actually began to hum softly. He didn't hum a recognizable song. Just random notes. Neither Clark nor Jay pushed him once the humming started. They focused on searching him for any other implants.

While Jay was slicing through the kid's underwear, Clark motioned privately for Laylea to turn around. She shared a room with Bailey and until four years ago Clark had never had any problem changing in front of her. But she shut her eyes.

They thoroughly searched the kid without finding any other transmitters. When they were sure, they stopped their threatening banter, stopped pretending they were other men. Jay took the young CF's face in his hands, looked him in the eyes and said, "You should sleep now."

The kid stopped humming. He took a breath, let it out, took another and his eyes focused on Jay's. "No."

Jay smiled gently. He lowered his head to the kid's ear, bringing his forearms in and pushing the points of his elbows into the kid's chest. He whispered, "I've given you the serum. You can't resist the serum. You know you must obey when you've had the serum."

The kid blinked. His lids drooped but he didn't sleep.

Jay insisted, "You must sleep now."

"No." The kid breathed the word almost as a question.

A third time. Clark held his breath as Jay spoke in the low tone. "You will sleep now. Serum."

His lids drooped. He blinked.

"Serum," Jay crooned.

The eyes closed and the kid sighed away into sleep.

They untied the rope and dressed him as best they could.

"Is it always that hard?" Clark asked stuffing the orange cord into a pocket.

"Has been lately." Jay pulled out his sewing kit. "I can't reach the new CF."

"So, you send them back?" Clark took a needle from him with a bobbin of blue thread.

Jay rubbed at his face. He hummed a few bars of *I Will Not Kill*. "You don't live out here. You can't understand." He threaded his needle. "I can't stop them. I don't have Sher's training in any of this. She gave me a one year crash course in conditioning."

"You're not conditioning." Clark repaired the rip in the kid's boxers with a rough stitch. "It should be easier to return them to who they were."

"Oh?" Jay said. "How do you like being who you were?"

"We're different." Clark pulled up the kid's pants. He basted the waistband back together. "These new ones aren't erased as well as us."

"And for a while that made it easier to help them break free. But they're being trained to resist me. And they're getting more messed up. I got through to this girl, could have been recruited out of ROTC." Jay ripped the thread with his teeth. "She actually remembered her name right before she leapt off the cliff face." Jay sang quietly.

"Why didn't you tell me about her?"

"I don't tell you about any of the CF who kill themselves." He heaved the kid over his shoulder and stormed into the forest.

Clark scrambled to gather Laylea, the hoodie, and the memory chips. "How many?" He tripped after his friend. "How many?"

Jay picked up speed. Clark slipped the chips into his pocket and held his little girl to his chest with both arms. He put on his own speed.

They raced back along the trail they'd just made. Around groves, over rocks, through the pond Laylea had had to hopscotch through. Clark caught up when the trail wove through a grove of sycamores.

"How many, Gamma?"

"Five."

Jay slowed. He barged so roughly through branches the barren limbs threatened to smack Clark. He turned away, following Jay sideways to protect Laylea.

"I couldn't take it anymore so I started letting them go. I work on them a little and try to wake them up but if it isn't working I switch to subconscious conditioning. I'm trying to get them to remember what they're told to forget."

He slowed to let Clark catch up.

"You're looking for home base."

"I'm looking for Trask." A pine bough rained needles when he reached overhead to slap it. "Every new CF knows the name."

"Any luck so far?"

Jay shook his head. "It's not in the mountains. I think the building they return to or maybe the dorm they're kept in has leaded glass windows."

Jay stopped in a small clearing. Not running, Laylea could appreciate the beauty of the mountains. A creek trickled by not far off, setting off Jay's harsh breathing. A ray from the lowering sun sliced across his dark face.

"I'm not rescuing anybody. I never have." One hand held the kid on his shoulder. He gestured wildly with the other. "All I'm doing up here is catching the Consortium's grenades before they're sent into the world. And after this long, we can't be their only training ground. I can't be catching all of the CF they send out."

"You want to go after the Consortium."

Jay took a deep breath. "I want to go after Trask." The muscles of his stomach visibly contracted. "I want to kill Trask."

Clark caught the kid. Laylea slid down his chest and pushed off his thighs to roll in the carpet of leaves while Jay fell to his knees and regurgitated every last bit of Bela's stew and Trey's bread. He heaved until only bile spilled into the leaves. Clark set the kid down. He lifted Jay by his jacket.

Jay clenched at his friend's shoulders. He whispered, "I am going to kill her" and heaved again.

Clark punched him. Jay collapsed.

Clark carried Jay away from the sick. He lowered his friend to the ground and lay beside him in the cold leaves. He did not sing the words but he hummed Sher's song. Laylea stood guard over the sleeping kid, watching the big man cry.

After forever, Jay asked, "Look up here?"

"It's from a movie," Clark told him. "You'd like movies."

Jay rolled to sitting. He rubbed at his belly. "Ow."

Clark flexed his hand and rubbed at the rapidly healing bruises. "Yeah."

Laylea barked. She licked her throbbing hip.

Clark sat up. "Sorry, little girl. How's our guest?"

Jay pushed himself to his feet. "Thanks, LG. I've got him." He hoisted the kid back over his shoulder and continued toward camp.

Clark recovered Jay's hoodie and shook it clean. He craned Laylea into his chest and followed.

"The nameless CF remembers movies." Jay looked over his shoulder. "I know how to build weapons. I've got all these diagrams and images of guns and drones and bombs in my head. He gets to remember movies."

"I remember plants." Clark hustled to walk beside Jay. "I can turn the pages of this gigantic book in my mind with step by step instructions on how to grow things and repot them and when to plant what and how to prevent pests and how to design and build any type of urban plot. But when I work in our garden, I don't remember the feel of dirt or the smells."

"The doc says smell is the strongest sense for bringing back memories."

Clark thought about that. "Movies don't smell."

They picked their way over a few felled trunks over a small creek bed. Clark thought about all the movies he and Sher had seen, hiding in the theater with a dozen other invisible people. He caught up to Jay again. "I should bring you some popcorn."

Jay offered, "Maybe you grew up in a city. You never had a garden but you had this book."

"An entire life," Clark said, "and all I remember is a book."

"All I remember is killing."

Laylea knew he didn't though. If Jay actually remembered killing, he'd be physically ill again.

"You should come down sometime. Watch a movie. Sit on a couch with a dog in your lap. Piss indoors."

"Still at the same place? In Foothills?"

"Yes sir. My lovely little cottage at the edge of the world." Clark followed Jay through the tight section of trees and bushes which had featured white fuzz before Laylea ran through them.

They paraded down a dip. Clark tripped over an exposed root and Laylea found herself on eye level with the kid's dangling hands. She yipped. Clark looked at her. She reached out of his arms to grab the kid's left hand in her teeth.

The pinkie finger ended after the second knuckle.

"You're right. I remember this kid. We used to deliver to him." The memory seeped into his brain. "Always brought him a Snickers bar."

Laylea barked.

"Yeah, then he swapped the chocolate for jerky."

"One of your normal hermits?" Jay asked.

"Normal," Clark laughed. "Yeah. It was he and his mom."

"Red makes good jerky."

"I offered him hers but he wanted this jalapeño bacon stuff. Always delivered to the same field."

"Is your memory fritzing out again?" Jay slowed as the path opened up under a canopy of orange needles.

"Long term's always fritzy." Clark said. "Isn't yours?"

Jay shook his head. He let Clark catch up. Laylea saw him watching the dad closely and she focused on behaving like a dog.

"In my defense," Clark explained, "he used to be pale tip to toe. Only reason I recognize him now is because I always wondered about how you both lost your pinkies."

"What?" Jay stopped.

"His left pinkie is cut short. Look." Clark lifted the kid's hand.

Jay laid the kid on the bed of fallen needles. He stared at their matching wounds. "The Consortium did this."

Clark set Laylea down beside the boy. "Have you rescued anyone else missing part of a finger?"

"Kim." Jay, in an automatic gesture of self-comfort, buried his fingers in Laylea's fur. "The one who leaped." He reached for the kid. "We have to keep going."

Clark stopped him. "I'll take him for a while. You could use some LG."

Jay chuckled. "A forest full of rescues and you're the only normal one, little girl."

Laylea licked his nose. She tripped over to where Clark bent over to lift the kid and licked his nose. For good measure, she stood on the unconscious boy's chest and licked his nose too.

The kid's eyes flashed open. His familiar ice blue eyes focused on the dirty dog and he started screaming. High pitched, relentless screaming.

Laylea yelped. She fell backwards, tumbling off his chest onto the pine floor. Jay wrapped his arms around the kid's head, crooning, demanding, trying to make him sleep again. But the Snickers kid kept screaming. Laylea whimpered. She cowered behind Clark. He picked her up and walked away from the clearing. The screaming stopped.

Clark turned, surprised, and walked back over to the kid with Laylea in his arms. The kid looked up, saw them. His pupils dilated until there was just a thin circle of blue around the terrified blackness. His mouth worked silently. Before he could start screaming again, Clark walked away.

He called from the shadow of the pines. "Can he be that scared of dogs?"

Jay focused on the kid. "Serum." He repeated the word at intervals, instructing the CF to sleep.

Laylea buried her nose under Clark's arm. The kid was Bailey's age and if the Consortium had cut off his finger, he'd been a CF since he was just a puppy. They were catching and conditioning kids.

"He's asleep." Jay came over to them. "I don't think it's LG. I think he remembers you both. He shouldn't. Something about being unconscious knocked the memory loose. He's not supposed to remember you and it hurts."

"That's awful." Clark flipped Laylea over to cradle her. "I guess you have to carry him the rest of the way."

Jay smirked. "You two go ahead, tell the others they should break camp and move on for the night. I'll let him rest for a bit before I follow you."

"Yeah. Let *him* rest."

Jay ignored the jab. "Pressure Trey to get Maggie away. She doesn't . . . ." He stopped before he gave away information he wasn't supposed to have.

Clark ignored the slip. As he walked into the forest, he called over his shoulder, "Yup. We'll save you some stew."

"You'd better."

Laylea barked.

"No, don't worry, little girl. I'll totally let you have his stew."

"There had better be stew for me when I get back." Jay cried louder as Clark and Laylea disappeared into the trees. "I cut all the vegetables!"

CHAPTER 38

SPRING 2036 - DEEP IN THE MOUNTAINS

A waxing gibbous moon lit the powwow clearing by the time Clark and Laylea reached it. They emerged from the trees to find all but two tents disassembled. Trey and Maggie disappeared into the far trees even as they approached the campfire.

"Left you some stew." Bela pushed her old bones to as close to standing as she ever achieved. "Jay can return the bowls when's convenient."

"Did you catch him?" Ahab took the stool and tucked it into Bela's already packed travois.

Flower strapped it down. "Where's Jay?"

"We caught him. Jay's stalling to give you all a chance to get away. You only have Flower to help, Bela?"

"Feranda had to leave once the screaming started. She took the twins." Bela waddled over to stand between the lead poles. "I been dragging this thing since long before I picked up these kids or her."

"Don't worry, Captain." Flower stopped him from following her. "Her hands don't grip enough to pick them up. Can you get this to Judah?"

"And this?" Ahab stacked his letter on top of hers.

Clark took the letters and handed Laylea to Flower. "Can you have

Bela give LG a once over? I did my best but I'd feel better."

"Sure." Flower licked her thumb and wiped at the blood on Laylea's face as she walked away.

"The kid must have gone through some of the tents. We've destroyed his camera and the memory chips." Clark slipped the IDs into Ahab's palm. "He also had these."

Ahab paled.

"Should I tell Judah to move?"

Ahab zipped the cards into his breast pocket, thinking aloud. "He couldn't have heard us talking from so far away. You're the only one who knows the name Judah is using. No. God, let him be safe, let him be happy."

"We have a code. I could tell him what happened and let him decide for himself."

"No." Ahab held out his rough hand. "You've been a great help to us, Captain. I don't think we'll see you again for a while."

Clark started to protest. But no one in Ahab's family was a CF. They didn't need Sher's help. He shook the man's hand.

"Good luck."

"You have ice packs?" Bela called as Ahab jogged off after his family.

Clark nodded. "Always carry them now."

"Get one on her hip. I reset the joint and it's going to swell. And get one on her head here over the cut but not over the eye. And make her rest."

Flower handed Laylea back to him. "You'll make sure Jay's safe before you fly off, right?"

Laylea barked once and nodded. The ladies laughed.

"What she said. You take care of—"

"Bela." Flower settled the travois harness against her hips. "Yeah, I've got her."

Clark shared a glance with Bela. "Feranda. You take care of Feranda. There *are* things that scare her you know."

"Like a little girl leaving for Denver who knows nothing about the world." Abuela used Clark's jacket to pull him down to her level. "My family might have room for another mouth."

"Thanks, Bela." Clark kissed her cheek. Laylea licked her hand.

The old woman wiped her hand but Laylea saw a smile quirk the corner of her lips before she shuffled off beside Flower. "Didn't know you liked the boy till he left. Story of the ages."

"I don't like him. I just want to go to school."

"What can they teach you that I can't?" Bela pushed a log out of their path with her walking stick.

"How to use a computer."

"Pff."

Laylea imitated Bela.

"Yeah. I don't know how to use one either." Clark turned away from the fire. "Let's get you on ice."

The nameless hermit stood just outside the circle of logs. He popped the inner packet on an ice pack and shook it. "She said you need two?"

Clark took the pack and held it on Laylea's head. "Yeah."

The older man took a second pack from his thigh pocket and activated it as well. "I can hold her. You should set up your tent before it gets too cold."

Clark glanced down at his girl. "That okay with LG?"

Laylea's eyes were pinned on the hermit. She barked quietly.

Clark looked up to see teddy lizard resting on St. Nick's shoulder.

He handed Laylea over. "Thanks. Left hip. You'll see when she licks it. Old war wound."

Clark gathered the Hotel bag from the plane as well as a camp cot that hadn't see daylight in a decade. With only the other CF in the clearing he felt free to pile himself up with extra blankets, first aid kit, and ropes as well. He dropped all the equipment beside Jay's raggedy tent.

He set the cot up in the open air and arranged some medical supplies and a sewing kit on the folded blanket. When he turned to pull the tarp out of the hotel bag, he found the hermit had dragged his own well-worn single man tent up beside Jay's. He unzipped the entrance and lay Laylea inside on the two ice packs.

Clark laid his tarp down to the west of the cot. He unbound a dark green roll of nylon on top of it. The hermit worked beside him. He jiggled the tent poles from the sack and unfolded them.

Clark bent over his work. "He's a CF."

"Odds were."

They erected the tent with the entrance facing in. Clark blew up his air mattress, threw some blankets inside, and then went back to the plane to get Laylea's bed. When he returned, the hermit had settled on a campstool beside the cot with Laylea sprawled in his lap.

Clark went over to him. "You don't have to stay."

The hermit repositioned the ice packs on the little dog's body. He looked up at Clark briefly and nodded, then balanced teddy lizard back on his shoulder.

When Jay came out of the woods with the Snickers kid over his shoulder, Clark was tying down the plane against a windy night. Laylea had rolled upside down. She'd turned the crook of the hermit's elbow into a pillow with one paw over his hand on her belly. She was half sleeping, half staring up at the silent one's face as he scritched her.

Jay had barely planted the kid on the cot when he woke, saw Laylea, and started screaming. The nameless one set Laylea and teddy lizard on the ground. He then leaned over the kid and screamed with him. He didn't touch him. Didn't scream at him. He just calmly caught the rhythm and pitch and screamed with the CF until the kid stopped in confusion.

"Hi."

The kid stayed quiet. Jay started to move in but Clark stopped him with a hand on his arm. They let the least healed CF take the lead. The hermit sat quietly, watching the kid for a bit. Then he let his gaze wander over to the moonlit plane.

The kid couldn't take his eyes off the man. "Hi."

The hermit looked back at the kid. He scratched his beard. Then he asked, like an afterthought, "What's your name?"

"Three... three nine seven."

"Two eight four was what they called me." The hermit was quiet a while, remembering what he could of the people who called him that. "But that's not who you are." He picked up the hose of his camelback, drank, and then handed it to the kid. He sat back, looking off at the trees while the kid propped himself on an elbow and took a long draught.

After a while the kid remarked, "I'm supposed to kill all of you."

"Is that what your heart tells you?"

The kid crinkled up his face at the hermit.

The hermit tried a different tack. "How do you feel about killing me?"

The kid thought about it. "I feel empty. I feel thirsty, missing, canyons." He drank again. "I'd feel better if I did what I'm supposed to."

"If you did what?"

"If I did what I'm supposed to do."

The hermit asked, "What are you supposed to do?"

The kid fell silent again. Clark knelt down to continue reweaving his orange bracelet. Laylea crept over to him. Jay hunkered down to pet her while they watched one broken man trying to help another.

The conversation went on in fits and starts for an hour. The hermit called Laylea over after a while by wiggling her teddy lizard at his feet. She crept over with tail tucked safely between her legs, ears pasted against her head. The hermit rubbed her ears till she calmed a little. He picked her up and set her in his lap scratching all along her flanks.

When the kid saw her, he sat up. But he didn't start screaming again. "You know Little Girl?"

The kid turned away and rubbed his third eye. Clark crimped the loose ends of the cord. He pulled out a Snickers he'd collected from the plane and moved forward slowly, offering the candy bar to the kid. The kid reached out automatically when he saw it.

"It's been a few years since I brought you one of these."

The kid spoke even as he unwrapped the chocolate, "I don't know you." He refused to look at Clark, turning instead back to the hermit with Laylea on his lap. "I don't know you." Tears streamed down his cheeks as he ate the Snickers.

They all sat quietly until he finished the chocolate. He crumpled the wrapper in his fist and lay back down on the cot.

The hermit scooped Laylea into his lap and Jay emptied his canteen while Clark wove the clasp into his cord and tied it off. He hooked the bracelet back around his wrist. The kid turned on his side and curled up. After a moment, he shut his eyes and whispered. "Tie me up with your orange rope. I don't want to kill you."

Laylea and the men looked at Clark. Jay held out his hand.

Clark turned his back on the kid. He whispered, "We have other rope."

"Kid said orange. He believes the orange rope will hold him. Right?" Jay looked to Laylea and the hermit for confirmation. They both nodded. "It's a mental thing, Captain. Give me the cord."

"I just finished weaving it."

Jay wiggled his fingers. A giggle twitched the corner of his mouth.

Clark pulled the bracelet off and undid his work. He and Jay worked it around the kid and the cot.

When they were done, Jay put a hand on his head. "You're safe now."

"You're safe now." The kid replied.

The nameless one covered the kid with a couple blankets and the trio of CFs stepped over to the fire.

Clark shook his head. "He's a mess."

"The doc taught me how to reboot subjects altered through *her* methods. This is butchery." Jay recalled that the nameless CF was one of the newer subjects. "Sorry."

"We adapt." St. Nick shrugged.

"I'll leave at first light. See if the doc can help." Clark noticed the bowls of stew. He offered one to Jay.

Jay took it and shoveled down three spoonfuls before responding. "I can't set the radio up this close to...." He looked east and interrupted himself. "I'll have to reboot him at least enough so that he's mobile."

"He can walk." Clark set his cold stew aside.

"I need to trust he won't run off."

"Can't you just carry him?" Clark took Laylea from the hermit and held her close to the fire.

"I'm gonna want to cut his tracker out here."

All three men reached for the scar on their backs.

Clark realized, "The Consortium will notice when his signal shuts down."

Jay added, "And come a-running to the spot it last transmitted from."

Clark explained to Laylea, "And Jay's too weak to carry him and move quickly."

Jay warmed his hands in Laylea's fur. "Jay's ready to go anytime your daddy wants to try him."

The nameless CF spoke up. "I have a sled. We can pull him."

Jay spun around. "You can't go with me."

"I can help."

Clark stepped between them. "It's not safe. He's still conditioned. You're barely unconditioned."

"I don't care. You got me away from the Consortium. You freed my mind. But what do I do with my freedom? I hide. I need to help this kid. I don't care if it's dangerous."

Jay stopped him. "Not your safety Captain's worried about. Mine." He looked at the lost man sadly. "You're still more Two Eight Four than a person."

"I'm not."

"You are."

Laylea barked at the same time that Clark suggested, "Pick a name."

"What?"

"Captain," Jay warned.

The hermit shook his head. "I can't give up on finding who I was."

"Deciding to have a future is not the same as giving up the past." Clark sat. He traced Laylea's name in the dirt as they used to do when she was learning to write. He still couldn't get past the L. "Captain isn't my name. And what I'm called at home isn't the name I was born with. But they're names that I've chosen for myself since I choose to live despite what was done to me." He looked up at the hermit. "I get that you think a new name will push your old identity further into the mist. But Jay sees it as you not wanting to give up Two Eight Four."

The hermit sat. "What does the doc say?"

"She says you're an individual. Just like everybody else."

The men laughed. Laylea took the opportunity to wriggle out of Clark's arms. She sat on the nameless CF's foot, leaning into him.

"Between us," Clark picked up his stew, "she wonders if the crazy is worse for Hardknock because he remembers his name."

Jay hunkered down. "Never considered that."

"Yeah. She says she's angrier than I am cuz she can remember her life before. She knows what the Consortium took from her." He took a few bites. "She's feeling pressure to live up to her name."

"Doc?" The hermit asked.

"Her other name. The one Jay gave her."

The hermit tossed Teddy Lizard to Jay. "How did you pick your name?"

"I didn't." Jay tried to scoop Laylea into his arms when she came after her lizard. "First initial J. Last name Doe. That's why I'd never pressure you to pick one."

"But he would feel safer if you did."

"And you, Captain?" he asked. "Was that your rank?"

"No, I don't remember having any rank. That's my woods name cuz I fly. Doc gave me my home name based on what I wanted to be. I was a little unrealistic in what kind of job a person with no social security number could hold. But it's a good name."

"And you do run a store, in a way," Jay pointed out as he dragged Laylea around on the ground. She'd gone boneless when growling and tugging hadn't won her the toy.

"I do." Clark smiled. "I do, don't I?"

"Gandhi."

Jay and Clark looked at the no-longer nameless man. Laylea seized Jay's inattention and ran with Teddy to tumble into Gandhi's lap.

"My name will be Gandhi Elgee."

Jay held out a hand. Gandhi shook it.

"Let's go look at some maps and make a plan. I'll teach you what I can and when the doc comes, she might teach you more."

"Nice to meet you Gandhi. LG is honored."

The little fawn dog showed her approval by licking her name-buddy's ear. She kept doing it as he picked up her teddy lizard and carried them both back to the triangle of tents.

GANDHI TOOK FIRST WATCH. Four hours later he was asleep in his tent as Clark and Laylea took over from Jay. Laylea scratched at the nylon hoping Clark would let her crawl in and sleep with him, but instead he set her to watch Snickers boy while he rolled up their tent. The boy looked harmless except for the orange rope that should be on the dad's wrist. Still she sat out of the boy's line of sight in case he freaked out again.

After he packed up the hotel, Clark refilled all the canteens and Gandhi's camelback with fresh water filtered from the creek nearby. He set one by the boy's head and another by each tent. He filled Laylea's collapsible water bowl and sat with her drinking from the fourth, petting her as she drank her fill. They cuddled for a wonderful while until Laylea fell asleep in his lap. She dropped immediately into a dream of running after the Rick's cat. She kicked at the dad, her muffled barks making him smile even as he thought about how many good people the Consortium had broken.

He liked his life. He liked living simply with Sher and Bailey and Woodford and yes, his odd daughter. But Bailey would be graduating soon and leaving for one of the seven schools that had accepted him. Maybe it was time to stop the conditioning. Time for him and Sher to finish what she started with Jay and shut down the Consortium for good. How, he had no idea. In fact, it seemed impossible.

Laylea yawned and stretched. She rolled to her back and slept with all her paws dangling out, belly to the sky, completely trusting that Clark would keep her safe. He chuckled and rubbed her chest. Impossible. This little girl was impossible. She could read and write and think and she changed the meaning of impossible. If a dog could do all that, maybe an amnesiac ex-killer and a mad scientist cum veterinarian could change the world a little. He and Sher even had thumbs.

Laylea woke. She stood on his chest, stretching. Then she got up and trotted off to the woods for a pee. Clark stood, stretched himself, and when Laylea came back he told her to watch the camp while he prepped the plane.

"Holler for me if the boy wakes and needs anything."

Laylea nodded and sat again out of the boy's line of sight. Clark brought the camp stove over from the plane and set it up. He filled a pot with water and set it over the flames. Laylea kept an eye on the fire and the boy as Clark went back to the plane.

Jay and Gandhi both woke as the sun rose, spreading a soft light over the camp. They each greeted Laylea and checked on the boy. Gandhi returned from a trip to the trees to sit by the boy. Jay went to the plane to confer with Clark.

When the boy woke, he panicked for a moment but quickly remembered that he had been tied to his cot and stopped struggling to sit up. Gandhi released the ropes. He helped the boy to sit up and massaged his arms where the cord had left marks. They stood and walked slowly off to the pit in the woods, the older man supporting the boy. Laylea got up and followed at a distance, not trusting Snickers. He said he was supposed to kill them all.

He didn't kill Gandhi in the woods. The three returned to find Jay and Clark making coffee and eggs. Snickers wouldn't go near Clark. He sat on the far end of the cot where Jay knelt in front of him and attached a blue nylon rope to one ankle.

"I'm sorry about this kid. How do you feel about killing us this morning?"

"My head aches."

Jay put a hand on the boy's exposed calf and lowered his tone, "Your head will ache every time you think of violence."

"I don't want to hurt."

"Don't kill us. You'll feel better." He returned to a conversational tone. "We're just gonna keep a leash on you for a little bit so you don't run off home and report on us. It's not so bad. Right, LG?"

Laylea met the kid's eyes as Jay took out his lighter and melted the nylon knot. She could see how tiny his pupils were, unnaturally small in the brightness of morning. He smelled scared. She tried rolling around and clowning to distract him but her heart wasn't in it. She was scared too.

The men packed away their tents and cleared some items from Gandhi's sled to give more room if they needed to tie the boy on it. Meanwhile the boy helped Clark fold up the cot. Throughout the morning, Jay and Clark used Sher's techniques to bring out the kid's humanity, to reach his feelings and condition his behaviors. Gandhi asked him questions as they worked and when they sat for breakfast.

The kid had few answers. Laylea thought he might cry as he shoveled the scrambled eggs into his mouth. She kept a wary eye on him.

When Clark stood to leave, Laylea leaped to his side. Jay had pulled a first aid kit out of his packs and was wiping his knife blade with an alcohol swab. He paused to give Clark a one-armed hug. Laylea got a nod. She trotted over to Gandhi and tagged his ankle. He gave her one long pat from ears to tail. Then she stepped over to the boy sitting beside Gandhi. She climbed carefully into his crossed legs lap and stood up on his chest. When she couldn't catch his eye, she barked once. He looked down. She licked his nose.

Then she leaped awkwardly from his lap and limped away to fly home.

"We'll extract the tracker after you take off then leave the area double-time." Jay escorted Clark to the plane. Gandhi followed.

"I'll be on the HAM at the usual times but if I haven't heard from you by Tuesday, we'll come out and check the message tree."

"Tuesday."

"Yes," Clark confirmed.

"Captain." Jay looked over his shoulder at Gandhi who grinned back. "What day is it today?"

Clark flushed. "Saturday." He took a breath, turning his face away from the CF as he lifted Laylea into the cockpit. "If we haven't heard from you, we'll meet you four noons from now."

Jay had seen the moment of anger. He put a hand on Clark's arm as if conditioning him, his voice naturally low with emotion. "I'd rather be here than killing people's brothers. Your wife broke us. But then she saved us and I will forever be grateful to both of you, my friend."

Clark faced him. "Someday it will be time to do more."

"Thoughts become words," Gandhi murmured. "Words become actions."

Jay nodded. "Someday."

Clark strapped Laylea into her ginger scented bed. He crumpled the top sheet of the pad where she'd written *kid has a mom*.

"In the meantime, we can look for his mother."

A small hope lit the CF's faces. Then the men returned to the boy as Clark and Laylea took off into the wide blue.

CHAPTER 39

SPRING 2036 - DEEP IN THE MOUNTAINS

Before the plane had lifted from the dirt runway, Jay knelt by Snickers explaining what he was going to do. He helped the kid remove his coat and shirts. The boy's chest glowed white. His skin looked so different on either side of the harsh line between tan and pale Jay wondered if the Consortium had been practicing skin grafting on him for some reason. Even with a six-pack, the pale chest made Jay offer the kid a blanket to hold against himself while he made the cut. Snickers turned him down.

This would be Jay's seventeenth extraction since the doc had talked him through taking out her own tracker. He never liked the cutting and the blood made him nauseas. But he knew it would keep the Consortium from finding the kid and taking him back in. They wouldn't be able to mess around in his brain anymore.

Maybe the kid had volunteered. Jay wondered if they weren't all volunteers, running from pasts that were worse than having no past at all. But the doctor had assured him that whatever he had volunteered for had not included all the things she had done to him. She'd done some research before demolishing the lab and she knew enough to know that no one knew everything, except maybe Trask. She was told that Jay had volunteered for his treatments with a full understanding of what was being done to him. But on her brother's advice she'd talked to Jay, awake and under hypnosis. She'd discovered he didn't have any idea what was really going on.

That's how the whole coup had started. That was when she had rebooted him and together they began their capture and release of Trask's Conditioned Forces. This boy would be their eighteenth rescue. The eighteenth victim. It would be nice if Clark could find the kid's mother. Unless the Consortium had killed her when they acquired her son as a volunteer.

Jay shook his head clear. He had to focus on the patient in front of him and put the countless other CF still lost out of his mind. He asked Gandhi to keep the boy calm while he worked. Then he wiped the skin clean with an alcohol swab and slipped the knifepoint into the kid's back just under the scar between his shoulder blades. The boy jumped. Jay paused until he was still then felt for the tiny capsule-like transmitter. With a twist of his wrist, he hooked the tip of the knife behind the electrical device and flicked it out.

Normally this was the easiest part of the process, cleaning the wound, bandaging it, and then showing the implant to the patient as proof. It had always been an eye-opening moment for the rescued CF.

Not this time.

As the transmitter popped out, Jay barely had time to notice that it trailed several wires thin as spider's webbing. The transmitter dangled from the kid's back by these wires. Jay leaned in to cut them. Before he could, the flash of a tiny explosion momentarily blinded him. In the same instant, the kid sprung to his feet, a fist speeding at Jay's head. Gandhi moved faster. He hit the kid in the side of the neck, paralyzing the boy for a moment with a direct strike to the vagus nerve. With the kid already falling, Gandhi guided him face down to the ground. The kid struck out when he regained muscle control but the old hermit took the wrist and yanked him forward to stretch him out to his full length. He pinioned the kid to the ground by twisting an arm behind him.

"Calm." Gandhi tapped on the kid's wrist with his thumb to show how easily he had him pinned.

Blinking against the flashes still sparking in his vision, Jay scrambled through the grass to the kid's back. The implant was slightly larger than any previous one and still connected to the boy via monofilament wires.

"What are these?"

"Take it out!" The boy screamed, tears turning the dirt beneath his cheek to mud.

Jay considered the blood and mucus surrounding the wires. He glanced up at Gandhi. The older man nodded and put a foot on Snicker's back to hold him down while Jay took a firm grip on the tiny tech. He held it as far away from the body as the wires would stretch and shut his eyes before he sliced them. A second small burst of light flashed.

Jay flipped his knife around and shoved the handle in between the teeth of the boy who'd begun convulsing beneath him. Gandhi dropped the boy's arm. He fell to his knees as he pulled the bandana from his head. Wrapping the cloth around a hand, he maneuvered the boy's head into his lap and used the protected hand to take the knife blade from Jay. Jay turned the boy's body onto its side, scanning the ground for sharp rocks or anything that could hurt Snickers if he hit it. Then they waited for the seizure to pass.

In moments, the body stopped convulsing and the boy started vomiting. He kept vomiting long after everything Gandhi and Jay had seen him eat had come up. When it became clear that he was heaving up only his own bile and showed no signs of stopping, Gandhi sat the boy up a bit and Jay, following Clark's example, punched him in the diaphragm. The muscle responded to the injury by relaxing. The kid didn't.

He cried over and over, "Please. Please."

Jay wiped the tears away, bending close with both hands on the boy's face, his elbows on his chest. "I took it out. You're safe now."

The boy altered his wailing refrain. "No. No. No. No. No."

"Why do you think you're in danger?"

"YOU!" he screamed. "You're in danger. I was a camera. Everything I saw. Everything I heard. They said if the tracker ever came out my body would be the transmitter to send it all to HQ." He curled into the fetal position, his tears turning into hiccups as the confession allowed his mind to calm.

"Everything." Jay rocked back to his heels. He looked at Gandhi, adrenaline souring his gut as his soldier's training took the fore. "Captain and I talked about where he lives. Where the doc lives."

Gandhi pulled the camelback off his shoulders. "Can you get there?"

"Three days." Jay took the water and went to his packs, pulling protein bars from the pockets. "It'll take me three days."

Gandhi wiped Jay's knife down and handed it back to the man. "Good luck. We'll go to the message tree."

"And try getting through to him on the HAM. It's in my camp." Jay hollered back over his shoulder as he tucked the knife into its sheath while running full out beside the plane tracks.

CHAPTER 40

SPRING 2036 - FOOTHILLS, OR

Laylea jackknifed to chew furiously at her foot. Before waking her, the burning had worked itself into her dream. She was inches from catching the Rick's cat when a bolt of flame shot from the German Shepherd fence into her body. The bolt concentrated into a white-hot spark simmering in the soft skin between the pads of her foot.

She blinked. She'd thought maybe a ray of sun had caused the illusion but the windows in the family room were still blacked out with shades and drapes. Woodford lifted his head. He shoved her with his muzzle but didn't tag her foot or hip. She adjusted and the old hound dropped back to sleep.

The dark room scared her. It felt like a storm was rolling in.

She climbed out of Woodford's bed, trying not to kick him, and downward dogged. She tilted her head in prep for shaking her muscles loose but her neck suggested that would be a bad idea. Her whole body still ached from being thrown against the tree. But that was better than being crushed by Snickers' fall.

She trotted out of the dark family room into the darker hallway. The mom had nailed black fabric over the small window at the top of the door. Laylea listened for anybody. Bailey and Sher were continuing his lessons in her tinkering room. She wouldn't be able to hear them in there. But she didn't hear Clark anywhere either. Outside the house, she heard music.

She continued into the dining room and nosed her way behind a drape. Standing on the sill and shoving the blinds out of her way, she could get a view of the neighborhood. The music came from a boombox on a folding table in the street down by where the German Shepherd had lived until last year. Smoke billowed from a grill beside the table. The scent of steak and grilled zucchini was probably her imagination considering how tightly the house was locked up. But she could see Mrs. Rick handing down pieces of something to that cat. The nice pregnant lady from the rental cottage balanced a full plate of yummy on her belly to the delight of Parker's little girl. She'd like Bailey to see the OLR swing dancing with Davis.

The smoke cleared revealing an unfamiliar face manning the grill. His pale, plump features stood out in stark contrast to the gaunt cheeks of Mr. Rick talking to him. Mr. Rick gestured toward Laylea. She ducked before remembering it was perfectly normal for a dog to look out a window. The strange man's eyes glittered. He closed the lid of the grill and walked toward the house. Laylea was about to bark a warning when he stopped in mid-stride. His eyes glazed over. He blinked three times and turned back around to return to the party. The OLR called him to take over for Davis.

A spark of pain dropped Laylea from the sill. She licked her arms in frustration, trying to reach her aching chest just like poor Herrhund had. She growled at her body. Her teddy lizard should be in the kitchen where she'd dropped him last night after they got home. She spent the evening being iced. Instead of sticking her in a bathtub of cubes like Bailey suggested, she'd been passed from Sher to Clark to Bailey every twenty minutes while a different achy part of her was held to an icepack. Bad hip, head, left ribs, right ribs, good hip and back to the beginning. No respite when she'd curled up in the curve of Bailey's legs and dreamt of snowstorms all night long.

Clark wasn't in the kitchen. The mantle clock read two-thirty which meant he'd be in his closet. She picked up her teddy and waddled her way to the closet door. It opened on the second scratch.

"Hello there. You looked so comfortable with Woods I didn't want to disturb you." Laylea pushed the door closed behind her.

"Jay Doe. Jay Doe. This is Cap n' LG. Come back." He bent to crane her up to the desk.

Laylea grabbed a pencil from her cup. She wrote *2:30, risking a trace?*

Clark looked at his watch. "Wow. I'd really like to hear he's okay."

There's a party outside.

Clark glanced at the note. He dialed to another frequency. "The Ruckers?"

Everyone.

"Uh huh." He wasn't paying attention.

She barked. *Can I have more drugs yet?*

He automatically reached out for her bad hip. "You hurting?"

Laylea tilted her head in a way that was half *duh* and half not willing to admit how much she hurt to a man who didn't really understand pain.

"Can you find Mom? I'd like to stay here a little longer."

Laylea leaned into his scratching. She wrote *He knows your frequencies. Be safe.* And crawled onto Clark's offered arm. He cracked the door for her but before she left she barked at him.

He finally looked down at her note. "Don't worry. I'll just listen."

Laylea crossed the hall. She set her teddy down to stand on the door and scratch with both paws.

"Hey Laylea." Bailey cracked the door. He scooped her up in one very warm hand. She dropped her jaw to laugh at his face again.

He ignored her, stepping back in among the coats to shut the door. He had to duck under the bar and shelf to push aside the inner wall. He held her in front of him as he squeezed sideways a few feet between the closet wall and the sand-filled inner buffer. At the final door, he set her down to release the secret catch. Laylea hopped over the two-foot-high threshold and turned to watch Bailey squeeze himself a quadrant at a time into the tinkering room.

What had been a large second bedroom when they'd bought the house was now a coat closet and walk-in pantry sized safe room. The walls were decorated with silver flame-retardant blankets nailed to which were dozens of examples of Sher's tech. Some of it was designed to enhance her magical abilities. Some of it, she thought, would work for anyone. Some were just straight-up bombs in fancy packaging.

Sher extinguished the flame in her palm. She looked like Bailey, like Katherine Coogan. "How bad?"

Laylea played dead.

Sher shook her head and her hair and features returned to the familiar fake ones the family was used to. She packed strange objects away in a giant metal-sided fishing tackle case.

"Bailey, you want to try one more time?"

"Mom, I'm trying all the time. I don't know how to fix it." Bailey held helpless blue hands out to his side.

"I told you to change your *hair*. Your *hair*."

"I've got hair all over, Mom. Want to see?"

Bailey was covered head to toe in blue hair. The hair on his head stood up in straight shocks of indigo. The normal crystal blue of his eyes laughed out of a face of marbled teal. The hands covering his giggling mouth matched his face while the nails stood out sapphire against his skin.

"No!" Sher headed for the passageway.

Bailey caught Laylea's eye. He flashed to his normal coloring. Laylea let out a chatter of barks to get Sher's attention. Bailey flashed back to blue.

"Well, come on, Lee. Are you drinking enough water?"

Bailey scooped Laylea up to look her in the eyes. "You and me, right? I trust you."

She licked his nose and then pulled her lips back in a grimace. She gagged until Sher turned to take her from her brother.

Sher pounded on the radio closet wall and door as they headed for the kitchen. "Jay can handle it. Trust him."

Bailey gathered ice packs from the freezer while the mom cut up a pill and shoved half into a cherry tomato.

On the counter, Laylea scratched out *A whole half?*

"Yes. You'll get a half every time Clark comes out of that closet. It seems like you've got full-body whiplash. It hurts but you'll heal." She held the tomato out for Laylea. "If I go out to see this kid I'm gonna want to hunt down Hardknock too."

Laylea wrote *I would have been crushed.*

Sher glanced over as she dried the utensils in the dish rack. "You very well could have been."

"Could have been what?" Clark held the swinging door for Woodford who couldn't push it open anymore.

Bailey answered, "Hardknock could have crushed Laylea."

Laylea started, *No. Hard*— But Bailey wrapped her in an armload of ice packs.

Clark took the dishes from Sher as she dried them. "The neighbors are barbecuing in the street."

"The Ruckers?"

"Yeah, the boys are out there. So are the Ricks and the renters and the new guy."

"From the German Shepherd house?" Sher perked up. "I haven't had a chance to shoe him yet."

"There's that. I was thinking more about how it might be conspicuous if we don't show up. They might start talking about all the shades being down."

"Even if they notice, it won't occur to anyone to talk about it." Sher spread her wet towel out on the oven handle and took a fresh one from the drawer.

Clark looked up from massaging Woodford's hips. "You woogied them?"

"Dad, she woogied the house."

"I can't woogie *things*—I don't know where you get your words." Sher shook her head.

"If I can't remember words I should get to make them up." Clark handed a stack of Tupperware off to Bailey.

"Mom," the kid turned to the pantry. "If no one can notice the house, why do we have to have the shades all drawn?"

"If someone manages to get close enough, they'll be able to see in, my blue son."

"So just add an early warning system." He shut the pantry door before his hastily stacked containers could fall out. "Like all the door bells ring if someone crosses the barrier."

"That is a very interesting idea." Sher handed the last coffee mug to Clark. "But again, I can't woogie *things*."

"Bails, you should figure out how to do that." Clark spun Sher to the kitchen door. "Come on. I want to be back on the radio by 9:30."

"You think I'm gonna hang out with our neighbors for seven hours?" Sher pulled away from him to examine Laylea's eyes. "Your pupils are a little constricted. You have a headache?"

Laylea nodded.

"Okay," her eyes rolled when she looked up at her azure son. "Read or nap. No movies. No roughhousing." She turned to look down at Woodford who put all his energy into raising his leg for a belly rub. "Yeah, you got that, old man?"

Sher bent to give his belly and chest some good loving.

"What? Blue boy isn't coming with us?" Clark kicked the rubber stopper under the swinging door so Woodford could get at his water bowl.

"Gotta stay home and puppysit, Dad."

"Gotta stay home and study for your Calc test, Bails."

Bailey carried Laylea past his dad and headed up the stairs. "That's what I said."

Sher joined Clark in the dour hallway. "He's staying blue to avoid a math test?"

Clark took their coats from the tree. "Oh no. A girl."

"He's avoiding a girl?" Sher paused with one arm in the jacket. "How did you find out?"

"How do you think?"

She pulled the coat on the rest of the way and reached for the door. "Thomas."

"Yep. Hey, boy." Woodford had joined them. He stood facing the tree, his nose on his leash. "You can come." Clark flipped the leash off the tree and clipped it onto the worn collar Woodford had gotten for Laylea's third adoptionversary. "Thomas says that Kylie told him Ginny wants Bailey to ask her—are we not going?"

Sher stood with her hand on the knob. "I can't open it."

Clark flipped the deadbolt. The door swung in and Woodford waddled out onto the porch.

Sher stepped up to the doorframe and stopped.

"We don't have to go." Clark offered.

He heard a little panic in her voice, "I can't. I can't move any farther than this." She took a step back and tried again.

Clark turned away from the door, "A mother witch's instincts? Maybe Bailey isn't faking it."

The concern melted from Sher's face. She took off her coat and hung it back on the rack. "That makes so much sense. I can't leave my child in danger. There is a chance he's done something internally.

"We should cut him and see if he bleeds blue."

"Get out." Sher shoved him away. "I will stay and be mother of the year."

"Mother of the decade," Clark amended. He kissed her. "And make sure he's studying for the test."

"I will." She stopped him for another kiss. "Thank goodness you're so smart."

"You'll think about how to help Snickers?"

Sher nodded. "And Hardknock."

One more kiss and Clark was out the door. He paused in the sizzle at the edge of the magic barrier wondering why his wife didn't think she could magic *things*. He'd love to meet her family if only to figure out how they'd screwed her up so badly.

Beyond the barrier, *Sing Sing Sing* blasted through the small neighborhood and Woodford's nose went into overdrive. The dog pulled him straight for the grill set up in the cul-de-sac. Laylea hadn't exaggerated. The entire neighborhood was out. The Ricks, whose first names never settled in his long-term memory, had their cat on a sawhorse table. With a new leg, Davis danced the pregnant renter around a card table covered with salads and steaks and drinks.

"Nice foot, Davis!" Clark gave him a thumbs up.

"Thanks, Mr. H. This is Vasavi." He stumbled on the name and checked in with the lady to see that he'd pronounced it correctly. She nodded. "Vasavi, that's Clark."

The man at the grill had been talking to Parker's little girl. His head popped up at Clark's name.

"Clark Hillen! So glad you made it out." He waved him over with a grill fork. "I'm Derrick."

Derrick wiped his right hand on the apron covering his crisp jeans and offered it to Clark.

"Nice to meet you Derrick." Clark transferred the leash to his left. "I'm Clark. Is this your party?"

The man shook his hand brusquely. He had a firm grip but the skin was awfully cold for him standing over a grill.

"Yes." He grabbed a Melmac plate from the stack beside him. "Yes, I meant to come knock on your door but kept getting distracted."

"That happens." Clark took the plate. "Did you just move in?"

"I'm very much looking forward to meeting your wife. Good to have a veterinarian right next door."

"Oh," The lack of an answer put him in mind of Sher conversing with a certain receptionist. "Do you have a pet?"

"Hm?" Derrick looked away at the food table. "Not yet. When I get one though. Now your son. With his friend visiting from Chicago and this meat grilling I thought we'd see him out here long ago. I'm dying to hear his version of how he saved Davis' life."

Clark's eyes flashed to Letitia Rucker. She knew Bailey didn't like to talk about that. Davis had even stopped thanking him. Why would they tell a complete stranger?

"We have a touch of the flu in the house." Clark noticed Derrick's pulse and temperature both rose and a little color filtered into his pasty skin at that though his face showed the appropriate sympathy.

"Sorry to hear that. Well, we're not worried about germs out here in the fresh cold air so you let them know they're welcome to come get some food. Need to keep their strength up."

"I guess we'll get their strength up when they can keep food down. But thanks."

The OLR appeared at his elbow with the renters in tow. "Clark, I'd like you to meet Vasavi and Jon. Vasavi is in advertising which she hates. Jon was an electrician and now teaches golf. Isn't that fascinating?"

She dragged Clark away from Derrick to show off her great granddaughter and tell him how very pleased she was Bailey had chosen Chicago. "I need somebody trustworthy to look after Davis."

WON'T LET you in DePaul if you fail the calculus final tomorrow.

"I'm not taking the calculus final tomorrow." Bailey adjusted the ice pack on Laylea's hip.

Y you're blue? She dropped the pencil to chew at her arm.

"Totes!" Bailey clawed her ears. "You're so smart."

Laylea shook off his hands. *B!S! You're afraid Ginny's little sister is gonna ask you to the band bash.*

"No." He flipped open the paper bag covered book. "Thomas said he'd tell me what's on it and I'll take it in makeup on Tuesday."

Thomas is no better at math than you! Laylea bent double to stare at her belly.

"Yeah, but Thomas isn't going pre-med."

She grabbed the pencil to scribble, *Who cares what he studies. He's getting away from his dad!*

"Hell yeah!" Bailey held a palm down by Laylea for her to low five.

Her face hit his palm as she dropped to the bed, licking furiously at her feet.

"You really hurt that bad?"

Laylea howled. She shoved Bailey's hand out of the way to write, *wish I human.*

"So Mom could woogie you."

Laylea snuggled onto the pile of Bailey's crossed legs. She tucked her nose into the bend of one knee.

"Maybe I can help."

Laylea raised her ears. Bailey massaged the muscles along her spine.

"The pain of whiplash is from the muscles swelling to protect the shock to your spine and whatever tearing occurred, right? So, if you promise to take it easy and rest, we can reduce the swelling. That might help."

Laylea raised her head and turned sad eyes on her brother.

"Okay." He rubbed his hands together. "I'll just tell your blood to keep moving."

The tightness and burning eased away as Bailey worked his way down her body. Laylea breathed deeply into his hands, overwhelmed with relief. He finished with a hand resting over her muzzle and she lifted her nose to trap the hand under her face. In her own magical way, she dropped instantly into a dream. No bolts of fire. No pain. Just warm sunlight on her face and a cool wind under her wings.

CHAPTER 41

SPRING 2036 - CONSORTIUM BIOTECH HQ, CA

W alter whistled his way into the office, Bayard trotting beside him like a well-behaved dog. The phone rang as they came in and Walter picked it up even as Trask rushed towards it, her eyes still on her computer. She barely controlled a scream when he handed it to her. She took the receiver as far from Bayard as the cord would allow.

"I don't want another lecture on electrochemical processing. I want clear images. These are not." Trask hung up the phone and went back to her desk. She stared at the blurry images on the screen, clicking from one to the next with small grunts of frustration. Open files spilled onto Walter's side of the desk with pictures of various CF subjects punctuating a mosaic of medical charts, maps, and timetables. Most telling, her suit coat hung on the back of the chair and her perfect hair had pencils sticking out of it. Multiple pencils.

The dog waited until Walter took a step past the privacy screen then he trotted over and stuck his nose in the trash. It held three plastic supersipper cups with chewed up straws and several protein bar wrappers. Walter ignored the dog's yip as he snapped the choke chain. Bayard followed as Walter spun into his chair.

"I had a productive day in the field yesterday."

Trask did not respond.

"It felt like an extended weekend, being out of the office on a Monday."

No acknowledgement. He fiddled with the buffalo.

"Did anything interesting happen here yesterday?"

His officemate pulled a picture blindly from the desk and held it up to the screen for comparison.

Spinning in reverse, Walter took Bayard with him to stand behind Trask. The images onscreen appeared to be primarily landscapes as seen through a bacon fat covered lens. Trask focused on the images that had figures in them. She grunted and closed the program leaving an audio-to-text file partially hidden by what looked like a music mixing program.

START OF RELEVANT BURST

397a: I am taking pictures of an encampment. There appear to be maybe a dozen or so people, half of them children. They have set up a cooking area and seven tents. I will try to get inside the farthest tents from the fire.

//

397a: There isn't much in this teepee. Found a wooden box that I've been unable to open. It was hidden deep in a pack of clothes. I'll break it open. Yes. I've acquired two IDs. The subjects are eating with the others in the main...

Sounds of a dog barking and then heavy breathing and crashing through trees.

//

Male 1: Look up here. Look up here. Look up here.

//

A yell of surprise. Sounds of snapping branches, grunts.

//

Male 2: Look out.

//

Struggling.

//

Male 2: I've got him. I've got him. Elgey Clark. Little Girl isn't moving.

Male 1: Laylea. Come on, wake up little girl.

//

Muffled voices

//

Male 1: What are you doing? I deliver this shit for money. If you want it, I'll deliver it to you for

---

"You haven't figured out who the two other gentlemen are?"

Trask sat up in a jerk. She rubbed her eyes and then her scars. "We do not have access to a usefully complete voice recognition database."

"Let me hear it."

"Walter, don't be ridiculous."

"Did your fellow take pictures?"

Trask sighed and pushed back from her desk. She brought her current supersipper to her lips only to discover it was empty.

"Good morning, Walter. Would you like to know how my day is going?"

He perched on her desk, his legs dangling, leash across his lap. "Talk to me, Luv."

"397a has not returned. This is the transcript of his auto-recorder, received late Friday. Yes, I'm sure he did take pictures but he has to manually upload them. And he did not." She tapped on the screen with a pencil. "I believe one of these men is Gamma Subject. This is the closest I've gotten to him. And I wouldn't have heard this for another week." She stabbed the pencil into her bouffant.

"Why such a time lag on your transcriptions?"

Trask explained as to a child, "The team reviews the uploaded files in order as they download to our system from the satellite. They are naturally always several days behind."

"The auto-recorder only records when there is significant sound?"

"Such as voices, yes."

"And the subject is searching the wilderness for your rescuers?" Walter plucked a map from her desk.

"For the escapees, yes."

"How many people can there be out there for him to be having conversations with?"

"You would be amazed, Walter."

"Still, several days behind time?"

She rubbed her eyes. "My team work eight hour shifts. 397a works twenty-four hour shifts, consecutively."

"Ah." Walter selected a pencil from the collection in her hair. "If only you had the budget to schedule round the clock staff. At least they have finally caught up to an interesting bit."

"The last bit." Trask grabbed the pencil from him and punched it at the days on her desk calendar. "They skipped to the most recently acquired audio when it was discovered yesterday that the tracking device had stopped transmitting on Saturday."

"And have you sent a team to his last known location?"

"Yes, Walter." Trask tapped the report. "But the escapees had two days head start. Nothing was found. Nothing will be found. Even footprints were wiped out."

Walter nodded approvingly. "Proof of how well you've trained your forces."

She inclined her head gratefully. "Thank you."

"Or how much they learned from the military before they came to you."

Trask shoved past the man. She stood glaring out the dreadful window. "They weren't all military. We had a history professor who had become a problem for the academy. I've gotten several easily manipulated candidates from a particular women's shelter outside Atlanta. Of course, more extreme programs assisted in relieving our prison crowding problem."

Walter looked up from the map. "I shudder to think what you would deem *more extreme*."

"Many survive," Trask retorted. "And two of them actually passed our final testing."

"Why do you continue to use the same testing grounds if you know Gamma is hunting there?"

"If our subjects can't avoid Gamma, they aren't good enough." She smiled. "He's still a part of my programming. I have integrated him as a part of the testing."

"And only your failures increase his forces." Walter rifled through the files.

"Not. Anymore."

"Your kid has been caught."

"We were hoping he would be. You see, I considered your suggestion of two-way communications. We initially ran into a power problem. Every time 397a blinked, his implant recorded the image from his retinas. As a single burst system, it is designed to get us as much data as possible in the event of capture and removal." She turned and glanced at her screen, hoping for a new message. "The images my lab is clarifying are these. Of course, transmission of this information means we have lost the subject."

Walter bowed his head in sympathy. "Another gone to the Gamma side."

"No. To power the data burst, the implant uses the body's electrical impulses."

"You were unable to find a survivable solution?"

"Uninterested." Trask turned back to the window. She twitched the curtain to hang straight. "The data burst was acquired by satellite early Saturday shortly before the tracker went dead. I presume our friends were delayed from destroying the implant as they tried to keep 397a alive. I feel there is some element in that delay that I should be able to use to my advantage in the next version."

Walter tapped her screen. "You've got mail."

Trask crossed back to her desk and opened the new images. They were better. "We're creating ground-breaking technology here, plugging into the brain-retina interface. I foresee some serious consumer grade applications if we can improve the translation software."

The first picture was still blurry, as if taken underwater, but it clearly featured three men. The man in the foreground had the clearest features. He walked towards the camera, or 397a as it were. A compact man—tall, bald, with muscles well defined enough that they could be seen stretching his dark t-shirt even with the poor resolution—his ink-black skin made him easy to identify.

"Gamma." Trask caressed the face on her screen with one perfect nail.

"Gamma is pretty." Walter observed as Trask clicked through some more shots until the other men's faces turned toward the subject. He stopped her with a hand outstretched. "Who's that?"

Trask tapped the older man's form on the monitor, a short, but solidly built figure with white hair and beard. "That is my professor, Subject 284."

"Not him." Walter snatched another pencil from Trask's hair. "This one." He tapped the third figure and then darted around Trask to sift through the pictures on the desk.

"At first glance, that could be my second deserter." Trask clicked through a few more pictures as the third man walked closer. "Yes. Theta subject." She brushed Walter aside and pulled a file from underneath most of the others. "He looks younger now except for that growing forehead."

Walter examined the picture of a man of average height with blue eyes, short brown hair, a crooked nose, thin lips and a slightly cleft chin and then crossed the room to his file cabinets, dropping Bayard's leash in his rush. He opened a drawer and flipped through the folders. Then he slammed that drawer and opened the one beneath. He found a collection of three ratty sheets of legal paper stapled together and brought it back over to Trask's side of the desk. The paper had little yellow left to it. It had been scratched and erased so much that it was now as thin as tissue.

"That," Walter slammed the papers down on the desk next to Theta's picture, "is Clark Hillen."

Trask was on her feet. "You've seen this man?"

"It was that vet we visited, when Nicole started acting oddly. I went back, the receptionist told me the doctor had a little fawn dog that would visit the office," he searched the illegible notes. "Laylea. I know nothing about them." Walter trailed off as he looked more closely at the image on the screen.

Trask turned to see what had caught his attention. "284 is carrying a little fawn colored dog. . . that looks an awful lot like Bayard."

The scarred dog had slipped away from the desk in the excitement. He looked up from the alcove between Trask's file cabinets and the window wall. Both scientists looked from him to the screen and back.

A corner of the mixing board program stuck out behind the images. It caught Walter's attention. "Play the recording."

Trask sat down and started the auto-recorded burst from the beginning. "Theta is a veterinarian?"

"No." Walter picked up the tissue paper, scanning down the invisible notes. "His wife is. I know nothing about—" He trailed off, glazed eyes boring through the paper. He grabbed Trask's pencil cup and sent it flying at the window. Pencils scattered. Bayard ducked. "I went to their home. It says right here I went to their home." His gaze flashed to the screen again. "I saw him when I went to her home." He flipped through the pages as the recording played and found what he'd been looking for. He turned the paper to Trask, showing her the address. "They have a son. Replay that. Go back ten seconds."

Trask clicked on the drag bar. They heard snapping branches and a thud. A rumbling bass coughed out *I've got him. I've got him. Elgey, Clark. Little Girl isn't moving.* There was a break in the recording.

"397a is a boy, yes?" Walter asked.

"He was," Trask confirmed.

"Are they speaking in code?"

A tenor voice spoke as if giving directions to the other man, *Come on, wake up.* And then that same voice raised in pitch, clearly talking to a dog, *Who's my good girl?*

"Stop."

Trask hit the space bar. Walter looked a million miles away. She turned back and pulled up her maps program. "Is that a two?" She pointed at the formerly yellow sheets.

"A seven."

She entered the address.

"Why's he tell the other fellow to wake up?" Walter thought out loud.

Trask copied the address and map and sent out a message to the hangar. She formulated a text and calculated who to bring.

"He's talking to her." Walter looked over at Bayard. "She's not a dud like you. She's smart and he knows it." He turned back to Trask. "Theta has my daughter."

"Let's go get them." Trask pulled on her jacket and stacked the relevant folders into her briefcase. "We're bringing support. Dr. Jones?"

"Yes." Walter scooped his notes from the desk. "Subjects Felix and King."

Trask raised her eyebrows. "Felix?"

"He's familiar with smart dogs."

She chuckled. "Not anymore, he isn't. I'll bring three CF operatives for muscle." She added the relevant names and sent out the text.

It was Walter's turn to chuckle. "What do you think I'm bringing King for?"

"Entertainment." Trask pulled a travel bag from the lower drawer of her desk, grabbed her suit coat, and strode out the door.

Walter slung his backpack over his shoulder and moseyed over to Bayard's corner with his usual good cheer pasted on his face. "Let's go get your sister. She has a debt to pay me."

Spring 2036 - Foothills, OR

Three days till zero hour. Six of the fourteen screens in his vacation home had fizzled out. They wouldn't go dark, even when he rebooted the entire system. They consistently broadcast snow across all signal inputs; audio, video, and data stream. The remaining seven were unwilling to display the feed from any but two of the cameras in the neighborhood.

The Director was beginning to regret this little adventure. It would get his doctor off his back. And he didn't want either Trask or Walter's divisions getting their hands on his target. This had to be his operation, his success. But everything that could go wrong was going wrong. And he had less than three days left.

Thank goodness Trask had recovered her suit jacket from the back of her chair. The embedded fiber optics had provided consistent feeds for fifteen years. The Director felt confident he could count on it today. He shunted the audio to the closet's left rear speaker.

Less than three days until the Consortium board's decennial summit and he had no world-changing accomplishment to present. He had not been able to get into the house. Only Theta and the stupid dog had come to his barbecue. What kind of teenage boy didn't run to the smell of grilled meats? The substitute band director's fiber optic feed worked perfectly. But the kid hadn't shown up at school the past two days. His friend had insisted he would show up for band practice even if he was too sick for classes. He'd been incorrect.

The only reason he hadn't sabotaged Trask and Walter's field trip was his hope they would smoke his gopher out. Or there was always a chance news of his only friend's accident would get the kid out of the house. Whatever happened, he had to grab Bailey Hillen in the next three days.

CHAPTER 42

SPRING 2036 - FOOTHILLS, OR

"Good news, Laylea." Bailey detoured by the front door. "Sorry, Woodford, I'm on Laylea watch." He unlocked the dog door and Woodford rushed outside. "Be safe." He returned to the couch with a bowl of cheese and cold roasted zucchini bits. "Thomas aced the test. He just skipped out after fifth period to bring it over." He whispered the last bit. "Guess I'll just have to miraculously lose the blue sometime in the next half hour."

Laylea crawled into his lap when he sat, crosslegged. She circled once and curled up in a tight ball with her tail tucked far under her chin. He set the bowl beside her nose.

She tapped his leg. *Again.*

"I don't think I should. I don't think I'm helping."

Laylea tagged his leg and shoved his pants up to lick his ankle. The only time she'd gotten any rest in the past two days was after Bailey worked on her. She sang out and bit at his hand.

"Okay."

She stretched out to her full length in his lap.

"Don't forget to pack layers. It's colder up there." Clark leaned in the archway. "You sure you guys'll be okay if we go?"

"Dad," Laylea growled at Bailey but he barreled on. "Laylea's getting worse."

The dad came into the room. He perched on the arm of the couch, a map dangling from one hand. "It's gonna hurt for a while. Sher said it could take a few weeks for the nerve endings to relax."

Laylea barked once.

"Dad, she's in a lot of pain. Shouldn't mom at least do some X-rays or something to be sure she didn't break any bones?"

Sher set her tinkering case in the hallway outside the doorway. "I'd treat a broken bone with just what we're doing. Pain meds and rest."

The phone rang.

"Can we increase the pain meds?" Bailey held a warm hand on her ribs.

Clark got up to answer the phone. "You're doing a great job with her. Good training for a doctor."

"Dad."

"Hello?" Clark plugged one ear. "Thomas? Hello?"

He lay the receiver in the cradle.

"What did he want, Dad?"

Laylea shoved her nose at his hand to make Bailey keep massaging her.

Clark came back to the couch arm. He set the phone on the coffee table. "I don't know. It was hard to hear him. He just said your name and then hung up. He was breathing pretty hard."

"Maybe he just took your math test." Sher shoved the coffee table out of her way. She knelt in front of Laylea to palpate her hips. "I don't want to increase the pain medication because she's already nauseous and you can see how small her pupils are." She stopped and stared up at her son as Bailey ran a hand over Laylea's ears. "We can't leave, Clark."

"What if Jay's in trouble? If Laylea gets worse, Bailey can call Armando."

"And what?" Sher stood. "Have Armando make a house call and see our son, the Cookie Monster?"

"No, Mom, Jay needs you. You have to go."

"Oh yes, Grover? And if Laylea gets worse?" she asked.

Bailey sighed. He blinked and shifted the pigment bend of his follicles. "I'll take her to the clinic."

"YOU COULD CHANGE ALL ALONG?"

Laylea cried out. Sher had never sounded so angry. The phone rang.

"That is the most irresponsible, unconscionable behavior. Your magic is a gift. A gift." She turned on her husband. "Answer the phone. Bailey, I let you avoid training because I trusted that you were mature enough to handle the morals of power."

"Hello?" Clark plugged his free ear again to hear over Sher's tirade.

"YOU! You, of all people, to scare me into thinking you would be stuck blue forever because I let you slide. You wipe that smile off your face."

Clark blindly reached a hand out to silence her. "Sher. Mr. Bevery, he's right here. He's not with Thomas."

Laylea's stomach churned and she struggled to sit up, not wanting to throw up on her brother. The burn started in her left foot again and shot through her hips to the right. She growled, chewing at her left leg and then spinning to bite at her right.

"Look at me, Bailey," Sher continued, yelling in a whisper. "I would never expect that kind of nonsense from you."

"Oh my god, no. No, he didn't. Sir, I am so sorry but you can't blame Bailey for—hello?"

Laylea whimpered. She snarled at her stomach.

Sher increased her volume when she heard the click of Clark hanging up. "Never from you. YOU who KNOW what can come of abusing your powers."

"Sher. Stop."

"He plays with magic like it's a game. Like it's a game, Clark. He's as bad as I was."

"Sher!" Clark grabbed his wife's arms a little too hard.

"Clark." Sher put her hands on his chest and made him relax his grip. "What's wrong?"

The dad turned to Bailey. He fell to a seat on the edge of the coffee table, staring at his hands for a script. "It's Thomas."

"What?" Sher recoiled from the grief in Clark's voice.

"Bailey, there was an accident." Clark choked on the words. "There was an accident and Thomas—"

"Shut up."

"Bailey." Clark laid a hand on Bailey's knee.

The boy swatted it away. "Shut up."

Laylea wailed, her head back, muzzle pointed at her brother's chin as she fought against the unseen force that was tearing her apart.

"Bailey." Sher found her voice.

Clark said the words. "Thomas died."

His mother reached out to lay a hand on his shoulder. Despite her pain, Laylea climbed up Bailey's chest to comfort him. He lashed out at both of them.

"No!"

He slapped away his mother's hand and shoved Laylea from his lap. The little dog fell backwards. A spasm sent her tumbling to the carpet between the couch and the table. Her yelping cut off when she hit the ground.

"Where is he, Dad?" Bailey pushed Sher out of his way. He tore his sweater from the back of the couch. "Where is he?"

"Laylea?" Clark croaked.

"Dad! I can save him!" Bailey screamed from the dining room. He had a hand up, ready to punch his way through the kitchen door.

Sher's voice filled with panic, "Lee?"

But Laylea ignored them. Her brother was in pain and about to do something stupid. She mustered everything she'd learned from years of watching her human family talk and screamed, "Bailey!"

Laylea lay sprawled on the floor of the family room, naked limbs crowded between the furniture. She pushed herself up on her new, thin human arms, a four-foot-long little girl's body in place of the twelve-pound puppy she'd been. Dirty blond hair hung raggedly in her flat-muzzled face. She shook it out of her eyes as she'd seen Sher do thousands of times. There was no pain anywhere. She looked in awe at the room around her. Colors had changed. She saw the vivid ugliness of the orange couch against the brown shag rug that Bailey had always complained about. Her fingers clutched at the long threads she'd chased as a puppy and she saw her thumbs.

"Laylea?"

Bailey stood in the doorway. His sweater fell from his hand and he dropped to his knees. Laylea tried to leap to him but her legs didn't work the same.

Bailey dove forward and caught her before her face hit the ground. "Laylea?"

She nodded and tapped his arm once for yes.

"Did you know?"

She tapped twice.

Bailey's eyes darted between his sweater and his new human sister. "I have to go," he moaned. "I can save Thomas."

She barked twice and remembered her voice. "Stay."

He whispered, "Did I do this?"

Laylea tilted her head.

"You can't save Thomas, Bailey." Clark tore his eyes from Laylea. "He's gone."

"He was coming to see me."

Clark stood. He circled the table to crouch beside his kids. "It's not your fault."

Sher hadn't moved since she'd seen Laylea transform into a girl. Her voice cracked as she said, "The Consortium is here."

Bailey grabbed his sweater. He wrapped it around his shivering sister. "You can't blame everything on the Consortium. I did this. He was coming to see me."

Clark started, "No—"

Sher raced to raise the window shades even as she pointed at the lights flashing from mirror to mirror overhead. Outside, two black SUVs pulled past the street sign. She screamed, "The Consortium is *here*. RUN!"

Even as they argued with her, Clark and Bailey found their feet taking them to their stashed run bags. Sher ran back to catch Laylea when Bailey let her go.

The girl turned her deep brown eyes up to her mother's false light ones and Sher's breath caught. She combed a stray lock of hair out her eyes. "Hi."

Laylea smiled and shivered.

"We've got to get you some clothes. There's nothing stashed at the cabin for a little girl."

Clark threw Bailey's PJ bottoms and Fozzie bear t-shirt into the room. He dropped his and Sher's go bags by the dining room arch.

"Scissors?" Sher called to him. She grabbed the bottoms.

"Mom."

Sher looked up from slipping Laylea's legs into the pants.

"Don' run."

She looked away again. "We have to run to keep you both safe."

"Stop em."

Clark handed his wife the kitchen scissors. He continued to the map he'd left on the coffee table. "Bailey leaves for college in five months."

"Six months." Sher cut the bottoms to fit Laylea.

"Mom." Laylea put a hand on her mother's chest. "Where?"

Bailey slowed when he hit the archway. He had his and Laylea's go back slung across his chest. "Your bags are in the truck. I put your tinkering case in too."

"Stop them." Laylea enunciated more clearly on her second try.

"We can't, Lee." Sher tore at the second pant leg.

Clark looked towards the front window. "We could try."

Laylea patted a fist against her mother's breastbone. "Safe. Where."

"I don't understand, Lee."

Bailey pulled his sister to her feet. He swung her into his arms. "Your excuses, Mom. You had to keep me safe."

"And we didn't know where Trask was." Clark stuffed the folded map into his pocket. "But we do now."

"Do now," Laylea repeated.

"But now we have Laylea to—" Sher stopped herself.

Clark put a hand on Bailey's arm to keep him quiet. Sher gathered the cut off ends of Bailey's old pajama bottoms. She set them and the scissors on the coffee table.

Sher stood. She looked at her husband. "He'll be careful if he has Laylea counting on him."

Clark nodded.

She put a hand on her son's cheek and gazed into her new daughter's brown eyes. "You'll take care of each other."

Laylea barked once. Bailey nodded.

"Alright. I'm done with hiding. Let's end this."

"This won't end here." Clark stopped Sher before she could storm from the room. "The Consortium isn't out there. Just Trask."

Sher faced the trio. She shook her head and her natural black curls and green eyes replaced her undercover features. "So, let's find out where she's working and blow up her new lab."

"We need a plan." Clark glanced out the front window. "We've got a minute before they'll be able to see the house."

Sher fingered her watch. "Bailey, get my case."

Bailey turned for the hall. The blast of an airhorn echoed through the quiet neighborhood. Bailey nearly lost his hold on Laylea as she popped back into a dog.

Silence reigned for a split second before they heard the crazed barking of an old dog defending his home.

"Woodford!"

Clark and Bailey beat Sher to the door but none of them got there quickly enough.

The shot rang out even louder than the airhorn.

Chapter 43

Spring 2036 - Foothills, OR

Bailey hit the door so hard Laylea thought they'd go right through. He got his hands sorted out from the clothes dangling off her paws and cracked the door before Clark could wrap him in a python grip.

"No! They'd shoot you too."

"I sent him out there." Laylea felt Bailey's tears raining on her head.

Clark growled from the effort of holding his son back. "It's where he spends most of his time, Bailey."

They heard car doors slamming and voices carried through the crack. A man with a smooth, deep, British accent said, "Look, Trask, we've found some volunteers."

Clark started at the sound of the voice. He almost lost the fight with his grief-blinded son. Laylea's ears ratcheted to the sound. She knew that sickly sweet smell. Her body convulsed in Bailey's arms. He fell to the ground in his effort to not drop her and found himself on the doormat with his arms around the blond girl version of his sister.

She croaked, "Walter!"

A scream from outside ended all debate. Little Ella. Bailey dragged Laylea to the side as Clark leaped over them and out the door.

Two black SUVs blocked the entrance to the cul-de-sac. An impeccably dressed woman walked towards the Hillens' home accompanied by a familiar man. Walter led a small dog on a tight choke chain. These three were followed by a small blond woman in a pantsuit with one inch heels, an older, heavily tanned white guy dressed in the kind of blue coveralls you might see in orange at a prison, and an Asian man wearing the slate and green uniform of a Conditioned Force soldier. This last man had slung the unconscious Ella over one shoulder, Davis over the other.

Walter called out, "Good morning, Hillens."

Clark scanned the neighborhood. Parker stood by the trampled rose bushes, brandishing a crimson airhorn branded with the cream-colored letters OU. The tiny OLR held him back with one hand. The Ricks' cat napped on the roof of their porch. Vasavi and Jon came out of the rental cottage as he looked that way. The pregnant wife had one hand on her belly, her cell in the other. She looked at it and shook her head at her husband. He took it from her and hit buttons with no more success. The Consortium team had apparently blocked service. Derrick and the Ricks must not be home or were wisely hiding inside.

"Nice to see you again, Clark," Walter continued. "I hope spring cleaning went well this year."

Bailey crawled across the porch to where Woodford's bloody body lay sprawled down the steps. The dog cried in little yelps as Bailey lifted him to his lap. Laylea echoed him from inside.

"I'd like you to meet my friends." Walter gestured to the older man. "This is Felix. The man with your neighbors is 511. And your wife has already met Dr. Jones. Where is your wife?"

Clark barely heard the man. Most of his attention was focused on ignoring the copper smell and constriction in his heart. He concentrated instead on the battle line forming in the street.

"251, 397b, come join us." Walter turned his back to wave at the SUVs.

A darkly tattooed arm holding a gun extended from the rear window of the closer vehicle. The weak smell of burnt powder dissipated further as the man climbed out, followed by a thin Swedish-looking woman in matching CF togs.

"King? Don't be shy." The far vehicle disgorged the largest human

Clark had ever seen. This SUV rebounded on its shocks when the enormous Polynesian stepped off the running board. He ambled into the street in a slouch rivaling Bela's hump. His knuckles actually scraped the ground.

Clark had only a moment to wonder what sort of experiments they'd been trying on this guy before Sher stepped onto the porch behind him and the heat signature around the woman leading the menagerie expanded.

Sher continued down the porch steps, trailing Woodford's blood in her path

Walter continued his cocktail party banter. "Trask, may I introduce Theta's wife, Dr. Hillen?"

Sher laughed.

Trask growled, "Don't try anything, Coogan. I'll kill the girl."

Trask made a motion at the Asian CF. He tilted his shoulders so Davis fell to the ground and swung Parker's little girl around to put his knife against her throat.

"No!" Bailey leapt over Woodford to the bottom of the steps. Before he could reach the street two darts from the Swede's stun gun stabbed his neck and he fell to the grass. Convulsions danced his body to the curb. Clark didn't move.

Trask laughed. "Nice father. I see our training has held."

"Where is Laylea, Dr. Hillen?" Walter asked as if her son weren't flailing on the ground. "We just want Laylea and Theta. No need to get yourself in the middle of this."

"Walter," Trask fixed her bangs. "Plans have changed."

"Oh?"

Sher opened her mouth to take a breath.

Trask put a lot of twos together and came to the reasonable conclusion that she shouldn't let her lead researcher speak. She screamed, "Collect them all."

Many things happened as Sher filled her lungs.

Dr. Jones fired a stun gun at Clark.

251, the tattooed warrior dashed for the house and the little blond girl hiding just inside the doorway.

Felix loped at Vasavi and Jon on all fours while Jon stepped in front of his wife with only a cell phone for defense.

King pounded his chest. He screamed a war cry and focused his gaze on Parker Rucker.

The Swede aimed a knife at Vasavi's belly.

The Asian CF wasted a moment smiling at Sher before he sliced Ella's throat. He didn't see Davis prepping to kick.

Trask herself ran at Katherine Coogan with a stunner in her hand.

Sher yelled, "SHOE!"

Parker, the OLR, and the renting couple all dropped to the ground to tie their shoes. Vasavi wasn't even wearing shoes. Clark pulled the inkless ballpoint pen from his pocket. And as Sher pulled off her watch and threw it into the air over the eight visitors, he flipped off both caps. He held it to his lips and sent two tiny silver spheres hurtling at the sparkly watch face.

Just before they impacted, Bailey rebounded from the ground. He hit the CF racing for his sister straight into Jones' stun gun darts and threw him back into the street. He spun and sent a fireball at the Asian's face.

Nine pairs of eyes followed Sher's sparkly watch as it spun across the sky. Even flying through the air himself, Tatts traced its path. When Clark's pellets hit the face, a bright flash of light blinded them all. Tatts hit the ground as a single high-pitched tone died slowly into silence.

Under this pitch, Sher intoned, "Still."

And the strangers were still.

Davis' titanium kick to the Asian's groin knocked the man over. Ella slipped right out of his frozen hands while Bailey's fireball sailed overhead to strike King. The Swede's knife sailed on course to sink into Vasavi's shoulder.

Bailey leaped over the unmoving cat-man Felix to reach the renter. He pulled the knife from her chest and ordered the body to heal itself. Jon cried out as the wound closed. He cried out again to find a puddle of water at his feet.

Bailey felt the contraction in Vasavi's belly before she noticed it. "Mom!"

Sher walked past Trask and Walter, past Dr. Jones who'd tried to condition her when they first met at the clinic. She stepped over the Asian and around the human gorilla to the Rucker's yard. Parker held Ella tightly in his arms while Davis leaned on his brother. Important bits of his leg had broken off or bent. Sher laid her hand on the shiner swelling his eye shut.

"I am so proud of you, Davis Rucker. You are fearless." She licked her thumb and wiped the spot of blood away from where the skin had been split before she healed it. She turned to the OLR. "You still park on Denny?"

Parker began, "How do you—"

But his grandmother cut him off. "I do."

"Get away." She held Ella's neck in both hands even as she turned so the renters could hear. "Let's get Vasavi to the hospital. She's gone into labor in the middle of the street."

Jon and Vasavi began chatting excitedly as Bailey practically carried her towards the Ruckers.

And another shot rang through the air.

A cement splinter struck Sher's leg. She turned. The dark skinned, dark haired, dark eyed CF covered in tribal tatts who had shot her dog stumbled towards her. His right arm raised, jerking and stiff until the gun pointed at her face. Sher took a few steps towards him, away from the Ruckers, until the little lines around his mouth and eyes tightened. One of his eyes burned into her. The other stayed still, staring up. He tried to speak but failed to even part his lips. He tried again. Sher saw his anger growing and the increasing tension in his barely controlled right pointer finger on the trigger.

"Speak," she told him.

"Stop." The word blurted out. He took a breath and started over. "Fix them."

Sher spoke low, "You don't want to shoot anyone."

"I do want to shoot you. Fix them first."

Sher looked over his shoulder at her porch. Clark stood as frozen in stillness as everyone who had watched the flash, the pen casing still at his lips. Woodford lay unmoving on the top step, his head in Laylea's human lap. She pressed Bailey's Fozzy Bear t-shirt against the growing pond of red on his chest and stared at her brother, silent tears running down her cheeks.

Bailey left the renters. He crept toward the showdown, his bare feet making no sound on the pavement. Sher didn't dare bring attention to him by telling him to stop but she couldn't keep from shaking her head. She turned her eyes quickly back to the CF in front of her.

"I won't do that."

The CF didn't expect this answer. "You have to."

"No. If I release them, they'll hurt my family and my neighbors."

"But I'll kill you." Tatts shook with frustration.

"I understand."

He gestured with his head at the others but didn't look away long enough for Sher to make a move. "And then I'll kill them."

She shook her head. "No. You won't. Parker was a fullback at OU and your friend over there knocked his daughter unconscious. You'll need what, five seconds to cock that gun again? He'll need two to knock you down."

"But you'll be dead."

"And none of your friends will ever move again."

Sher spotted Bailey out of the corner of her eye. He'd circled back to the sidewalk, moving more quickly now that he was fully out of Tatt's line of sight. She willed him to stop. But he crept over to the Swedish CF and slipped the gun from her holster.

The CF facing Sher was now having to keep an eye on her and Parker. "What's wrong with you?"

"I'm thinking with my heart."

He stared at her. The man holding the gun in her face couldn't understand. He started to look around in agitation. He needed sense. He needed orders. Sher calculated how much she could move to keep his attention on her without scaring him into shooting. But then they both heard the click of the safety on the gun Bailey had taken. The CF turned.

Before he could aim, before Sher could launch herself into him, the CF was flung backwards. Sher found herself tackling her son. His shot flung her back into Parker before they both crashed into the cement.

"No!" Laylea howled from the porch.

The tatted man lay struggling to gasp in a breath, his gun forgotten, a knife buried to the hilt in his neck.

Bailey tripped forward to reach his mother and nearly collided with Jay racing past them. Jay slid to the CF and wrapped an arm around the man who was panicking, clawing at the hilt as he suffocated. Sher reached up to her own chest in a daze.

"I'm sorry. I'm so sorry." Bailey held her, wailing into her dark hair.

"It's alright." Sher coughed. Blood splattered into her hand. "I'll be okay." She pushed him away, watching Jay.

Tears pouring down his face, the ex CF held Tatt's tortured face in his hands. He sang as he snapped the man's neck and pulled his knife out before laying the body gently to the ground. Sher reached him as he turned away retching. She put a hand on his forehead, forced him to look into her eyes, and spoke low, "Calm."

Bailey's fingers went numb. The Swede's firearm fell from his hand as he focused on the exit wound healing on his mother's back. The hole in her sweater had been seared by the heat of the passing bullet. Bailey turned.

Parker lay flat on the street. His eyes stared blindly at the sky.

CHAPTER 44

SPRING 2036 - FOOTHILLS, OR

Bailey couldn't help but see Parker the way his father had taught him. He saw no pulse in Parker's neck. No rise or fall of his chest. His gaze floated up to Davis. Before he could speak Jay knocked him aside.

Jay used the knife still bloody from Tatt's neck to rip open Parker's jacket and jersey. Sher slid her hands in before he was done. She glowed with an aura that stood her black hair out like Parker's afro. Heat rose around her, burned away the clothes touching her hands. It sucked all the moisture out of the air and dried Bailey's tears.

With a sucking pop, she pulled the bullet from Parker's body. A quick brush of the wound and Jay tilted the man's head and breathed into his mouth. Sher ripped open his shirts and healed the wounds but Bailey didn't see the heart start. He crawled in to start compressions. She pushed him away.

One hand to the sky she pulled energy from every living soul in the street. Bailey felt his heart pulse in his chest, reaching for her. He could hear every heart beat in sync.

Sher slammed her hand down onto Parker's chest. "LIVE."

She whispered the word and everyone recoiled, their hearts released.

Parker's heartbeat deafened Bailey, Jay, and Clark.

Sher collapsed against Jay. Ella broke from her uncle and ran to her daddy. Vasavi cried out against another contraction.

Jay brushed Sher's hair from her face. "Sher, you have to—"

"Woogie them. I know."

Parker opened his eyes. He smiled at his crying little girl. "Did I fall down?"

Sher reached a tired hand out to hold Ella's hand on her Daddy's bare chest. "You fell down. But now you have to get the nice pregnant lady to the hospital."

Ella leaned over Parker. She whispered, "Daddy, that lady wet her pants."

He whispered back, "She's having a baby, Sweetheart. Go get Grandma's car, would ya?"

She giggled. "I can't drive."

The OLR helped Parker to his feet. "I'll drive. Come on, Vasavi. Time to be a woman."

Jay helped Sher stand as the renters joined the small crowd. Shaking Davis' hand she woogied him. "We're lucky you noticed her stumble. The baby could have been hurt." She put an arm around Vasavi and hand on Jon's back, ushering them along. "You can trust the Ruckers. They're good neighbors."

Parker helped Davis while Jon and Ella walked with Vasavi. Sher reached a hand out to the OLR but Letitia pulled her into a hug, "Do what you must but you can't make me forget what you've done for my family."

Sher stumbled. She leaned out of the hug to meet Letitia's eyes. "Your family will always be safe in your home."

"Hm." Old Lady Rucker looked away at her rose bushes. She watched as the neighbors skirted the SUVs. And when her eyes were clear, she turned back to Sher. "Roses are a mess. You bury Woodford where he always liked to dig."

She patted Sher on the shoulder and then hustled after her boys, past the SUVs, and out of the neighborhood.

Sher took Jay's hands in hers. "Hi, Jay."

He kissed her bloody cheek. "Hi, Sher."

"Thanks for coming to visit." She crushed Jay's hand. "Time to finish what we started?"

He nodded. "First take care of Clark. And Woodford." He offered Bailey a hand up. "Help her."

Jay swallowed his gorge as he checked King's pulse, closed his eyes. He checked each of the six remaining invaders to verify the Still order held. Tears sprung to his eyes but his stomach stayed calm when he knelt by the Asian. The CF's Still order would hold forever. Jay cursed the Consortium.

The Ricks' cat dashed from under their azalea bushes. She leapt at the Still dog by Walter's side, batting him with extended claws. Laylea bared her teeth. She growled.

"Stop it, cat!"

"I got it." Jay gratefully turned away from the dead men. He kept low, moving slowly. "Ts ts ts. Here kitty, kitty."

The Rick's cat whacked Bayard's muzzle one more time. She flipped around in mid-air to aim the same claw at Jay. He hissed at her. Another amazing contortion and she landed already running full out back to her roof.

"What an unpleasant creature."

Laylea looked up at Sher and Clark. "See?"

She pressed Bailey's t-shirt against the wound in Woodford's side even though the blood had stopped flowing. She didn't even notice Bailey wrap his hands around hers. Frozen Clark held all her attention.

Sher brushed a hand down her husband's back and set another on his forehead.

"You're free," she whispered.

Clark wrapped her in his arms. He dropped down to squeeze Laylea and Bailey into the desperate hug.

Bailey broke away. "Mom. Save Woodford."

"I can't." And there was no arguing with the despair in her voice.

"She saved Parker." Bailey shoved his father's arm off his shoulders.

"Parker's human, Bailey." Sher took Bailey's place trying to pry Laylea's fingers away from her fur brother. "You know I can't—hip." Sher sat up, a surge of energy lit her face. She dove over Woodford to lay her bloody hands on Laylea's left hip.

"Hey Sheriff, if you're fixing things, I've been running for two days. My legs could use some of your magic touch." Jay stood at the foot of the steps with the Still dog in his arms. "You guys have any rope?"

Bailey pulled Laylea's collar and leash from the go bag still slung over his shoulder and tossed it down. Laylea unclipped Woodford's woven collar and threw that to him. "This one'll fit better."

Jay smiled.

"Thanks, kids." He collared the dog and laid it in the grass, slipping the leash around a porch rail before he clipped it onto the collar. "I actually meant so I can tie up these guys before the cops get here. I don't want to have to steal Clark's jewelry again."

"There's rope in the garage." Clark rubbed Sher's back. He brushed Woodford with one hand as he leaned over to kiss Laylea's head. "Come on, I'll show you."

The two CF went around to the driveway.

Sher caught the glint in Trask's eyes. "Forget about it." She walked down the steps. "You're never getting them back." Sher turned from Trask and bent to the Still dog. She gripped his nape with one hand while she placed the other carefully over his small face, "You can move."

The body relaxed and Sher tensed, slipping her hand down to hold his muzzle in case he tried to attack. Bayard rolled off his side. He sat up and looked at Walter. But he made no move against Sher.

"He won't bite you, Mom." Laylea watched through the stair rails.

The scarred dog looked up at Sher. Sher released his muzzle and he lay down. She adjusted the collar so the fur didn't stick up around it and then turned to deal with Trask.

"That's my brother's collar," Laylea told Bayard. "He was a good dog."

Bayard turned his eyes to watch his old friend, Lieutenant Lazar, now called Felix. He was glad the man hadn't hurt anyone. He wouldn't like to do that.

Sher took her time approaching Trask. She noted the scars covering the woman's face. She brushed back her strategic bangs to see the worst of it. Then she circled away, unwilling to stay in such close proximity.

"You didn't even know I was here. You were coming for Theta." She searched the two leaders but found neither carried a gun. "I never thought of using him as bait."

She'd watched her son take the Swede's gun so she turned her eyes on the Asian. He lay flat where Davis had kicked him, his hands still up, still holding the knife to the missing Ella's throat. Sher unsnapped the holster at his side. She took his gun, avoiding his sightless eyes.

"Hey, might not be so hard for me to use a stun gun." Jay stopped by Trask. "I'll just take this."

Clark wrapped rope around Trask's ankles.

"Don't bother, Clark." Sher flipped off the safety.

Clark and Jay exchanged a glance. They backed away as Sher approached with the gun gripped tightly in both hands.

Jay hummed. Clark asked, "What are you gonna do?"

Sher faced Trask. "I'm addressing a problem."

Jay couldn't help himself. "Hello, Problem."

Clark saw Walter's pupils dilate in defiance of Sher's magic. "But you wrote this great song."

"That song is for you."

"The song should be for everybody, Sheriff." Jay resumed humming.

She raised the weapon.

"Mom?" Laylea pulled herself upright.

"Go inside, Laylea. Bailey, take your sister inside."

"No, Mom." Sher looked over at her son. His hair flashed blue. "Aren't there rules?"

She turned back to Trask. "That's why I'm not using magic."

Walter's pupils grew wider.

"Mom, not her. Orders." Laylea's words devolved into a growl. She clung to the post.

Bailey interpreted. "Trask gives the orders, right? So the Consortium will just replace her."

Jay laid a hand on Sher's shoulder. "They're right. We can do more good if we let these two lead us to their bosses."

Sirens reminded them Vasavi had tried to call 911. Sher's arms shook.

"We can't kill her. We can't let the cops get them." Clark stood beside her, facing the face of all the evil Sher had done, to him, to Jay, to so many others. "Let's get the Consortium, Sher. Let's get them all."

"I promised you I'd keep Bailey safe."

"He'll be safer at school than with us, now."

The gun lowered. Jay took it from Sher. He flipped the safety and wiped it clean before tucking it into the Swede's holster. "Let's get them all into one vehicle before you—"

Sher punched Trask's face. Clark leapt forward to catch the supervisor of Homo Sapiens Research.

"Sheriff, you have to fix that. She's gonna wonder how she got a broken nose."

"She got it in the car accident that killed three of her volunteers."

"No, we have to leave them here." Jay's tone lost all its laughter. "Their DNA might get them back to their families."

Sher looked around at the dead bodies and the blood. Without looking at Trask, she placed a hand on her face.

"Bailey, get the cat-man." Sher rubbed a hand on down Trask's chest and then Walter's to relax their muscles. Clark caught them.

Sher did the same to help Jay carry the Swede. When Bailey arrived with the running form of Felix, she fixed him too. Jay and Bailey fit the volunteers into the back seat and belted them in while Sher wrestled Trask into the driver's seat. She leaned in to adjust the seat and caught Walter's eyes watching her.

"You're a witch," he mumbled. "That's how you made our best warriors."

"Shh, Walter. She only calls me that in bed." Clark clicked the seat belt over his lap.

Walter flipped his eyes to Theta. "I'll find Laylea, you know. After all, she's my daughter."

"She's a dog," Clark pointed out.

"Well, her mother was a bitch."

Sher snapped her fingers in front of Trask's face. "Trask, does Walter have any children?"

"He has puppies. He slept with a were dog."

"Is Walter a shapeshifter?"

"No." Trask rolled her head to the side to look at Walter. "But he thinks his great grandfather was a bear." She laughed.

Jay piped up from the back, "Can you make him forget all about Laylea?"

Clark answered, "It would be too extensive. They came here looking for her."

"He'd be so messed up people would notice," Bailey added.

Sher grabbed a fistful of Walter's hair to turn his face toward hers. "Walter, Laylea is not your daughter and she will never be your subject." She released the man and gestured for Jay, Clark, and Bailey to back out of the SUV before she snapped her fingers again and addressed the Consortium visitors. "You found no one in Foothills. You sent King, 511, and 251 to search for Theta and the dog. When you hear," she looked around, "the airhorn you will go back home. No one is following you. You are perfectly safe."

Sher backed out of the SUV and slammed the driver's door. Bailey dashed over to get the OU airhorn from the Rucker's yard.

"Anything else?" Sher looked from Jay to Clark.

Jay took the airhorn from Bailey. "Say goodbye to your kids. I'll pull the other SUV around."

Clark spun to stare at the porch. Laylea had made it down to the third step. Bailey jogged to the house.

He shouted over his shoulder, "I'll take care of her, Dad."

Sher took Clark's hand. "She'll be safe with him."

"Yeah, but we just met her."

"No, Dad." With her brother's help, Laylea met them on the sidewalk. "I'm still me."

He pulled her into a hug that left her feet dangling in the air. He ignored the sirens.

"I'll get the car." Bailey ran for the driveway. Sher followed.

"You're not mad you can't come with us?" She helped him drag open the garage doors.

"I can't, Mom. I don't know what I am but I think everyone was safer when I was blue and locked in the house." He threw his bike in the truck bed.

"Take mine for Laylea." Sher pulled the two go bags from the bed to make room. She tossed them at her feet on the passenger seat floor.

Bailey tossed her bike in as well and climbed into the driver's side. His mother popped back into her blond hair for just an instant.

"I tried that hiding from the world thing. I liked it. I liked just being your mother." She put a hand on his knee as he pulled up to the curb and then lifted it away. "You take your time to just be Laylea's brother. I think that's gonna be a lot right now."

Clark opened her door. "The sirens are getting closer."

Sher handed him the bags.

Bailey ran up the porch steps while Sher helped Laylea into the truck. He lifted Woodford.

"No." Clark stopped him. "You can't take him."

"We can't leave him here." Bailey held the dog to his heart. "I'm leaving Thomas. I won't leave Woodford."

"You can't risk having him in the truck if the cops stop you."

"What do they care?"

"I don't know. But they'll want to call your parents."

"Lay him in the sunlight, Bails." Laylea called. "The Ruckers will bury him."

Bailey arranged Woodford with his wound down. He curled him up so all his feet lay together the way he liked.

Jay pulled the second Consortium SUV up in front of the truck. He hopped out and went to the scruffy brown and white mutt still watching everything from the grass.

Clark grabbed Bailey into a hug and carried him down the steps like he was a little kid. "If we haven't made it to the safe house by the time you need to start school, go. We'll find you in Chicago."

Sher added, "You can trust Orin with everything."

"We about ready?" Before anyone could answer Jay blew the airhorn. "Better be."

While Sher and Clark transferred their bags and the tinkering case to their stolen SUV, Jay unclipped the dog's leash from the collar.

"You can come with us if you want to or—" Jay stopped midsentence as the little dog ran past him and leaped in the open driver's door of the SUV. Jay followed him. "Let's go."

A single siren screamed from only a few streets away. The SUV driven by Trask had turned around and headed out of the neighborhood.

Sher and Clark kissed their children one more time.

Sher looked into the familiar eyes set in the new face of her little girl. "I am your mother."

Laylea woofed once. She turned to the dad, her Dad, and licked his nose.

Bailey climbed into the driver's seat. Clark closed the door.

Sher patted the roof twice, "Quickly now. Before the police get here."

Bailey leaned out the window as his parents rushed to hop in the SUV.

"Hey!"

Clark and Sher looked out their windows as Jay pulled away. Laylea leaned out of the passenger side.

They both called, "Fair winds!"

Their mom and dad's voices were torn away by wind as they yelled back.

Bailey made sure Laylea was belted in. He looked back at the house he'd lived in for his entire life. He thought about running back to close the front door but a siren blast made him focus on avoiding the bodies as he drove away from his home. Past the rosebushes. Past the leaning trees of the cul-de-sac. He turned right where left would have taken him towards school.

"It's you and me now, Lee. You're not worried, are you?"

She barked twice.

He looked over. The Laylea he knew sat surrounded by clothes.

"Maybe a little worried?"

She barked once.

"Me too."

CHAPTER 45

SPRING 2036 - FOOTHILLS, OR

The Director flipped through the five working views. A figure appeared behind the stone wall leading to the deep forest. He brushed dirt from his gray Consortium issued pants. The sun was still high enough to keep him warm, especially with his enhancements but he wore a homespun poncho over his issue snap-front shirt. Likely the poncho was to help him blend into the trees. He ran so quickly out of the shot the Director lost him. Scanning the few monitors around him he caught a glimpse of the man near the entrance to the street where an old sycamore leaned precariously against a hemlock. The figure dug at the roots like a dog. Soon he circled the trees and threw his body at the trunks. Three body slams and a sustained push knocked both trees down across the street.

The CF surveyed the bodies. He snagged a handful of King's pant leg and dragged him by one foot. He tossed 251 over one shoulder and 511 over the other. The Director was thrilled to see his cameras facing the house had resumed broadcasting. He watched the CF take care to haul his catch up the porch steps without disturbing the dead dog.

Red and blue lights flashed through the branches of the downed trees as he disappeared into the so-called Hillens' house. The Director disconnected his audio feed and blacked out the screens though recording continued. He tried to leave his monitoring room with the headphones still plugged into his console. They jerked him back and he whipped them off his head and threw them at one of the inoperable screens.

A high school letter jacket waited on the banister for just this kind of moment. He buttoned it closed over his technical fiber shirt and reached the porch just in time to lock eyes with the CF holding the dead dog in his arms on the Hillens' porch. He nodded. The man slipped inside and closed the Hillens' door.

The Director jogged over to the downed trees. A driven young policeman had climbed his way past the hemlock. He eyed the Sycamore with little enthusiasm.

"Officer, hi." The Director waved cheerily.

"Sir, is everyone okay?" The officer pulled a tablet from a pocket on his tool belt.

"I am everyone, I think." The Director looked behind himself as if to confirm. "I'm okay."

"We had reports of shots."

"We've had a good deal of excitement here, officer, but no gunfire. I just moved here but I thought Foothills was a peaceful town."

"Normally is." The cop's tablet flashed and went blank. "Dead boring in fact. But there was a shooting on Elm an hour ago."

The Director put a hand to his mouth. "That's awful."

"Are your neighbors okay, sir?" He punched the power button several times.

"No neighbors here. A woman went into labor when the trees fell. They've all gone to the hospital."

The tablet finally flared to life. "Who's they all?"

"I don't know. Sorry. I just moved here." The Director waited while the boy fiddled with settings. "Probably need to get this tree out of here, ya think?"

"I called City Services. They might be a while. Do you need help?" He looked up.

"I'm okay. Plenty of food in the house." The Director shrugged. "No job to go to."

"Sir," the officer stuffed the computer back into its pouch. "I can't conduct this interview with a tree between us. I'm going back to the station to get some help. Here's my card." He flicked three cards through the branches before one reached the Director's outstretched hand. "Call if you need us."

"Thank you, Officer Young. I'm sure I'll be okay."

The Director waited to see Young contorting himself through the branches before he turned away.

"With a woman in labor, you said." Young grunted. "How did they get out?"

The Director looked back. "Human ingenuity is amazing."

The Director strolled along the street, pausing at each bloodstain on the concrete. The CF met him at the curb.

"Nice cleanup. I hadn't expected my Biotech team to be so prepared."

The man held an appropriately subservient pose. "Trask works for you."

"Yes. I'm the Director." He brushed a strand of the Asian's hair from the soldier's shoulder. "You should consider my orders above theirs. The blood will need to be scrubbed before the City Services arrive."

"I know how to clean blood."

"Good. I'll keep an eye on things from my station. If you need help, give me a sign." The Director turned to return to the comfort of his monitors.

Behind him, the CF began humming. The humming grew into singing.

Another soul today. Her life is in my hands and I will not throw it away.

He turned to see a green book descending at his face. There was no time to duck. He was thrown to the ground by the blow. The CF pounced on him. He punched the Director in the neck and the Director found he couldn't scuttle out of the way. He couldn't hit back. He couldn't speak.

"No one else will hurt Little Girl."

The CF lifted the Director in his arms and carried him up the Hillens' steps.

"My name is Tracy Hardwick. I remember why I was in prison. I remember everything Trask and her scientists did to me."

Hardwick laid the Director in a pile with the dead CFs and King. The dog lay on a table, his head resting on a bundled jacket. The CF pushed through a swinging door leaving the Director alone with the corpses. He wanted to scream. He couldn't see anything but the dog and the front door. He couldn't hear anything outside of this room.

Hardwick returned carrying a red gas can and a shovel.

"No one else will hurt Little Girl."

He poured gasoline around the Director and the bodies. He splashed some into the rooms all around. He set the can down in the doorway. The Director heard him walk into the room behind him. He passed through the Director's line of sight tucking a worn patchwork lizard into his thigh pocket.

When he returned to the gas can, he had the dead dog in his arms, its head resting over his shoulder. The CF picked up the shovel and gas can and started out the door.

The Director tried to scream. A sad little groaning was all he could manage.

The CF turned back. "I'd like to kill you. But I can't. Jay fixed me. I don't kill anymore."

He trailed gasoline out the door, down the porch steps, and into the street. He poured gasoline over each spot and puddle of blood ending near the yard across the street. He dropped the empty can and lowered the dog to the grass. The shovel glinted red in the early evening sun as Tracy Hardwick dug a hole and buried the dog beneath some rose bushes. He bowed his head over the spot.

The Director heard sirens in the distance. Sirens coming closer.

Tracy Hardwick didn't seem to hear them. He stayed still over the little grave for several moments.

Then he raised the shovel over his head and struck it against the cement.

A spark caught the gasoline. The gasoline erupted in flames. The flames raced along the winding path, washing away the blood. It followed the path up the porch steps, into the house. The bodies burned. The house burned.

But there were no cameras in the house. No microphones. So nobody heard the Director's screams as he burned looking out over Woodford's rosebush grave.

The only surviving footage showed a cat prowling on a glowing porch roof with audio of a clear tenor singing.

I find
my mind
By listening to my heart
Together they will keep my soul from fracturing apart.

AFTERWORD

Thank you for reading my book. I hope you enjoyed it. If you had a good time with this story please take a moment and leave a review on Amazon. I'd love to hear what you think and it helps me figure out what you want to read next.

Sign up at Wyrdos.net to be the first to know all the latest on my books and audiobooks. I promise I won't inundate you with mail and I will not share your email with anyone. Just ask my sisters. I don't share.

You can also connect with me on Facebook, and on Twitter I'm @gwendolyndruyor.

WereHuman 2 - The Warrior's Son

By Gwendolyn Druyor

Fire can burn a house to the ground in under ten minutes. It can burn fifteen miles of forest in under an hour. You're going to walk into that fire. It's up to you how you come out the other side.

- Dunavent Fire Department training manual

CHAPTER 1

SPRING 2025 - DUNAVENT, WA

Bayard was an eight-week-old puppy when his Mama abandoned him.

He woke to her long fingers digging him from the pile of his sleeping brothers and sister. One of the bike shop rags she'd stolen was tucked in between Rhemy and Laylea. Mama had to tug it out. Rhemy and Laylea were always tussling when they were awake. But after the excitement of escaping from Walter and crouching hidden in the car for hours, the big boy of their litter had fallen asleep with his chin draped over Laylea's neck. Laylea woke when Mama tugged the little towel. She stretched up to nip at Bayard's dangling paws. He kicked her nose.

Then Mama had shut the car door and the tears had started. She walked across the street to the firestation's side door, crying the whole way. Bayard shook with her heaving chest. His mama's tears tingled on Bayard's tongue. They wouldn't stop falling. Her tears soaked into his fur. He couldn't catch them all on her cheeks.

It was dark out and cold and Bayard was sleepy. He protested when Mama set him on the hard rubber mat in front of a door. She wiped her eyes with the deep blue rag she'd stolen from Rick's Bike and Ski where they'd been hiding and bundled it on the ground.

"Curl up here and you won't be so cold." Mama choked the words out.

Bayard had never heard her voice catch before. He tilted his head at her as he climbed up into the rag. He tripped and fell into them, landing with all his paws in the air. Mama laughed. Bayard lay there, his tail slapping her knees.

On his back, he could see the yellow sign covering the bottom half of the door. It read *Don't abandon your baby. Safe Surrender.* He didn't know what the letters meant, of course. He didn't know why his mama had taken him away from the litter and laid him here.

His eyes swiveled back to her familiar face when her laughter morphed into a sob. He rolled out of the rag and tried to climb into her lap.

"I can't keep you. You won't be safe with me. Walter will never give up. I can't let him hurt you anymore."

Despite the protest, she scooped him up and buried her face in his scruffy fur. Her bouncy brown curls blended into the mess of his fur. He licked the makeup hiding the black diamond over her eye. She was his mama. He'd know who she was no matter what she looked like. But the humans in the lab they'd been born in had always made a big deal over her having the same diamond when she shifted into dog form. She used to give them milk when she was a dog. She'd slept with them all curled in her belly the night before but she had no milk anymore. She licked all of them clean, but Bayard thought she'd spent more time with him. He was shaggier than the others. She chewed through the knots in the tufts of fur springing from his floppy ears and between his toes. She'd fallen asleep with Bayard tucked right under her muzzle. Her favorite, he thought.

The sound of a footstep made his Mama spin.

A quiet voice murmured, "I can take the baby, if you'd like."

The well-muscled man had tufts of white in his hair like the white tuft on Bayard's right ear. He stood with both hands at his sides, a gym bag hanging from one shoulder. Mama had hid the litter in a gym bag to escape Walter. Bayard hadn't liked not being able to see out and defend her. But this stranger's gym bag wafted thick waves of salty musk when the air turned, so maybe it only held workout clothes. The man looked like he worked out a lot. He didn't show off his strength like Walter holding Mama too tightly or cracking unfunny jokes or locking doors. He stood balanced on both feet in a way that felt like he could dash forward but would also go away if Mama asked him to. He waited for her to speak.

"No. Thank you. This was a mistake."

Mama started to walk away but the man still kept his voice down as he called after her. "You said it won't be safe with you."

"He." Mama shot the word over her shoulder. "He's a dog."

Bayard watched the man over Mama's shoulder. His brow crinkled before he spoke, just as quietly as before. "I have an awful memory for faces. I'd never remember you."

She stopped walking.

"If you're running from someone who would want to hurt him—or you—you couldn't do better than the Dunavent Fire Department."

She turned. Bayard swiveled his head to keep his eyes on the grizzled man. The man averted his eyes from Mama's face. He caught Bayard's eyes.

"We could use a smart dog around the firehouse." A glint in his eye made Bayard think the man might be smiling at him.

"He's a special dog." Mama loosened her fierce grip on him.

"I can see that." He strolled over and scooped the blue rag off the ground. "Never had a son myself. But he looks like a good boy."

Mama swallowed. Bayard felt it. "He's a very good boy. Loyal and brave." She kissed his head. "Fiercely protective."

"Sounds like just the kind of dog we could use around here." He kept the rag in one hand and held out the other. "Name's Lazar. Lt. Lawrence Lazar."

Mama wiped her eyes and then brushed her hand dry on her shoulder before she shook the lieutenant's hand. "This is Bayard. He's eight weeks old. Just weaned."

"We've got a great vet, two blocks over. We'll go visit her later today and she'll set me straight on everything Bayard needs." He paused. His eyes flicked up to Mama's face for an instant. "Everything he needs that I can give him."

She met his eyes and Bayard rose as she took a breath deep into her lungs.

"I'm an early riser." Lt. Lazar took a step back. He nodded his head at the firehouse. "None of these lazybones will be up before five, unless the bell rings. You can take a moment."

Mama nodded, but the fireman had already turned away. He strolled over to a hose and started watering a plot of dirt beside the building. Bayard saw him sniff the bike shop rag before he set it, with his bag, on a bench.

Then Mama spread her hand on his chest and Bayard looked up into her red-rimmed eyes.

"You are important, Bayard. And special. Sometimes you'll just feel different. Never forget that you are important." For a moment it was like she couldn't breathe. Then she blinked her eyes dry and kept going. "I didn't believe your grandmother when she tried to teach me that sometimes you have to leave those you love in order to protect them. But now I understand. Now, when she can't help me." She kissed his head and his ears and his muzzle. "I love you so much."

She turned towards the lieutenant and then away and then back again. "This is crazy. I can't leave them. I'm his mother. He needs me."

Lt. Lazar released the grip of the sprayer. He set the hose down in the dirt and grass and brushed his hands on his chinos. Then he stood and caught Mama's eyes.

"If you'd walked away, I'd have let you. But there's something telling you that your baby would be safer away from you and I don't know if that's a mother's instinct, or a psychic knowing, or just a smart woman aware she's in a heck of a lot of trouble. But there's something."

He walked over to them and slipped his hands into his pockets. Mama leaned towards him when he spoke.

"You have to make a choice, right now, what kind of mom you're gonna be." He let that sit for a bit before he reached out a hand to Bayard.

He didn't try to pet him. He didn't try to take him. He just held his hand out so that Bayard could sniff the soapy, sweaty, earthy scent of him. Bayard tucked his nose under the rough fingers and the man scratched his ear like a natural.

He looked into Bayard's eyes as he said, "Trust yourself. This is a decision that stays with you forever."

Bayard leaned out and nipped at the man's fingers when he took his hand away. He liked that hand.

Mama lifted him up to her face again. She buried her nose in his chest and kissed his head. "I will love you for always, Bayard. Never doubt that. If it is ever safe, I will come find you."

Bayard stretched his neck out to lap her face one more time and then he found himself in Lt. Lazar's arms, cradled against a rock hard chest while he watched his mother trip off the curb and break into a run to reach the far side of the car. He thought maybe she was going to get the others. But she didn't. She climbed into the little car holding his still sleeping brothers and sister.

The click of the door closing echoed through the silent street. Bayard jumped. He cried out for her.

Was it because he'd bit Walter in the lab and they had to run away to the bike shop? Was it because he cried in the bike shop? Walter would never have found them again if Bayard hadn't cried. He clamped down on his whimpers, shivering instead in Lt. Lazar's unyielding arms. If he didn't cry, maybe Mama would come back.

Mama didn't come back.

Mama drove away. Mama took his brothers and sister and everything he'd ever known and drove away down the long, long main street of Dunavent. She rolled straight through the red light two blocks down like she couldn't get away from him fast enough.

His cries piled up in his throat, choking him.

Lt. Lazar's minty breath warmed Bayard's tear-slicked head. He whispered, "Hang tough, Bayard. I've got you. We're gonna be okay."

Chapter 2

Summer 2016 - Horace County, UT

Gamma Subject had just tossed an improvised grenade at the Horace County Morgue doors when he woke up the first time. It didn't occur to him that he was missing years of his life. He didn't, in that moment, know what memories were, much less that he didn't have any. He only knew that his handlers at the Consortium had sent him to fetch a man. It was his mission as a CF, a Conditioned Force soldier. His mission must succeed.

He dropped to the ground behind a well-lit exam table and covered his ears with his hands.

The fortyish-year-old man crouched there already stared at Gamma. Arterial spray decorated the front of his lab coat and his face. Blood dripped from his thick brown hair and down his glasses, but the guy didn't blink his baby blues. Gamma wondered at the amount of blood and tried to calculate how many people he must have killed in here to cause that kind of Jackson Pollack red period piece on the poor coroner.

With an almost involuntary twitch, the coroner raised the scalpel in his left hand. That was what alerted Gamma to the fact that the guy hadn't covered his ears. He grabbed the coroner's hands and put them to his ears, then covered his own again. He squeezed his eyes shut and then looked to see if the coroner understood.

Just in case, he said, "Boom."

The guy shut his eyes.

Gamma was up and racing out of the room before the concussion blast died away.

He was aware of the things he was doing. He smelt the chemical reek of the explosion as he leapt through the smoke and over the heads of three military figures rolling in pain under the remnants of the door. He saw the rows of gurneys stacked two deep all down the hallway. He felt his own hands grabbing at toe tags and dog tags, looking for a particular name.

He couldn't have said what the name was, but he would recognize the symbols printed on the wrist-band when he found his target. Gamma stopped searching the tags and started grabbing the corpses' wrists. His CF, Conditioned Force, enhancements meant that he barely needed to look to know the symbols weren't the ones he'd memorized. One after another, he worked his way down the hallway until he grabbed a wrist that stopped him cold.

Unlike everyone around him, this man wasn't wearing dog tags and he wasn't dressed like a soldier. He also wasn't dead.

Gamma's instincts reacted to the threat. He gripped the warm wrist in a hold that would keep the man down. He didn't recognize the symbol tattooed across the man's fingers, but he knew the symbols on his wrist-band. He'd found his target. He bent to haul the body away. But then the real threat rolled out from under a gurney.

Gamma felt like an observer as the soldier rolled into the middle of the cold hallway. Her hat fell off, freeing an explosion of red curls as she shot him in the shoulder. Gamma's blood splattered over the target, who remained on the gurney, inert and oblivious to the drama unfolding around him. Gamma jerked backwards as the bullet tore through his shoulder. He noticed the pain. He took the pain quietly, assessed the damage as minimal, and dismissed it. The soldier who'd surprised him shot again. This time, Gamma dodged it.

Quick as a wink, he yanked the soldier to her feet by the front of her deep green shirt. It was nearly the same color as his Consortium-issued coveralls and offset her wild red hair nicely. She nearly dropped her gun. Gamma knew he should snap her neck. But he just looked her up and down as a throb in his shoulder told him he should have used his other hand to lift her.

The red-headed soldier was short. Her pulse ran fast but steady. He had no memories to compare her scent with, but it excited him. He noted the symbols on the name patch over her left breast pocket, but he couldn't read them. All he knew was they didn't match the target name he'd been taught to recognize. He'd found his target. He needed to concentrate on extraction.

Gamma didn't know why but he knew that the red hair didn't make sense against the soldier's features and skin tone. He noticed all this in an instant before letting himself be drawn to her pale blue eyes. A hazel ring circled her pupils.

She stared back, taking in his dark skin and CF uniform. He watched as terror made her pupils expand, nearly obscuring the hazel before she blinked and brought her gun up to shoot him again. By the time she pulled the trigger, he'd tossed her into the two soldiers racing down the hall behind her. Her shots went wild.

He turned back to the target, who was wearing civilian khakis and a blue-gray t-shirt, and heaved his sagging, bloodied body off the gurney. Gamma tossed the target over his shoulder and hauled ass for the morgue. More military crowded into the long hallway to defend their dead. Gamma dodged their bullets. He tossed trained soldiers aside like rag dolls. Even with a grown man slung over his shoulder, they were no match for him. They were so weak and slow as to be another species.

Just before he reached the blown open doorway to the morgue and the blue-eyed coroner inside, he heard an unexpected pulse. One of the bodies lying on the inner row of gurneys had a heartbeat. Gamma watched himself from that observation center deep inside his brain. He swatted off the unending barrage of attacks with one hand as he scanned the left-for-dead soldier with the weak but steady heartbeat. He detected critically low body temperature, all limbs nearly fully connected to the subject's torso, with electrical nerve connections just coming back online. Dr. Coogan had requested he keep an eye out for possible volunteers with a strong spark of life. This abandoned boy qualified in spades.

Gamma (he knew that wasn't his name but his designation) was aware that a normal human could not complete such observational analyses without tools. A standard-issue person could not, for example, see the spark of life just beneath another person's skin or (Gamma looked at his flexing fingers) their own. A normal human would just see a tow-headed boy cut down before his prime.

A battalion barreled, screaming, into the long hallway to defend their dead.

"Fire at will."

Gamma wondered what they'd been doing so far. He dropped his target from his shoulder onto the nearly dead boy's gurney as he turned to face the new arrivals. A few dozen bullets grazed him, but nobody got another direct hit. He flexed the still-bleeding shoulder as he assessed the situation before him. The redhead lay on the ground where he'd thrown her. She aimed her weapon at him from low, between the legs of a gurney. She was smart. The rest lined up as ordered, as the British had done at the birth of this country.

Gamma shook his head. He didn't know what that meant. He didn't know who the British were.

He couldn't get two bodies out while dodging bullets and fighting the soldiers one at time. He needed a break from the bullets. He needed a barricade. And he had the perfect building materials all around him.

Gamma grabbed a gurney and threw it, body and all, down the hallway. Standard-issue humans found it difficult to shoot their friends even if they were dead. He followed the first gurney with another and another until a blockade of metal and bodies piled up.

Gamma turned back to his bodies to find the target sitting up, one tattooed fist cocked up and ready to fly.

In a voice torn by ages of abuse, the target hissed, "I'm gonna kill you."

Gamma punched him in the throat. The man bounced off the nearly dead boy and almost rolled to the ground. Gamma ducked and let the body's momentum help him haul the target and the boy to his shoulders. He dashed back through the hole where the door had once hung. He meant to run straight to the stairs and up to his waiting van, but he found himself detouring around the secondary exam table. The coroner lay flat, hands over his head, one still holding a scalpel.

Gamma crouched at the foot of the table, tilting his head close to the ground to catch the doctor's eyes.

When the man looked up, his pupils were blown wide behind his blood-streaked glasses. Gamma heard his heart speed up. Salt water fell from one blue eye, distorting the Pollack pattern.

Steady heartbeat, healthy reflexive response. Gamma smiled.

He felt the smile wasn't enough. He should say something to the nice man.

He said, "Boom."

After a moment's confusion, the doctor nodded. "Boom."

Gamma nodded back. Then he stood as easily as if he were holding a raincoat over his shoulder rather than two humans. He danced around the recently and not-so-recently dead corpses scattered about the room and headed out the way he'd come in. The morgue's back door was set low in the earth with a six-foot long, four-foot wide bunker carved out beside the stairs. The coroner had planted a garden in the wasted space.

Gamma liked that. A man in charge of death day after day had created a haven of life for himself. A trickle of unfamiliar warmth seeped into Gamma's veins, making him smile for a second before it was over-taken by the adrenaline driving him to complete his mission. He wasn't done until the target had been delivered to the Consortium. He left the garden with a sigh.

The laundry pickup van was waiting right where he'd left it. He opened the back doors with a kick and tossed the two bodies inside. Blood sprayed the inside of the truck as they landed, the target's bare feet bouncing off the back of the driver's seat.

Gamma spared a glance to see if anyone was coming for him. But the hospital personnel were too busy in the crowded ER turnaround to notice him. They were focused on triaging the survivors of the chemical spill that sent Gamma's target to the morgue. Nobody was bothered by an ordinary laundry van.

Gamma hopped into the back of the van and shut the door. He looked down at his captures. The men could have been father and son. Both white as good ol' boys. Both with messy sandy blond hair and sharp jaw-lines. His target's face, though, was covered in acne scars whereas the nearly dead boy had only one perfectly round pockmark below his left eye.

The van was crowded with the two bodies and pallets of clean sheets. Gamma had to duckwalk through it all to reach the cab. He stopped when the card stock tag tied to the nearly dead boy's foot brushed his arm.

Gamma tilted his head to better hear the calming susurration of the string slipping out of its simple bow knot. The card showed the symbols *J. Doe.* A lot of people in that morgue were named J. Doe.

Gamma tucked the card into the thigh pocket of his coveralls and climbed up to the driver's seat.

It was nothing to drive off the hospital grounds and out through the small town. Everyone was busy with the chemical spill Jay had caused. Gamma drove the speed limit, stayed within the lines, and pulled over for all emergency vehicles. He was prepared to shoot anybody who bothered him, but it was not necessary.

The part of him that had woken up was grateful for this. That part of him didn't want to kill anybody. If it weren't for this part of him, Gamma knew he would have been a good CF and killed the redheaded soldier and the coroner. They'd both gotten too close a look at his dark face, distinctive in this brown and white town.

He slowed to turn left into a private carwash, twenty miles out of town. Business was slow. Only one car was being hand-detailed by a guy in the front drive. Gamma cruised past him to the automated tunnel. At the entrance, he drove the front tires into the indicated grooves and rolled down his window to punch a set of memorized symbols into the keypad below the touchscreen asking what level of service he'd like.

The van jerked forward as the conveyor belt pulled it into the long, dark bay. Gamma relaxed as the front doors passed between the plastic strips blocking the entrance. He felt his body reabsorb the adrenaline that had been driving him. He'd completed his mission. The target was in Consortium hands.

He pulled all of the guns and knives from his many pockets and tossed them on the passenger's seat. He hung the forehead camera from the rearview mirror. He kept J. Doe's toe tag.

The van door was opened for him and he stepped carefully past the attendant onto a secondary conveyer belt which veered west, taking him away from the van, away from his target and the nearly dead boy. He'd be carried through a washing process himself to remove all evidence of his mission. He'd be asked to remove all of his clothes and they'd be burned. He couldn't keep the toe tag.

The new awareness inside of Gamma wanted to keep the toe tag.

His eyes had instantly adjusted to the darkness inside the facility. He could still see the pale light shining through the swinging rubber slats of the carwash entrance. As he reached the bench where he was to remove his boots and all his clothing, the man inside Gamma decided.

He dashed for the light.

He hadn't gone two strides before a chainmail net sprung from nowhere and slammed him down on the belt. Magnets engaged in the suddenly still floor, trapping him. And then an older man dressed in a bespoke gray business suit stepped onto the belt. Gamma felt like the age-spotted face and tight silver curls should be familiar to him. The man used both gloved hands on a silver-tipped cane to lower himself beside Gamma. He spoke in a tone so quiet, nobody but a CF could have heard.

"Disappointing. Your commanding officer warned the Consortium to just kill you but they believed your stubborn will might prove beneficial once conquered. You can't run from them. You won't ever get away. The Consortium *will* rule the world. And they are going to clean up your mess. We don't leave witnesses."

He reached into the inner pocket of his jacket and removed a pair of bright sliver snippers and a plastic bag. He removed one glove and laid the scarred bare hand on Gamma's face. His quiet voice seemed to echo in Gamma's mind as though he'd heard these words before.

"You are mine. You follow my orders before all others. Remember this."

Gamma remembered. This was the third time this silver-haired old man had conditioned him this way. He struggled against the net, against belonging to anyone.

"Still."

Gamma stopped moving.

The silver man leaned away and the magnets released. The net flew into the darkness high above. The floor jolted into life. But Gamma stayed as he was, flat against the slowly, inexorably moving belt.

"Give me your writing hand."

Gamma didn't know what writing was. He thought he might have known once. His left hand raised almost of its own accord and offered itself to the silver man.

"This is your third strike."

Gamma felt the man take his hand but pictures flashed in his head of somewhere else, some other time, long ago. He saw a different man towering over him, taking his left hand in dry black fingers. Gamma stood with this man, a man he called *Dad*, in the middle of a field of packed dirt and carefully mown grass. Children, other children, laughed and shouted and threw balls in the distance. But young Gamma stood with his head down as his Dad crushed his hand and hissed at him for striking out. He held the metal bat in that way that promised Gamma would see it again when they got home.

The silver man kneeling over him on the conveyer belt picked up the snippers. "I will give you a gift to help you remember your promises to me." He held Gamma's hand by his pinkie finger. "Do not disappoint me again."

In his memory, Gamma heard his dad saying the exact same words over and over: on the ball field, at the lake, in the principal's office, in his bedroom, at Mom's graveside. The silver man's accent was more cultured, vastly more educated but the words echoed between the many pasts and the present, seared in Gamma's torn mind.

In the present, the silver man cut. The tip of Gamma's left pinkie fell into the waiting plastic bag. Gamma didn't scream. Some cue in his brain wanted to but he'd been conditioned to take pain quietly.

The silver man recovered his cane and pushed himself upright. Holding the scissors, the bloody bag, and one loose glove, he stepped off into the darkness just as Gamma slid under a doorway of plastic strips and into the shower portion of this post-mission sequence.

The silver man hadn't released him so he could not move. His bleeding hand remained in the air, dripping O-negative onto Gamma's chest. He couldn't close his eyes through the spray of water, soap, the scrub brushes, or the rinse. He simply rode the conveyer, his mind screaming and flashing through moving pictures of his dad, until he reached the attendant whose job it was to spread depilatory lotion on his entire body.

The attendant screamed. It was almost a relief to Gamma. She made all the horrific sounds he dreamed in his head. She eased his pain that way. She did nothing to ease his pain or bleeding in any other way.

Soon enough, a co-worker came and then their supervisor called his boss and a vehicle detailer came over to rubber band a rough, paper towel around the finger and apply pressure to the radial artery in the wrist until a recovery team arrived to fly Gamma Subject back to Dr. Coogan.

The real man deep inside Gamma's messed-up brain had a lot of time to think. He thought this wasn't right. He thought he could remember a time when he'd been in charge of his own actions, when he hadn't killed people or stolen bodies just because somebody told him to. He thought of the terror in Redhead and Blue Eyes' faces and knew why the Consortium had cut him off from his consciousness. He thought he'd like to know what Blue Eyes had done to wake him up.

He didn't think about the silver man.

He'd forgotten the silver man.

ALSO BY GWENDOLYN DRUYOR

Wyrdos urban fantasy series

WereHuman 1: The Witch's Daughter

WereHuman 2: The Warrior's Son

WereHuman 3: The Hunter's Heir

WereHuman 4: The Wizard's Mutt

Voices of Reason(AVAILABLE FREE TO NEWSLETTER SUBSCRIBERS)

Shifter School

Shifter Ghost

Dee

Laylea

Junior

The Wyrdos Tales: Three Book Bundle

Doug vs. The Boogeyman(AVAILABLE EXCLUSIVELY TO NEWSLETTER SUBSCRIBERS)

Mobious' Quest fantasy series

Geoffrey's Queen

Hardt's Tale

Callie's Crown (COMING SOON)

Killer on Call thriller series

Ecstasy

Gin

Morphine

Valium

Pot

Absinthe

Killer on Call 6 book Bundle

Justice (AVAILABLE EXCLUSIVELY TO NEWSLETTER SUBSCRIBERS)

Second Edition, February, 2018
ISBN 978-1-948421-03-4(ebook)| ISBN 978-1-948421-13-3(print) | ISBN 978-1-948421-10-2(audiobook)

Cover design by Logan Prather
Editing by My Two Cents Editing

Published in the United States of America.

Wyrdos.net